DANCE
OF THE
ASURAS

N. PATEL BAXI

Cover design, map, and interior artwork by Tairelei Book Cover Design

Development Edit: Emily Golden at Golden May Editing

Manuscript Critique: Mallori Sorenson at Fiction & Fable Editorial

Line Edits: Taylor Q. at Earley Editing, LLC

Proofreading: Krista Dapkey at KD Proofreading

Published by Baxi Books, LLC

www.npatelbaxi.com

1st ed. February 2026

E-Book ISBN: 979-8-9998184-0-9

Paperback ISBN: 979-8-9998184-1-6

AUTHOR'S NOTE

This book features mature content, including graphic violence, explicit sex scenes, prostitution, assault, death of loved ones (mentioned), imprisonment, captivity, and mentions of trafficking (not to any of the main characters or shown on the page). It is not intended for anyone under the age of eighteen.

Regarding worldbuilding, South Asian culture (from multiple regions) as well as religious mythology inspired this story and its themes. In no way do any of the story messages or explanations represent facts from those religions or ideologies. Dance of the Asuras is a work of fiction, and should be read as such.

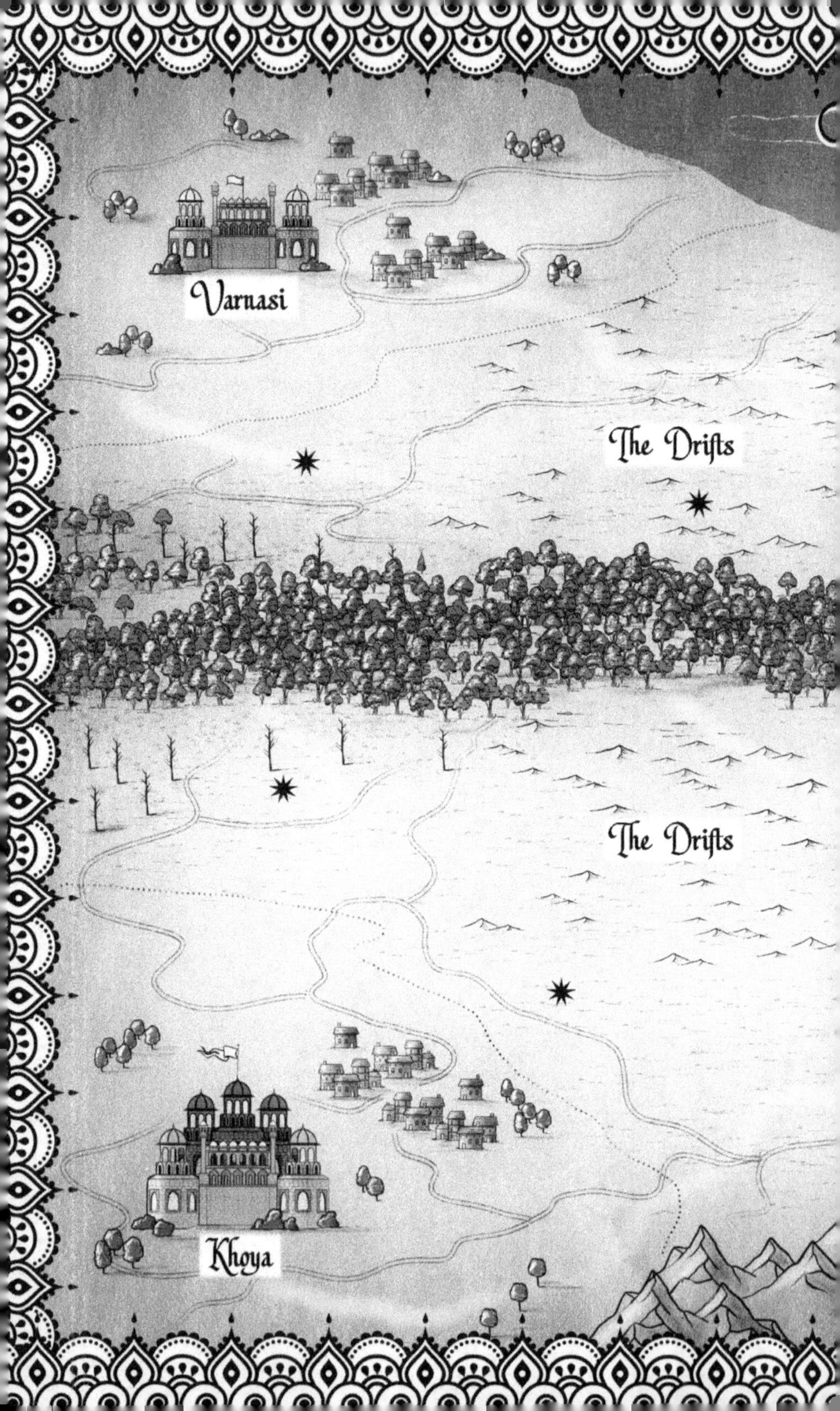

Varnasi
The Drifts
The Drifts
Khoya

a
Nila Ocean
Zehan's checkpost
st
of Three
Kalank
Naraka
Vajra

CONTENTS

GLOSSARY

In this world, there are multiple characters, places, and things that are pulled from the Sanskrit or Hindi language. While most are easily understood through context, others may require a reference guide which is summarized below. Please note, these are not exact or real definitions, but how they are used in this story.

1. Asura – a divine being, an antigod known to be evil or benevolent.
   Asuras mentioned in this book:
   Abhi – Asura of Pride
   Shama – Asura of Sloth
   Lobha – Asura of Greed
   Krod – Asura of Anger
   Rahi – Asura of Lust
   Shoka – Asura of Despair
   Issa – Asura of Envy
   Nadi – Asura of Fear
   Hans – Asura of Violence

2. Deva or Devi – a divine god or goddess, known to be benevolent or evil. When speaking about more than one god or goddess, the term devas is used.
   Devas mentioned in this book:
   Rati – Devi of Desire
   Kama – Deva of Love
   Yama – Deva of Naraka

3. Rakshasa – a powerful, malevolent demon that can possess magical abilities or shape shifting qualities.

4. Svarga – realm of heaven, referring to the celestial abode of devas and virtuous departed souls.

5. Naraka – realm of hell or the underworld, where departed souls are

tormented for their sins or negative karma.

6. Prithvi – realm of earth, where mortal humans live until their souls leave their bodies to enter Svarga or Naraka.

7. Grahan – eclipse, a powerful time for rituals that celebrate the devas.

8. Lehenga – an ankle-length skirt mostly worn by women.

9. Dupatta – scarf worn in various fashions; around the waist, over the shoulders / head, looped around neck, etc.

10. Payal – anklet with small bells, generally worn during traditional indian dancing.

11. Sherwani – a knee-length coat buttoning to the neck mostly worn by men.

12. Dhoti – garment mostly worn by men that wraps around the waist and extends to cover most of the legs.

13. Kurta – a loose shirt that can be short or knee-length worn by both males and females.

14. Diya – A traditional oil lamp, usually made from clay, filled with oil and a cotton wick that can be lit with fire.

For the darkness that beckons,
And the light that always tugs us back.

CHAPTER ONE

One day, dance will be the death of me.

But not today. The stubborn voice in my mind repeated the phrase like a sacred mantra.

Baanu's belt cracked against the floor for the umpteenth time and a faint whimper escaped from one of the other dancers. I flinched but did not let my body visibly react to our keeper's wickedness.

"Again, my dearies," Baanu demanded as she clapped counts of eight with the flat part of her palms, providing us with a faint rhythm to follow.

Sheer loathing laced my sweat as I fought through heat exhaustion, the sharp clang of my belled payal the only thing keeping my full attention to the sequence.

The sharp smack of leather greeted stone again, creating echoes that made my inner ears hurt. I clenched my jaw and stretched my arms an inch farther, ensuring my elbows were straight. In my long tenure as a courtesan, I had been on the receiving end of that belt too many times, and I would not let poor posture be the reason for my feet to bear another wretched scar.

"Keep up!" Baanu exclaimed as another wave of nauseating heat crashed over me. "This day has just begun, and we have far too many sequences to go through." Her features resembled a hyena readying to strike.

Blood and sand marred our dance floor. A gilded fortress surrounded us with high-windowed walls that hid us away from the famous spice markets of Khoya Kingdom, though I could still smell faint notes of fresh cumin and chilli. Barren of any greenery or shade, the oblong courtyard was a trap for the intense heat.

We'd been dancing for hours with no breaks to catch our breath or sips of water to replenish.

One graceful step at a time.

I took another sharp inhale and spun on the balls of my feet, ignoring the fervent black dots that swam in the corners of my vision. My cotton kameez and leggings were soaked with sweat and practically translucent. But I was too close to freedom to quit now.

Six more full moons, I reminded myself. *A few more months and then I'll leave this mediocre life.* No more waking up at the crack of dawn to practice, no more dancing until blisters oozed crimson spirals, and no more living solely for the benefit of others.

"Again," Baanu commanded in a sickly-sweet voice that made my insides twist like a dupatta being wrung out. The courtyard was empty besides us, a few guards, and a servant who stood behind Baanu holding a bright pink umbrella over her head providing her with shade. Baanu twisted the tainted brown strap around her wide wrist. "And this time, I want to hear the footwork. Niya, take the center."

I swallowed my groan as I took my rightful place. Hearing stomps on a sandy concrete floor was impossible, especially for the younger dancers who were still learning how to create the perfect clap with their bare feet. But Baanu always expected her dancers to go above and beyond.

Even if it killed them.

She counted off from the beginning, and we moved in tandem, with me at the center of the diamond formation. I motioned through the steps, a dull jab radiated from the edge of my heels to the center of my arch.

I used to say that the only thing that made me feel free in this world was dancing to a tabla, but now, the beats suffocated me. I missed dancing without boundaries and letting the lyrical song guide my steps.

The set finished. We froze in place. From the corner of my eye, I caught a dancer crumple to the ground, but I kept my gaze locked on Baanu.

Baanu's eyes narrowed. "Get up, Ruhi, or you will run the set again alone with my full attention." We all knew better than to help her and break the final formation.

Ruhi slowly pushed herself up. Her brows created a shadow over her eyes, exhaustion written all over her face. I kept my hands over my head, staying as still as possible. Only fools exert themselves in this climate, but Baanu drilled us like this every day, forcing our bodies to acclimate and teaching us endurance for performance nights.

Most of the time, I didn't mind dancing out here because it was the only time I felt freedom within the walls of the palace. Lacking the liberty to do what we pleased was one of the many unfortunate parts of being a courtesan in King Murkha's court. Daytime was for practice; nighttime was for work. Our purpose was to serve as entertainment and a luxurious pastime for the royal court's visitors—flirting with them, urging them to drink, and pleasing them with our beauty.

Baanu rolled out her shoulders as if she had been dancing. "You may rest."

We all released our stiff postures at once. Most fell to the ground, but I remained standing and rolled my shoulders out. *Rest.* That word meant nothing to Baanu. She always watched, waiting for someone to make a mistake so she could pounce on them with her claws.

At least I don't have to perform tonight. Every month, I received one night off and today was that lucky night. However, it was bittersweet as it was only because *he* was coming that I was able to get a break.

Ruhi handed me a water sachet. I glanced at her foot, which had a nasty lash, but she didn't appear to be in pain, likely conditioned to the sharp sting of Baanu's belt. She wiped her forehead with her dupatta. "No one can rest in this blasted heat," she muttered so only I could hear.

I let out a loose laugh and pour lukewarm water into my mouth like a waterfall, without touching my lips to the rim. The arid air made my nostrils flare, stretching my hooped nose ring uncomfortably.

"Yes, Soraya, what is it?"

All the dancers shifted their attention back to the front. *Oh nine hells.* This wouldn't be good. Soraya stood in front of Baanu with a straight back and her hands clasped together.

"I'm just wondering what the lineup will be for tonight's performance?" She asked, shooting me a glare. "We all know it will be different," her voice dripped with bitterness.

I rolled my eyes. I was too old for this. "No need to be vague, Soraya. Just say it."

She placed a hand on her hip. "I don't need to, Niya. Everyone here knows you're favored." She turned back to Baanu. "I'm just saying, we lost two dancers this past month, and if she isn't dancing tonight, the set will look off."

Ruhi frowned. "We all get one night off a week, Soraya. She gets only one a month."

"She's off the *only* night that matters," Soraya shot back. "We'd all trade places with her, even you."

Ruhi scoffed, handing me the small leather pouch. "You're just jealous that she is the best dancer in the region. We have her to thank for the full courtroom each night. Men are not coming for us. They are coming for her. They only want *Mohini*."

Something hot trickled through my chest.

Baanu's stage name for me had made its way to every nook and cranny of this scorched and dry land. Every man who visits King Murkha's court is eager to watch the famous dancers of Khoya Kingdom and drown in their delicate gait. But more than that, they travel hundreds of miles to sit on the edge of their seats for the finale, thirsting after the person who made them whistle and pant.

And that person was me.

Soraya scowled. "Yet, the great Mohini somehow gets out of dancing for our most prominent guest." The other dancers bristled around us uncomfortably. "I wonder why that is? I'm sure he is just as eager to watch you as everyone else in this deva-forsaken land."

Her words had merit. I did have the only night off that truly mattered. Tonight was a full moon, which meant I wouldn't have to step foot on the marbled floor. I was favored—amongst Baanu, amongst the king, amongst everyone who came to the court to watch us perform.

Aside from Ruhi, the other courtesans hated me for it. I didn't blame them, but I also didn't feel guilty. I paid a price for my talents, one that ate away at me every single time I bowed to start a dance.

"Do not forget that I've been here longer than all of you put together," I said stiffly. "I've earned this right."

Soraya scoffed. "Keep telling yourself that if it helps you sleep better, but we all have worked our way up to get here. Many of us danced in the hot streets until we could barely stand. We've all earned the right you speak of."

I don't bother answering her. She was right in a way. All of us danced our way to the most famous stage. All of us worked hard to get here. But I was still more valuable than the rest. Not by choice, but by circumstance.

But I wouldn't be dancing for much longer. After seven years of serving as a courtesan, my contract was finally ending, and the deal I'd made all those years ago would finally come to pass.

Seven years of service and in exchange you'll be given safe passage to Varnasi.

Baanu's promise of freedom drove me to the dance floor each night. I clung onto her words like a prayer. I submitted to this court and flirted with sleazy nobles for information about their kingdoms and coaxed greedy traders into making horrible deals. All for the day I could finally go to Varnasi, a kingdom of paradise in Tyaga.

People of Varnasi were not forced to live in slums or serve as slaves. Everyone could be whatever they wanted to be. But the city was on the other side of the Chayya Forest, and the passage was dangerous. If the person traveling wasn't someone of importance, chances were they wouldn't make it. Either they became food for the various creatures and demons that lurked along the path or they became lost within the forest for good, fated to roam its twisty trails forever. As I had no desire to do either, bargaining with Baanu was my only way out of this miserable kingdom.

Serving in the palace as a courtesan was a mundane and degrading life, but it'd kept me safe for the past seven years. After King Murkha overthrew Queen Orna and destroyed our kingdom, the smaller surrounding villages became obsolete. My options were to become a courtesan, or starve on the street. So I agreed to play the pawn in Baanu's and King Murkha's snakey games. In return, I was fed, housed, and clothed. It was more than I ever expected to have after my parents were murdered.

"Girls," Baanu called our attention with the fake sweet voice she often used. She had been quietly watching us go back and forth, no doubt wondering how she could use it to her advantage. "Normally, I would dismiss your pathetic concerns, Soraya, but today, I'd have to agree with them. We will have to run the sequence tonight with all dancers on the floor."

My heart stopped. *What?*

Baanu's beady eyes landed on me. Rushed whispers traveled through the dancers as they all flicked confused or satisfied glances toward me.

This was a joke. It had to be.

Ruhi's expression turned grim. Soraya tried and failed miserably to hide her smile.

I waited for Baanu to laugh and tell us she was merely kidding, but the short plump lady stood resolute before me.

I opened my mouth to protest, to tell her she was out of her mind if she thought I would step onto the stage, but I struggled to form a cohesive set of words. I couldn't perform tonight because tonight was a full moon, and the Prince of Hell would be our guest.

And if I had to face *him,* there was a strong possibility that he would mark me as his.

CHAPTER TWO

The concrete floor burned my soles as I stared at the woman who had controlled every facet of my life for over a decade.

"Be ready in the receiving room by six sharp." Baanu waved us away like we were bothersome fruit flies.

Sweat rolled down the sides of my face, turning cold. The prince was the most ruthless and powerful person in all of Tyaga and the informal ruler of Naraka, a separate realm that was the manifestation of hell on earth.

Legends say the goddess of death herself had gifted him a piece of her magic, giving him the ability to send someone into madness with a flick of his wrist. No one knows why he was chosen or how, but he was the enforcer of punishment. He showed no mercy to his prisoners, and he let his rakshasas, the demons native to Naraka, run amuck through Tyaga, killing humans for sport.

The dancers around me shuffled away with their heads bent, not wanting to be within Baanu's gaze any longer. I stood rooted to the ground, unable to move until I got some answers. She couldn't expect me to agree to dance tonight when that was not part of our deal.

"Niya," Ruhi urged. "Come on."

Soraya threw another smug grin my way before she slinked off with the others. I shook my head stiffly, watching Baanu, who stared right back with an all-knowing smile. "You go."

Ruhi opened her mouth like she wanted to protest, but I gave her a pointed look. I knew which battles to fight, and this was one of them.

I lifted my chin as I approached Baanu, ignoring the subtle throb every time my heel pressed into the hot concrete. She shooed away the servant holding her pink umbrella, who bowed curtly leaving us alone.

"It's my night off," I reminded her, trying not to sound accusatory.

Seven years of service. That was the deal we had made. I had always gotten the night of a full moon off specifically because the prince attended the court. I had a deal with Baanu and the king because they needed my *other* talents. And they knew if they were to place me center stage, they would lose me to him.

After all these years, *why now?* Was it because my contract was ending soon? Was this some convoluted way of getting me to stay longer?

"I wondered if you would do this." Baanu fiddled with an absurdly large black diamond mounted to a gold ring on her index finger. "If you'd muster the courage to question me. I was sure you wouldn't, but I stand corrected."

"Why?" I asked, ignoring her comments, and not bothering to voice the full question.

Baanu shrugged. "That stocky old merchant bought Mahi out, Kashi is too young to debut. We're down a dancer, and the lines would be uneven."

I almost scoffed at how rehearsed her sentence sounded. Uneven lines and unseasoned dancers had never stopped us before. Hardly any courtesan lasted more than a year here. I didn't buy it. After staying true to our bargain for so long, why would she risk it now? "Is that all?"

Baanu flashed her stained teeth. "We need you to use your *influence* on a particular commander in attendance."

I straightened. *Influence.* She meant my abilities outside of dancing, because not only were the courtesans of Khoya entertainers, we were also the king's spies.

Khoya Kingdom had nearly doubled in size through trade agreements and alliances with neighboring villages that were run by smaller councils. But all the intel and persuasion that fed those negotiations came through us. After a seductive charm hooked him, a thirsty man would drink just about anything. They drank our lies like their own gospel and confided their truths without hesitation.

I folded my arms. "Who is the target?" It must be important if they needed me to be the spy.

"Commander Ezhil, a personal friend of the prince who handles most of his territory negotiations."

The muscles along my spine tensed. I had heard other nobles speak of Commander Ezhil. He is the only known acquaintance of the prince, carrying out most of the prince's extortion and violent threats. I couldn't fathom why any human would willingly serve the prince, and that told me all I needed to know about the man.

"Why do you need to interrogate him?"

Baanu bristled. "*That* information is above your paygrade."

Ezhil would not be an easy shell to break, and I already had a contract in place with Baanu and the King that stated I did not have to dance on full moon nights. "I won't do it," I maintained. "This was never part of our deal."

"You're right," Baanu agreed. "It wasn't, but I'm willing to adjust the terms of our agreement if you agree to dance tonight and use the entire array of your abilities."

"Adjust the terms?" I tilted my head. "How so?"

Baanu's lip curled. "Dance tonight, but not as *Mohini,* where you are front and center. Dance as another normal courtesan, with your face hidden. Help us get the information out of Ezhil, and I'll arrange for your departure to Varnasi."

My mouth parted. It was too good to be true. "You'll let me go just like that?"

Baanu clasped her hands together. "I don't doubt for a second that you've served me well over the years, Niya. I admit it will be difficult to not have you drawing in the crowds, but this court is well established now, and our success will and must continue with or without you."

"Forgive me for having a hard time believing this," I said carefully. "You've repeatedly tried to bribe me to extend my contract." Over the past few months, Baanu had brought up my departure a handful of times, encouraging me to stay a bit longer with promises of flexibility and fortune. And now she was giving me a way to end the contract earlier?

Baanu moved closer. She was at least five inches shorter than me, but her personality made up for our height difference. "Your contract is ending soon anyways; I'm simply offering you a way out earlier. We desperately need the information Ezhil has, and I'm a woman of my word. You'll be out of here before sunrise if you agree."

Baanu was many things, but she always followed through on two things—her goals and her promises. I knew that. She was the mastermind behind the grand frivolity of Khoya Kingdom. Her rigorous dance practices and perfectionist expectations are why every evening men drank until dusk faded into dawn, enraptured by their own senses.

When Baanu first saw me dance, I recognized the emotion that crossed her face. It was admiration laced with ego. She knew I would be her winning hand. That's why I struck a deal with her years ago in her small establishment. The dingy hut where she first started her raunchy business was probably not much larger than the small square concrete slab we stood on now. She needed outstanding performers, and I needed a home that wasn't the slum.

Over the years, she's used me to grow closer to the king. She started with the nobles in his court, drawing them to my performances until no one wanted to attend the royal court for frolic. The attention forced the king to approach Baanu, and two days later, we shifted to the palace as his court entertainers. I was the reason for her success, and my payment was eventual freedom. Letting her use my talent for her own gain was the only way I could get to where I wanted to be. And freedom was now within fingertip reach.

But you risk becoming one of his Chosen.

The dancing wasn't the problem; it was what came afterwards. Because the prince did not just come to indulge in our beauty and then quietly leave. The prince took courtesans from various courts. His *Chosen* as he called it. And now, I'd be on that floor tonight, another rose available to be plucked. If he did choose me, I'd be trading one prison for another. Building a life in Varnasi would remain a wish that would never come true.

Baanu seemed to read my thoughts. "Since you're not dancing as *Mohini* tonight, you'll be wearing the same veil as the other dancers. It will be easier to *focus* that way. Besides, everyone knows the prince has a type."

Another wave of nausea rolled over me at the way she said the fact so nonchalantly, even though it was true. The prince always had a knack for spotting and selecting one of the younger and newer courtesans. But that didn't remove the risk of him choosing me.

"What will it be, Niya?" Baanu crooned, examining her perfect fingernails. "What is one more dance?"

One more dance, and I'm free.

I swallowed as my desire to leave this place slowly won over my mind. This offer was too good to let go, especially if I could blend in with the other dancers. I was too seasoned for the prince's taste, and my face would be hidden with the veil. If I didn't take this opportunity, Baanu or the king would undoubtedly use some other ploy to keep me here.

This was a chance to leave now. I had to take it.

"One more dance, Baanu," I promised. Warning pressure built in my chest, but I buried it deep. I'd been a courtesan long enough. "After tonight, I am no longer yours."

Baanu dipped her chin and gave me a crooked smile. "Ensure it is your best dance yet, Niya." Meaning, make sure Ezhil is thoroughly under your influence.

I dipped my head, letting the request fall on deaf ears. By now, she should have realized every dance was my best because when it came to bringing life into music, I did not know how to give any less.

CHAPTER THREE

The palace walls dripped in shades of gold and blue. Bundles of white baby's breath were woven into the curtains and around the pillars to contrast the gaudy fabric that weighed down the entire palace.

Baanu strode ahead of us through the brightly lit halls with her nose held high. She led us toward the throne room, where the king's council and his guests would congregate for the evening. We stayed silent as we followed her, letting the soft chimes of our coin belts mark our presence.

My hands fidgeted with the loose folds of my lehenga, if one could call it that. The flowy fabric was thin but hugged every curve, leaving little to the imagination. The plain skirt had a slit that ran up to my upper thigh, revealing a thin gold chain that wrapped down my leg and hooked into my coin belt. It matched my plain gold bangles, earrings, and tikka that felt cool against my tawny skin. The same shade of burgundy flooded through my top, and a series of strained strings held it over my breasts at the back.

Dozens of maids in marigold salwars with blue veils scurried past us with plates of food and trays of drinks. The smell of spiced curry and milk sweets hit my nose in a heady wave. My stomach growled, wishing I could shove down a potato puff.

I stumbled a step as a wave of nausea crashed over me. Ruhi nudged my shoulder. "Get it together," she hissed.

I nodded, clutching my stomach and pulling my shoulders back. Ruhi had danced in front of the prince multiple times and survived. Though, I don't know how she had done it so many times without vomiting.

It will be fine.

The prince was notorious for taking new and untrained courtesans. He won't want me. Perhaps if he had seen me at the tender age of twelve when I first started dancing, he would have taken me. But now, at nineteen, why would he bother?

I was the best dancer here and the oldest. Sia, Priti, and Fareeha were barely sixteen and constantly fumbled on footwork; they all had higher chances of being selected as his *Chosen*. I clenched my fists together as unease churned low in my belly.

I closed my eyes for just a second to imagine tomorrow when I'd be on my way to Varnasi. *One more night, one more dance.* The thought settled me as I opened my eyes again, focusing on the task at hand: get on the marbled floor, identify my target, and focus on commanding his attention.

We entered the servants receiving room next to the throne room, a tight space with a few lit fire torches. Servants were bursting through the door every two seconds with empty and full plates.

Baanu whipped around. She wore her finest navy silk gown paired with a double-chained pearl necklace. "I won't bother saying perform well." She locked eyes with each of us with merciless intention. A sweeping chill traveled down my spine. "You know what will happen if you don't." Without another word, she left us in the dark space, letting us fester with our jittery nerves.

"Has he arrived yet?" Ruhi whispered next to me, trying to peer through the small window in the door. "I want to get this over with."

"We haven't heard any screams yet, so I'm assuming no," I said flatly. Ruhi gasped, as did some of the other courtesans. All of us had veils that covered half of our face, but I could still make out the deep-seated fear in their irises.

My eyes reflected the same sentiment.

Soraya folded her arms. "For once I agree with Niya. It's no secret the prince takes joy in the suffering of others. Last time, he almost killed a noble for saying something he didn't like."

I remembered because I was in the back, pouring brown liquor for a noble. I could still hear the bone-rattling scream of that fully grown man.

"Still, do not say such horrible things," Ruhi said grimly, fussing with her wine-colored chiffon lehenga. "Take a few deep breaths, all of you," she said with soft command. A few of the dancers around us let out airy breaths. Others sat down to stretch and get into their performance mindset. Ruhi looped her arm through mine. She dropped her voice down to a whisper. "I'm going to miss you, you know. Promise you'll write."

I stared at her arm looped through mine. I confided in Ruhi about my deal with Baanu. Courtesans normally didn't last very long here. Within a year, most dancers, like Mahi, became mistresses after someone bought them out, or the prince took them, or Baanu kicked them out for not performing up to expectations. I had made it a point not to become close to the others, not wanting to feel their loss after they left. But Ruhi somehow wiggled her way into the tight bubble I kept around myself.

She had become my friend...my best friend if I was honest. "I'm not much of a writer," I said quietly. An odd sort of pressure built behind my eyes. "But find me when you get there." The standard contract Baanu set with new girls was ten years, but no one ever made it that long.

Ruhi snorted. "I don't think the devas have written Varnasi into my fate. My karma from my past life has already dictated it. Sometimes, it is best to take comfort in whatever liberties you can find within the bounds of the life you are given."

She referred to an old belief, one that said our past lives dictated our future ones, but I wasn't so convinced that was true now. "The devas have abandoned us," I said thickly. The only gods people prayed to these days were the Asuras, the antigods who were the overseers of Naraka and doled out torture and torment. "They no longer control our kismet, but people like Baanu and the king do."

Naraka hadn't always been accessible to humans. It had been brought closer by Rati, a devi who went rogue after her lover was slaughtered before her.

Before, there were three realms—Svarga, where the devas lived; Prithvi, where the humans lived; and Naraka, where the demons lived. But Rati closed the eternal gates so that the gods and antigods could not travel through them.

Another beat of silence passed, then Ruhi nudged me with her shoulder.

I sighed. "Perhaps. But don't underestimate—"

Muffled voices beyond the door cut her off. All of us stiffened as the chatter became louder.

The king's voice rumbled above all of them. "We've been eagerly waiting for your arrival. There is much to discuss." I held back a snort at the king's feigned enthusiasm. He enjoyed seeing the prince just as much as the rest of us, yet like every monarch in this territory, he openly greeted the devil at his gates. "How is Naraka faring? I've heard you imprisoned a few of King Aatank's soldiers, forced them into your world. I'm curious to why you are in need of measly foot soldiers when you yourself control the rakshasas? Ones, I've heard, can take down twenty humans at once."

The orchestra swallowed the answer to his question. Servants walked through our space with dark liquor bottles and trays of exotic fresh fruit and expensive nuts. All probably selected based on the prince's favorites.

Each agonizing minute ticked by as eager chatter filled the room.

Baanu's voice flowed through the cracks of the door. "Welcome! Welcome, council members, noble gents, and, of course, his Highness of Naraka," her voice softened a hair. "The Khoya Kingdom is known for many things in Tyaga—fine silks, premium spices, intoxicating potions—and while our neighboring kingdoms may try to rival us in these fine goods, there has always been one thing they will never be able to beat us at...our knack for entertaining."

Someone in the crowd whistled. Ruhi let out a breath of indignation. I chuckled under my breath. Men acted like such fools when it came to pretty women.

Who was I kidding? Men acted like fools when it came to anything.

"Enough of this prolonged speech. Bring them out!" someone shouted, and murmurs of agreement followed.

I swallowed the lump that had formed in the back of my throat.

Baanu chuckled. "We are restless. Worry not, your patience will be rewarded. Our *best* dancers have been selected for tonight. And as always, the bid will take place immediately afterward."

"There will be no bid tonight," a deep, smooth voice cut through the room.

My heart shuddered at the sheer power in that voice. I had heard it before but never gave it any mind; now, the effect on me was instant.

"Ezhil and I are only two outside humans here tonight, and we have no interest in bedding your women. And as my rakshasas are not allowed in this hall, holding a bid is pointless," the voice added.

Ruhi and I exchanged a look. The crowd's primary interest was the bid at the end of the night. Every kingdom's court in Tyaga was different, but in Khoya, courtesans were not forced to sleep with onlookers. We were given a choice. As an incentive, we are given a hefty cut of the earnings, but any sexual activity had to be consensual.

That was not the case in surrounding kingdoms or in Naraka, if rumors were true. Other courts forced courtesans to comply, instead of letting them choose.

I had never seen a map before, but I knew there were four kingdoms excluding Naraka—Khoya, Varnasi, Tavas, and Dhana. Aside from Varnasi, they all had harsh climates and ruthless monarchs. Which made conflict for resources a sport, and the lost lives of soldiers frequent.

Tyaga held no reprieve for anyone.

"Very well"—though she didn't sound happy about it—"there will be no bid. Bring them in," Baanu announced.

I could taste the relief in the air. I had participated in the bid on multiple occasions. In most cases, it was because I was trying to gather intel on a target, but other times, it was because I spotted someone attractive and needed the release. But not having the bid this evening was favorable. I could get on and off the floor without any fuss.

On cue, the door in front of us swung open. On catlike feet, we all filed out onto the marbled floor. The amount of gold in this throne room could feed the entire kingdom for over a year. Men dressed in equal amounts of gold and fine silk sherwanis sat amongst maroon and evergreen cushions. Their gazes were hungry and wanting.

I looked down at the golden floors as that was protocol upon entering the room. *Just another dance.* I took my place at the center of the troop in the back. The few beats of dead silence calmed the blood pounding in my ears. The first string of the oud was pulled, and like a pack of lionesses on a hunt, we all began to move.

Impress and sway.

The qanun joined the oud, closely followed by the subtle *thumps* of a tabla. The tempo increased, and the instruments began to draw me in. Their sounds perfectly synchronized with each of our steps. With a graceful twirl, we all switched formations, so that I was now at the front and the other girls fell around me into an inverse triangle.

The music softened, and I lifted my gaze, letting it caress the room until it collided with Zehan's.

Air stalled in my lungs.

I'd always seen him from a distance, stealing glances while I served the other guests in the back, but I'd never let the full beauty of him hit me squarely in the chest.

His eyes were darker than a night with no moon. Underneath the clean beard, it was easy to make out chiseled cheekbones that gracefully blended into a pointed nose. His ebony hair was ruffled across his oddly pale forehead. He sat lazily on his cushioned seat with one leg propped up to rest an elbow. He had an ethereal beauty that could only be explained by the fact that he transcended mortal existence. Power and cruelty radiated from him like heat from glowing embers.

The glass of amber liquid he was readying to take a sip of froze on his lips as his eyes lingered on me. His Adam's apple bobbed. My stomach lurched. The music picked up again, and without breaking eye contact, he downed his drink in one long, slow swig. He wore an indigo sherwani that had white fabric embroidered with gold droplets twisted into a subtle knot at the shoulder and draped across his broad torso.

He leaned back as an arrogant, alluring smirk crept onto his handsome face, and I almost forgot the next step.

Don't get distracted. I had a job to do. On Zehan's right, King Murkha sat with a full belly and an eager expression. He regarded Ezhil, who was busy eating grapes on his other side. Objectively, Ezhil was much more built than Zehan, yet his features were softer, more worn and classic.

I caught Baanu's gaze. She dipped her chin a millimeter. She had said that I should wait until the king leaned in to speak with Ezhil. King Murkha leaned in to speak to Ezhil while Zehan was busy refilling his glass. *That is the signal.*

My sights settled on Ezhil like a hawk. The tabla beat picked up, and I twisted my hips sharply so that my coin belt flapped followed by a slow inch-by-inch roll of my torso. We danced in perfect synchronization across the floor, captivating the hungry men in the room, demanding their attention.

Zehan motioned the waitstaff to bring him more drink. Instantly, servants entered the room from all sides. I turned sharply as the music continued to crescendo. My steps became more intricate, and when the next quick rapt of the tabla ensued, I released invisible tendrils of magic toward the crowd. I was careful to target only Ezhil and the guests—not the servers and definitely not Baanu or the king.

Like frost spreading through a forest, my audience became captivated by the lure of my magic. Eyes glazed over and mouths parted. The trance, as I called it, caused an ensnarement of senses and euphoria. They cheered louder for more, clinking their glasses repeatedly against each other. King Murkha grinned with a puffed-up face as the crowd's rowdiness took on a new form. For him, this was music to his ears. He enjoyed it when his courtesans held his guests' desire captive.

That was precisely what I was doing. My enchantment forced them to sit, watch, and want us until I released them. Of course, they wouldn't know I was using magic. They were aware of what was happening around them, but their focus and attention would continuously find the dancers on this floor.

King Murkha leaned in closer to Ezhil, and I gave another flood of power into him, encouraging him to pay heed to what King Murkha was saying and reveal whatever secrets he may be keeping. It took effort to hold him under the trance, like an invisible shield around him wanted me out.

I despised how icky my magic made me feel, but it was how I survived so long as a courtesan. It was a curse disguised as a blessing.

I gracefully spun, moving closer to Ezhil, but someone else caught my attention.

Zehan observed me. Without looking, he plucked a grape off the vine and tossed it into his mouth. He didn't have the same wide-eyed expression as the others. My insides plummeted.

He was unaffected by my magic.

I released another swell of magic to keep the crowd under my influence, giving an extra dose to Ezhil as he continued whatever conversation he was having with King Murkha. Zehan's thin lips formed a slow, menacing grin.

He knows.

But he couldn't. My magic was invisible, and we were all dressed in identical clothing. And if he did, why was he not stopping King Murkha from speaking with Ezhil?

I stumbled on the next set of eight counts, lagging a beat too slow. Baanu's pursed her lips. But I was too busy trying to decipher what was happening. I had never met anyone immune to my powers. Was it because he also possessed magic?

Music faded away as my ears pounded with my own heartbeat. Zehan continued, rather languidly, picking up pieces of fruit from a servant's trembling tray, clearly not in a trance.

Ignore Zehan. Focus on Ezhil.

My magic ebbed and flowed with the tune, wearing me out, but the king hadn't finished his conversation with Ezhil.

The commander, of course, wouldn't realize why he suddenly had a loose tongue, he wouldn't even realize he had revealed anything of value. Zehan turned toward Ezhil and cocked his head. *Does he know what I'm doing? Does he know what the king is up to?* Tendrils of my magic flared over the crowd, causing them to jeer like a wild troop of chimps.

Another drumbeat led to another swell of magic. No matter how much lustful magic I pushed out, Zehan would not succumb. He simply watched us with grim intrigue.

To my relief, Commander Ezhil leaned away from the king, his eyes glassy and relaxed. The song turned soft as it approached its melodic end, and I knew it was time to reel my magic back.

My shoulders dipped gratefully as I released my hold, and subtle fatigue loosened my limbs. The watchers whistled and clapped as we bowed with our hands folded in front of us. Ruhi gave me a reissuing look as we filed into a line and bowed.

After so many years of being held captive by my own fate, I was free.

King Murkha appeared satisfied with whatever he gleaned from Ezhil as he settled back into his obnoxious throne. Yet, the whole performance had felt off. Ezhil leaned towards Zehan to say something, and the prince nodded. My gaze found Baanu, who stared at me with a strange smile. Maybe she was bitter that I would be leaving her.

We turned to leave the hall, but Zehan slowly stood up and took a few steps forward. The hall fell silent.

My veins filled with ice as Zehan's long index finger lifted and singled me out.

"You, with the bright-green eyes."

CHAPTER FOUR

B lood drained from my face.

"You are my Chosen," Zehan said.

No demand. No room for argument. He stated it as if it had always been.

The gold walls closed in on me. Every muscle stiffened, but my mind raced. *No.* I was supposed to leave this forsaken kingdom once and for all. I practically tasted freedom on my tongue.

"No," I breathed, inadvertently too loud as Zehan's head snapped up. As horrible as it was, I was *sure* that he would select one of the other dancers. Ruhi pressed into my shoulder. Thoughts spiraled in my head. *Why does he want me? I was older. I was experienced. I am everything he never chooses.*

Zehan tilted his head. An amused smile played on his dark lips. "You have been here a while, have you not? Then you know I never go back on my selection, courtesan."

My magic bristled, still alive and awake from being used so thoroughly. Perhaps it was desperation or perhaps it was beckoning me to take control of the situation. I lifted my chin. "Well, there is a first for everything. My answer is *no.*"

Zehan's arrogant gaze felt like a pulse of uncomfortable heat from the glaring sun. My senses heightened tenfold, and a low churn stirred near my navel. He slowly approached me like a predator on the hunt, hyper focused and purposeful. I fought the urge to step back, pressing my toes firmly into the smooth cool floor.

"No what?" he asked, leaning in. He yanked down the veil that covered half of my face. I let out a small gasp, or maybe it was his breath that hitched. His shoulders became even more rigid as he scanned my face, pausing on my hooped nose ring and then my lips.

"No, I will not be your Chosen," I said quietly. The other dancers froze with wide eyes, like gazelles scoping out their surroundings. I had won my independence. I might damn myself, but I had worked too hard to lose now.

He chuckled. "I'm assuming you are not stupid enough to actually believe that you are in a position to refuse me, courtesan. It's clear you have a wide array of *talents.* Ones that you'll still be able to exploit in Naraka. I assure you the realm is not what humans have made it out to be."

I blinked at that statement. If he was trying to make the situation better by assuring me living in Naraka would not be so bad, he was failing miserably. I clenched my jaw, not letting my fear deter me. "As of five minutes ago, I am no longer a courtesan for Khoya Kingdom. That was the deal I made with Baanu. You cannot take me."

"Interesting." He pulled back, studying me. He clucked his tongue and twisted around. "Baanu, is this true?"

Baanu spoke to me but answered him. "I have no utter idea what she is referring to." Her expression was stony.

"We had a deal," I said through gritted teeth. "I—" The heavy gold adornment in the room suddenly became overwhelming.

She betrayed me.

There could be no other explanation. I had worked for Baanu for years, and she had never fallen back on her word. She *always* followed through on her promises. Why now? Unless she was upset that I would be leaving and wanted this to be her parting gift.

I turned to King Murkha, readying to appeal to him. He must honor the contract I had agreed to with Baanu.

Zehan beat me to it, looking sideways at the king. He was at least six inches taller than the balding man. "Murkha, I thought our deal where I supply your army with weapons in exchange for a courtesan was permanently sealed."

"It is and shall remain so." King Murkha didn't bother sparing me a glance and kept his tone diplomatic. "Mohini's era in Khoya Kingdom had to end at some point."

In that moment, my hatred for him and this court grew to an impossible level. My magic hackled, threatening to lash out like a whip, but I shut it down. I shook my head, trying to refuse what I already knew was true.

I no longer belonged to this wretched kingdom; I belonged to one far worse. Because a promise to a prince far outweighed a promise to a courtesan.

A corner of Zehan's lip tugged up as he leaned forward The smell of burning coals and something sweet tickled my nostrils. "You heard him, courtesan. Say your goodbyes and pack your bags. You belong to me now." He held out his hand.

I stared at it for a beat and shook my head. Maybe I was stupid for challenging the ruler of hell, but I didn't care. "No." King Murkha and Baanu looked mutinous, but I had nothing to lose. Punishment at their hands was better than being taken as a prisoner to Naraka. If I stayed here, leaving this life was attainable. If I went to Naraka, I would never escape because *no* courtesan had ever returned after being chosen. Naraka was a one-way ticket.

Zehan lifted an eyebrow. "You will be far more interesting than any of my other Chosen." He turned his back to speak to Commander Ezhil, dismissing my refusal. "Prepare the horses. I want to be on our way within the hour."

No, no, no. This can't be happening.

"What is wrong with you?" I yelled, unable to control my tongue. The dancers and audience grasped in horror, like I had gone mad, which I might as well have. "What kind of cruel, senseless person gathers joy in taking people against their will to a place that hates humans?"

Zehan's back tensed. I'd momentarily forgotten my place. He was a prince, and I was a lowly courtesan. I had no right to yell at him; my words were punishable by death if he felt like it.

Yet, dying seemed easier than becoming *his*.

Zehan twisted around and stalked back to me like a crazed wolf. "Ask me that again. This time to my face."

I pushed my lips together as he leaned into me. I held back the deep shudder that fought to come out.

"Do it, *courtesan*," he growled. I didn't open my mouth. I held my ground. He sniggered. "Fine. Have it your way." He lifted his hand in front of my face and snapped his fingers.

Ruhi screamed. She fell to her hands and knees like she had been stabbed by a blade. Her shriek of agony made my eardrums explode. I attempted to help her, but Zehan grabbed my upper arm, digging the pads of his fingers into my supple flesh, holding me in place.

Soraya rushed over and knelt before Ruhi, whispering words of comfort, but the screaming persisted as Soraya hovered her hands over her, afraid to touch her. "Accept your fate, Niya," she said with harsh words, eyeing me with pure hatred. "Or her death is on *you*."

I had seen Zehan perform this kind of magic before, where it left no physical wound. To a messenger from Dhana for delivering him news he didn't want to hear. Ruhi screamed again.

"Stop!" I sobbed and turned to Zehan. I tried to twist my arm out of his grasp, but it only made him tighten his grip.

His expression held no sympathy, not even an ounce of remorse for what he was doing. "You can stop it, courtesan, in more ways than one."

What did he mean by that? It wasn't like my magic would help. I couldn't stop this. I wouldn't know the first place to start. My magic was only good for bringing out unsaid truths and deep desires. I had never used it to help someone.

Ruhi's piercing cry made my insides writhe. Zehan didn't even flinch. Hot tears slipped from the corners of my eyes.

"Please," I begged, hating the fact that I was at his mercy. Ruhi's features scrunched, her body in a fetal position on the floor. "Please spare her."

Zehan's expression darkened. "Do not beg. It's unbecoming." He snapped his fingers, and Ruhi went silent, crumpling flat onto the floor.

"Challenge me again, and I'll make sure every dancer here doesn't wake," Zehan said viciously. He grabbed my chin, pinching my cheeks with his index finger and thumb. He dropped his voice to a whisper, one that trailed along the curve of my ear and down the back of my neck. "And I'll make sure all of Tyaga knows of your so-called *talents* outside of dancing. Do I make myself clear?"

Any doubt I had of him knowing about my trance magic ended.

I stared at him dumbfounded. I swallowed and nodded. Even if he hadn't threatened Ruhi, he had me trapped. My magical abilities were a well-kept secret. Only Baanu and King Murkha knew of its true depth and scale. There were rumors, but no one *truly* understood. Most thought a deva had given me a boon to captivate and seduce. But little did they know that it wasn't just lusting magic, it was coaxing magic. One that both King Murkha and Baanu had repeatedly exploited.

And now the Prince of Naraka knew about it too. Which was dangerous. If people found out about the full extent of my powers, it would place a target on my back. At one time, it was common for humans to possess magic, but not anymore.

"Good," Zehan said, releasing me. I closed my eyes as the small pebble of hope I'd felt right after the performance fell to the bottom of the pond. More tears slipped out as two pale fingers, with a mere snap, ripped away everything I worked so hard and so long for. "Now, you will come with no more complaints, correct?"

I let my hatred shine as I glared back at the prince. With grim acceptance, I nodded, letting my self-made doom descend upon me.

"Good," he said, assessing me with the same expressionless mask. He strode out of the room without even bothering to say goodbye to his host. Ezhil gave a sharp bow to King Murkha before glancing my way with piqued interest and then following behind his master. Muffled murmurs trailed them as they vanished out of the hall.

I rushed over to where Soraya kneeled, and together, we helped Ruhi stand back up. Her entire body was trembling. "I'm so sorry, Ruhi," I said quietly.

Baanu muttered commands to the servants and other dancers. I glowered at her, but she kept her eyes averted. She had thrown my loyalty away like a tattered rag. I knew Baanu was wicked, cunning, downright wretched, but I hadn't pegged her for a complete liar. I should have recognized this was a trick.

Ruhi squeezed my hand tighter. "It isn't your fault," she said through soft tears. Even after being put through whatever pain Zehan placed on her, she was showing me nothing but kindness.

My heart plummeted. *I had been so close to freedom.* Baanu's betrayal, King Murkha's indifference, Zehan's viciousness—it was all too much to grapple with. I'd been chasing a life that lived with no boundaries, where I wouldn't have to answer to anyone. With one quick snap of his fingers, Zehan had ripped that dream away. Two more hot tears streamed down my cheeks.

After tonight, after what he had just done, there was no doubt in my mind that Prince Zehan was as vile as everyone made him out to be. He may have forced my hand in agreeing to come with him to Naraka, but I wouldn't stay an obedient Chosen. I would find a way out of his grasp, a way to escape this fate. I wouldn't give him the satisfaction of capturing me.

Zehan may have picked me as his rose, but he failed to see one thing.

I had thorns that would prick until they drew blood.

CHAPTER FIVE

Moonlight streamed through the latticed windows, creating symmetrical diamond shapes across the sandstone floor. The liveliness of the night had died, and along with it, my hopes for a better life. Anxiety warred in my mind as I quietly followed the palace guards towards the entrance and my new fate.

Fifteen minutes. That's all I was given to change out of my skimpy outfit into something more travel-friendly and pack my things, which consisted of an heirloom necklace and a small satchel.

A line of servants and maids peered out the doorless openings to glimpse Mohini departing Khoya, whispering as we passed. My chest caved in on itself as I recognized so many of them. I hated my role here, but it had also been a home full of people I knew. A familiarity that would be hard to part with.

The rest of the courtesans were huddled in the vast oval foyer. Magenta drapes *swooshed* in symmetrical patterns along the wall. It was customary for every dancer to have a send-off when they left. However, I never imagined I would be the one walking out. Soraya stared at me with smugness; I had half a mind to comment but refrained. Spitting out venom took energy I didn't want to spend.

Ezhil waited at the entrance with a grim expression. Zehan casually tucked his hands into his pockets, nodding to King Murkha like he agreed with whatever the old king spewed his way. Zehan's gaze flickered my way and did a double take.

My heart rate picked up as the arrogant bastard smirked at me like we were old friends. I wanted to bolt. Take my chances and run into the desert and pray to the forgotten devas that I make it through Chayya Forest alive.

My footsteps slowed down as I approached the front door. Fate closed in on me. My feet stopped moving altogether when I saw Ruhi with tears still streaming down her cheeks.

A wave of emotion flitted through me. Ruhi reached her hand out, and I grasped it in solidarity. She leaned in so her forehead rested against mine. The guards behind me tensed, readying to break out contact, but Zehan held up his hand silently telling them to wait.

"Are you okay?" I whispered.

She dipped her chin an inch as she lifted her head so we were eye level. Her pupils were a bolder shade of hazel. "What am I going to do without you?"

"What you've always done," I said quietly. "Survive."

She clasped my hand tightly and pulled me into a brief hug. "If I don't see you in this one, I'll see you in the next lifetime."

I kept my chin high as I walked toward Zehan and his entourage, ignoring the way his intense glare made me want to combust.

My eyes flickered toward Baanu, who held no sympathy. She simply stared at me with emotionless indifference. It was clear there would be no formal acknowledgments or goodbyes. Our contract had been terminated. What happened to me was none of her concern.

Anger thrummed under my skin. She was the reason I was in this mess. And after everything we'd been through, she couldn't produce a teaspoon of compassion?

I sighed with resignation. Lashing out at her would not change anything. I would still be Zehan's Chosen and dragged to Naraka. Baanu was what this kingdom made her. I could not fault her for it. We're all shaped by the events of the past.

I pulled my satchel over my shoulder and passed over the threshold without another glance, shedding the last unwanted attachment I had to this place.

I couldn't remember the last time I had been on this side of the palace. Murkha normally kept us hidden inside, heightening the mystery and novelty of Khoya's courtesans. During the day, soldiers drilled in the front yards, land-scapers cleaned the outer walls, and carriages trotted down the long driveway. But now, it was unusually empty and deathly silent, as if Murkha wanted to keep my departure a secret.

A chill crept into the tips of my fingers and toes. In the silvery moonlight, I could make out a long line of onyx carriages and black horses at the foot of massive concrete stairs. *I am finally leaving.*

Yet, I headed to a place much worse than Khoya.

I wrapped my long, printed dupatta over my head and looped it over my shoulders and arm. The urge to run out into the open night fell over me, but I knew it would be difficult to escape with King Murkha's soldiers roaming all over the kingdom. No, I'd have to wait until we got out of this city, perhaps when we stopped for a break. I knew Naraka was at least a day's worth of travel. That time was all I would have to figure out an escape plan.

I opened my satchel to pull out the extra shawl I had packed, but instead, found a crinkled-up piece of paper sitting on top. I quickly glanced back to where Zehan and Ezhil continued to converse with Murkha. I faced forward and slowly opened the note.

Niya,

I hope you see this letter before it is too late. I pray to the Asuras that you stop at Sahra, one of Zehan's check posts. Find the man named Ameel and tell him I sent you. He might be willing and able to get you to Varnasi. He knows the major traders and merchants from there. He might ask for payment.

You can trust him. He frequents this court often and owes me a favor.

Your Only Friend,

Ruhi

A small kernel of hope flared within me as I tucked the note back into my satchel. She must have slipped it into my bag when she hugged me. That clever friend of mine was more conniving than I gave her credit for.

I smiled as I let her perfect handwriting sink in. If Ruhi trusted this man, then I would, too. Besides, what other options did I have? And as for payment,

I had a plan for that as well. A diamond pear on a black beaded necklace burned between the crevice of my breasts.

I scanned the dark desert, letting the soft sounds of sand being whisked by wind calm my nerves. I just needed to get to Sahra now.

"If you're thinking about escaping with that fancy magic of yours," Zehan interrupted, startling me, "I wouldn't."

I snorted. Tucking my hand with the note underneath the dupatta I had just wrapped around myself. "I'm not an idiot."

I *had* considered using my magic to trance a handful of guards to help me escape. I'd probably get out of the palace and past the main gates easily, but once King Murkha or Zehan sent their guards to fetch me, I wouldn't be able to influence that many minds at once. Not to mention, crossing the desert terrain, or the Drifts, as travelers called it, without food or water wouldn't bode well for me.

Zehan chewed the inside of his cheek. "No, you're not."

I blinked. Was that his way of being nice? My trance itched to come out and test itself over him again. What was it about this man that made me want to turn this desert into an ocean.

As if he could read my thoughts, he chuckled. "At least you won't be a bore. Do not fret, there will be plenty of opportunity to release some of that energy you're keeping bottled up."

My mouth parted. Zehan blatantly pointing this out to me brought up the same burning question that had bothered me since my performance.

How did he know about my magic?

I had replayed my performance in my mind repeatedly, wondering how Zehan had realized I was using powers, but I couldn't pinpoint it. When I received this magic, I had been told that it would be unseen and undetectable. In the seven years I had used this ability, no one had ever fully grasped what it could do, but somehow, in just a few dance sequences, Zehan had.

"We're all set," Ezhil called as he trotted down a few steps past us.

"Then we are done here." I felt Zehan look sideways at me, but I didn't return his glare. "Let's go."

I mutely followed them to the carriages. Zehan snapped his fingers. One of the carriage doors swung open, revealing a sleek inside with black seats. He tapped the door, looking back at me with a rogue grin. "In you go, courtesan."

I stood rooted to the spot and shot him a defiant glare.

Zehan's smile only darkened. He jerked his chin to the door. "I can also place you in there myself if you would prefer."

I quickly stepped into the carriage and slammed the door shut in his face.

Sahra couldn't come fast enough.

***

A high-pitched whistle startled me awake.

"Whoa," someone called out.

I sat up as the carriage rolled to a stop. I blinked a few times, momentarily confused by my surroundings—black interior, smooth leather seats that smelled like musk and smoke.

I wiped the tiredness from my eyes and brought saliva to my mouth so my tongue would stop sticking to the roof of my mouth. I had fallen asleep while letting my imagination and fears run wild.

If I wasn't able to escape, what would happen once we got to Naraka? Would Zehan throw me into a cell? Would he feed me to his rakshasas? Would he force me to become his consort? The questions stacked on top of each other.

Sunlight peered around the edges of the black curtain. It was midday by the looks of it, which meant I had been asleep for hours. But it was still too soon to have arrived in Naraka.

Tyaga was mostly made up of desert until it greeted the edge of Chayya Forest, but that was miles away. Zehan had strategically established checkposts throughout the kingdom, providing tired travelers with supplies and direction. But everyone knew it was all a front to hide his darker dealings. His demons not only stole from travelers but took some as prisoners as well. And now, they were my only hope of escaping.

"Five minutes," a voice roared outside. The same voice shouted commands, but I couldn't make out what they were because it sounded like hissing or a strong lisp.

I rose to my knees and slowly peeked through the edge of the curtain and held back a scream.

Dozens of rakshasas roamed the sandy plains. They were all sickly shades of brown and red with bull-like horns or razor-thin teeth. Bile rose in the back of my throat. I had seen rakshasas—some with multiple heads, others with monstrous faces that resembled demonic animals—before, but never so many in one place.

This must be Sahra. Which meant Ruhi's contact, Ameel, might be here.

Prince Zehan stood like a phantom with his arms folded loosely across his biceps. His skin was pale in the sunlight, and in his dark clothing, he seemed wholly out of place.

Commander Ezhil stood next to him with one hand on his dagger, along with a rather bulky rakshasa in a black and navy uniform, whose bulging white eyes were visible even from here.

Zehan let out a deep laugh. The rumble of it licked up my spine. Rakshasas were the most vicious and manic creatures to walk this land, and the prince conversed with them as if...they were friends.

Small tents were erected all around the area. On the other side of the gate, a long line of carriages waited to be searched and sent through. I had heard countless nobles complain about these checkposts in Khoya. The rakshasas searched every nook and cranny of the carriages that traveled through these parts. They stole any precious goods and some even took small children or females. What they did with those they took, no one knew, but the demons made travel between kingdoms difficult.

Zehan's eyes and ears were everywhere.

My head pounded as someone screamed. Two giant rakshasas dragged an older man as he kicked, attempting to break free. They forced him to his knees before Zehan. Another human with a low bun and shawl wrapped around his torso stood next to the demons.

I pressed my nose into the window and opened the curtain farther to get a better look. Streaks of blood ran down the captured man's face. His clothes were tattered and ripped, like he had been tortured for days.

"Let me go," he sobbed with a broken voice. "Please."

Zehan strolled up to him. I wanted to come out of my hiding place, go to the man, fight for him, do something—*anything*. I pulled the latch on the carriage door, but it was locked. *Damn him.* Panic seized my heart and gave it a small squeeze. If I couldn't leave this carriage, how the hell was I going to escape?

I watched the old man, enraptured by the events unfolding. In the next blink of an eye, white light swallowed the man whole. *What was that?*

Zehan smiled as he flicked his wrist, diminishing the light around the man. "You and your cronies were simpleminded if you thought you could get past my rakshasas. This is the second time we've caught you bringing people over illegally." He leaned down until he was right in front of the man's face. "So, let me be crystal clear. If we ever see you passing through this region again, the rakshasas will kill you. If you try to fight now, they will kill you. If you continue to give them a hard time during your imprisonment... They. Will. Kill. You. Do you understand?"

The man nodded vigorously, half-conscious. Nausea bubbled in the pit of my stomach. How could Zehan justify punishing a man so ruthlessly? The man was old and had clearly been mistreated. Even if he had been bringing people here illegally, those people might have needed to escape. What was the harm in transporting a few illegals to a new place if it helped them have a better life?

Zehan rose back to his full height, his lip curling in disgust. He snapped his fingers, and the man screamed while convulsing on the floor. My nails dug into the carriage walls while Zehan's gaze flitted to my carriage, like he knew I was watching and loathing every second.

Use your magic.

I didn't know what else it could do aside from the trance, but I couldn't just sit here and do nothing. Another shriek from the man made my power flood to my fingertips. I let out the invisible magic, but as soon as it hit the carriage wall, it fizzled out. I bristled. This carriage contained magic to prevent me from using mine. All I could do was watch helplessly.

Zehan dropped his hand. He stared at the man with utmost loathing. "Take him out of my sight."

The rakshasas led the beaten man away, and the human with the low bun turned to Zehan. "He will be harder than the others," he said.

"Yes," Commander Ezhil said, "but they always come around. Either by words or force."

"What's wrong, Bidal?" Zehan watched the large rakshasa with bulged eyes. "You have that expression like you have something to tell me but don't want to."

Bidal looked reluctantly at his prince. His thick skin was a deep ash gray, and he had upturned fangs that were the size of my middle finger. "We haven't seen Darsh in a few days."

"Shit," Zehan said, running a hand through his wayward strands. "I haven't felt anything since the last one." His voice shook. "Have the guards interrogate every departed soul in Naraka. Use any means necessary. I want him found." Shadowy white tendrils, like steam, released from his frame.

Who was Darsh? And was that worry on the prince's face?

"We'll start right away," the rakshasa nodded.

"How many departed souls is that now?" the man with the bun asked.

Zehan's expression darkened. "Eight."

Departed souls? Were those the people who lived in Naraka? What did he mean when he said he *hadn't felt anything since the last one?* I stared at Zehan, trying to convince myself that his expression reflected something akin to worry.

The doors to my carriage suddenly clicked open, and I squinted in the bright daylight. My voice caught in my throat as a huge rakshasa pulled me out by my upper arm and onto the dry earth. I kicked and tried to pry myself out of the demon's iron grip, but it flung me onto the ground.

"Move, human," the rakshasa grunted. "I don't have all day."

I gasped and twisted around to face one of my many captors, refusing to cower before the beast. My lips opened. This demon was female. It was clear by how her armor protruded at the breast and the thick double-twisted braid that fell to her mid-back. Red rings circled her pupils, and piercings decorated one of her horns. Female demons were rare and mostly used for breeding, but based on her armor, she was part of Zehan's guard. She stalked toward a small outhouse about fifty paces away, motioning for me to follow.

The human that had dragged the old man before Zehan approached us, he smiled at my escort. "Sunitra," he addressed. He glanced at me and then back at the demon behind me. A smirk curved onto his lips. "Babysitting again, I see."

I straightened. *Babysitting?* Did he think that forcibly taking a female from her home was okay?

Sunitra scoffed. "It's better than your job." She jerked her chin at the rakshasas carrying the frail man away. "What is that? Four this month? I hope his highness has given you a raise, Ameel."

He let out a hearty laugh. Sweat broke out on the small of my back. *Ameel.* How could this man be the same one that Ruhi was talking about? He was interacting with demons. He was doing Zehan's bidding. He wasn't fazed at all that I was a prisoner.

"I've been given plenty more than a raise. No complaints on my end." He placed a hand over his heart, and to my utter surprise, smiled at the demon.

He fell into step with Sunitra behind me. They conversed about normal things that made me almost trip more than once, causing Sunitra to bark at me to walk properly. *This* was the man that could get me to Varnasi? Could I trust him?

There is no other choice.

If I didn't convince Ameel to help me get safe passage, escape would be impossible. Naraka wasn't just a city; it was a realm with a formal gate as an entrance. One that was said to be controlled by Zehan himself and created by the power of devas. It wouldn't be easy to walk out.

Sunitra chuckled at something Ameel said, then tapped me on the shoulder, causing me to recoil internally. "You have five minutes to finish your business, then it's back into the carriage." She motioned to a rickety shack next to the outhouse where I caught the corners of Ameel's shawl entering.

I balked at her. "You're not standing watch?

Sunitra barked a laugh. "Where the hell are you going to go, courtesan?" She walked backwards toward the line of carriages and pointed at me. "Back to the carriage in five minutes."

I didn't linger. I entered the makeshift outhouse for thirty seconds and peered back outside. My ears felt hot as I observed the rakshasas wandering the checkpost.

If I didn't escape now, I would have to live amongst them. I scanned my immediate surroundings one more time. No one seemed to be paying attention to me. Zehan was also out of sight. I took a deep steadying breath and slipped into the shanty next door.

Ameel leaned over a narrow table of flat maps, his tunic rolled up to his elbows as his fingers drummed on the wood. He studied the scattered documents intently. I cleared my throat.

His head snapped up. "Did Sunitra just leave you in front of the building? The outhouse is next door—"

"I'm one of Ruhi's friends," I pulled out the note from Ruhi and handed it to him. "She said you might help me leave with one of the traveling caravans. I'm trying to get to Varnasi."

Ameel's eyes softened as he read the note. "What is your name?"

"Niya."

Ameel sighed as he handed me the note back. "I'm sorry, Niya." He rubbed his hand on the back of his neck. "I wish I could help you. I do, truly, but I can't."

My heart sank. "Please, this is my last chance. I'm willing to pay any price," I add quickly. I untucked my necklace so the diamond shined brilliantly.

Ameel shook his head as he saw the necklace. His eyebrows pressed together. "You don't understand. It's not about—"

"Any price you say? Now how would someone like you have the means for that?" a deep voice said behind me.

I whipped around. Zehan leaned against the splintery door frame. A dark grin stretched from ear to ear.

I didn't answer as Zehan looked over my head, silently communicating with Ameel.

Zehan moved toward me until the back of my thighs hit the map table. He towered at least a foot above me, if not more. "I have to admit, for a courtesan, you have some uncanny nerve."

Ameel came around the table, eyeing both of us, like he stood ready to jump between us when one of us decided to lash out with our power.

A few long seconds of silence passed between us. Intense heat rose from below my navel to my cheeks. I pushed it back down, locking it away. Zehan slowly looped his finger through the black chain at my neck and pulled me toward him, inches away from his mouth. The chain dug into the skin on the back of my neck. My breath turned shallow as he examined the diamond then dropped it.

My pulse raced like I had been dancing for hours.

"Where were you planning to go?"

I licked my dry lips. Zehan tracked the movement. "Varnasi." I didn't see a point in lying to him.

A muscle tensed in his jaw. "And why are you interested in Varnasi?"

"Why does anyone want to go to Varnasi?" I said with awe, already imagining the possibilities the city would offer me. "A fresh start."

White shadows rushed out of him and wrapped around my waist. The sensation was similar to a coin belt being fastened around my bare skin. I tensed, waiting for the agony to strike.

But it never came.

I fluttered my eyelids open, and the hazy white light retracted back into his fingertips. The muscles in my back tightened.

He looked a bit pale, or maybe it was the way his complexion felt out of place here, like it lacked color. He rocked back on his heels. "I will arrange for your safe passage to Varnasi."

I froze, unsure if I heard him correctly.

Ameel frowned. "Zehan—"

Zehan shot him a look. Ameel, to his credit, openly glared back with defiance.

"What's the catch?" I interrupted.

"I need your particular set of magical abilities." Zehan shrugged a hand into his pocket.

I glanced at Ameel, who didn't appear surprised that Zehan had casually mentioned I had magic. Unease fell over me. "So, you did choose me for my power." That's why he cut a deal with King Murkha and Baanu to take me as his Chosen, though it didn't explain why he took all the other girls before me. "Why do you need it when you have your own?"

"All magic has limitations, even mine. And it will be far more fun to watch you wield it."

I wanted to ask precisely what his magic did. I'd heard stories, of course, and I'd seen what he did to Ruhi, but the hard look on his face told me he wouldn't indulge my curiosity. "What specifically do you need me for?"

"For the past six months, departed souls have been going missing from my realm. Eight, to be specific. I don't know how or where they are going, but I'm convinced someone in surrounding courts is responsible, and I want your help in finding out who is betraying me."

"You want me to use my magic on your suspects," I replied.

Zehan nodded. "By being my Chosen and serving as a courtesan of my court, it will be easier for you to get close to the Asuras."

I gaped. "You want me to use my magic on the *Asuras?*" I had never used my magic on any other being except humans. Demons were one thing, but using my magic on the antigods? I didn't even know if it would work, but if I revealed that bit of information, it might make me completely disposable. "Why can't you ask them yourself?"

Zehan smirked. "Because I don't want them to know about the departed souls going missing yet, and as I understand it, your magic not only lets you trance an individual, but it temporarily stalls their memory. Meaning they can be under your influence and not realize what they are saying or doing. Is that correct?"

I pursed my lips together. *How does he know so much about my magic?*

"I thought so," Zehan smiled, taking my silence as an answer.

I folded my arms. "And if I decline to help you?"

Zehan prowled closer, my head filled with that familiar burning coal scent, but this time I could distinguish the other smell a little better. It was spicy, sweet, and...minty.

His hot breath grazed the edge of my ear. "Then get used to the black walls of your carriage because it will be the same color as the bars you'll be behind in Naraka. I can either play nice or not, courtesan. You'll find that there are no in-betweens. Not with me."

I glared at him. "I have a name, you know."

He lifted a brow. "Not interested. So, what will it be, *courtesan?*"

I frowned. "That isn't much of a choice." It was black bars or marble dance floors. Neither appealed to me.

Zehan waved his hand. White strings wrapped around my waist like a taut rope. He tugged the end of it, forcing me forward. Ameel sighed and returned his gaze to the map.

So much for his help.

"What the hell are you doing?" I tried to break the hold of his magic, but it only tightened, seeping coldness into my arms. A shiver racked my body. "Let me go," I seethed.

Zehan yanked again, pulling me closer until I was inches away from him, close enough to see the tiny flecks of gray in his black eyes. "Come as an escort on my arm or a prisoner on my leash. This is the fairest choice you'll receive from me."

I struggled for another minute, trying to break the white strings, but they didn't budge. I groaned with frustration. Zehan's smile grew wider when I slackened against his white tendrils. "Damn you."

Zehan chuckled. "Save your curse, courtesan. I've been damned for a long time."

I chewed on the inside of my cheek. I felt trapped in a sneaky deal. *Again.* The memory of my bargain with Baanu flooded my mind. "How do I know you'll keep your word?"

"You don't," Zehan said dully. "But what do you have to lose?"

My head felt heavy on my shoulders. I had nothing and everything to lose.

Zehan said his primary suspects were the Asuras, which meant I would have to get close to them, talk to them even. The small essence of an idea formed in the deepest corner of my mind.

I could convince them to give me a boon.

I hid my magic from most of the world for a reason. Back when the devas were still present, humans were more inclined to have power because boons—gifts for being loyal devotees—were given out frequently. After Rati became the Goddess of Death, the devas simply stopped visiting humans, and slowly, over the centuries, they were forgotten. The only way to get a boon these days was from an Asura, and they were not keen to hand them out.

Asuras were ruthless and held significant power, enough to take on a weak deva and win.

It was wishful thinking to believe they would grant a random mortal a favor, as Asuras were not known to be generous, but I had something I knew they would be interested in. *Power.* I'd trade my magic for freedom. At minimum, they would at least consider it.

I slipped my hand into his and gave it a slight shake.

The fresh wound from Baanu's betrayal still bled in my chest. Instead of stitching it up, this bargain felt like adding turmeric to the injury to slow the blood loss.

This deal would not heal me completely.

But a healing wound was better than a bleeding one.

CHAPTER SIX

My stomach growled ferociously. It had been hours since our last stop, and thoughts of starvation and dehydration had passed my mind more than once. I stared blankly at the dark rolling sand hills that stretched for miles, letting every jostle of the carriage amplify my anxiety.

What would Naraka be like?

I'd of course heard the rumors. Naraka was said to be a decrepit land, blackened by the sins of humans, where not even the simplest flowers could bloom.

And then there was my bargain with Zehan.

Serve as my courtesan.

It was clear Zehan chose me for my magic, but if that was the case, why did he take all those other Chosen? Many believed that Zehan's Chosen became his consorts. But what happened once he grew tired of them? What purpose possibly did they serve in his court games and realm politics?

I let out a ragged sigh. Learning that truth wasn't why I was here. My goal, though seemingly impossible, was twofold: befriend an Asura and convince them to give me the boon of freedom.

The carriage slowed as it approached a peculiar lone flat-topped tree in the middle of the Drifts. The horizon behind it was purple-pink rather than the familiar midnight blue. Stars blinked down at me with a lure I could not ignore.

I rubbed my eyes with my index finger and thumb, wondering if I was seeing a mirage.

A whistle signaled again, and my carriage halted. I listened for any movement outside but was greeted with pin-drop silence. Perhaps we had finally stopped for another break.

I hesitantly tried my door handle, surprised when it opened easily. Sunitra stood, waiting for me with her hands firmly behind her back. I stepped out onto the first step, my hair whipped chaotically out of its loose braid. I hugged my torso in a feeble attempt to give myself some warmth from the cold desert night.

Zehan appeared in front of me almost as if he formed out of thin air. His black overcoat billowed around him. His expression was solemn, his features sunken a bit.

He snapped his fingers at me. "Let's go, courtesan. We only have a small window to do this."

I pushed my lips together as I followed his broad frame to the tree. When we were a few feet away, Zehan whipped around and grabbed my hand.

"Hey!" I said as his grip tightened, threatening to cut off circulation.

A small dagger with an emerald-encrusted pommel appeared in his other hand, and without warning, he slid the blade along the curved line between my index finger and thumb down to my wrist.

I hissed through my teeth. "A little warning would have been nice."

"Why bother with manners when you already believe we have none?" He roughly guided my hand to the tree and placed it on the bark, causing crimson streaks to fill the cracks.

Muffled whispers traveled across my skin, and I became very aware of the fact that Zehan watched me intently, like he was waiting on something more to happen. I flexed my fingers on my other hand, feeling a subtle zing go through them.

Suddenly, a translucent film, like a portal, embedded into an enormous silver gate, appeared next to the tree. It was large enough to fit an entire carriage or crowd of people.

I gaped. "Is this...?"

"The Gate of Three, or the door to Naraka," Zehan said, looking at the large silver fence.

Stories existed about the three eternal gates. Two sat on Prithvi—one that led to Naraka and the other led to Svarga. The last one connected Naraka and Svarga, serving as a doorway between heaven and hell.

A faint swirl of rainbow floated in the gate, the light bright enough to attract a whole swarm of mosquitos.

"Mortals are not normally allowed." He faced me. "However, since you were marked by me and offered your blood, you are granted entrance."

I looked at him. "You sound as if I should be grateful."

"You should," Zehan said stiffly. "Living humans are not traditionally welcome in Naraka, because it wasn't built for them. It was created for the dead. If you tried to enter or *leave* without a mark by a higher being of the realm, it would shred your soul. The infinite thread of your existence would cease."

I swallowed hard. A warning to not try to escape by my own means. Lucky for me, Asuras were also higher beings that could help me leave. *If* they were in the mood to make a deal.

The caravan made its way through the portal. One by one, they disappeared behind the hazy light.

Zehan watched me with anticipation. Like he was waiting for something to happen. It set my nerves on edge. A prickle of cold air washed over me, making the hair on the back of my neck rise as I passed through the gate.

My vision went white. A whisper of words that I couldn't quite make out grazed the top of my ears. It was as if I was being greeted by a familiar force. The haze cleared, and my breath caught in the back of my throat.

Nothing could have prepared me for what stood on the other side.

A vast landscape with lush greenery that was most certainly not ash and ruin. Homes sat at the bottom of a great round hill, and a large brightly lit city glistened beyond that. Mountain ranges cascaded like white and gray waves in the distance. Even the air smelled faintly of flowers.

The sky was not black, instead, it was a clash of day and night. Stars glimmered around a brilliant white moon nested within swatches of purple and midnight blue. On the opposite side, a perfectly round and fiery red sun hung low with the promise of power and wonder.

"*This* is Naraka?" I turned in a slow circle, soaking it all in.

I had never imagined hell would be more beautiful than earth.

Sunitra grunted behind me. "I don't know why your kind is always this surprised. Did you think we lived in swamps and ditches?"

Not ditches, but I definitely thought there would be a few swamps.

The portal had caused us to appear in front of a massive fortress with flying buttresses protruding at various angles. An intricate stone masterpiece with hundreds of detailed carvings of humans and devas and rakshasas. Leafless vines webbed along the horizontal edges. Cobalt stones latched together at the bottom around the entire structure. It vaguely resembled a deva temple I had visited as a child before King Murkha's armies destroyed it.

The large rakshasa with the upturned fangs I'd seen speaking to Zehan earlier hissed to some guards stationed at the archway. They stomped once in acknowledgment and opened the massive wooden doors.

My fingers and toes were now numb. It was even more freezing here than in Tyaga, and the shawl I had did little to retain warmth.

My rib cage constricted. The carriages had vanished. Zehan was also out of sight. In my ogling of the palace, I hadn't noticed everyone integrating back into their normal lives.

A short man with deep-brown skin hopped down the stairs. "Oh, wonderful! You're back. The palace had become too silent without your dolent growls, Bidal." He winked at the beast.

Sunitra snorted as Bidal shot her a look. I had to clench my jaw to keep it from falling open. I'd always thought the humans in this realm would look like some manic version of their earthly selves, not so...*normal.*

"Kal," Bidal grunted as a way of greeting. "Take this one to her room." His bushy eyebrows fell over his eyes. He studied me for a beat too long and then turned to Sunitra. "Stand guard."

Clearly, he didn't trust me, but that was fine, because the feeling was mutual.

Kal turned his attention to me, bowing gracefully. "It is wonderful to meet you, uh—"

"Niya," I replied.

"Niya," he repeated, nodding to himself. "My name is Kal. I am your personal butler and have been assigned to keep you company and ensure your well-being while you reside with us."

I snorted. "I didn't realize that Zehan cared about my well-being." I folded my arms. "I do not need someone to watch me. I can fend for myself."

"He knows that. However, you're in hell. You can't go waltzing just anywhere," Kal said seriously. "And watching you is Sunitra's job. Come now, I'm sure you want to rest after the journey. I'll show you to your rooms."

I followed the short butler not through the main doors, but a side one. Perhaps Zehan didn't want anyone to know I was here. A thought that was confirmed when we stepped into a vast dungeon that reeked of decay and rust. I clasped my hands together to hide the tremble in my fingers.

"Keep walking, courtesan," Sunitra said, nudging me forward to keep pace with Kal.

We passed a dozen rooms with dark black doors, though I couldn't see who was inside the cells. It was as if a permanent black shadow had been placed over the prisoners. Demons guarding the doors saluted my captors as we passed. Their eyes widened with interest when they spotted me but quickly returned to the void space above my head.

My heart hammered wildly. What if the bargain had all been a trick to get me here and lock me away in one of these cells? I scanned them. I didn't see or hear another Chosen. I couldn't fight off a rakshasa on my own, and even if by some miracle, I did, where would I go? Zehan said I couldn't leave without his mark.

Kal slowed toward the last cell. I held my breath, searching for ways to delay the inevitable, but instead of shoving me into the iron impound, he continued up a set of rickety stairs to a brightly lit corridor. Human servants dressed in white-and-teal uniforms filled the hallways, some carried trays of food or hookahs while others scrubbed the pillars and floors with small cloths.

I glanced back at an amused Sunitra—or maybe she was angry. It was hard to tell with the permanently contracted eyebrows.

"Are you a departed soul?" I asked Kal. It was all I could do to distract myself from the fear that had started to drill a hole in my head.

Kal nodded. "For the most part."

"Do all departed souls look so..." I didn't know how to ask.

"So human?" Kal's voice held a smile. "Yes. Departed souls remain in the same physical form they last had on Prithvi." He opened another door, motioning me inside. "Ah, here we are. I will be back in the morning to show you around the palace."

I had a million questions for the small man but didn't want to ask with Sunitra watching me so keenly. So instead, I just dipped my chin.

The door shut behind me, leaving me alone in a massive luxurious bedroom. Paneled windows made up one entire wall. Deep teal curtains were tied back, giving way to a perfect view of the dramatic sky. The lit village nestled in the valley below had somehow become brighter now, and miles away. I could barely make out snowcapped peaks.

My jaw slowly inched towards the floor the deeper I went into the room. It was five times the size of my living quarters in Khoya with a bed large enough to sleep an entire family and a full sitting room and crackling fireplace. This space was fit for a noble guest, not a nighttime dancer.

"Not the hell you were expecting, courtesan?" a smooth voice drawled behind me.

I twisted around. Zehan had an elbow propped on the fireplace mantel. *Damn him.* How the hell did he appear so fast? A slight smile played on his lips.

I squared my jaw. He had shed his black coat and overly fashionable kurta, leaving a plain royal blue shirt that was rounded at the edges and rolled up to his elbows. The material clung to him, emphasizing every hard and soft indent of his muscles.

No, this was definitely not the hell I was expecting, but I wasn't about to admit it. "It's Niya," I snapped. "If we are to work together, I would like to be called by my actual name."

"Again, not interested," Zehan said.

I folded my arms. "I may be your courtesan, but I won't be disrespected."

Zehan laughed. "Disrespected? Is this how you define that?" He gestured to the room around us. "Perhaps I should show you what real disrespect looks like." He grabbed my wrist, and before I could react, he faded like a fog dissipating after a dewy morning, taking me along with him.

We were transported to a dingy room surrounded by black bars that had a makeshift cot on one side and an empty bucket on the other.

I braced my hands on my upper thighs and retched, but there were no contents in my belly to come out. "By the Asuras, what did you just do?" I said between deep gulps of air.

"We traveled by Vayu, or through the wind if you will," he said, straightening his cuffs, like the fact we had just disappeared from one place and appeared in another was completely normal. "You could do it, too, if you wanted."

"No," I snapped. "My magic doesn't do that."

"How do you know?" Zehan crooned.

"Because I just do." I didn't. From what I had learned about my magic, it removed the masks people wore and brought out a person's true feelings. But I had never fully explored what else it could do, and I wasn't about to start now. I didn't enjoy using this *gift*, if you could even call it that.

"Suit yourself. But one day, something will force you to test its limits." Zehan shrugged. "I hope I'm there to watch."

I slanted my eyes. Why was he so concerned with my magic?

I opened my mouth and almost told him to fuck off, but I bit my tongue. That wouldn't go well nor help me with my overarching plan to leave this place despite how intriguing I found it.

"When will I get to meet the Asuras?" I asked, switching topics. The faster I could meet with them, the faster I could bargain with them for a boon. I didn't trust Zehan to uphold his end of our deal. I had to figure shit out on my own.

The corner of his mouth twitched. "All in due time."

I ground my teeth. "At least tell me about them," I asserted. "It's better if I know the personalities of each Asura if I am going to use the trance on them."

Stubborn personalities were harder to manipulate, and I had a feeling every Asura would fall into that category. They were ruthless and known for mind trickery. It would be a feat to successfully use my magic on them without detection.

"I will tell you everything you need to know. For now, enjoy your comforts, courtesan." He vanished into a cloud of smoke, leaving me alone to bid my time in a dark old world.

I banged my arms against the bars. My bangles clinked against them, a few breaking into tiny pieces on the dirty floor.

"What a bastard," I said to no one.

CHAPTER SEVEN

Time didn't exist behind iron bars.

Hours, maybe days, had passed in the dark cell. The putrid stench of the dungeon had seeped its way into the deepest layer of my skin. Zehan had left me to fester in this pit of filth, where diminished hope threatened to take over my mind. I kept it at bay by focusing on what I would do when I was finally free of this deva-forsaken palace.

I lay on the small cot studying my necklace, watching as the diamond glimmered. It had been years since I had worn this necklace, always refraining from pulling it out due to fear that Baanu would snatch it the moment her gaze latched onto it. The memories the black chain held caused a new ache to surface.

I dropped the necklace, letting the weight rightly resettle between my breasts. I stared up at the dirty brown ceiling.

I am a courtesan of Naraka.

The thought washed over me like a bucket of frigid water.

Never in a million years would I have believed that this would one day become my fate. And while I knew what my bargain with Zehan entailed in theory, execution of his plan would be difficult.

Zehan needed me to use my trance on the Asuras, but I also needed to speak with them alone to bargain for a boon. Those two things were not agnostic from each other, and Zehan couldn't know what I was up to.

I had to find a way to hide my part of his plan from him. But how would I even do that? I let out a groan of frustration. The plan wouldn't even happen if I didn't get out of this damn cell.

"Niya?" Kal's tiny voice slipped through the bars. I looked up at the butler. I jerked my head up. Sunitra stood behind him, glaring at me with folded arms.

Kal fished in his pocket. "I'm sorry you were thrown in here. His Highness sometimes lets his stubbornness and temper get the better of him."

I scoffed. "Sometimes?"

Kal winced. "Okay, maybe a little more than sometimes." He pulled out a thick black key.

I stood with piqued interest. "What are you doing?"

Kal's eyebrows pinched together. "Letting you out of course. Unless you want to stay here?"

"No," I said sharply as he inserted the key into the door and it creaked open.

"Come now, this way," Kal fussed.

Sunitra sniffed. "You smell."

I rolled my eyes. "I'm surprised you find this scent repulsive when it's yours."

Sunitra snarled, her hand immediately traveling to the sword at her waist. "Why you little bit—"

"Sunitra, stand down," Bidal said from the top of the stairs. "You can't kill her."

Sunitra sighed. "Fine, I won't kill the human." She grabbed my upper arm, not minding her abnormally long nails leaving scratches on my skin. "Not today at least," she added under her breath so only I could hear.

It would be a miracle if I lasted a full day roaming this realm.

***

Kal and Sunitra led me back to the same room Zehan had found me in before he used his magic to transport us to his dungeon. The curtains were swept aside, revealing a stunning view of the sky and sprawling grounds. I had never seen land so abundant. Not a single patch of desert visible for miles. I shook my head. It was a shame that the sinners had all of the resources.

The sun was higher now, overshadowing the dimmed moon, like the two orbs constantly battled each other for dominance. The sky was brighter, a turquoise shade that had a hypnotic effect.

"All right," Kal said, nodding toward the side door. "Bath."

I didn't argue.

I spent the next hour scrubbing myself clean with a soap bar that smelled like eucalyptus and sage. I wrapped myself in a floor-length black silk robe and walked out into the room. Kal set down a massive tray with a kettle, fruits, and breads on the small coffee table.

My mouth watered at the vast spread. It felt like I hadn't eaten in days. Kal busied himself around the room, pulling out clothes and laying them on the bed while humming to himself.

"The tailor will be here in a few minutes to take your measurements for dance outfits. Once you've eaten and freshened up, we can explore the palace a bit."

I stared at him bewildered. "Are all departed souls this cheery?"

Kal grinned. "No. Only the ones that have lived longer than a human lifespan here. I am also one of Naraka's oldest residents." He paused in the middle of fluffing a pillow to look at me. "You know, I don't know how many centuries I've been here. I've lost count." He moved into the bathroom with a set of new towels.

"You've been here longer than the prince?" I asked. I was curious about the prince's role here and the inner workings of the realm. I knew that Zehan had only been here for a century or two. Before he came into the picture, Rati ferried the souls after she removed Yama, the first Deva of Naraka, from his throne.

But for a soul to stay that long here could only mean...

My eyes rounded. "You were sentenced to eternity here." I bit into the bread, which was perfectly crispy on the outside but soft and warm on the inside.

Kal gave a sad smile. "Yes, but don't pity me. I did have a choice in the matter."

I found that hard to believe. What could Kal have done in his mortal life to earn him an eternity sentence here? And how could he have had a choice? I thought the souls that passed through Naraka had no choice when it came to their sentence.

The desire to ask was overwhelming, but it wasn't my place, nor was it my business, so I changed the subject. "How many departed souls are here?" I asked between a bite of papaya that fueled me with newfound energy.

"Oh, too many to count. We have an entire town as you saw on your way in," Kal said, the corners of his eyes crinkled. "Were you expecting half-dead humans with deformities and barren lands?"

"Maybe," I admitted. "People don't speak very much about Naraka. They only speak of—"

"Svarga," Kal finished. His gaze darkened. He studied out the window, like he was lost in a memory. "Yes, humans have exaggerated the heavens to be this wonderful, perfect paradise, but in actuality, like Naraka, it is its own unique prison."

I picked at my plate with a fork. Kal had been in Naraka for centuries, so he was biased. However, even I had to admit that the very little I'd seen of Naraka thus far was not what I had expected.

"If you've been here for this long, does that mean you were here when the devas fell? Before Devi Rati took over this realm."

Dozens of tall tales explained how the devas met their downfall, describing an internal dispute between two gods over a lover. The conflict created divides and eventually led to one goddess taking matters too far. Rati, the Devi of Desire, destroyed the other devas along with the gate to Svarga so that no one could go in or come out.

She made her way to Naraka, and after she defeated Yama, the original deva who ruled over this realm, she took his seat of power and became the Goddess of Death. With time, she grew tired of passing verdict on departed souls, so she brought Zehan from Prithvi and made him the prince. She delegated the task of sentencing souls to various paths of afterlife to him.

Kal's irises were a striking light brown, almost orange. "Yes. Yama was fierce and cunning before he was locked away. But he had a weakness that Rati exploited. It destroyed him and everything he had built." Kal looked like he wanted to say more, but he shook his head. "Things were rough here for a while, but it has become much better after His Highness took over day-to-day ruling." He jerked his chin to the tea kettle. "Drink it before it gets cold."

I poured myself a cup of golden-brown liquid, inhaling the scent of cinnamon and cardamom. I took one sip and instantly let out a low, indecent groan. All thoughts of devas and Asuras vanished as my attention was wholly on the milk tea before me.

"By the Asuras." I hadn't had chai like this since I was a little girl, sitting on my father's lap. A memory of drinking my mother's chai from a saucer was one of my last cherished moments with them. My insides warmed with comfort. The ginger, the black tea, the whole spices, the mint—all of it was perfectly balanced.

Kal chuckled as he moved over to make the bed. "I'll give your kind words to the chef."

I slurped another bit of tea. "Why was Zehan chosen by Rati?"

"Ah, the only person who can answer that is Zehan. He can be stubborn when he wants to be, but for the most part, he uses his magic to help the souls that pass through here."

My eyebrows pinched together. "How does he help?"

The only time I had ever seen the prince use his magic was when created pain and suffering. Ruhi's piercing shrieks rang in my ears. Zehan *helping* people felt utterly foreign.

"Zehan can read fates," Kal said.

Goose bumps erupted along my arms. "What do you mean he can read fates?"

Kal finished making up the bed and moved to dust the bedposts again. "You humans really don't know anything about him, do you? Zehan's magic lets him see threads of a person's past life. Once a soul enters Naraka, they are given an audience with Zehan, and he looks into their soul. Of course, their past is not always clear. Sometimes, he can read everything, and other times, he cannot. But he uses what he sees to decide how they will be punished for their sins."

My mouth hung open. I had never known. I don't think anyone on Prithvi knew. Had he used his magic on me to read my life decisions? "Can he read the past of the living?"

Kal shook his head. "Not that I know of. Then again, there is much I don't know about his magic, as he isn't very forthcoming with his ability. As I understand it, he can only read the fates of those who have passed on Prithvi and souls that are waiting here in the in-between world. After a mortal passes on Prithvi, they can take one of three paths depending on their life's karma. They can attain true peace if their soul goes to Svarga; they can be reincarnated into a new body on Prithvi; or they are forced to stay in Naraka and be tormented for the rest of their soul's existence. Zehan helps pass judgment on them."

I studied the butler, bewildered. "So he decides if they go to Svarga, reincarnate to their next life, or stay here?"

That was a shit ton of power.

Kal nodded. "Sometimes the Asuras have a say if the sin belongs to them. Most departed souls have clear paths; however, sometimes, if the sin is truly abhorrent, the soul must go through the Asura Trials, where they go head to head with their sin or fear. And if, for some reason, a departed soul's path is still in limbo, then the Goddess of Death makes the final call."

"That's a big task," I said, unable to hide my surprise. To be responsible for every soul that passes through hell must be exhausting.

"It is," Kal agreed. "But I think Zehan enjoys it. At least, on most days." The butler chuckled to himself.

I frowned. Zehan's magic sounded like a curse, but he *helped* souls navigate their afterlife. That fact created a fissure in my beliefs about the ruthless prince and this realm.

Someone knocked. "Are we ready for a fitting?"

An older lady wearing a servant's uniform walked in with a bundle of fabric. She gave me a soft smile as she placed colorful folded clothing on the table. "My name is Gauri. Here are some basic kurtas and lehengas for the daytime. But I need to take your measurements for the rest." She waved a frail hand at me. "Come now, don't be shy. Much to do before the next Antam." She pulled out one of the small ottomans for me to step up on in front of a floor-length mirror.

I stared at the lady's graying hair, she must have passed on Prithvi at an older age. Her features held kindness, and I couldn't help but wonder about her mortal life and how in nine hells she ended up as a maid in the palace of Naraka. "What is Antam?"

Kal spoke. "Every week, when a new batch of departed souls arrive, Zehan along with the Asuras gather to meet them. That is when you will perform."

My fingers twitched. "And when is the next Antam?"

"In one full moon."

That was weeks away. A lump formed in the back of my throat. I hadn't asked Zehan about how long it would take to question all the Asuras, it could take months to interrogate them.

Gauri's stared at my face in the mirror. "Do not fret, my lady," Gauri said, using a string to mark my size. "All will be well. You will look absolutely stunning while performing. I'll be sure of it."

Looking great was not what I was worried about in the slightest.

Dancing for a room full of demons? That caused adrenaline to overflow my veins. But the sweet old lady continued to chatter cheerily, asking me questions on what I liked to wear. I had to think before I responded because I had never been given the autonomy to choose my clothing.

After a few more minutes, Gauri took her leave, promising to return with a large selection to choose from, though she mentioned I likely wouldn't have a choice in what I wore for the Antam which was not surprising at all. Zehan would likely choose something see-through and wholly inappropriate. It was nothing new in my job.

"What about you?" Kal asked quietly when Gauri had left, leaving me slightly flustered from the entire interaction. He had moved to stoking the fire with an iron poker, his back faced me. "I am told you have magic. What can it do?"

My mouth went dry. Zehan told Kal, which meant he trusted the butler.

I cleared my throat. "I can place people under a trance, making them want me more than anything else in the world. But I can also convince them to tell me their deepest desires. King Murkha and Baanu exploited the ability. I was their most-prized spy."

Yet, they sold me out like it meant nothing. Their loyalty to me had been thin as rice paper, easily crumbled. Or perhaps they were deathly afraid of Zehan, but regardless, they didn't even attempt to keep me.

"It isn't common for humans to have power these days, is it?" Kal speculated.

I clenched my fists, digging my long nails into the heel of my palms. We were entering a conversation I wasn't sure I wanted to have.

"It's rare." I kept my tone neutral. "But not unheard of."

Kal stood up and stared at me. "Who gave it to you?"

The memory of a beautiful meadow full of bright-purple hyacinths turning to ash flooded my mind. His question was innocent, but the answer was anything but.

I stood up quickly. "I'd like to see the dance hall, and I believe you promised a tour." At some point I would also need to learn about the Asuras and their quirks, and Kal had to be knowledgeable about them and everything Naraka. I just had to get him to talk.

Kal blinked rapidly at the sudden change of topic but bounced on his feet. "Of course, forgive me." He clapped his hands together. "In fact, I'll give you the full tour on the way. His Highness's art collection is a hidden wonder."

My brows hit the top of my hairline. "Art collection?" The prince did not strike me as the type to admire the work of creatives.

"Probably the best one in Tyaga," Kal said with a boyish grin. He tossed a shawl at me. "Here, it stays cold here. We can also visit the gardens, the fountains, and the town at some point as well."

I smiled to myself, placing the wool scarf over my shoulders. The butler was perhaps the quirkiest person I had ever encountered, but I couldn't help but be grateful for his kindness that, for a few minutes, made me forget I was in the realm of cruelty.

CHAPTER EIGHT

I could have wandered the shaded stone corridors for hours. Every room and floor had something new to discover. With perfectly preserved oil paintings, written works inlaid into the walls, and exotic plants that seeped floral notes into the corridors, the palace was a treasure chest filled with invaluable artifacts. Though, sheer curiosity wasn't what drove my eagerness in learning all about the castle.

It was a contingency plan in case I needed to leave undetected. I had marked every entrance that seemed accessible, and surprisingly, the place was relatively unguarded. It appeared that the prince held an open door policy.

Kal proved to be a riveting guide, knowing about every art piece and how the prince acquired it. It was impressive, but the question that roared through me was *why?*

Why collect art and priceless relics created by mortals and bring them to this realm where only immortals dwelled?

I walked amongst the various shelves of the library, running my hands over the leather spines. "How did the prince manage to gather all of this?"

Kal followed my gaze around the room. "Most pieces you see here were purchases, but a few were what we will call *forced* gifts."

"So, in addition to being a cruel and heartless leader, the prince is also a thief?" I mocked as I stalked over to a shelf full of dusty books. All first editions. "Figures," I murmured. I pulled one from the shelf with a fancy gold cover and black lettering.

"I think he prefers *insistent collector* rather than *thief,*" Kal clipped.

I snorted as I inserted the book back into its place. *An overly attractive collector.*

I bit my tongue, shocked at the thought that had just crossed my mind. I shook my head. "Where is this one from?" I pointed at a white blade sitting on the mantel above the fireplace. It had a blackened silver handle and no adornments, yet something made it eerily alluring. Like the weight of the world would fall upon its wielder.

"Ah, that," Kal said, coming to stand next to me with his arms firmly clasped behind his back. "That is the Ashti, believed to be carved out of a deva's bone and possesses the power to drain power from a deva. It is said that Yama, with the help of his asuras, killed a deva for trespassing on his land."

I could practically feel the power wafting off the tip of the blade. Did it hold power now? I lifted my hand, letting it hover over the white shaft. In my village, the elders had told us stories of the Devas. Yama was widely believed to be the most ruthless and merciless one, twisting fates for fun. I shivered and wondered if Rati was just as cruel.

I turned to Kal, leaping at my chance to understand more. "How does it all work? The hierarchy with Rati, the Asuras, and Zehan?"

"Rati is the ultimate puppeteer. Both the Asuras and Zehan answer to her," Kal said. "Think of it like a king and his nobles. The nobles all have separate roles or regions to manage, but they will ultimately follow the king's orders. The nine Asuras were created by Yama, but their loyalty will always lie with the true holder of Naraka's power."

I knew most of the lore. Rati used to be the consort to Kama, the Deva of Love, who did not take just one but many partners. Foolishly, he used one of his arrows to force another devi to feel attraction to him. That devi's soulmate was the Deva of Creation, the most powerful deva of all time. When he found out, he became angered and sent Kama to Naraka in imprisonment for five centuries. But on the day Kama was to leave and go back to Svarga, the Deva of Creation killed him.

Betrayed and depressed, Rati spiraled with vengeance. She locked all the devas in Svarga, forcing them to abandon us. She spread that news on Prithvi and turned her attention to Naraka, which she saved for last. After seven months of battle, she finally overruled Yama and forced his Asuras and demons to bow to her.

I turned to Kal. "There are nine Asuras? I thought there were only seven—greed, lust, pride, envy, sloth, anger, despair." I ticked them off with my fingers. "What am I missing?"

Kal gave a small smile. "Two of the worst sins—violence and fear."

I wrinkled my nose. I could understand violence but fear? "How is fear a sin?"

"Every human has some inherent fear, but too much can become a crutch." Kal tilted his head. "People lie, steal, and kill out of fear."

"And how does the Asuras' power work?" Was it like Zehan's? Or did they all have their unique abilities?

"They have similar capabilities. The ability to move through areas using the Vayu and inflict various types of pain of course, but they were created to be naturally inclined toward power that symbolizes their own sin. For example, Krod, the Asura of Anger, can quickly call upon fire."

My throat tightened. What would happen if an Asura realized I was using my power on them? Would they turn and use their magic on me?

I just needed to speak with them first. If I convinced them to give me a boon, maybe I wouldn't have to use my coercing magic at all. Or if I used my magic enough to get them to want me then it would give me a chance to pitch my case to them. Though, it would be tricky. Kal said all the Asuras attended Antam, so I would have to target only one or two Asuras at a time.

"I still don't understand why Zehan cannot simply ask the Asuras themselves," I muttered quietly. Why go through all this trouble to bring me here and use my magic on them? "Wouldn't the Asuras also want to find the culprit behind the murders?"

"Not if the murders are somehow aiding them in gaining power," a deep voice said. I twisted around. Zehan leaned against the door frame with his arms folded. He wore a plain dark linen kurta paired with light cream pants. Nothing extravagant or bold. He could have fooled me for another common merchant.

I shook my head. "Quit doing that."

Zehan feigned confusion. "Doing what?"

"Barging in on my conversations," I exclaimed. "Standing there with...whatever that pose is." His expression lit with bemusement.

"Highness," Kal bowed, beaming at the prince.

Zehan motioned him to rise. "None of that, Kal, you know that. And does my intruding bother you, courtesan?"

"Everything about you bothers me," I sniped back. I turned my back to him, returning to examine the bookshelves.

"Leave us," Zehan said.

I stiffened, immediately wanting to kick myself for my habitual sass. *Do not let him intimidate you.* I had already made a deal with him, he wouldn't go back on it if he really needed my magic to find whoever was behind the disappearances. However, if I wanted to maintain the ability to walk around the palace, keeping my mouth shut would help.

The door creaked shut. I felt Zehan encroach into my personal space, and his dark glare on the nape of my neck. Uneasy warmth spread into my belly.

"We don't need to talk to each other," I said bitterly, keeping my back to him. "Our bargain never claimed I had to interact with you."

"Ah, that is where you are wrong," Zehan said, his voice drifting closer to me. "I gave you the morning to sleep in and tour. Now we go over logistics. You'll need to be very careful with your powers, courtesan. The Asuras have ways of detecting outside magic."

"It's Niya." I turned around fiercely. My jewelry chimed softly. "And I don't need your help. I'm well versed in my magic." It was a half-lie, but he didn't have to know that. And if he thought I would give any information about my magic to him, he obviously didn't know me as well as he thought.

Zehan smirked. "I knew you had sharp teeth, but I failed to realize how sharp they truly were."

I glared at him. "Good, perhaps that will prevent you from getting too close."

Zehan chuckled, the deepness of his voice curling around my throat. "I'm not afraid of being bit, courtesan."

I clamped my mouth shut. The retort tickled the tip of my tongue, yet I didn't want to waste time bantering. I needed to discuss other things with him.

"Is your power weaker than the Asuras? Is that why you need me to coerce them?"

"The Asuras and I are probably at the same level when it comes to magical prowess." Zehan gracefully pushed off the door frame. He walked to a tray which had a decanter full of sura in it. He poured a knuckles length and downed the reddish-black liquid in one go.

Zehan twisted the empty glass in his hands. "I want you to ask them if they know anything about the disappearances. With your influence on them, they won't have a choice but to be truthful. Easy."

My palms were sweaty, causing the book to slowly slip from my trembling fingers. "My magic didn't work on you," I stated. "Why do you think it will work on them?" My plan wasn't actually to do what Zehan wanted with the Asuras. I would use my magic if needed, but to serve myself. Not him. But right now, I needed him to think I was on his side.

"I was waiting for you to use your magic, and I always have my shield up around me—something, you should learn. The Asuras, on the other hand, won't be expecting your magic, so the time to strike will be during your performance at the Antam when you have their full attention."

"You said they could be killing departed souls for more power. Why do you suspect that?"

Zehan's lips formed a grim line. "I felt them being ripped away from the realm. The souls are not just dying. Their very essence of life is being stolen."

"Wait, you physically felt them being torn away from here?"

"I'm tied to this realm. I know every departed soul that enters and leaves."

I gaped at him. "All of them?"

"Every single one," Zehan mumbled. He ran his hand over his beard. "So, I need your magic, and I need it working well. You can put people into a trance and manipulate them into trusting you. You can convince them to reveal their secrets." He ticked each fact off with his slender fingers. "Anything else?"

"No," I said.

Zehan smiled with all his teeth. "Lies."

"I don't know what you're talking about."

Zehan gave a half shrug. "You could do a lot of the same things I can if you would free yourself from the invisible chains you've wrapped around your wrists."

My cheeks warmed. I folded my arms. "Why on earth would I want to use my magic in the same way you do?"

"Well for starters, you're not on earth. You're in hell." Zehan prowled closer until my back hit the shelves, and his face was inches from mine. He looked down at my exposed collarbone and sucked in a tight breath as his eyes trailed back up and bore into mine. "And second, you might need those powers here. The realm and its inhabitants will be intrigued by you and your magic. It wouldn't bode well for either of us if you draw the *wrong* attention." He leaned in further, giving me the perfect whiff of smoke and sweet mint. "You cannot give yourself away during court. If the Asuras and Rati realize what we are up to, they will be knocking on my door, and if that happens, no one can save you. Not even me."

My pulse quickened as something hot sparked within me. "I don't expect you to save me," I whispered back. "Why would I when you do the opposite each time you visit a kingdom? You take a Chosen each month and make them live here in some dark corner until you decide when they can be free. Your rakshasas kill foot soldiers from other kingdoms in such gruesome ways that their bodies cannot even be recovered. And the check posts you've placed around Tyaga are notorious for trafficking women and children. So, you can sit and pretend you care about the souls here or say you'll save me if it came down to it, but we both know the only reason you would do that is because it is self-serving. You don't need me. You need my *power*."

Zehan let out a frustrated sigh. He opened his mouth and closed it, like he was battling some internal conflict. He pushed away from me. "Kal," he snarled.

Kal hopped back in. How someone managed to stay so cheery in a place like this was beyond my understanding. "Yes, Your Highness."

Zehan's black pupils ignited with a spark of fire. "Put him under your trance."

"Why?"

"Because I asked."

I folded my arms. "Putting your commander under my trance wasn't enough?"

Zehan's eyes narrowed. "Are you worried your magic isn't up to the task?"

Irritation pulsed through me. "Of course not."

"I—" Kal fidgeted with his shoulders hunched. He squished his eyes together and then opened one of them to peer back at me. "I-is this going to hurt?"

"Possibly," Zehan replied.

I glared at the prince. "Don't listen to him. You won't even remember what happened."

Zehan's lips tugged down. Cold. Ruthless. "Do it."

I didn't move. I stared at him defiantly. I told him I would use my magic on the Asuras not on anyone else.

Zehan pried the book from my fingers. He drummed against the cover of it. "Now, courtesan. Or do you want me to use my magic on Kal until you comply?"

Kal audibly swallowed. "Niya, I would much rather be under your magic than his."

Infuriating man. I'd prove it to him once and for all that I didn't need help. I pushed my lips together and focused my attention on Kal.

I rolled my shoulders out, ignoring the warning presence from the overgrown shadow assessing me. I focused on the feel of my magic. It was heavy and overbearing and filled with greediness. That's how it always felt, but since arriving here, its presence was stronger and pliant.

I concentrated on Kal who had hunched his shoulders and squeezed his eyes shut as if he were waiting for a bout of pain. I funneled invisible threads of magic toward him, yet as soon as they got close, they hit a wall just like when I used my magic on Zehan. I gritted my teeth and pushed strands of magic toward Kal, trying to find an opening in his invisible shield. Whenever I got close to worming my way through it, the shield would somehow reinforce itself.

I let out a huff of frustration. Kal didn't have magic. How was he shielding against me?

Kal opened one eye. "Are you doing it?"

Zehan watched me smugly. Like he knew exactly why I was scrunching my nose up in focus.

I curled my fists. "You're shielding him, aren't you?"

His smile widened. "Weak," he said.

I wanted to scream but pushed my lips together in concentration. I changed tactics with the threads of power that only I could make out and attacked his shield at different sides. It was sloppy and unsophisticated, but after a few minutes, my magic speared into him, like breaking the surface of a frozen lake.

Kal's eyes grew large, and his expression became relaxed.

I smiled triumphantly. I eased up my magic so that he wasn't fully taken by the trance. The trick was to leave him conscious enough to know what he was telling me, so it made him feel like he gave up private information willingly.

He stared at me with longing and desire, and I fought the urge to laugh. He looked ridiculous.

"Command him to tell you a secret," Zehan demanded.

I gaped at him. "Absolutely not."

Zehan tsked as he lifted his fingers, readying them to snap whatever horrid magic he held onto Kal.

I grumbled, "Fine!" My hate for the man grew with every minute I spent with him.

I looked back at Kal who still stared at me with unfaltering devotion. "Why did you choose to stay in Naraka?" I had no reason to invade Kal's privacy. He had been nothing but kind to me. I just needed to prove to Zehan that he was under my grip.

Kal's smile stretched across his face. "It is all I have ever known, and it is also where I met my wife."

Truth. I felt his words vibrate with nothing but love and longing. My mouth parted. "You have a wife?"

Kal's smile faltered. "I had a wife. She was beautiful and radiant, almost as much as you." He took a meaningful step forward.

Zehan's shoulders straightened, and he dropped his hands by his sides. "Let go of him."

My blouse felt too tight. This was precisely why I hated my magic. People wanted me, even if they were deeply in love with another. I sighed, releasing my hold over him.

Kal's shoulders relaxed, and he let out a *whoosh* of breath. He blinked a few times. "Well, are you going to do it or not?"

"Not bad, courtesan." Zehan ruminated, even I could tell he was impressed. He inserted the book back into its place onto the shelf, his shoulder brushed against mine. A blush crept onto my cheeks. His breath skirted across the top of my ear. "But it still took you some time to get past my shield. You will practice three times a day until the next Antam, which is when we'll truly learn whether you are stronger than you believe yourself to be." He tapped my large nose ring and the small charm at the bottom of the hoop tickled my top lip.

I shuddered. I wouldn't be dancing in front of just humans, I would be dancing in front of Asuras and rakshasas. Would they be as grimy as the nobles in King Murkha's court? Would they roar or claw at me? Fear wormed its way into me. "Does your Antam partake in a bid?"

"No." Zehan's features twisted into something harsh. "My court is civil and well-mannered. No one will touch you without consent. Besides, they will likely believe you are with me given you are one of my Chosen. And they know better than to go after what is mine."

I didn't know how to reconcile that fact with my own preconceived perceptions of Naraka. Is that why Zehan forbade the bid in Khoya? But if that were true, why would he take girls at the check posts? It didn't make sense. "You won't get a thank you if that's what you're waiting for," I said. "But now that you've brought it up, where are your other Chosen?"

"That is none of your concern."

"It is. I am one of them, and I'd like to know what you originally had in store for me."

Zehan ran a hand through his hair. "Despite what you believe, you are not a prisoner here."

"Right. Sure. Tell that to the massive rakshasa you've placed outside my door to watch me day and night."

Zehan ignored my sarcasm. "I will be gone for the next few days. Practice. I will receive daily reports of your progress. And trust me, you don't want me as your teacher." The finality in his voice signaled this conversation was over.

On that, I agreed with him. Spending more time with Zehan than required was not something I was interested in. I sucked in part of my cheek.

You are not a prisoner here.

That was a lie. As long as I was stuck here, I would never be free.

My palms felt clammy. Too much depended on this Antam. Finding which Asura was responsible for taking his souls was an impossible task. What if none of them are? Where does that leave his investigation and my bargain?

I wasn't fooled by his words. Devils didn't have integrity. As soon as Zehan got what he needed, I would go from being his most valuable resource to his most expendable.

I was his asset. That's all.

A means to an end.

CHAPTER NINE

I t had been a week since I had last seen Zehan. And to his credit, my bedroom door was never locked from the outside, and I was given whatever I needed when requested. I was able to roam the vacant halls at my leisure, although the guards trailed me like leeches. Aside from practice with Sunitra and Kal every evening, I was not restricted from anything.

No rules, no curfews, no shackles.

Yet, it wasn't enough.

Zehan claimed I was free, but I was still a captive mortal in Naraka. Trapped in a bargain that forced me to dance. It's like I had never even left Khoya.

"That was the fastest you've gotten Sunitra under the trance. Well done, Niya," Kal approved. He stood next to me in one of the palace's sparring rooms. It was larger than the entire throne room in Khoya. "His Highness will be pleased with your progress."

I clucked my tongue. Of course Zehan had Kal providing him daily reports. I flicked my wrist, and the lustful gaze vanished from her large round eyes as her shoulders sagged with relief. If fumes could leave her ears in a physical form, they would have in that instant.

"Your turn, butler." Sunitra shook out her arms and rubbed her temple. The rakshasa was stripped of her general armor and daggers. "I'm tired of feeling the delirious need to fuck Niya on the mat. I should be training her how to carry a sword, not helping her seduce men."

I held back a laugh. Though the demon initially intimidated me, I realized Sunitra had a hard shell, but she hid her softness and understanding inside.

"No way," Kal said, shaking his head. "She already practiced on me five times this morning." He gave me a meaningful look. "I've never seen magic like yours before, Niya. It is barely detectable and subtle enough to make me believe I am just attracted to you and want to win you over."

"Let's hope it acts like that on the Asuras." I had no idea if my magic would work at all on the Asuras, but I didn't voice that deeper concern.

"It will," Sunitra reassured me. Though, it did little to convince me. "Your magic is powerful."

My power trembled. "I think I've had enough magic practice for today." I rolled out my stiff shoulders. I wanted a hot bath. The constant cold here was unbearable. Not to mention that in twelve years, this was the first time I had gone multiple days without dancing, and the lack of movement had made my limbs tight. It unsettled me in a way I couldn't quite understand. I thought having a break from dance would be refreshing, but it had had the opposite effect.

"Excellent. Let's go down to Vajra," Sunitra said.

"Absolutely not," Kal said. "I don't think His Highness—"

"What is Vajra?" I interrupted.

"The town where the departed souls live," Sunitra said.

I lifted my eyebrows. "Is this the same town you mentioned to me when I first arrived here?"

"No," Kal stated as he twisted his fingers together, blinking rapidly. "We will not be going. Who knows who we will run into there, and if His Highness—"

"Zehan told me I could do whatever I pleased. I think visiting the town where his people reside won't pose a threat if they are as well-mannered as he makes them out to be."

Sunitra clapped her hand on Kal's shoulder, and he stumbled a few steps forward. "Live a little, butler."

Kal glared at the demon, rubbing his shoulder. "This is a bad idea."

I laughed. "Would you rather tell Zehan you let me go down to Vajra with Sunitra alone or that you accompanied me?" I turned to head toward the door.

Kal cursed. "If Zehan murders me, I'll make sure my soul haunts you both for eternity."

***

Minutes later, we were walking down the hill towards a small town center. Apprehension hummed in the misty air as we walked on uneven cobblestone. It was midday, but you would have no way to tell with the sun and moon both present in the sky. I didn't want to admit that I was giddy to visit the town. The truth was that this realm intrigued me beyond understanding.

I tightened my overcoat around me, feeling my inhale trap itself in my lungs. "Is it always this cold here?" I grumbled. My toes were numb. My nose was red. Even through the thick wool gloves, my fingers tingled.

"Yes," Sunitra and Kal chimed together.

"Great," I said, as we turned the next corner. "How much farther until—" The words died in my throat.

Black lanterns strung across a massive bustling town square. Dozens of carts filled with various trinkets, exotic fruit, and spices filled the street. The smell of fresh food made me salivate. Carriages trotted through the alleys in front of stores with extravagant window displays.

My pace slowed, letting it all sink in. Departed souls and rakshasas strolled the market, laughing with each other. The two species were congregating and working together to create this quaint village. This wasn't just a city of departed souls, it was also the city of demons. In Prithvi, rakshasas went on human hunting parties. They hated us. And we hated them. It was simple.

Yet everything I saw before me made it anything but that.

"Insects will fly into your mouth if you do not shut it, courtesan," Sunitra said, a smile in her voice.

I clamped my mouth shut, masking my awe, but it was too late.

A few bystanders stared at us as we approached. At first, I thought they recognized Sunitra and Kal, but they were staring at me. Their curiosity skated down my spine.

"Can they tell I am not a departed soul?" I asked Sunitra.

"Yes." She offered no further explanation.

"Why are they staring?" I asked in a low voice. "Surely they are used to having mortals amongst them."

"No, they are not." Again, she did not provide any extra information.

I frowned. Zehan had said he made bargains with his other Chosen, and then they were allowed to leave. Yet, none of the others had ever come to Vajra?

"Let's hurry this excursion up," Kal said, glancing around his shoulder, no doubt worried Zehan would pop out from one of the stores. It wouldn't surprise me, as the prince appeared everywhere I didn't want him.

He looked up at the sky and then back at us. "Okay, let's plan to head back to the palace in an hour. Niya, purchase whatever you need or want, just tell the shopkeepers to put it on Zehan's tab."

I didn't even know where to start. As we walked past the carts, merchants yelled out facts about their goods, though many became quiet as I passed, like they had never seen a mortal before. "Is this the only town in Naraka?"

"Yes. Well, there is Kalank, but only the worst sinners are sent there. Smaller clusters of cottages and villages are scattered throughout the realm but think of this as the main city of a kingdom," Kal said.

Sunitra nudged me forward towards the vendors. "Come on, courtesan. Don't be shy now. Aren't you used to people staring at you all day and night?"

I sighed. "Your bluntness has no bounds."

"I'm a demon, for Asura's sake. Being direct and aggressive is in my nature."

"Are you sure you're not trying to hide behind that bluntness, Sunitra?" I mused. "Because I think you actually enjoy my company." The rakshasa poked at me, but I didn't think it was coming out of pure loathing.

Sunitra shook her head. "I'll start praying to the devas if it means I can get rid of you. Serving as your sitter is a punishment. I don't know why His Highness felt my talents would be best utilized walking around as your shadow."

I chuckled as the rakshasa continued to murmur her jabs. Vajra had a variety of stores. Some sold familiar items such as incense, books, jewelry, and sweets. Others sold items unique to demon taste such as horn piercings, clawed gloves, and raw meat.

"And this town...has it always been here?" I had grown up believing so many horrible things about this realm, but seeing the exact opposite was disorienting.

I was a bit stunned that no one on Prithvi knew how beautiful and resource heavy Naraka was.

"Sort of." Kal stiffened as a gust of wind pushed back his curly hair. "It looked quite different when Yama was in power."

"*Different?* It was a wreck of a place before Zehan got here. Vajra didn't even exist. The entire realm was just one big ruin. The first deva believed this place should be miserable." Sunitra glanced over her shoulder. "He made everyone live in a constant state of sorrow. His Highness built it back up, created laws and districts, made it into a home for the departed souls who chose to stay here."

I pushed my lips together. How could the darkest corners of the cosmos be a home?

The street finally flattened, and after another block, we turned onto what seemed to be a main intersection. A crowd of roaring rakshasas gathered at the center, blocking off one of the streets.

"Shit, Krod is here," Sunitra muttered.

I followed her gaze to a tall, lanky man wearing slim pants, a tunic, and a light brown embroidered jacket. He looked human with his broody eyes, thick eyebrows, and square jaw, yet at the same time he didn't. His features held demonic characteristics.

His voice boomed over the crowd. "Let this be an example of what happens when someone tries to cheat me."

My gut twisted. A young man, bloody and battered and barely conscious, kneeled before him. Bile traveled up my throat.

"Who is that?" I whispered.

"The Asura of Anger," Sunitra said grimly. "He frequents the town to pass time with his games, and almost always finds a way to dole out some torture."

Unease settled into my bones alongside the arctic chill as I observed the Asura of Anger. The harsh wind hit us at full speed, causing strands to fly out of my loose braid.

"Any other takers?" Krod plopped back down on a chair, flipping the cards through his hands.

"What is the game?" I asked quietly.

"That's just it. You don't know. Krod decides in the moment," Sunitra said grimly. "The odds are always against you."

I frowned. "Then why would anyone want to play?"

Kal stared at the Asura. "Because before the game begins, the terms are set, and each player gets to decide what they want from Krod. It can be practically anything within his means."

Like a boon. My head pounded.

"No other takers then?" Krod smiled wickedly, leaning back to prop his feet on the makeshift table. "Who would have thought hell would house a bunch of cowards."

"I'll give it a go," I called out.

CHAPTER TEN

Sunitra grabbed my upper arm, tugging me back. "*Are you mad?*" People stared at us. Hushed chatter fitted through the crowd. "This is not a simple game of kabaddi. You'll get yourself killed."

"And then Zehan will kill us," Kal gulped.

I pulled myself out of Sunitra's grip, standing as tall as I could. "Believe it or not, I'm rather good at kabaddi."

It had been over a decade since I'd played the contact sport where players took turns running to the opposing team's half of the court to tag their players and then return safely back to their own side. But in my village, I had been the star player.

"And if I am killed, then at least you won't have to watch me any longer." I stepped forward, hearing a string of curses behind me.

Krod tilted his head. "So, you are Zehan's new Chosen. The one he decided to keep." His eyes traveled down my body with acute interest. I squirmed internally. "He has always had good taste. But I must warn you, this isn't a game for the faint of heart. I'm on rather good terms with the prince right now. Messing with his new toy seems like the type of thing that would ruin our current relationship."

I straightened. I hadn't realized news of my arrival had become a source of gossip, and I definitely was not Zehan's *toy*. However, it explained all the gaping stares.

The one he decided to keep.

What did that mean? Zehan said he wasn't in the business of keeping young girls against their will, so if they weren't here, where were they?

"I assure you I am anything but the faint of heart." I placed my hands on my hips. "And I hadn't realized an Asura would fear a relationship with a minor prince."

Krod let out a sharp laugh. "Well, I certainly see why the prince has taken to you so quickly."

Kal moved to stand in front of me. "Y-your Highness, she doesn't know how our realm works. We really should be on our way, the prince—"

"Never said I couldn't play a game," I finished for Kal, moving to stand beside the butler, shooting him a death glare. I smiled back at the Asura. "Are you really going to go soft for a human?" I didn't know much about Asuras, but I suspected they probably hated to be challenged.

A muscle in Krod's jaw twitched. My bait worked. "Very well. Come, courtesan, let's see what cleverness you hold."

Sunitra cursed again and muttered to Kal. I sat across from the Asura, ignoring the whispers that traveled across my skin from the growing crowd.

"Make your demands," Krod said, shuffling the cards.

I swallowed hard. "If I win, you give me a boon."

Krod's eyebrows hit the hairline of his small forehead, but the surprise quickly faded. I waited in silence, holding my breath.

"Fine," Krod said. "If I win, you either give me your darkest secret or you give Zehan a night off and come dance for me in *my* court." He held out his hand.

I exhaled, sharply. I wouldn't give the Asura any additional information about myself. I had no idea what Krod's court would be like, and signing up to dance at an Asura's court felt like the worst possible idea. However, I could not let this opportunity go to waste.

I shook his hand, and a whiff of magic snapped between us, sealing our deal.

"The game is simple." Krod shuffled the deck. He laid out nine face cards—all queens with different colored crowns. "Find the Queen of Shadows amongst the other cards." He picked up the card with the darkest queen. Her expression was indifferent, and wispy shadows dripped from her steel crown. Krod placed the card back in line with the others. Using his magic, he flipped them all face down.

I marked the card, keeping my eyes glued to the slightly bent edge at the top right corner.

Slowly, the cards shifted positions. I ground my teeth. A thrill of adrenaline reverberated down my spine as I focused in on that muted brown card.

"What do you want a boon for?" Krod asked with a small lazy grin. "Is Zehan not providing you with what you need?"

"I'll tell you when I win," I replied. "Why do you want me to dance in your court? Are you lacking dancers?"

"No," Krod said. "But Mohini is not only famous in Khoya, your name has made its way to this realm as well. Tell me, are you enjoying the floors of Naraka?"

I didn't look up from the card. "I wouldn't call dancing for hell's demons an enjoyable activity."

Krod barked another laugh. "Perhaps not, but warming Zehan's bed must come with some level of contentment. Many departed souls would trade their sentence to be in your position."

My jaw dropped. "I am *not* his mistress."

"I didn't say mistress." Krod flicked his wrist as the cards moved again. His lips spread into a wicked smile. "He just made it seem like you were *his*."

I scoffed as the cards moved again. "What's the difference?"

Krod paused the movement of cards. His tone suddenly shifted as he whispered, "Oh, my dear, trust me, there is a difference."

My eyes flickered to the Asura. It was all he needed to shift all the cards when I wasn't looking.

Shit. I skimmed the edges of the cards, looking for the one with the bent edge. The fourth card from the left had it, but I deflated when I saw that the card next to it had an identical bent edge.

Where did that come from?

"So, my dear, where is she?" Krod sniggered with malice, like he knew exactly why I anxiously pressed my hands together.

He added the bent edge to the second card. Somehow, he must have known that was what I was tracking. I frowned at the Asura and tapped a cold finger on the card to the right. It flipped over. My stomach dropped as the female dressed in white smiled back up at me from the card.

"Ah." Krod snapped his fingers and the cards vanished. "Better luck next time, my dear."

"You cheated," I blurted. He manipulated the cards. I was sure of it. "I want another game."

Krod's features twisted into something from a nightmare. He rose and placed both of his hands on the small table. "Did you really expect an Asura to play fairly?" He flashed his teeth. His own sin coming forth. "Now tell me your darkest secret or you'll receive the time and date for your court appearance in the coming week." His eyes glared with something sinister as they traveled down my body. "Don't bother bringing clothes. I'll have ones made for you."

Despite the cold brewing through the air, my skin burned. My magic sparked against the edges of my fingertips. I didn't have to play fairly either. If he wouldn't willingly give me a boon, perhaps I could persuade him to give one to me.

I didn't give myself time to debate. I barreled trance magic at the Asura, breaking through his shield, but given his size, it took a lot more magic to bring him under.

My head pounded with adrenaline. Another sharp breath led to another pulse of magic. Krod opened his mouth, but like all my targets, his eyes became hooded.

His intrigue rapidly shifted into a deep need to reveal his truth. He dropped his voice low and leaned toward me so only I could hear his next angry words. "I'm sorry I had to cheat, my dear, but I could not let you, an undead human girl, beat me at my own game. Besides, winning would have provided you with no benefit as I cannot gift boons."

I kept my magic in check, reinforcing it within Krod. I bit my lip, feeling my hope dwindle. "Why not?"

"That right was taken from me years ago after I unleashed my sin on Rati. She siphoned some of my power. Boons take more than a mere snap of fingers. They are fed by the devotion of followers or torment of sinners."

My magic struggled to maintain its hold. "Which Asuras can still give a boon?"

Krod's expression was blank. "Lobha, Rahas, and Hans are the three Asuras who can grant boons with no limitations. Perhaps the others can, but I am not too sure. We are siblings in one way, but rivals in another."

I felt the truth in my bones as my magic purred. I pursed my lips. The crowd became restless as they watched us converse quietly. No doubt, they were waiting for Krod to dole out some sort of punishment.

Krod opened his mouth again, eyeing me with devotion that made my skin prickle. He was readying to spill whatever secrets he held on the tip of his tongue. I could let him give in to his need to reveal his deepest, darkest desires. I wanted to embarrass him for underestimating me, make him drop to his knees and beg for my forgiveness.

But I knew what it was like to be robbed of choice. I refused to do that to someone else, even if he was an Asura.

Before I pulled my magic back and released him, I asked, "Have you had any interactions with departed souls as of late?"

"Only those who were sent to my court as punishment for committing my sin. Which have been far fewer since Zehan provides too much mercy when sentencing," he spat out like sparks from a match.

What did that mean? Zehan made it seem like the souls that had vanished were under his purview, not any of the Asuras. "And aside from those who are indebted to you? Have you heard of any departed souls going missing?"

Krod's eyebrows pinched into the center of his forehead. "I have not. Though, I don't pay much heed to what occurs here in Vajra or within the courts of my siblings."

Truth. He was telling the truth. I nodded curtly and let the trance fall away from him.

"I... *What?*" He frowned with confusion but then his expression hardened.

He knows I manipulated him.

That was new. Normally, my magic was subtle enough to not be noticed. The splashes of red covering Krod's face said otherwise.

"What just happened?" Krod's hold on his sin finally snapped. He threw the makeshift table with his magic. Flames erupted around us. My stomach lurched as he strode toward me. "You wrench. How dare you—"

White shadows suddenly appeared in front of me, wispy and light. They materialized into a solid form with broad shoulders and sleek black hair.

For once, relief washed over me as Zehan materialized.

Zehan shoved Krod back with a hand. "If you hope to continue breathing in this realm, I'd take a step back." He looked around at the spectators. "Disperse now."

The crowd instantly cleared. Sunitra and Kal glanced at each other.

My teeth chattered like a child getting out of a bath.

Zehan let out a slow sigh and stared at me like I was the biggest annoyance in his life. He snapped his fingers, and invisible warmth suddenly encased me like a fur blanket. I released an involuntary sigh as my body settled into the magical heat. The corner of his lip kicked up.

By the Asuras. Why did I let him hear the satisfaction?

"Zehan," Krod said smoothly, but caution laced his voice. He played with his deck of cards, like he wasn't at all bothered that Zehan had just threatened him. He licked his lips as his attention turned back to me. "I see why you've decided to keep her." He didn't mention the use of my magic on him. Perhaps he was ashamed to admit that he succumbed under my influence. Or maybe he was still figuring out exactly *what* I did. "The others will be intrigued by her."

"I don't doubt it." Zehan stepped closer to the Asura, inches away from his face. White shadows rose around us, taking the form of monstrous wolves with demon-like fangs. A few departed souls screamed.

Ice filled my veins as the wolves surrounded us. They growled at the Asura and scratched the floor, readying to pounce.

Krod, to his credit, did not blanch. He blinked at the wolves like they were harmless cattle. "Is this dramatic gesture really necessary?"

Zehan's voice carried with the whipping winds as he spoke. "I thought I made it clear to all of you that she is off-limits. Consider this warning as a thank you because of our arrangement regarding Ezhil."

"Is that a threat?" Krod seethed.

"Yes," Zehan said. He stepped back and calmly fixed the lapels of his coat. "I trust you'll remind the others."

I stiffened. Despite the cold, a prickly wave of heat banged against my rib cage. The wolves snapped their jaws. The sheer authority in his voice made the ground beneath my feet tremble.

Krod eyed the wolves, no doubt wondering if it was worth the fight or not. "Very well," he snarled. "But tell your plaything to be more careful. I'll do you this favor, but I won't be this understanding next time." He glanced at me one more time. And just like Zehan had done with white shadows, the Asura faded into a dark-orange mist.

Zehan clasped my upper arm, yanking me back toward the ominous castle in the distance. The wolves around us vanished. "If you are done fraternizing with Asuras, we'll be going now."

"I thought it was my job to fraternize with them."

"It is your job to interrogate," Zehan clipped. "Not to play games with them." Before I could respond, he caused us to travel with the wind.

We were transported back into my bedroom.

I placed a hand on the nearest couch, forcing back down the breakfast that was attempting to make its way onto the plush carpet. "By the Asuras, a little warning would help," I said through gritted teeth.

"It's more fun watching you struggle."

"You. Are. Such. A. Bastard."

"And you are a nuisance, so we're equal." Zehan rubbed the palm of his hand against the end of his beard.

My patience wavered. "If I didn't interrogate Krod, how else would I know that he wasn't responsible for your missing souls? He had no idea that they were even gone."

Zehan blinked. "You used your magic on him? That's why he was about to attack you. I thought your magic was undetectable."

"I thought so too." I shrugged off my overcoat and threw it onto the couch. I moved to the fireplace to warm my hands. "He knows I used some kind of manipulation on him, but I don't think he fully knows what I did." I'd have to be more careful with the other Asuras.

Zehan's gaze narrowed. "If the Asuras can sense your magic, perhaps it is not best to place you in front of them."

"No," I said tersely. I needed to meet with the others. If Zehan decided I was not useful to him, he might change his mind and keep me in Naraka. I shivered. "I just can't be the one to question them. You have to do it while I use my magic on them."

It was a tactic I used with Baanu and King Murkha. They would make trade deals and learn of neighboring kingdom secrets during my performance when their guests were fully under the trance.

Zehan dipped his chin. "How are your practice sessions going? Will you be able to get multiple Asuras under your influence at the same time?"

"Is that doubt in your voice, Prince?" Having to use my magic on even one Asura was going to be difficult, but I couldn't back out now.

He flicked his wrist. "Not at all. I'm simply ensuring the famous Mohini is not getting cold feet."

"Worry about the interrogation, Prince, and I'll worry about the dancing." That and a way to convince the Asuras to make a deal with me.

A corner of Zehan's mouth quirked up. "Your dancing, courtesan, is *exactly* what I worry about."

CHAPTER ELEVEN

Dark suns and bright moons filled my dreams.

I stretched out my arms in the plush silk sheets, appreciating the gentle stretch in my spine and arms. I couldn't remember the last time I'd woken up so rested. For my entire life, I had shared a room with someone, and though I didn't mind Ruhi, she kicked. *Hard.*

Over the past two weeks, an odd sort of peace had fallen over me as I created a routine here. Aside from mandatory practice sessions in the morning, afternoon, and evening with Kal and Sunitra, I was free to do whatever I pleased. The only condition was that I was accompanied by a chaperone, which was admittedly frustrating, but it was preferable to being trapped in my room. Even Sunitra had further warmed up to me, taking me to Vajra when her schedule allowed, and aside from wayward glances from the residents here, no one bothered to speak to me.

Zehan occasionally dropped into my practices and forced me to use the trance until I could barely stand. But for the most part, the Prince of Naraka stayed out my way.

I scrubbed myself clean in a large stone bath big enough to fit at least four people. It had become a daily ritual to lounge here for an hour, letting the citrusy steam seep into my skin. I never had the luxury to take long, solitary baths in Khoya. The courtesans had one hour to use the shared bath, and we didn't linger in there if we didn't have to. The water was cold, and the deep underground cave it sat in smelled like dead fish.

In fact, I had many luxuries now that I had imagined I would only get in Varnasi.

I no longer had to abide by Baanu's strict schedule of four hours of sleep. My meals here were not restricted to dry vegetables and plain rice. Every time I sat down at the long asymmetrical table in the dining room, a steaming pot of chai waited for me along with a feast laid out with every sort of food imaginable. No one slapped my hand if I tried to take one more roti. I wasn't ordered to show more skin or forced to look down when entering a room full of nobles.

Of course, I wasn't foolish enough to let the pleasantries sway my perception of this place. This was hell. The side I was seeing was just a tiny part of the very large realm that was known to do very bad things. As much as I appreciated the fact that no one was controlling my every move, I still needed to leave. Varanasi was still the goal.

Freedom always would be.

I stood slowly, welcoming the chill after stewing in the water for so long. I pulled on a plain long kurta and palazzo pants. Antam was tomorrow night, and my nerves had coiled themselves tighter than a ball of string.

Aside from Kal and Sunitra, Zehan didn't want anyone to realize I had any magical ability. However, after my encounter with Krod, we could not be sure that the other Asuras did not already know. There were too many things that could go wrong, yet Zehan's plan and my secret plan had to continue.

I placed two bobby pins between my teeth when I heard it. A hauntingly beautiful voice echoed through the hallways. Warmth spread through my chest. He sang in the language of the devas, with a timbre I didn't know was possible for a man. I rose, abandoning my unfinished hair to follow the sound.

I peered outside of my room. Sunitra wasn't here and neither was the guard that was normally stationed. I was warned to not go anywhere without someone, but going for just a little while wouldn't hurt anyone. It wasn't like I could escape this realm and the castle was mostly empty at this time.

I grabbed my dupatta and shut my door. I followed the alluring voice to the ground-level floor of the palace and into a room full of windows. Morning sunlight poured into the rectangular space, and soft notes of anise and cinnamon hung in the air. An older man with a turban sat with his eyes closed, lost in the lyrics. His nimble fingers moved swiftly over the strings of a lute. I leaned against the door frame, watching like a secret admirer.

The man finished his song with no care in the world, and not wanting to remain hidden any longer, I clapped. He startled, his gaze landing on me. He quickly rose and bowed with his instrument in hand. "I am so sorry, my lady. Did I disturb your sleep?"

"Please, call me Niya." I shook my head, moving into the room. "And not at all. Your voice is incredible."

"Thank you," he said, placing a hand over his heart. "I'm Raga. The head musician of the orchestra. I was just warming up before thinking through the music for tomorrow night."

A head musician? Similar to Gauri, I wondered how he wound up here. "You will be at Antam."

"Yes," he sat back down on a flat, round cushion. "Actually, I'm glad you're here. I would love to see your style of dance so we can ensure we play something you are comfortable performing to."

"Happy to, but I am sure whatever you play will be perfect," I insisted. Baanu had trained us to perform in any condition, and with or without music. "In fact, I love being surprised." I enjoyed the challenge of having to dance to a song I'd never heard before.

Raga's eyes twinkled. "Good to know. Maybe just a few sets to see and then I can work with the rest of the musicians to come up with something."

A few sets turned into dozens by the time I left Raga. It had been weeks since I had danced, and sweating out some of my pent-up energy and nerves felt good. I made my way to the kitchens, hoping to find food, when I approached deep voices arguing behind closed doors.

"How are you so sure she is the one?" That voice belonged to Ezhil.

My eyebrows lifted. How was he in Naraka? Did Zehan mark him to enter the realm as well?

"I just know," Zehan said. "But regardless, we'll know for sure tomorrow."

Were they talking about me? I crept forward a few steps and pretended to study the carvings on the wall. There were two rakshasa guards on this floor, one on either end of the long hall.

"You're taking a lot of risk, Zehan. Rati and the Asuras have spies everywhere. The rakshasas gossip. Everyone knows you have a Chosen in the castle." Another familiar voice said. "They likely already know what you're up to. Whatever action you want to take, you need to do it sooner rather than later." Was that *Ameel?*

One of the guards twisted his head at me. I took a few more steps forward, letting my hand graze the walls as if they held words that needed to be transcribed.

A hand thumped on the table. "I will not rush this. I need to be sure. If my suspicions are correct, then there is a way out of all of this."

"We all agree that you shouldn't let the opportunity pass. We are concerned that you won't take it because of your ridiculous morals," Ezhil fired back.

"What Ezhil means," I couldn't see Ameel's face but I could hear his glare, "is that you have the tendency to be overly righteous."

Confusion filtered through me. Zehan righteous? It was laughable. Whatever Ezhil and Ameel believed about their master was heavily misguided.

"After tomorrow, I'll know for sure and then I'll make a decision. Right now, there are more pressing items. The missing souls for one and then the rising conflicts between these amateur monarchs are another."

"I'm visiting Queen Oeshi tonight," Ezhil said. "I believe I can talk her out of it, but you know Oeshi, she will want more."

The tension in the room leaked through the cracks.

"Oeshi isn't the only one, Zehan. Travel is easier through the Drifts now and more land is becoming overrun by humans. Look at these maps." Papers shuffled on a table. "News is spreading throughout Tyaga and beyond about the abundance not only in Varnasi but also in Naraka."

"They won't be able to get into Naraka," Zehan said.

"Don't underestimate mortals," Ameel said. "They find ways to do the unthinkable. Look at your courtesan and her magic. How did she even come to possess it?"

So much for Kal and Sunitra being the only ones who knew about my magic. Heat traveled up the sides of my neck as no one answered the question.

Zehan's words came out like a growl. "Very well. Ezhil, see where you can get with Oeshi and if she demands more, then don't give in. I'll go see her myself during the next full moon."

"Understood," Ezhil said. "Now that we are done with business, can we please get to the game." Chairs screeched back like someone was sitting down.

"The politics on Prithvi are cumbersome. If we didn't have to safeguard–"

"Niya."

I jumped, twisting around with a hand over my chest. "Bidal, you scared me."

The rakshasa towered over me, and despite how tall and large he was, I hadn't even heard him approach. Or I'd been too busy eavesdropping.

He looked grim, but that was always his expression. "Are you lost? And where in the nine hells is Sunitra?"

"Not lost, I was just meeting Raga to discuss tomorrow's performance and then found these walls. . .well, interesting. And Sunitra had to run drills this morning." Technically, she told me to wait for her before leaving but that was before Raga's voice had lured me to him.

He leaned back on his heels, clearly not believing a word I said. "Sesh!" He barked.

The lanky guard at the end of the hall jogged to us. He saluted Bidal. "Yes, general."

"Escort Niya back to her rooms and have lunch brought to her," Bidal instructed, his words sharp. "The courtesan needs to rest before tomorrow's big performance."

Sesh dipped his head, motioning me to step in front of him so he could trail me. I turned away but Bidal stepped forward. "Zehan may have given you permission to do whatever you please, but if you wish to remain safe and well, it would be unwise to act as a shadow in these halls."

"Is that a threat?" I folded my arms. I knew Bidal did not like me, hell, none of the rakshasas did, but it was as if he acted as if I was a burden. Yet, it wasn't even my choice to be here.

"No, it's a warning," he said. The general spun around and walked to the opposite end of the hall. His footsteps were now loud and clear.

"Is he always that bitter?" I asked Sesh.

The demon just lifted a brow and gestured for me to walk.

So that was a yes.

I allowed Sesh to lead me to my rooms, taking the opportunity to let my thoughts dissect what I had heard.

How are you sure she is the one?

I was sure Ezhil was referring to me, but what did it mean? What was Zehan trying to prove with my magic? I wasn't naive. As soon as Zehan finished using me for his interrogations, who knew whether he would keep his bargain. He would likely dispose of me like he had his other Chosens.

It was also apparent that Zehan wasn't just the ruler of Naraka. He played his own games on Prithvi but it wasn't clear for what end. Why was he so involved with the humans? It sounded like he was trying to prevent war, but why did what the monarchs did on Tyaga affect him?

"Whatever you're planning, I'll figure it out." I murmured to myself. Zehan claimed he was using me to interrogate the Asuras, but what if there was more? I wouldn't let myself become a pawn in his schemes or anyone else's for that matter.

That was my old life, one I had left behind as soon as I walked through the Gate of Three.

CHAPTER TWELVE

The black walls closed in on me.

Deep breaths. That's what Ruhi always said while we got ready. *It will be over before you know it.* A fresh wave of anxiety washed over me. I had never possessed stage fright, but dancing in front of demons on hell's stage made this a challenge I wasn't sure I could overcome.

Antam was going to start in an hour, and despite having performed hundreds of times in front of thousands of people, this one felt infinitely more nerve-wracking. I finished lining my eyes with kohl and started on jewelry but every movement was jittery.

I picked up a beautiful crystal-and-pearl tikka and laid it at the top of my head along my center part. My fingers shook as I slid the bobby pin at the back loop until I felt a slight tug in my hair.

A knock sounded at the door.

"Come in." I rose and placed a foot on the velvet chair to fasten one of two bright silver payals around my ankle.

"I was able to finish just in time for tonight," Gauri said, carrying a bundle of black fabric that she placed on the small table in front of the couch. "I am sorry it took so long. There were some last-minute adjustments that had to be made."

Kal walked in. He blinked a few times as he took in my adornments, makeup, and half done-up hair. He whistled. "The court guests won't know what hit them tonight."

I couldn't help but smile as I finished securing the second payal. The tiny bells chimed lightly with every step. I picked up the bundle of black fabric. "Is that what I'm wearing?"

Gauri practically bounced on her feet. "I hope you don't mind the color. His Highness had it tailored specifically for the occasion. I believe his exact words were, 'This will help her dance more freely.'"

I huffed with indignation, unbundling the fabric and wondering what flimsy material he had picked out. I lifted up the first piece—a black blouse with long loose sleeves and a red zigzag pattern. The material was top quality linen, thick and sturdy. The entire bodice was handmade with mirror work and vermillion thread. The craftsmanship alone on the outfit could have cost a fortune.

"This is—" I caught myself. *Gorgeous. A work of art. Absolutely breathtakingly beautiful.* I swallowed. "Unexpected."

"Glad you find it amenable to your taste," Kal said with a knowing look. "I'll wait outside while you get dressed."

Twenty minutes later, Gauri finished pinning up my dupatta while I gaped at myself in the mirror.

The lehenga featured the same mirror and thread work at the bottom, woven intricately to look like flames rupturing into the night. I twirled, letting the skirt flare around my legs, lifting at least a foot off the ground. The outfit was ideal for dancing. It was airy yet secure. It was sophisticated and somehow, utterly me.

Something new stirred in the deepest pit of my belly. Zehan had impeccable taste. It was clear from the way he dressed and from his vast art collection, but his reasoning behind *this* dress made a foreign emotion erupt within me.

One that I did not want to linger on.

I opened my door to find Kal, waiting with his hands behind his back, ever the gentleman. His brows lifted as he took in the dress. "You look—"

A low whistle sounded from my right. "I understand why they call you Mohini."

Commander Ezhil approached us, clean-shaven, his hair perfectly combed. He wore a deep maroon sherwani with gold paisley print. While Zehan was handsome in an edgy, dark way, Ezhil was the opposite. He was much more charming and personable. "You're enchanting."

I would have been more shocked if I hadn't heard Ezhil already speaking with Zehan yesterday. "What are you doing here?"

He grinned. "I have an open invitation to this court."

"Yes, but I thought living humans were not allowed into Naraka," I said, remembering the gate that we had walked through when we first arrived.

"They aren't," Kal said coolly. "Commander Ezhil has special exceptions granted to him by Zehan."

Ezhil's angular eyes flicked toward Kal. "Run along, butler. I'll escort her to Antam."

Something flashed in Kal's face before he schooled his features back into neutrality. "As you wish. Good luck tonight, Niya." He gave me a tight smile before spinning on his heel and heading off.

"Are you always that rude?" I asked. "Or only to those you consider beneath you."

"I consider no one beneath me. Kal just irks me to no end with his chirpiness," he said. I rolled my eyes. Ezhil sniggered. "I have a silver tongue when required."

"I'm very much aware of that." It was primarily why he was Zehan's negotiator in the other kingdoms. "You're popular amongst the courtesans of Khoya." Ezhil was a frequent attendee at court and had participated in the bid his fair share. And well, the courtesans talked.

He laughed. "Am I really? And what do the beautiful women of Khoya say about me?"

I scoffed. "I'm not in the business of gossip." But if I was, what I had learned about the commander would only fuel his ego.

"Ah, that's right. My mistake, you're in the business of intel. It was always so interesting to me that King Murkha knew of big territory negotiations before they occurred."

I opened my mouth. How did he know about that? And why did I care? Spying and gathering information for Murkha and Baanu was no longer my job.

He held out his arm to me. I spotted small tattoos on each of his knuckles. "Shall we? You don't want to be late to your little power show, do you?"

I blanched. "Zehan told you the full extent of his plans?"

Ezhil's expression turned gleeful. "You don't approve?"

"No." I folded my arms. I had believed Zehan trusted no one. At least, that was the perception he gave off. And if he did, I hadn't expected it to be the broad man before me. "Just unexpected," I said.

The sentiment was becoming a theme tonight.

Ezhil knowing about my powers made me nervous. What if he revealed it to the humans in Prithvi? I wanted a clean slate in Varnasi, where no one knew who I was or tried to use me for their own selfish wants. He was a master blackmailer and could easily use this information against me.

"Relax, firefly," Ezhil said. "I'm not what you think. I wouldn't dare utter a word about your powers. I didn't then, and I won't now. Zehan would eat me alive. But we are going to be late if we don't go, and Zehan might kill me for that, too. And I'd prefer to live for another night."

I stiffly threaded my arm through his. "Did you do something to piss off Zehan to get the wonderful opportunity to escort me?" Servants and rakshasa guards scurried around us, dressed in crisp clean uniforms.

"Something like that," Ezhil replied. "And I wanted to make sure I wouldn't fall at my knees seeing you again. Your magic did a number on me that night. I couldn't get you out of my head for three days, and I couldn't figure out why until Zehan told me what had happened. The bastard kept me in the dark until I went to confess to him that I thought I wanted to bed you."

I stared at Ezhil and broke into a laugh. My first real one in probably months.

Ezhil smiled. It was so genuine that it made my chest thud. "Glad my suffering provides you with humor."

"For what it is worth, I am sorry," I said. I had used a stronger dose than usual on Ezhil. Sometimes, the lingering impact of my magic was that it created a longing to see me again. It was what continually drew nobles and travelers to my door. "I generally don't let it strike that hard but that night I was distracted." By the fact that my magic hadn't impacted Zehan.

"Don't worry about it," Ezhil said. "I know you were just doing a job. And like I said, Zehan forbade me from telling anyone else."

"And just because he forbids it, you won't say anything?" Mistrust still laced my tone.

"You're asking the wrong questions, firefly. But, yes. I owe Zehan a great deal and wouldn't betray his trust for anything, which in turn, means not betraying yours. Whether you choose to believe that fact is up to you." He gave me a pointed look.

"What do you mean—" I abruptly stopped talking as we stepped into the massive throne room, decorated with hundreds of candles, white roses, and baby's breath. Dozens of people were seated on either edge of the throne room. But that hadn't snagged my attention.

No, what had caused me to stop in my tracks was Zehan, looking like divinity in the flesh, standing in the center under a five-tiered chandelier.

He wasn't in his usual black or dark green or midnight blue. It was a luscious cream kurta fully embroidered with russet and garnet thread paired with a layered necklace inlaid with pearls of various sizes. A silk khaki dupatta wrapped around one shoulder and then looped through the opposite arm. He was freshly groomed, his beard shaped to perfect precision. A vintage gold crown inlaid with black diamonds and sapphires sat on top of his dark waves.

My skin prickled with needles of heat.

He spoke with another short and bulky rakshasa that had spiked jewelry wrapped along the lengths of his arms. Two weeks ago, I would have been distraught at the sight, but now, they didn't seem so scary. They seemed...normal.

Ezhil let out a cough-laugh that made me wince out of my own self-inflicted trance. Zehan's eyes snapped to Ezhil and me, arm in arm.

My cheeks flamed. I couldn't form coherent words no matter how hard I tried. His smoky gaze traveled down my dress and back up to my face, lingering on my ruby-red lips.

My pulse picked up at the same time white steam whiffed off his frame. What was it about this man that drew me to him like a mosquito to a candle?

He walked toward us, not bothering to bid adieu to the rakshasa he had been conversing with. I forced myself to look away, hoping it would reduce the light flush that undoubtedly bloomed on my tanned cheeks.

Zehan stopped in front of us. "Ezhil, I trust there were no issues with Oeshi."

"None whatsoever. Krod upheld his end of our deal despite recent events," Ezhil confirmed, his eyes flickering to me for a millisecond.

I held in my gawk at the mention of the coastal queen. Queen Oeshi normally didn't engage with anyone in Tyaga. Her territory had been out of conflict for over fifty years. Tavas greeted Nila Ocean, giving her access to both land and sea resources, but I doubted it was as abundant as Naraka.

Ezhil held Zehan's gaze like they were conversing silently. The commander released my arm and bowed to me. "Good luck tonight, Niya." He winked. "I'm sure I'll be seeing you around."

"Let's hope not," I remarked. The commander only smirked before parading off to speak with other guests, leaving Zehan and me alone.

"You look exquisite." Zehan chirped, giving me a heavy whiff of the addicting smoky and sweet-mint scene that constantly clung to him. If I could, I would wrap the smell around me like a cloak. "And your entrance has been duly noted by everyone in this room, courtesan."

The use of that nickname diminished my haze.

"Niya," I clarified for the millionth time, but as usual, my quip went ignored. I cleared my throat and looked around the room. He wasn't wrong, dozens of eyes were on us. Few were wary, most were curious, and some were downright smug. I ignored all of them, my gaze traveling to something far more interesting near the throne.

The Asuras lounged in their seats, four on one side and three on the other. They all stared at me.

My heart thudded. These creatures were the most feared ones in the entire realm. Krod was amongst them, with his head tilted in a fiery red sherwani.

Zehan placed a hand at the small of my back, sending warm shivers up my spine as we walked around the room. It took all my effort to not lean in and let the pad of his fingers dig a little deeper into my skin.

His voice rumbled through me. "The one next to Krod is Lobha, the Asura of Greed. The bored looking man with the cream shawl and his leg folded across his knee is Shama, the Asura of Sloth. Next to him, in the purple is Rahas, her sin is lust. On the other side of the throne, Abhi, the man with the boyish grin and turquoise scarf, and Issa, the female with the light-brown hair, are the Asuras of Pride and Envy, respectively. And then the last one, the female with the deep blue gown is Shoka, the Asura of Despair."

I swallowed. An intense aura engulfed them. It was clear they all held their own sorts of power, but I was too afraid to ask what they specifically were. "And the two missing seats?"

"Nadi and Hans," Zehan said. "The Asura of Fear and the Asura of Violence. They rarely make appearances at these things, much like Rati."

Tension clawed itself through my chest. Hans was one of the ones that could grant boons, which meant there were only two Asuras here that I could work with—Lobha and Rahas.

"What if I can't use my magic on all of them at once?" I had used my magic on crowds before, but they hadn't been shielding against magic. It had been easy to influence them. These Asuras would not be the same.

Zehan clucked his tongue. "I feel fairly confident that Nadi and Issa are not involved. Krod already revealed to you that he did not know souls were going missing. Shoka has the most souls under her purview, so I do not see why she would need to take departed souls to increase her power. Shama is fifty-fifty, he is extremely calculative, so he could pull something like this off, but he is not as power hungry as the rest." He moved his hand from my back and readjusted the cuffs on his kurta. "Lobha, Rahas, Abhi, and Hans are the ones I'm most skeptical of, so let's focus on the ones that are here. If we can't get to all of them tonight, there will be other opportunities."

"Got it. Cream, purple, and turquoise." It was easier to remember the colors of their outfits versus their names and features. Jitteriness flitted through me. I clenched my hands together.

Zehan noticed. His lips pushed together in a fine line, his exhale tickling the tops of my cheeks. "Do not forget, courtesan. You hold the power to easily command this room."

My nerves diminished, replaced by shock. Was Zehan giving me a confidence boost? Magic filtered through me like cold water sliding down slippery pebbles.

Focus on the task. I needed my senses clear of whatever this uncomfortable heat was if I was going to coerce the rulers of demons.

Zehan led me to a seat beside the staircase leading to the thrones before he walked up to his dark throne, which was a step above a line of smaller thrones where the Asuras sat.

The prince sat and lifted one leg to rest on the other. With his hands poised on his kneecaps, he donned a mask of unreadable darkness. "Bring them in." No formal welcome. No niceties. Just straight down to the devil's business.

The main doors swung open, and a group of humans shuffled in close together. Their gazes were guarded. They crowded into the center of the room like a pack of frightened ewes. They paled as they registered the demonic creatures in the room. I was sure the skinny boy with spiked hair was going to faint.

"Recently departed"—Zehan's voice vibrated with cosmos power—"as it has already been explained to you by the gatekeepers, your time in Naraka is dictated by actions committed throughout your mortal life." He glared at the small group. "I will glimpse into your past life to see the sins you've committed to pass judgment and provide you with a sentence. For those of you who have embodied multiple sins, you will have to go through the Asura Trials. There, you will be tested on your vices." His tone held a sharp edge.

The Asuras seated in line with him kept their expressions in check, giving nothing away. I moved to the edge of my seat, unable to hide my interest as Zehan called the first name.

"Ruhi Turan."

CHAPTER THIRTEEN

A loud ringing sound filled my ears.

No. He couldn't have meant *my* Ruhi. She was safe and sheltered in Khoya.

Yet, when a petite girl with straight black hair down to her waist took a few steps forward, surprise racked through me.

"Ruhi?" I said, my voice barely a whisper. Zehan's back tensed. Why was she here?

Her anxious eyes locked on mine, widening further. "Niya?"

I tried to stand, go to her, snatch her away and face whatever hell was brought our way, but thick white bracelets formed around my wrists, creating the sensation of needles pricking every time I moved.

Zehan.

I scowled internally. I tried to twist out of them, but the effort was fruitless. I even tried to use my own magic on them, but it simply bounced off. I sucked in a tight breath as the cuffs grew tighter. I could make a scene, but that wouldn't help this situation, if anything, it would only draw more attention to me and, worse, to Ruhi.

Zehan tilted his head at Ruhi, not letting his mask fall. "Do you admit guilt to performing sins in your mortal life?"

Ruhi quivered under Zehan's intense glare, likely remembering what he had done to her in court. My stomach lurched.

"Yes," her voice trembled.

That couldn't be right. Ruhi was the kindest person I knew. She would never do anything wrong.

Zehan's eyes flashed gold, like he held the rays of the sun in his stare. I dug my fingernails into my chair's velvet armrests. Zehan's white shadows pounced on Ruhi.

What was he doing to her? I moved dangerously close to the edge of my seat.

My magic swirled within me, building like a storm to save Ruhi from Zehan's dangerous fog. But the wrist clamps tightened their hold, like they knew I aimed to break them apart. The white haze around Ruhi cleared in seconds.

Ruhi's eyes were big and anxious, like a rabbit that had been spotted by a fox, but she inched her chin up with unwavering confidence.

Zehan also smiled like they shared some secret. "Ruhi Turan, despite your crimes, you have lived a righteous life. I see why you stabbed Daman."

Ruhi flinched.

Stabbed? My mouth parted but I quickly pushed my lips together. Ruhi wouldn't hurt a fly. There must be some mistake.

Daman. That name sounded familiar, yet I couldn't place it, but whoever it was had done something horrible. I could see it written all over Ruhi's face.

Zehan's voice softened. "I assure you that once Daman arrives here, he will serve a *very* long sentence under Hans. Your sentence is one month in Naraka, and then, you will reincarnate into your next life cycle."

What did Daman do to her? My shoulders tensed. At least she wouldn't be here for long. I hated that her life had ended, but seeing her after her death created an odd sense of comfort.

Ruhi bowed in acceptance. In seconds, her entire life had been judged. She was swallowed once again by the crowd of departed souls she entered with.

The next soul was called forward.

Zehan's sentences ranged from living in Naraka for years, shackled to an Asura for torment, or solitary imprisonment. However, more frequently than not, the souls he judged had committed sins that were somehow...justified. Most of them were in dodgy situations that forced them to act. Only one soul was sentenced to the Asura Trials, a hefty man with a bald spot who abandoned his children, causing them to perish on the streets.

I thought he deserved a punishment far worse.

The range of sin didn't surprise me. I knew from my life in Khoya that people were not inherently good or bad. They were always a mix of both. Ruhi was a prime example of that.

However, what did cause me to second-guess my entire set of beliefs was the potential fact that Naraka was not evil or good, but somewhere in between.

My skin prickled. This world has done nothing but push back against everything I had known since stepping into it. Every rumor I had heard about the realm and its prince were not entirely false but also not the whole truth.

Yet people like Zehan always had ulterior motives. I witnessed it repeatedly in Khoya Kingdom. Those in power always wanted more and knew how to play games to get what they wanted. They never thought about the pain they were causing on others or the ripple effect their decisions created. Zehan might help his subjects here, but he was still a tyrant to the living humans.

Zehan looked brutal sitting on his perch like a white raven. I noticed the increasing slouch urging his shoulders forward and the slight darkening under his eyes. It seemed I wasn't the only one who felt a power drain after too much use of magic.

The last of the souls were sentenced and flanked by rakshasas as they left the throne room. I wanted to go after them to see Ruhi, but I had a job. *Later.* I'd find a way to see Ruhi, a vow to myself.

"Now that is done." Zehan rose from his seat like he was about to give a grand speech, but instead, his ebony eyes landed on me. The white bands around my wrists vanished.

"We have a special performance."

***

Demons and tortuous souls watched me like they were being let in on a dark secret.

No one whispered or even appeared to breathe as I made my way to the center of the stone floor. Blood rushed to my face. Normally, when I walked onto a stage, I was greeted with cheap whistles, not this incredibly tense mixture of sharp silence and keen interest.

My court is well-mannered and civil.

I was amazed at how right Zehan had been. Even respected it a smidge.

Servants walked in systematically with trays of sura and glass hookahs, standing at the edges of the hall to fetch anything guests may need. I faced the crowd and bowed at the hips to His Highness and his demonic court.

Krod's deep purple lips sniggered. I ignored the bloodshot eyes of the Asura of Anger and zoned in on Lobha and Rahas, who sat on either side of Zehan. They were my first targets to entrance so Zehan could question them. Abhi was two seats away from Lobha, so it would be futile to target him if Zehan couldn't speak to him. I also needed to give them just enough magic to make them want to speak with me afterwards.

Zehan's goal was to interrogate to find a killer, but mine was to negotiate to get a boon. I hadn't worked out how I would get the chance to speak with them, but in my experience, if they received enough of the trance magic, they would seek me out themselves.

I closed my eyes briefly to block out the jitters and worrisome thoughts. *This is just another night on the floor, another night of bringing men to their knees.*

Except instead of men, they were creatures of hell.

Easy.

I found Zehan again, lazily slumped in his seat with a dark smirk on his face. I was transported back to the last time we found ourselves in similar positions. He held my gaze as he took a long drag from a hookah pipe, then deliberately tilted his head back to release a velvety plume of smoke.

Something throbbed below my navel, hot and heady. A sudden urge to swagger up to his iron throne and inhale his released smoke overcame me.

I shook out my hands. *Focus.* I needed my magic to work, and these wholly inappropriate and jarring thoughts about the ruler of the underworld would hinder my success. His lips curled up at the corners, as if he could read the deceitful thoughts swirling in my mind.

I faced my audience of gruesome beasts. Their sharp upturned teeth flashed, and their slitted eyes passed judgment. I rolled back my shoulders. This was just another dance. Another performance for mongrels.

I briefly touched the cold floor and then my heart, giving a silent thansk to the devas for my talent and this floor to showcase it on, despite it being hell's stage.

Zehan arched an eyebrow as he lifted a hand in a half wave. "Begin." His voice rippled through the room with a force that could sway even the most powerful winds.

Like puppets, Raga and his musicians strummed their chords. A palm slapped a bayan. A breath filled a flute. Raga's yearning voice filled the room. This music was nothing like Khoya Kingdom. It was reminiscent of the fervent music I'd heard as a child.

Emotional. Mysterious. Transformative.

My eardrums pulsed with a deep need for *more*. I smiled at my music givers, urging them to continue. Raga gave me a toothy smile, like he could read my thoughts, and he urged the others to pick up the beat.

I kicked out my foot in a slow circle, getting a feel for the unique vibrations of the song. A sense of rightness flooded my being. I drew my hands up and twisted my wrists to give the visual of flowers and then let the music overtake my senses, guiding my steps and spins and expressions.

The musicality shifted as the belly-stirring thrum of the sitar joined into the fold. My heart swelled. This was not the lyrical tone of death and hell, but of life and creation. A melody that told a story, ebbing with natural highs and lows.

I don't know how much time passed. I was so enthralled by this music that I forgot to release my trance magic, but as I took in my audience, I realized I didn't need to. The rakshasas and departed souls watched with rapt attention like they were already under my influence.

This soul-reaching rhythm was why I had become a dancer in the first place.

I felt Zehan's full attention on me, with equal parts light and darkness. His throat bobbed, and his fingers tightened on the armrests of his chair. I stumbled on the next step.

By the Asuras. Focus.

I shifted my expression, embodying the persona of Mohini, the seductress. With one sweep of my arms, I released the trance over the audience. The invisible shields and locks around the Asuras were similar to the one Krod had around him.

I worked on Rahas first, giving her just enough trance magic to turn her interest into lust, which wasn't hard given her sin. On the next spin, I switched to Lobha, chipping away at the tight coils of disdain he held around himself.

I winked at Zehan. His nostrils flared. That was the signal we had agreed upon, but Zehan stared at me two beats longer than necessary before he finally leaned toward Rahas like he was telling her a juicy piece of gossip.

An uncomfortable jolt zinged through me at the sight of him so close to the beautiful Asura. The beat of the tabla became faster as the song sped up. I allowed myself to be swept away by the soulful lull of instruments. The minutes ticked by as I glided across the stage, captivating my audience, feeding them more of my trance with every spin.

I was so immersed in my art that I almost missed the doors to the throne room bursting open. Bidal walked in with a solemn expression. The music abruptly cut off, and my hold over both Lobha and Rahas broke like a twig being snapped in two. I paused mid-pose. My heavy skirt twisted around my calves finishing the circle for me. I looked back at Zehan, breathless.

He stared right at me like he also had woken from a hazy stupor. I had been so caught up in my own whimsical steps that I had forgotten where I was and who I was dancing for. Zehan fingers dug into the massive chair's armrests. His heated gaze sent a bolt of lightning through me.

What was happening? Was I attracted to Zehan? *No.* It was just the high from the dance. The rush of adrenaline from being able to dance with abandon overwhelmed me.

Zehan stiffened, and his expression turned stormy as Bidal whispered in his ear. He stood up swiftly and murmured to Kal, who stood next to him. "My attention is needed—"

The door swung open again and one of the most beautiful women I had ever seen walked through it.

The way she held herself made the hair on my arms rise. Similar to Zehan, she looked ethereal and something *more* than a mere mortal. Her features were too perfect—high rogued cheekbones, petite sharp nose, plump red lips. Wild black waves cascaded over her breasts and down to the top edges of her hips. The room fell into silence as everyone rose out of their seats to bow.

"This is a first," Zehan said, he was standing along with the rest of the Asuras. "You generally find these events boring, Rati."

My heart drummed. *Rati*

The Goddess of Death.

CHAPTER FOURTEEN

Numbness spread through my fingers and toes. The only known deva left in the cosmos stood before me.

Rati's steely gaze locked onto me, and her head tilted with intrigue. Her layered lehenga fell to the floor in wafting dark-red waves. She dripped with silver jewelry—her earrings dangled to her shoulders, her arms were strewn with heavy bangles, and at least five ruby-encrusted necklaces wrapped around her long neck.

"I was bored." She said to Zehan. "I came to see if the rumors were true. That you brought a new Chosen to your court. I came to see what the fuss was about."

"I see. Well, your presence is a welcome surprise," Zehan said tersely. "Though, we were just ending for the evening."

Rati tsked. "What do you mean? Clearly, I interrupted a performance. Do carry on." She strode up next to him and perched on his armrest. She patted his seat and waived her hand at me like I was nothing more than a maid. "Continue, my dear."

Irrational irritation flickered through me, but I kept my expression neutral. I had to obey.

Zehan looked like he could kill with one blink. "My Chosen is finished with her performance."

Rati shifted her jaw, turning to me. "I said *dance.*"

The musicians began to play a melody that was off-key. My feet moved with a will of their own. A surge of wrongness went through me. I glanced at the Raga, whose face was scrunched up in pain.

She controlled us with her power.

I tried to force my arms down and my feet to halt but all that did was cause sharp pain to shoot into my limbs. I gritted my teeth. With a one-worded command, the devi had turned me into a puppet.

Zehan snarled something to Rati, but she did not move, only relaxed farther onto the armchair. The Asuras watched with caution as Zehan's normally calm, stoic expression turned into one of wrath. Krod smiled gleefully, his head whipping back and forth between me and Zehan.

I gasped again. Zehan's head snapped toward me. Every time I tried to stop, the pain intensified. Tears sprang to my eyes, and I prayed for the stone floor to open and swallow me whole. White smoke circled around my feet and rose to form a see-through barrier.

Rati's control faded away, and my body sagged in relief. The music abruptly died on a high note. My cheeks felt flushed.

Zehan bent forward to whisper in Rati's ear. It appeared...intimate. Faint tightness coiled in my lower belly. Then Zehan rose to his full height and held out his arm to Rati, which she took with a winning smile. Unease slid down my spine.

"Carry on with your festivities," Zehan said in his stiff ruler's voice.

As he passed me, he shook his head barely. *Don't continue with our plan* is what his gaze suggested, along with other emotions I didn't care to evaluate.

They swept out of the room and the doors shut with a heavy thud, leaving me alone in a room full of rakshasas.

Hushed voices erupted through the hall. Kal was by my side in the next moment as I attempted to slow down the heavy rise and fall of my chest. "His Highness told me to escort you back to your rooms."

That same coil tightened further. Of course he did. But I wasn't about to let tonight go to complete waste. "I'm not going anywhere."

Two Asuras vanished through Vayu. If I didn't attempt to get a boon now, I'd have to wait until the next Antam to meet them, delaying my departure to

Varnasi even longer. Yet after my interaction with Krod, using my magic directly when seven of them were here together didn't seem like the best idea.

Maybe I don't need to use my magic to get them to make a deal with me. I could be charming without my ability. Baanu named me Mohini for a reason. The name meant enchantress and was based on my ability and knack for getting nobles to do exactly what I needed.

I pushed my shoulders back and walked purposefully toward the Asuras.

Kal hovered behind me like a fly that had found its fruit. "I must insist that you go back to your room."

"As we've established when we went to Vajra, following orders was not part of my bargain with Zehan."

Perhaps it was the fact that I had just lost control and needed to regain it, or maybe it was the indescribable emotion at seeing Zehan's mouth graze against Rati's ear that made me reckless.

Ezhil held an arm out in front of me. "Run along, firefly. Your services are no longer required." The warning in his voice was clear.

"I don't need Zehan to do my job," I clipped, skirting around him. Lobha's eyebrow lifted at my eager smile. "Zehan was supposed to interrogate them while I danced, but I have no idea if he managed to do so after Rati's interruption. We can't let this opportunity go." I gave Ezhil the response he expected when really I just needed to speak to three of them alone to make my own case.

Ezhil kept up with me and spoke from the corner of his mouth. "No, but as you are already aware, Asuras can be tricky. They hardly ever speak their mind."

So Zehan told him about my interaction with Krod. Just how close were the commander and prince? "I'll make that judgment for myself. Shoo, Commander. Your guidance is no longer needed."

Ezhil let out a low curse.

I tilted my head as I stepped up to the Asuras. I paused, realizing I had no idea of an appropriate greeting. Deciding I should treat them as a lord or noble, I bowed.

Lobha let out a rough laugh. "There is no need to treat us as royals. We are anything but."

I rose. "Perhaps not, but I've learned a little bit of respect can go a long way."

"Beautiful *and* clever," Lobha admired. "Fitting qualities for the most famous dancer in Tyaga."

Mohini is not only famous in Khoya. Krod had warned me, yet it still surprised me that the worst of humanity also found appeal in Mohini. In me.

"Amongst many others." I shrugged.

"You are quite the dancer, Niya," Rahas purred. Her rust-colored corset blouse and silhouetted skirt hugged her form perfectly, emphasizing every curve. "A shame that you were not able to finish your performance."

I lifted one shoulder. "I am sure there will be more chances."

"But of course," Lobha said. "However, it seems you are not the only one the prince pays attention to." He glanced back at the door where Rati and Zehan had disappeared. He moved a step closer and took a large sniff. "You smell absolutely delectable."

"And she is Zehan's," Ezhil added matter-of-factly.

Magic twitched in my fingers. *How dare he.* "I belong to no one." I shot Ezhil a look. This rumor about me being an item Zehan claimed irritated me to no end.

"Interesting." Lobha moved closer. The tiny streaks of gold in his emerald eyes became too close for comfort. "And here I thought the Prince of Naraka was too soft for any indecency."

"You thought wrong," Ezhil spat out.

I was angry at Ezhil's comment, but I could use it to my advantage. Greed was an easy emotion to heighten. "Again, I do not *belong* to Zehan. We've merely come to an agreement of sorts." I fluttered my lashes.

"Oh?" The Asura towered over me. Ezhil tensed. He was *massive.* "And what agreement is that?"

"I ensure his needs are met, and he returns the favor," I said matter-of-factly. "Now I know what it's like to sleep with the Prince of Naraka. Though, his *performance* could be described as mediocre at best and definitely could use some work."

Kal gasped behind me.

Lobha's pupils dilated. I could practically feel his greed and ego tearing at his insides, urging him to act on his wants. Lobha's voice dipped a few octaves. "We can remedy that. Perhaps you'd want to experiment with other creatures. Ones that can guarantee a good time."

I flashed a sly smile. "An interesting proposition that I'd like to hear more about." I rose on my tippy-toes to whisper in his ear, fighting the scent of raw meat, which burned my nostrils. "But not around so many ears."

"That is easily fixed." Lobha held out his arm, and I threaded my arm through.

Kal guffawed. Ezhil looked like he wanted to haul me over his shoulder like a sack of rice and stomp out of the room.

Rahas clucked her tongue, flicking her eyes between all of us with sharp intensity. "I grow tired from the lust-filled emotions in this room. I am going, brother. I'm sure we will meet again, Niya." Without another word, she vanished through Vayu back to whatever piece of hell she resided in.

Lobha led me out of the throne room and into one of the palace's many gardens. Eyes trailed us, but no one seemed surprised that one of Zehan's Chosen was wooed by an Asura.

I led us away from the stationed guards into a massive outdoor garden with a towering fountain. I shivered as coldness from the ground seeped into my toes. I kept a tight hold on my magic, noticing I wasn't as drained as I normally was after dancing.

As if the darkness in this realm fueled my sinful magic. "Do you frequent the court often?" I asked.

He grunted in confirmation. "I always like to learn what new art pieces Zehan has added to his collection, though the bastard hardly lets me see it. I also like to see who the new departed souls are. Sometimes there are nobility amongst them, and they make excellent conversationalists. They are also the easiest to lure into my sin. The fortunate are greedy."

If Lobha enjoyed the company of departed souls, I doubted he would be responsible for them disappearing. My head immediately went to Zehan, wondering if he had managed to ask them if they were involved.

Do not forget why you are here. Zehan had nothing to do with my conversation right now. And it sure in hell wasn't why I was outside in the deathly cold, alone with an Asura. "I bet the departed souls frequently ask you for favors, boons even," I hedged.

Lobha raised an eyebrow like he knew where this conversation was headed. "They do, but I rarely grant them. I highly doubt you'll be able to pay the cost, Mohini."

"How do you know if I haven't even asked yet?"

"Because the only way to receive a boon from me is to hand over all of your emotions aside from greed." Lobha faced me. "You'd have to give it all up. Your ability to be angry, happy, sad." He circled around me. The straps of my blouse became too tight. "You give up your ability to feel lust or love."

My heart rate sped up. That was a steep price. *Too steep.*

Yet even though I knew it was preposterous, I still considered it. I wasn't keen to feel much emotion anyways, and perhaps not being able to feel anything would be easier than having sympathy for things out of my control.

I internally scowled at my thoughts. Living with only greed as an emotion was absurd. "And there is nothing else you will take in exchange?"

"Well, perhaps I can make an exception." His eyes glazed over again as he leaned his nose to my hair and breathed deeply. I could smell the sour smell of sura on his breath. "By the Asuras, you smell good. Maybe if you were to stay in my court for some time, I could be convinced otherwise." Revulsion racked my body.

Why were so many of the Asuras male?

"Brother," a dull voice spoke behind us, "are you trying to get yourself killed?"

Lobha groaned and stepped away. "At least if I had been killed, I would have died in a lustful embrace. You couldn't wait a few more minutes, Shama?"

Unlike his siblings, the Asura of Sloth, didn't have a cold expression or sharp features. His wintry eyes were bright, and his smile soft. An air of ease surrounded him. It was hard to believe he was an antigod. "Zehan wouldn't have made it an easy death." He held out his hand to me. "Niya, it is nice to make your acquaintance. Everyone in there can't stop talking about you." He pointed at the throne room. "You've done quite a number on their egos. Abhi is having a field day."

I stuck my hip out a little more than I needed to. My coin belt jingled. "I'm happy I could impress. Though Lobha has done no such thing."

Shama chuckled. "Your first mistake was believing that the Asura of Greed could impress you."

"Oh, and what about you?"

Shama leaned forward with his hands shrugged into his pockets. He towered at least a foot and half over me. The smell of the ocean hit me at the same time. "Try me."

I fought the urge to roll my eyes. Naraka wasn't the only realm full of powerful shameless flirts.

Lobha plopped down on the edge of the fountain and ran his pudgy fingers through the water. "She wants a boon."

Shama stilled and shared a pointed look with his brother. "Does she now?" The blue in his irises deepened. "And does your precious prince know what you're up to?"

I didn't know what to say. I shivered. Zehan would not react well when he found out about my plan. I had never expected him to *not* learn of it, but I had hoped that when he finally realized what I was up to, it would be too late, and I would already be gone.

"Hmm." Shama's grin widened. "I thought so."

I shrugged, feigning the underlying fear I felt at the thought of Shama revealing everything to Zehan. "What I do in my spare time is none of the prince's business as far as I'm concerned."

"Yet, it is always my business." Zehan's powerful, arrogant voice sent a brush of tingling warmth down the back of my neck.

I cursed every wretched Asura.

<h1 style="text-align:center">CHAPTER FIFTEEN</h1>

Zehan emerged from the dark shadows of the courtyard. "You have a knack for wandering, courtesan. Do I need to leash you?"

I scoffed, ignoring the way my knees buckled at the timbre of his voice. The nerve of this man.

"Zehan," Shama drawled, tilting his head. "How did your *meeting* go with the goddess?"

Next to him, Lobha sniggered. "We were just becoming familiar with your new Chosen."

My jewelry felt like pounds of gold instead of ounces. If Shama and Lobha told Zehan what I was up to, who knew how he would react. What if he went back on his bargain? What if he put me back into his dungeon and never let me see the light of the sun and moon?

Zehan was expressionless as he casually unbuttoned the top of his sherwani. "Yes, well, I only choose the best. I'm sure Krod has informed you both all about her." He ignored Shama's question altogether.

She is off-limits. I don't make empty threats. His words to Krod came flooding back to me. Zehan glared at the two Asuras, and I wondered if he would summon his white wolves again. I had somehow become a part of their political rebuttals. My body felt like it was constantly being slammed into a concrete wall.

"Of course." Shama smiled wickedly. "Yet, my sources tell me you sleep in separate rooms. And Niya was entertaining Lobha just now for something *quite* interesting. I heard she also sought out Krod in the Vajra. So I do wonder how strong of a claim you actually have on her. Perhaps...she's looking for something else."

Shit. He was baiting Zehan. Hovering on a delicate line to reveal my secret. Shama challenged me with a manic sort of gleam that said, *Your play.*

Every conversation I had with an Asura was a trial in itself. I didn't know what game Shama was playing, but I couldn't let Zehan realize what I was doing.

Zehan opened his mouth, but I cut in. "Just because he doesn't enter through the doors of my room doesn't mean he isn't in there. Don't you all travel by Vayu?"

If Zehan was surprised, he kept it to himself. Lobha and Shama glanced at each other with amusement. They already believed Zehan and I were sleeping together, I might as well play the part to keep my secrets safe.

A large hand wrapped around my waist. I tensed as Zehan fitted me into his frame. The coldness I felt disappeared, only heat and comfort engulfed me along with the smell of the mint-flavored hookah he had inhaled in the throne room. I attempted to pull away to get some space, but Zehan's hand pushed me back into him.

I forced my next exhale out slowly. This is just part of my role as his courtesan. Nothing more.

Lobha let out a rough laugh and clapped his hand on Shama's shoulder. "It seems your sources overlooked that tidbit, brother."

Shama didn't look convinced.

Lobha drummed his fingers against the curved edge of the fountain. "I see why you stole her, Zehan. Though I'm still pondering how in nine hells she tolerates you."

"Wouldn't you want to know, Lobha." Zehan said impatiently. He swiped a thumb down my spine. I straightened. "Come, let me show you the latest art I've brought back. I think there is a piece you might like to have."

That drew Lobha's full attention. "Lead the way."

"I doubt the art pieces would interest you, Shama, but you're welcome to join." Zehan's lips moved against my temple. I flushed, and if he hadn't been holding me, I might have fallen.

"Can you find your way?" His expression tightened. "Or do I need to have Kal escort you."

I let out a loose laugh. "I can find my own way. I've been here long enough."

He gave me a measured look. I had gotten under the Prince of Hell's skin, which brought me a great deal of satisfaction.

I gently twisted out of his hold, which was a grave mistake because the cold air wrapped around me ferociously. My body screamed at me to stay close to him. "I'll see you later?" I asked innocently to maintain appearances in front of the Asuras. Zehan and I had other matters to discuss and I refused to wait until morning.

"Later," Zehan promised.

"I'm sure we'll meet again, Niya," Shama said. Without another word, he dissipated into the air.

I left Zehan and Lobha, fighting to not look back at the prince. His stare drilled into the back of my head as I exited the garden. When I reached my room, I shut the door firmly behind me and slumped against the door frame, finally letting the delayed drain of energy and exertion fill into my muscles.

Ruhi was here. I failed to get a boon. Nothing had gone according to plan.

Krod was a bust. Lobha had requested too much, leaving Rahas, Hans, and Abhi as my only options. I'd have to get to Rahas at the next Antam. As for Hans, Zehan said he rarely attended court, so I had no idea how to reach him.

But I had to find a way before one of the Asuras revealed my secondary plan to receive a boon to Zehan. Clearly, the rulers of this realm did not have *friendly* relationships, only mutually beneficial agreements. No doubt the Asuras would wait until an opportune moment to leverage a secret like this.

It's what I would do if I was an Asura. I did it all the time in Khoya. I would flirt with the same noble for weeks, slowly gathering critical details about their courts, and then use that information as selling points to their competitors with the ultimate goal of supporting King Murkha's trade agreements.

I took a deep, shaky breath, releasing the pent-up tension from the evening's events. My gaze traveled to the sky through the windows, as it often did. The moon at its peak height offered enough light that I didn't need lanterns. The sun was at the edge of the horizon, its brightness muted by the darkness. In the distance, I could barely make out the shadowy mountains where the unruly Asuras took up residence.

It was so beautiful that it hurt.

I reached for the curtain, to shun away the mocking landscape when I heard my door knob twist with a small click.

Zehan stood under the archway. Ruffled hair. Darkened expression. Relaxed gait.

Utterly devastating.

I hated it.

And I hated him. I reminded myself. No matter how overwhelming the Prince of Hell's presence was, I couldn't let him disorient me.

My hands dropped from the curtain as he shut the door slowly so he could lean back against it. He crossed one leg over the other. "I thought we had a plan."

"No, you had a plan," I clarified. "One that failed, so I used my backup plan."

"Luring away an Asura–"

"I want to see Ruhi," I blurted before he could finish his lecture. I *had* to see her. I thought I would never see her again, but fate had other plans. She was here, *in Naraka.* She had been killed, and I needed to understand what happened.

Zehan didn't hesitate. "Done."

My shoulders sagged an inch. "Just like that?"

Zehan shook his head. "Your amount of distrust for me is baffling."

I flushed under his scrutinizing gaze but turned away to take off my jewelry. "I don't know why you're surprised when you haven't done much to earn my trust." Faint tiredness laced my voice. My jewelry clinked against each other as I created a pile on the vanity, filling the silence between us.

"I am sorry about Rati," Zehan said with quiet wrath. "It won't happen again."

"It's fine." The whole debacle shook me, but it wasn't too different from being in Khoya. My actions were constantly controlled. This had been extreme, but most of the people in Tyaga who had any authority had no morals. And yet...Zehan stopped her. "Thank you for intervening."

"If you would dig deeper into your powers, perhaps next time, you will not need my help." He shifted on his feet. "You did well tonight."

I paused, not expecting any praise from him, but then slowly pulled off my earrings. I sighed as the weight lifted off my ears. The jewelry, though beautiful, weighed more than a heavy sack of coins. I rubbed my lobes between my index finger and thumb, offering relieving pressure. "Were you able to question Rahas and Lobha?"

"Lobha didn't do it, neither did Rahas." Zehan ran a hand through his hair. "If you would have just waited for me to debrief you...leading on an Asura was reckless. Even for you."

I busied myself with the clasp of my necklace. "I had no idea if you had successfully questioned them before you went gallivanting off with Rati, so I took matters in my own hands."

Even though the missing souls were not my problem, I wanted to be able to find who was responsible. Somewhere out there, departed souls were being taken against their will.

Maybe some of them deserved it, but maybe they didn't.

Zehan raised his eyebrows. "Gallivanting?"

"You know what I mean," I snapped. "What did the devi want anyways?"

"What Rati always wants—praise and attention. What did *you* learn from the Asuras?" Zehan eyed me suspiciously.

"I didn't get to it. The Asuras know I have magic. It's a smidge hard to get them to reveal things," I said with an air of indifference. I slipped off the ruby gemstone choker.

Zehan tracked the movement, his eyes lingering on my bare neck. Stripping myself of the jewels and garments always made me feel raw after performances.

"Well, because of your interaction with Lobha. Shama knows we aren't *actually* sleeping together, which is a problem because it's what I led all the Asuras to believe. So, I'll be stopping by your room each night."

I blanched at the implication. "You want me to act as your mistress."

Zehan shrugged. "Everyone already believes that is our arrangement. As long as I enter your room at night, Shama's sources—whoever they are—will report to him, and no one will know our ruse. I can leave by Vayu as soon as I enter. It's essentially what you told Shama and Lobha I'm doing."

"You don't seem worried about the fact that an Asura is tracking you within your own palace."

"This is hell, courtesan. The ones who rule it don't play fair." Zehan dropped his hands as he prowled forward. "And it was you that confirmed we are in a physical relationship. Not to mention, you had the audacity to imply my performance was not up to your standard."

I stifled my laugh as I unpinned my tikka and ran my fingers through my long wavy hair, and Zehan homed in on the action. I lifted one shoulder, wanting nothing more than to face-plant onto the luscious silk sheets. "If I'm going to pretend to be your mistress, you'll have to deal with whatever I say outside our room." I should be more concerned with this new arrangement, but I wasn't. It made sense, and I didn't need Shama prying more into my plans.

Zehan closed the distance between us. He lifted my chin, assessing me. "Perhaps I should give you a demonstration so you can remember it whenever you're speaking of us outside these four walls." He slowly trailed one of his fingers down my bare neck. "Though, something tells me you won't be able to keep up."

Blood rushed to my head. This was headed in a dangerous direction. The soft caress of his fingers juxtaposed the roughness of his voice.

I drew my face away from him. Defiant. "Please. I'm the most famous courtesan in Tyaga. My reputation doesn't only stem just from my ability to dance." My voice didn't have the bravado I hoped for. I tugged off my gold bangles, tossing them onto the vanity. The only metal left on my person were my payals around my ankles and the gold nose ring and attached chain that hooked into my hair.

A small smile tugged at the corner of his lips. "Ezhil is right. You fit this realm perfectly."

"I do not," I seethed. Any association with this realm was not a compliment. "And for the record, Ezhil was the one to indicate I was your *pastime*. I assumed you have that kind of relationship with your previous Chosen. All I did was let Lobha and Shama believe it."

Zehan studied me with half-lidded eyes. The moonlight from the window hit him at the perfect angle. Staring at him too long felt hypnotic, like he could see both the light and dark parts of my soul.

I walked past him and placed my foot on the emerald velvet bench at the foot of the bed, sliding up my skirt to take off my anklet.

All thoughts left my head when Zehan sat down on the bench and perched my foot on his knee. With deft fingers, he unfastened it.

I let out a sharp exhale. "*What* are you doing?"

He tossed the payal on the bench next to him. "Proving a point." He cut me a look that said not to argue. But by the Asuras, I wanted to challenge him. I attempted to pull my foot from his grasp but he held on, letting his fingers brush against my ankle. A series of warm shivers skated up the back of my leg to the base of my spine.

I swallowed. *Hard.* This made me feel all sorts of ways that I didn't want to feel. *Ways I couldn't feel.* He was the Prince of Naraka, for deva's sake. And I was a simple courtesan.

Zehan examined the raised scars on the top of my foot. "Who did this to you?" he asked with quiet rage.

I laughed. "Don't you know? Dancers' feet are always ugly." I pried my leg out of his hands, but he held on.

His brows furrowed as he squeezed the top of my foot. His thumb swiped softly across my toes. "Niya."

I had a visceral reaction to the way my name rolled off his tongue. My chest rose and fell like I had danced for hours. He chose *now* to finally say my name. That same foreign emotion from when I first saw him at the Antam ignited within me.

I had harped on him for not using my name, but now I wanted him to keep saying it like a chant that called upon the devas.

"Baanu didn't like messy footwork," I said, my voice was airy and raspy. Nor did she want our arms, back, or face marred. Scars on the legs and feet were easy to hide with long skirts, and besides, no one watched a girl's feet when she danced.

"I'm sorry." Zehan loosened his grip and motioned for my other foot. "You truly are the most extraordinary dancer I've ever witnessed. Your elegance, your movement, your expressions. People say they can feel the emotions in a song, but I feel them when you dance. Somehow, I feel free when I see you embrace your grace." The darkness around him lightened.

I couldn't remember the last time someone complimented my talent instead of my beauty or without the influence of my trance. "Thank you," I said quietly, placing my other foot in his open hand.

"And for the record"—his grip tightened. The pads of his fingers traveled up the back of my calf. He applied more pressure the higher he went. He paused, giving me the option to remove my leg, but I didn't. He smiled smugly as he moved his hand higher—"my *performance,* as you described it to Lobha, doesn't need improvement. I'm meticulously slow, attentive, and..." His fingers disappeared under my lehenga to skim the dip behind my knee before curving into my inner thigh. His lips brushed my knee. "I don't need fingers to make you beg."

My breath hitched. I wanted to abandon all common sense and let him prove that statement. I fixated on his fingers and the deep black of his eyes. My own logic dictated I should stop this. I hated the devil sitting before me, yet I wanted to stay glued to him like sap on a tree.

White shadows left his other hand and wrapped along my leg. Cool. Warm. Exhilarating. "Do not forget, courtesan. I'm the prince of all sin, including *lust.*"

His magic wrapped around my waist, breasts, and throat like a vine. Soothing. Caressing. Maddeningly arousing. I bit my tongue to prevent the small whimper that had built in the back of my throat from escaping.

This crossed every single line there was.

Did I care? *Yes.*

Did I plan to stop him? *By the Asuras, no.*

I felt drawn to Zehan in a way that made me question everything. Maybe my attempts at bargaining with Asuras had made me impulsive, or maybe I just wanted the distraction for a minute. I wanted to feel bliss and peace and freedom.

"When you're ready to take the edge off, courtesan, just say the words. Any time. Any place," Zehan murmured. He was sitting inside my mind, reading my thoughts off a scroll. The hand under my skirt traveled farther upward toward the ache that needed immediate attention, while the other lifted my foot gently off his knee and then he ran his thumb down the center of my arch.

I tilted my head back and basked in whatever the hell this was. The place where my sole touched his knee burned. The barest touch, and I was unraveling.

He is the Prince of Naraka.

I stiffened as the thought wormed through my head. I pushed my lips together. I couldn't let anything get in the way of living without restraints. Including my emotions.

Zehan grazed his fingers back down my leg like the tip of a feather quill. His magic unwound its tendrils, making me instantly want them back. He stood up, causing my foot to slip from his knee. He moved closer, letting me taste the smokiness of his breath from the hookah. "Good night, Niya."

I blinked a few times. The rush of heat still clouded my mind.

Zehan tensed but appeared less shocked than I was. He smirked like he had won a gamble and vanished through Vayu.

I muttered a curse. Entangling with him, even if it was just physical, had untold consequences.

Yet, as I stared at the carved ceiling waiting for sleep to take me under its influence, a dull ache flooded into my muscles. Thoughts of a conflicted prince and his white shadows swam through my mind, inviting me to join him.

Truthfully, I was not sure how long I could stay away.

CHAPTER SIXTEEN

I shoved the memory of last night into the darkest corner of my mind.

At least I thought I had until I arrived at breakfast and saw Zehan sitting at the head of the long dining table, leisurely sipping on chai and reading a thick red-leather-bound book. This morning he wore a plain cream tunic that tied diagonally with straight pants. He looked incredibly normal. Yet, every nerve ending within me caught on fire.

At once, everything came rushing back. Zehan's calloused fingers running up my thigh, the moonlight hitting his face, and his magic holding me in the most sensual choke hold I've ever had the privilege of experiencing. But it was the way he looked at me in awe when I was completely raw. When I was no longer Mohini, but simply Niya.

My cheeks flamed.

"Good morning, courtesan." Zehan's eyes flitted up at me as he took a long sip from his steaming teacup. "Sleep well?"

The way his voice slipped beneath my skin almost made me trip. *Infuriating man.*

My feet started moving again. He knew I didn't. Or he wanted the servants bustling around us to believe I didn't, given our new arrangement.

I wrapped my shawl tighter. "Prince." I sat across from him and poured myself a generous cup of chai. I took one sip and let out a long sigh. "The only thing I will miss about this place is this damn tea."

Zehan chuckled, but his hard gaze softened a smidge.

We stared at each other. I had never shared a meal with him. I ate and spent my days here in solitude or with Sunitra and Kal. Aside from our interactions regarding the bargain, I hadn't spent quality time with Zehan.

Nor did I want to.

My time here was limited. Getting to know the man in front of me was counterproductive. I stiffened, looking away from the high cheekbones and thick black hair that my fingers wanted to entangle themselves in. "So, when do we go meet Hans?" I asked, taking another sip.

Zehan raised an eyebrow at the sudden change of topic.

"Rahas and Lobha have both checked out according to you. Hans and Abhi were your last two suspects, but Hans doesn't attend Antam." I slowly shaved the skin off a mango with a blunt knife.

Zehan placed his book down and uncrossed his legs. "I had hoped the Asuras had nothing to do with any of this, but I was especially hoping Hans was not involved."

I nodded. If the Asura of Violence was involved, then this was bigger than Zehan originally thought. Hans was his first creation, his strongest and most deadly servant.

"And you believe that a play for power is what this culprit is after?"

"Yes. What else would a bunch of sinners deal in? Power is all we have to lose."

I added a spoonful of sugar to my chai. "Don't they have unlimited power?"

"No. Asuras become stronger when they torment departed souls, which is reliant upon me sentencing sinners to their courts. I sentence them when appropriate, but I offer more leniency than my predecessors."

I rubbed my temples. "The only time someone is after power is when they are trying to interfere with the existing reign. What Hans or another Asura is trying to take is Rati's throne?"

"It is plausible, but not possible. The Asuras are bound by the laws of this realm to serve whoever is in the throne. And I cannot use my magic against Rati at all."

"Why not?"

"Because my magic is a boon from Rati, and boons cannot be used against the deva or devi who gifted them to you. There are laws, even amongst gods."

I tucked away that information. "How does your magic work?" I saw him use it last night on the new souls that had arrived here, and Kal had told me what it could do, but I still didn't understand the inner mechanics.

"I can use my magic on a soul only once, and I can't control what I see. Sometimes what I see are just glimpses of moments that could be interpreted a multitude of ways. I don't dictate what they see. A higher force guides me. Truth be told, I can't explain it." His eyes slid toward me. "Similar to *you*, I do not yet understand much of my magic."

I didn't respond. I knew I hadn't unlocked the full potential of my power. I worked hard to keep my magic separate from my identity. I strictly used it only on the dance floor because it could not be trusted.

"So Hans would likely benefit from the increase in power?" I concluded. "Especially if you've been sentencing fewer souls to him."

"Even though Asuras can't take Rati's throne, it doesn't mean they wouldn't benefit from added power. It would give them clout to bargain over their siblings, enhance their existing power, or even the ability to move through realms. But Hans..." Zehan shook his head. "That's just it. Hans is unique. He doesn't necessarily have a need for departed souls. Unless it's to feed his pretas."

"His what?"

"Pretas are his minions in a sense. They feed on the darkest parts of departed souls. When a soul is sentenced to his court, they generally deal with his pretas. And Hans feeds on them for his power."

Like a food chain. Nausea rolled over me. "Do all Asuras feed on souls?"

"In different ways, but yes. Souls being punished for their sin are critical to their lifelines. They all specialize in different ways of torture and punishment based on their sin."

Lobha said as much last night. It was clear he got his well of power replenished by interacting with those who were greedy by nature. "Why haven't you told the Asuras about the missing souls? Maybe they would help."

"The Asuras and I tolerate each other. Aside from Antam and regular court visits, we do not choose to interact. I haven't told them because they will immediately go to Rati, and the last thing I want is the Goddess of Death getting involved," he grumbled.

"You don't like her," I stated.

"Rati likes to play games. Her entire existence is focused on making everyone around her miserable. Like most beings here, she likes to bargain and make deals, but they can never be trusted. She always saves a twist for the end."

"But isn't she why you're here?" I wave my hand at the beautiful room around us. Rumors said that Zehan had tricked Rati into giving him this position, others said he slept his way into her good graces. The latter was something I did not like to ponder too long on. How else did a young boy convince the Goddess of Death and Asuras to make him king of their realm? "You approached her for all of this."

"That is simply a tale made up by mortals. I never *asked* to be here, Niya," he said softly. "You're not the only one chained to a fate that you're trying to escape."

The cold sank into my bones. I wrapped my arms around my torso, remembering who I was and why I was here. I was his Chosen.

"Perhaps not, but unlike you, I didn't have much of a choice," I reminded him, though my tone didn't hold as much bite. Perhaps we were both looking to be rid of our invisible shackles, but the difference was that he held the key to unlock mine.

"I suppose you didn't," Zehan admitted, closing his leather book.

The mango slipped between my fingers and clanked onto my plate. Was that *sympathy* in Zehan's tone?

Two massive ogre-like rakshasas covered in dull silver armor and multiple weapons entered the room. Rati strutted behind them in a heavy embroidered gown and long jacket.

"Devi Rati," Zehan said, not bothering to stand, "you're still here."

My mouth parted. *Still here?* Had she spent the night?

I pushed my lips together. Why did I even care? What the devi did was irrelevant to me.

"Do you blame me for wanting to spend more time with you, Zehan? I heard the rest of the Antam last night went well. The remaining Asuras had much to say after you retired for the evening." She made a clicking sound with her tongue as she moved into the room. Like a python about to strike, she tilted her head at me. Power rolled off her in waves. *Too much power.* "Aren't you going to introduce me to your little friend?"

I felt like the smallest, insignificant creature on Prithvi.

I rose, unclear of the damn rules of this realm. Was I allowed to speak to her? Could I even look her in the eye? This was a freaking devi for Asura's sake, the only goddess that could still move through all three realms.

"My latest Chosen, as you are very much aware," Zehan said with an air of indifference, like he was conversing with one of his subjects instead of the most powerful person in the universe. "Mohini, the famed courtesan from Khoya Kingdom. She was just leaving—"

"You are a very talented dancer, Niya," Rati said.

Zehan stiffened at the use of my real name.

Rati's heavy, kohl-lined eyes bore into me. I froze. Unable to move, unable to speak as she ran a long finger through a few strands of my hair. "She *is* beautiful, Zehan. Yet, I forget how utterly delicate and weak humans are in their Prithvi forms."

I gripped the edge of the table to prevent myself from batting away her hand. She was a more powerful and dangerous version of Baanu. "I may be delicate, but my nails are sharp."

Rati arched one brow as she turned to Zehan, who sniggered. "Her talents both on and off the stage must far exceed your expectations, *meri jaan,* if she sits with you at your dining table. We both know how difficult it is for you to be satiated."

Something hot and rough erupted underneath my skin. *Meri jaan.* I remembered the way my father looked at my mother when he called her that. The term of endearment always elicited comfort and warmth, but hearing Rati say it to Zehan? My head, my heart, every piece of me irrationally protested.

Zehan relaxed further into his chair. "She is beyond comparison with anyone else," he said smoothly.

That wiped the smug expression off Rati's face. Something within me bloomed at the subtle praise.

Play the part. A mistress. Nothing more. Nothing less. I allowed my lips to curve upwards and batted my eyelashes dramatically.

Once a courtesan, always a courtesan.

A pulse of magic warped around Rati as her features twisted, but she recovered just as quickly. "I see. Well, in that case, I'd like to see her perform in front of my court."

A chill slithered into my chest.

"Absolutely not," Zehan said, his nostrils flaring.

Rati stared at Zehan as if he had slapped her. "It was not a request," she barked. "Do not forget who *owns* you, Zehan." A cold gleam surfaced in her eyes. "I expect her to visit my court."

Zehan snapped his jaw shut hard enough to crack a tooth. "I thought the agreement we had when I took over ferrying souls for you is that you would let me bring in a Chosen at my discretion without interfering."

"It was," Rati said, "but it isn't now."

I tensed. Zehan's court was one thing, but Rati's court? Even my nightmares could not conquer the cruelty that probably took place. Did she even have a stage to dance on? She didn't strike me as one to consider dancing as entertainment.

She smoothed over her irritated features and ran a hand down her lehenga. "Until then, meri jaan." She walked toward the door. "It was nice to meet you, Niya. I look forward to our next encounter."

"As do I," I answered. My skin crawled with heightened awareness of her power. I would not let her scare me.

Without another spare glance back, the devi disappeared behind the door.

Zehan let out a long sigh and rubbed a hand over his face. He looked tired, like sleep had not found him.

I picked up a piece of mango and shoved it into my mouth. "She is lovely by the way."

"She is a devi." Zehan shrugged like that explained everything.

We stared at each other in silence until he walked over. He picked up one of the mango pieces I had sliced and slipped it into his mouth.

"When will I have to perform in Rati's court?" I kept my tone light, like the subtle action of him eating off my plate did not affect me.

"As I said to Rati, you will not be performing in her court. I don't say things I don't mean, Niya." Zehan leaned forward as he braced a hand on the top of my chair and one on the table, cocooning me with his broad frame.

My shoulders slumped forward. "But—"

"Niya?" A familiar voice tugged at the deepest threads of my heart.

My head whipped to the small petite brunette who had just walked into the room flanked by two guards and Sunitra.

I popped out of my seat. "Ruhi!"

CHAPTER SEVENTEEN

Ruhi slammed into me, her arms wrapping tightly around my neck.

I let out a cry-laugh while returning her embrace. I had believed I would never see Ruhi again and that she would remain a courtesan in Khoya. The familiarity of seeing her made me feel so much warmth despite the constant cold that filled this place.

I released her and grabbed her shoulders firmly. "How are you here?"

Zehan watched us like a hawk, but something about his body language was softer. He turned and left the room without another word. Sunitra stood at the door with her hands clasped behind her back. She must have brought Ruhi here on Zehan's orders.

Ruhi looked at me, stunned that we were seeing each other in the flesh. "After you left, I became the head dancer. Everything was going fine until Daman Basu from Tavas attended court. You know, that older man with the slimy hair and crooked nose."

Disgust filtered through me. I remembered. He had a long forehead and brown-yellow teeth. He always participated in the bid and had a type—beautiful, young, *new*. He was also known to have no limits or respect behind closed doors.

I gripped Ruhi's shoulders. "He didn't hurt you..." I trailed off, not even able to say the words out loud.

Ruhi's sharp eyes took on a new edge. "No! No. But he got angry that I wasn't partaking in the bid. He demanded that the head dancer should always participate. King Murkha, true to his word and court rules, let me have the choice. But afterwards, when we were dismissed from the dance hall, he sought me out. I tried to fight him off, but he was so drunk. He pulled out his dagger and stabbed me." She shuddered as tears traveled down her golden cheeks. "I knew I was dying, but I couldn't let him leave without punishment. I pulled the dagger out and threw it at his back. It struck him, but he lived."

My magic hackled within me. "It's okay. It's over now, and you heard Zehan last night, Daman will meet his fate one day. What about Baanu and King Murkha?" My lips formed a thin line. "Let me guess. They did nothing."

"Of course not. Daman is an asshole, but he is also an asset. You know that Tavas doesn't send many emissaries. They couldn't piss him off over a random courtesan. It would risk their entire relationship with Queen Oeshi."

She was right. If Queen Oeshi's emissary was hurt or killed, she would mark that kingdom as her next target.

Tavas was the seaside kingdom that was on the far east corner of Tyaga, known to be the strongest kingdom in Tyaga. They mostly kept to themselves and only sent sleazy men like Daman out to kingdoms for diplomacy and alliance building.

It was naive to think King Murkha and Baanu would exact retribution for Ruhi. Baanu didn't give any shits about the well-being of her dancers as long as she was still filling her vanity with more gold jewelry. And King Murkha was aging and needed to be seen as fully in control. If Queen Oeshi detected even an ounce of weakness in either of them, she would exploit it.

"How are our previous masters faring?"

Ruhi snorted. "Their prominence across Tyaga is quickly falling since you left. Turns out, aside from having the famed Mohini and spice, they have little to offer. King Murkha still has a foothold in the southwest part of Tyaga, but I overheard a few nobles speaking about Queen Oeshi and her plans to expand Tavas' territory. So I'm sure they've already forgiven Daman for his transgressions."

That aligned with what Zehan, Ezhil, and Ameel were speaking days ago as well. I shouldn't be happy with potential war on the horizon, but a sinister smile made its way to my face. I wouldn't be that upset if Khoya crumbled.

After everything King Murkha did to me and my people, he deserved his falsely obtained legacy to be destroyed.

Ruhi looked around at the ornate stone pillars and the plentiful gardens. "This place...is something else. I have a small home in the town at the bottom of the hill, which is probably the most beautiful place I've ever seen. And my neighbor is a purple-blue demon with horns that are pierced in twenty different places."

We stared at each other and then burst into a fit of laughter. It was ridiculous really. Two lowlife dancers now living with the demons from our nightmares, conversing with them like they were acquaintances. From the corner of my eye, I saw Sunitra's lips curve.

Ruhi sat down in one of the massive wooden chairs and picked up the last mango slice from my plate, already comfortable in the palace of hell. "So, what is the devil prince like?" Ruhi could fit in anywhere, speak to anyone. It was one of the things I loved most about her.

"You know what he is like," I said, lifting my eyebrows. "He is the devil."

"Is he though?" she asked curiously.

I gaped at her. "Ruhi, he used his magic on you in court. To *hurt* you."

Ruhi shrugged and pursed her lips. "Aren't you the one always harping on about how people's actions are not always so simple?"

I shook my head. "Yes, but this is different, and you know it. Did his magic yesterday somehow sway you into his good graces?" How could Ruhi, out of all people, justify Zehan's actions?

"He did use that horrible magic on me," Ruhi admitted. "But last night when he used his magic, it was different."

"Different," I repeated slowly. "What do you mean?"

"It was..." Ruhi squirmed in her seat. "Warm and invigorating."

She had gone mad. "Invigorating?"

"I don't know how to explain it." She threw her hands up in the air. "But it was filled with something *more*. Whatever he did in court that night was, of course, wrong in a hundred ways, but it seems like there is more to him. We've always believed he enjoyed watching everyone around him suffer, but he sentenced everyone fairly yesterday. Don't you think?"

My jaw slackened. "He should have sent you straight to your next life cycle. Why make you serve any sentence here when you didn't do anything wrong?" Her actions were exacted in self-defense. "I don't think that is fair."

"Perhaps there is a waiting period, and I am not fully beyond any type of sin. I did *stab* someone." Ruhi lifted one shoulder. "Regardless, I'm glad he gave me the sentence." She covered my hand with hers. "Because I got to see you in death."

Heaviness fell over me. I stacked my other palm on top of hers. "I'm sorry this happened to you, Ruhi."

"Don't be sorry for me, Niya. The life I had in Khoya wasn't worth living." Ruhi's smile was a mix of sorrow and relief. "And I'll meet you again in my next life. I'm sure of it."

Ruhi and I spent the entire afternoon together wandering the hallways of the castle, our laughs cutting through the silence that constantly lingered in the air. Sunitra mutely followed us wherever we went like a shadow we couldn't rid.

I shared everything that had transpired since I left Khoya: my bargain with Zehan, my plan to get the Asuras to give me a boon, meeting the Goddess of Death, my new label as Zehan's mistress. The only detail that I hadn't disclosed was whatever the hell happened last night in my room. Something I planned to avoid discussing at all costs.

"Let me get this straight," Ruhi said, plopping down on a massive outdoor swing. It was chilly outside but bearable with our shawls. "Zehan made you his Chosen so that you could help him solve a murder case? And if you are successful, he will get you to Varnasi?"

"That is our deal, yes." I leaned my back against one of the thick chains that allowed the carved wooden bench to hover above the grass. "Now, if he actually keeps that deal is another thing."

"And what? He just happens to be friends with the monarch over Varnasi?" Ruhi asked with skepticism. "Doesn't the ruler have to personally grant entrance for every new resident?"

I nodded. "I would presume he has a relationship with whoever is in that seat. He probably schemes with them the same he does with Murkha and Oeshi." Everything Zehan did was for selfgain.

"Which is why you are also seeking out the Asuras for a boon," Ruhi reiterated. "In case he doesn't follow through."

I shushed her, looking around the courtyard. I didn't want eavesdroppers to tell Zehan.

Ruhi rolled her eyes like this was not a concern. "It's odd though. If the missing souls are a new development, why would he have taken any Chosen before you? I mean, where are they?"

I placed my bare feet on the bench, fixing my lehenga so it covered my toes, and tucked my hands under my knees. "I've been trying to gather the answer to that myself. He claims they aren't here, and I haven't interacted with any other mortal. But then, where did they all go?"

Ruhi pushed against the ground so the swing swished back and forth. "Well, I guess now that you are publicly labeled as his mistress, you'll have plenty of time to ask him when he makes a pit stop at your room each night."

I snorted, leaning my head back onto the chain so I could see the sky that never ceased to amaze me. Today, the moon was winning the fight, staying just a bit higher than the sun. I closed my eyes for the briefest moment, reminiscing at the way Zehan's magic wrapped around my throat and waist. He had made me feel things I hadn't felt in...well, ever.

My eyes snapped open. *Shit.* I wasn't just attracted to him. I yearned for him. I wanted Zehan.

No. I refused to accept that thought, to even let the tiniest part of me dwell on it further. Zehan was my captor, not my protector. I wasn't falling into the trap of mixing those two things.

Movement and stern voices caught my eye from the side. Bidal was a few steps in front of Zehan and Ezhil.

"They don't know what they are doing. Ameel is doing everything he can to keep them at bay, but they are insistent." Ezhil muttered. Bidal cleared his throat loudly when he spotted us staring at them, then Ezhil dropped his voice to barely a whisper.

Ruhi tilted her head, still watching them. "Were they referring to—"

"Your Ameel?" I finished for her. "Yes. Who, by the way, I met at Sahra like you said."

The tops of her cheeks reddened. "You saw him?"

I smirked. "Yes, and he was unable to help, though, I got the sense he *wanted* to. That bastard over there interrupted us, and it seems they are friends."

Zehan sight found me, and heat cascaded from the top of my head to the tips of my toes. I busied myself with twirling the end of my long braid. I felt his smile slide beneath my skin.

Ruhi whipped her head to me. "Ameel? Friends with the Prince of Hell?"

I nodded as I fidgeted in my seat. "Just like the commander over there. They're some weird fucking trio. They don't act like mere acquaintances. They joke with each other and act like...brothers."

I had noticed the way Ameel looked at Zehan at Sahra, as if he saw behind his infuriating complex. And even Ezhil had made excuses for Zehan while escorting me to Antam.

Ruhi wrinkled her nose. "That is weird. But I guess even the devil needs family."

Sunitra walked over to us. "We should head back to Vajra, Ruhi."

We stood up, and Ruhi gave me a tight hug. I squeezed her back. "You're still here for a whole month, I'll see you again."

Ruhi grinned at me. "As long as we don't have to dance."

"Deal," I smiled, feeling lighter than I had in days.

I watched as Ruhi left with Sunitra. She dipped her head low toward Zehan, which he returned. Ezhil winked at her with a roguish grin. She turned around and waved, her face brighter than I'd ever seen it.

I waved back. A kernel of emotion flared. I had never fully appreciated her friendship in Khoya, but I wouldn't dare take it for granted. Not when her time here was limited.

Zehan's stare burned with emotion I couldn't decipher. I dipped my chin the barest I could. *Thank you.* He didn't have to bring Ruhi here. He could have made it so I could never saw her, but he gave me today, and I would always be grateful for it.

I turned to make my way to my room when I felt a princely presence behind me. Blood rushed to my head when he fell into step beside me.

He didn't say anything. He simply walked close to me. His arm brushed against mine, causing a ripple of heat to shoot to my fingertips. He nodded to guards and staff, but their curious eyes flitted between Zehan and me.

Of course. He was coming to my room to show everyone—and Shama's spies—that I was his. I flushed as heat rushed to my head.

He held open the door to my room, and I paused on the threshold, unsure why. It wasn't like anything was going to happen once we were in the room, but anticipation had bubbled up to my throat.

He lifted an eyebrow.

I sighed and stomped into the room. When I heard the door shut, I whipped around, my lehenga brushing the floor with a soft flare. "Go aw—"

Zehan appeared inches from me and looped a finger through my necklace and twisted it towards him. "Whose wedding necklace does that belong to?" He jutted his chin at my small pear-shaped necklace.

I stilled. "Why?

He half shrugged. "Call me curious."

I doubted that but it wasn't like the necklace was a key to anything. "My mothers. I-it's the only thing I have left of my parents. I know only married women are supposed to wear one of these, but—"

"You want to feel closer to them," he finished.

I ran a hand over the necklace. "Something like that."

A quiet spell fell over us as we stood staring at each other. I cleared my throat. "Thank you again for—"

He pressed his index finger to my lips. My nostrils flared at his scent. "You will meet me outside at the front gates tomorrow morning."

I spoke against his finger. "Back to commands, are we?"

Zehan let his finger trail down to tilt my chin upwards. "I think you enjoy my commands, Niya."

I snorted. "That's prosperous."

"Is it?" He crowded into my space, so our breath mingled. "Then do explain why the tops of your cheeks are beginning to turn pink?"

He winked. *Damn him.*

He laughed, dropping his hands away. "Tomorrow, the front gates, courtesan."

I pinched my eyebrows together. "Where are we going?"

The rogue twinkle in his gaze sent my pulse racing. "To pay Hans a visit and see how strong your powers really are."

CHAPTER EIGHTEEN

Kalank was the promise of Naraka.

Tucked away in a crevice between two snowcapped mountains, a massive stone structure had been built into the rock formation. This was what the place mortal humans imagined when they spoke or thought of hell. It was where the nine Asuras dwelled, where sins were forged and broken.

And it was where we stood now.

I craned my neck to get a full view of the fortress. High ominous walls towered hundreds of feet above us with black-tipped towers. A sense of foreboding fell over me along with the overwhelming stench of rotting corpses.

I swallowed. "This is...not like Vajra."

Winds wailed around us, whipping my hair away from my face. I tucked my chin into the long overcoat that Gauri had tailored to fit my frame perfectly. Bulky clothing like this didn't exist in Khoya. Wool or fur would have caused a stroke.

"No, it isn't." Zehan was next to me in his black fur-lined coat that made him look devastating in the best way. Snow flurries peppered his black hair. Age would not negatively impact his attractiveness. My mouth watered like I had been starved for days.

"If you're done staring, let's go over the plan," Zehan said with a sly smile. He scrutinized the stone entrance. There were no guards stationed outside. The entire place looked abandoned.

"Walk in, let you question Hans about the departed souls, wait for your signal, use my magic, and then we take our leave." I ticked off each step with a frozen finger. "Easy," I said, though my magic cowered and I doubted this place would be anything but easy. I prayed to the forgotten devas that I would have the opportunity to appeal to the Asura alone.

Zehan slid his gaze to me. "You forgot the parts about sticking close to me, not wandering off, and not speaking unless spoken to." His breath created small plumes of mist in the air.

I waved him off. "D-details," I stammered.

Sunitra snorted next to me, earning her a smile from me. I was secretly glad she accompanied us. Otherwise, the long carriage ride over here with Bidal and Zehan would have been painfully dull.

Bidal cut her a sharp look from Zehan's other side. "Stay in form, Sunitra." He looked back at the handful of guards we had brought with us, signaling them to wait out here.

Sunitra schooled her features into seriousness, but she managed to give me a quick wink.

"I still think there is a glaring issue with your *plan,*" I muttered. The plan was really a loose guide in my mind. Hans was the strongest Asura, which meant it would take a lot of skill with my magic to get him under the trance *and* keep him from realizing he was being influenced.

Zehan held out his arm to me. "It's unfortunately the best one we've got. You see now why I've had you practice using your magic. But in this case, it will be a little different. Unlike with the other Asuras, we won't need to hide your ability." His confidence was unwavering. "You'll see. Hans likes playing mind games, so go along with it but keep a straight head."

What did that mean? The warning made me loop my arm into his a little too tight. "H-how are you so sure? It doesn't work on you," I reminded him while fighting a shiver.

Zehan snapped his fingers, and instant warmth embraced me like a long-lost friend.

I groaned. "By the Asuras, can you please place a permanent bubble of heat around me?"

His lips tugged at one corner as he led me up the steps. "Your magic would work on me if you really wanted it to. Magic is only as limitless as the bearer."

The oversize door creaked open into a gaping black hole. Two rakshasas walked out dressed in silver-and-black armor with two blades crisscrossed on their backs. They physically looked the same as Zehan's guards, but they didn't carry the same ferocious expressions I had become used to. These rakshasas had been beaten down, like time had failed them repeatedly.

"Hans is expecting us," Zehan uttered with cold dominance.

They bowed to the prince, but their expressions held resentment. They didn't show respect to Zehan out of goodness; it was out of duty.

"They don't like you," I murmured. "Why?"

"Because they were sent here by me. This is Rati's court, and the abode of the Asuras."

I whipped my head to him. "That is a detail you should share in advance next time," I hissed.

Zehan only smirked. "So, you agree there will be a next time?"

I guffawed. "That's not what I meant—"

"Keep denying it, courtesan." He walked in.

Denying what? Sunitra's shoulders jostled with silent laughter. I narrowed my gaze at her but hissed at Zehan, "If this is Rati's court, won't she want to see us?" Didn't she want me to perform?

Zehan stiffened. "Techincally, she asked you to visit the court, which you are doing now."

Is that why he decided to come "visit" Hans in his home? So I indirectly fulfilled the devi's request?

We passed over the threshold. A shiver of whispers raced across my skin. It was the same sensation I had when I entered Naraka through the Gate of Three. A pleasant and unpleasant welcome. But this time, I understood the words.

Pranam meri mara.

I shook my head, attempting to rid the wispy phrase from my ears. Zehan dubiously watched me. Had he heard the whispers, too?

The door closed behind us, and the skylight vanished, replaced by the warm glimmer of fire torches lining a vast circular foyer.

The smell of damp skin and decay hit me first, burning my throat. I blinked a few times, adjusting to the dim light. My gut twisted as the room became clearer.

Departed souls sat slumped against the walls covered in dirt and grime and tattered clothing, their wrist and ankles shackled. They were clearly underfed, tossed into this abyss like rats. Their human features were dulled, gaunt from whatever horrors they faced here.

We proceeded into the narrowed tunnels. Guttural moans and cries trailed behind us. Instinctively, I grabbed Zehan's arm, digging my fingernails into his coat.

This is what Naraka truly is at its core. Echoes of torture, spiritless air, and death marked every inch of this stoic structure.

Zehan tugged me closer to him, and for once, I didn't want to pull away.

Even the departed souls glowered at us with feverish intensity, as if every single drop of hope they held for redemption had been slaughtered.

They stared at Zehan with loathing, and I was willing to bet that if they had any morsel of energy, they'd try to rip our hearts clean out of our chests. "So everyone here hates you, and by association, they hate me?" Somewhere in the distance I heard a faded scream.

Zehan smirked, but it didn't reach his eyes. "Do not forget *why* these souls are here, courtesan."

Murders. Rapists. Thieves. Humans that ruined livelihoods out of greed, pride, and lust.

"I haven't," I said. "Though, it's good to know that an allegiance with you won't always save me here."

"You don't need saving, Niya," Zehan said, his expression softened. "It is I who needs to be saved by *you.*"

My heart dropped into my stomach like a stone.

The rakshasas stopped us in front of an archaic door that had words and symbols carved deep into the iron. One of the creatures yanked open the door.

"Only you two." The one with a series of tattoos on his arm pointed at Zehan and me.

Our two guards stepped back. "We'll wait here," Bidal said with quiet assessment.

The chamber was devoid of light, and the forest-green walls were jagged. The air was thick with the stench of sulfur. The tables in the room were lined with blades and hooks and other torture devices. Shadows lurked in the corner, twisting into contorted, grotesque shapes.

A surge of magic caused my body to shake.

Hisses spoke into the darkness, and then a slick voice entered the pit of my mind. *This is unexpected, Zehan.*

I gripped Zehan's arm tight enough to leave nail marks. Did I just hear someone speak into my mind? The darkness I thought was shadows in the corner grew and morphed into a fleshy creature with black skin wrapped in a black cloak.

Hans.

The Asura rose two feet over Zehan with large striking burnt orange eyes. He grinned, revealing a mouth full of razored teeth. He didn't look like the others, unless what they displayed at court wasn't their true forms.

Zehan gave him an equally off-putting smile. "Aren't all of my visits, Hans."

The creature chuckled in my head. He opened his mouth, but again, only a series of hisses escaped his lips which translated into that same spooky voice filtering through my mine. *Yes, but you never bring your Chosen. One with her soul completely intact.*

I stared at the obscure creature and his talons that I hadn't noticed until now. Is that what he used to rip souls out? My throat had gone dry. And a maddening thought crossed me. If he could speak into our minds, could he also read them?

A smile coasted onto his rippling face. *Read them, manipulate them, destroy them.*

I straightened. That is why Zehan had said I wouldn't have to hide my ability from him.

Zehan sighed like his precious time was going to waste. "Her soul may be intact, but it is *mine*," Zehan said slowly. "Everything she is *belongs* to me."

A tiny match lit in my chest. Men had always staked their claim on me, but the way Zehan did it felt permanent. Like he stated what had been written in the cosmos.

His words mean nothing. We are playing roles. None of this is real. My fingers loosened on Zehan's arms, but he tucked my hand in between his arm and torso with no way to pull free. Heat flooded into me.

Hans watched me with a glint in his eye. *Indeed. Perhaps only to make a statement. But I appreciate it. You know us Asuras love a good tease.* His voice vibrated like a string after an arrow was released off a bow. *What is your business, Prince?*

"Like you don't know." Zehan dusted off his sherwani. The essence of casualness. "Departed souls are going missing from Vajra. Have your pretas indulged in food that doesn't belong to them?"

At the mention of his creators, wraithlike beings appeared in the corners of the rooms. They shrieked like they were in agony and snapped their jaws.

Goose bumps erupted along my arms. Zehan stepped forward so his shoulder was slightly in front of me. Magic pulsed on my fingertips, ready to pounce. To leech off whatever thoughts this beast hid inside his darkness.

Hans let out a loose laugh as his pretas wailed around us. *I have no idea what you speak of. And my pretas know their bounds, Prince. Do you know yours? Does your Chosen know why she was truly brought here?*

The magic building in my veins winked out. "What is he talking about?"

"Nothing of significance," Zehan said tightly. "Don't feign ignorance or attempt to play games, Hans. I felt those souls being ripped from the realm. Tell us what you know." He flicked his wrist, and white shadows rose behind him. His wolves were back, except now they were larger, their heads reaching the top of mine.

That was the signal.

I ignored the way the pretas displayed their razor-sharp teeth and pushed away my questions and focused on redirecting my magic to Hans. The invisible tendrils were greeted by a shield, but before I could figure out a way to get past them, they vanished altogether.

My magic reached Hans in seconds.

His voice spoke into my mind and rattled my very bones. *Unlike my siblings, I welcome your magic on me, meri mara.*

CHAPTER NINETEEN

Meri mara, the same words I had heard upon entering Naraka and Kalank. But it was Han's first comment that made my stomach flip multiple times.

Zehan warily observed the Asura. Had he heard what the Asura called me? Did that mean that Krod, Lobha, Shama, and the other Asuras knew I had used my magic on them?

Zehan cannot hear us. But yes, they can sense your magic just as well as I can.

My head pounded with questions. Why hadn't any of the Asuras said anything? Why let me use my magic on them? How did they recognize my magic?

If you want answers, I will speak to the courtesan alone, he said it to both Zehan and I, but by the way the Asura stared at me, I knew he was referring to the questions that swam in my mind.

I leaped at the opening. "Done."

"Absolutely not," Zehan twisted his head sideways. Magic rolled off him like white smoke scurrying away from its fire. The wolves snarled, creating a clicking sound with their jaws.

I gave him a pointed glance. "If this is the way to get the information we need, so be it."

Aside from understanding how the Asuras knew about my ability, I still needed a boon. The pretas shrieked again, the pitch grating against my eardrums.

"Niya," Zehan warned.

I ignored him and his secrets. I didn't know what Hans was referring to when he made that comment about Zehan's Chosen. But that was a riddle for another day.

I lifted my chin. "Five minutes alone, but only if you tell me the truth—all of it." I needed information not only about the missing souls but also about the boon; leaving the proposition vague was for my benefit.

Hans may be horrifying, but Zehan had said Hans liked mind games, and by the way his lips widened, it was clear this was the most entertainment he'd had in a long while. In truth, I understood it. Being in a decrepit place like this, who wouldn't want to interact with other people.

Deal. Hans talons and teeth sharpened. *Except I will answer only seven questions. See yourself out, Prince.*

"I'm not leaving." Zehan folded his arms, keeping his eyes set on Hans, letting white tendrils leak from his frame menacingly. His wolves closed in around me. "Speak to her mind-to-mind, but I'm staying here."

"I'll be fine, Zehan," I muttered. Though, I wasn't sure if I was trying to convince him or myself.

A muscle in his jaw ticked.

Five questions, Hans said.

Damn these Asuras.

"Do you want to know who is after your departed souls or not?" I said sharply. The stubbornness in Zehan's gaze did not waiver. I sighed. "I can handle myself. I've been doing it for years."

I slid my arm out of his tight hold, and for a moment, I thought he would grab my hand and entwine his fingers with mine.

"The wolves stay." He said with no room for argument. "I'll be right outside." He said to me before slipping out of the room, leaving me alone with the greatest monster in Naraka.

Hans continued to read my thoughts. *There are monsters and creatures that dwell in this realm that are far worse than me.*

My nerves twisted into a knot. "How can you sense my magic?"

Your magic has a signature on it. Time stopped passing as the creature glided toward me. His talons hovered inches from my face. *It has been a long while since I have felt its presence.*

That response sparked a million other questions. I would have to be more specific. "Why did the other Asuras not tell me?"

We wanted to see what you would do with it.

I frowned. That wasn't much of an answer, but I had already wasted two questions.

Hans's smile stretched from ear to ear as he read my inner turmoil.

I sighed, folding my arms. "Do you have anything to do with the missing souls?" I needed something to give back to Zehan.

No, but I do know that every soul that vanished saw the rishi a few days prior.

Who is the rishi? The question was on the edge of my tongue before I stopped myself. "How do you know the souls visited the rishi?" The way Hans spoke about the departed souls made it appear as if he was interested in finding the culprit as well.

I received word a few weeks ago that souls were disappearing. I have been racing to find the culprit, as are the other Asuras. My pretas dug up that bit of intel after the last disappearance. I tried questioning him, but the old man revealed nothing.

"You're all trying to find out who is responsible for the missing souls?" My brows pushed together. That meant none of the Asuras were involved in the disappearances. But why were they so invested in the culprit? The Asuras did not strike me as a vigilante group.

I hadn't asked the question out loud, but Hans answered it anyway. *Departed souls vanishing from under our purview does not only impact Zehan, it impacts all of us. Every soul that enters this realm makes us more powerful by default, having them stolen away makes us appear weak.* Hans prowled even closer to me. *Last question, meri mara.*

"That is not my name," I stated.

His breath smelled sickly-sweet, like milk gone bad. *For now.*

I opened my mouth but stopped myself. He was baiting me to lose my last question. He knew what I wanted but was simply testing me. To his credit, my curiosity had piqued; though not enough for me to give up what I came here for.

I straightened. "If you have spoken with the other Asuras, then you know what I am after," I said. "A fresh start in a new place without any power, and I want you to give it to me. So, my last question is what do I have to do to gain a boon from you?"

Nothing, because I cannot offer you a boon. None of the Asuras can.

My gut tightened as magic flared around me in rippling cold waves. Zehan's wolves herded closer to me, one of them with the small ears brushed against my shoulder.

"The Asuras used to have the power to supply boons, but over the last few centuries, Rati's rule and Zehan's mercy have stripped us of our full power."

Black flashed across my vision. That means the other Asuras had lied to me. I went over my interactions with Krod, Lobha, and Shama. They all seemed to know things about me that I didn't know about myself. And despite threatening to tell Zehan what I sought, they hadn't yet. Why?

"What are you—"

The doors slammed open. The wolves snarled viciously.

Zehan was slumped against the wall, clutching his head. Bidal was holding him up on one side, Sunitra on the other.

I rushed over and kneeled beside him. "What happened?" I had a feeling I already knew the answer.

"Another soul has been ripped from the realm," Sunitra said.

Zehan's eyes suddenly went wide and started to glow silver. A sharp grunt slipped his lips as his body convulsed.

"Ruhi," he bit out. White tendrils of power flitted around him as he clenched his jaw.

The world tilted on its axis. Ruhi's soul was being ripped from the realm.

Zehan cried out in agony. The wolves whimpered as if they could feel their creator's pain.

I looked up at Sunitra and Bidal. "Where is Ruhi?" We had to find her.

"It's too late," Sunitra said with kindness.

"No, it isn't. Go. Find. Her." I barely contained my rage. Sunitra only returned my glowering with pity.

My breathing sharpened as another grunt of pain escaped Zehan's lips.

Bidal kneeled next to Zehan, looking grim. Zehan's silvery eyes found my face. They held sorrow and confirmation. *Ruhi was gone.*

I couldn't process it. I *wouldn't* process it. Zehan's next deep yell made it hard for my chest to expand with air. "Tell me what I can do to help." My voice was thin and fragile.

Bidal shook his head. "There is nothing. It will run its course."

Sweat rolled down Zehan's temples, his tunic was damp. Panic seized me. I hated being useless, and I couldn't stand the sight of him in pain.

Use your magic, meri mara. Hans watched me from the same spot.

I didn't question the Asura. I didn't ask what he meant or how he knew.

My magic flared and poured into my veins at his words, like it automatically knew what to do. I slowly lifted my hands over him and allowed the invisible strands to funnel into him.

Zehan was too weak to hold up a shield against me, so I easily slipped in. I had never used my magic in this capacity before, but I thought of calmness and trust. I thought I saw a thin string of black stream from the tips of my finger, but it must have been a trick of the light, because it was gone with the next pulse of magic I pushed into him.

Zehan let out a sharp sigh. Seconds trickled by, and his shoulders relaxed. His breathing evened out. His eyes were no longer silver, but once again a brutal black. His expression slackened, but he controlled his emotions well. My magic hadn't overpowered him or put him into a full trance.

Calmness gravitated between us like a feather falling to the ground, but then Zehan's face vanished and I was thrusted into a different time.

***

A boy with sharp features ran barefoot behind a darkened carriage, sand stuck to the tears that streamed down his face. A beautiful dark-haired female sat in the back of the carriage shaking her head at the boy, urging him to stay put. But the boy ran until his feet blistered and his breath turned ragged. He stopped in front of a veiled realm, translucent and shimmering. A dark queen greeted him, running her hands through his long tresses. She leaned forward and whispered something in his ear. The boy wiped his face with the back of his hands as his jaw tensed with determination.

***

My power trembled at the intrusion. I was thrown back out into the present, heavy and drained. I gasped as power sharpened my senses.

Zehan's wide-eyed expression grounded me. The shape of his nose matched the little boy's. I opened my mouth but couldn't speak. Magic had taken everything out of me, or maybe it was his magic, because in my tranced state, I no longer knew the difference.

CHAPTER TWENTY

"We leave now," Bidal ordered, pulling me out of my stupor.

I still kneeled next to Zehan glancing back and forth between his face and my hands. I was shaking. *What in nine hells just happened?* The power I had just released...

"Come on, Niya. Get up." Sunitra hauled me to my feet.

Ruhi.

Thoughts jumbled together as I tried to make sense of the facts and unsaid questions. Someone might have said my name, but all I could think about was the way Ruhi hugged me tightly last night and our plans to meet again. She couldn't be gone.

Bidal lifted an unconscious Zehan and flung him over his shoulder.

I will see you again, courtesan, Hans mind-spoke, jolting me out of shock. The Asura's form rippled, blending with the aesthetic of this deva-forsaken palace. *When you are ready to accept who and what you are.*

I stared at him, unable to hide my confusion. The Asura's form blurred until he was no longer there at all.

"Niya." Sunitra placed both hands on my shoulders and shook slightly. "I need you to walk. Can you do that?"

"Yes," I said weakly. My ears filled with a sharp ringing. But I focused on moving my feet and keeping up with the rakshasas' large steps. They were worried about something. I felt it in the way they rushed to get out of here.

And when we turned the next corner, I understood why. A formidable group of demons blocked our path.

The head of the group was one of the guards that had let us in, the one that had stared at Zehan with utter loathing. "Leave the prince, and we'll let you be on your way," he spit out.

Sunitra tensed. My next swallow hurt as I took in their hungry expressions and low snarls. Magic flickered in my veins like it was attracted to the pure vengeance of the group.

Bidal's voice sharpened. "Move out of the way, Oman, so I don't have to make a mess."

I glanced at Zehan flung over Bidal's shoulder, his features scrunched like he was having a painful nightmare. Now would be a great time to wake, Zehan, I thought to myself. But the prince did not even stir.

Oman's lip curled. "Are you really going to side with that sap of a human rather than your own kind?"

"We are all the same kind in Naraka," Bidal said simply. "What has gotten into you? Is this place not vile enough? I had hoped that you would change being here, but I see I was wrong. Your fate was right to bring you here, brother."

My gaze whipped to Bidal. A deep crinkle had formed between his brows. Zehan had sent Bidal's brother to Kalank?

Oman spat at his feet. "You are no brother of mine." The large rakshasa pulled out the sword in his belt and tossed it into his good arm. He flashed his sharp teeth at me. "I'll take the whore as well."

Bidal pulled out his blade with one swift movement. Sunitra did the same. Fear gripped my soul so tightly I thought I would become a permanent inhabitant of Naraka. How in nine hells would we get out of this?

Oman used two fingers to produce a sharp whistle. Demons lunged for us from all sides. Sunitra roughly shoved me to the wall so that she was serving as a barrier between me and the rakshasas. Teeth snapped, throats growled, and claws scratched in the dark corridor, but Sunitra moved lightning fast. In a matter of blinks, she had about five demons wounded and groaning on the ground.

Black blood sprayed onto my face as Sunitra's blade swung down. She was a harbinger of death. And now, I realized *this* was why Zehan had assigned her to me. It wasn't a punishment like she had claimed in the dungeon.

It was because she was his best warrior.

Bidal fended off demons with one arm, holding Zehan in place on his shoulder. He yelled as he cut down one demon after the other without breaking a sweat.

More demons rushed toward us. Oman watched as Bidal fought against them, like he was biding his time, waiting for his brother to tire.

We were outnumbered. Sunitra and Bidal wouldn't be able to strike down every demon in this place. Oman strode toward Bidal, whose back was turned, with purpose on his face. I pushed off the wall and ran toward the rakshasa as Oman lifted his sword, readying to strike.

"Stop!" I held out my hand, and all at once, every rakshasa froze in place. Their expressions of rage slackened to awe. They dropped their arms and waited. I sucked in a shallow breath. This was stronger than my normal trance magic. Like Rati, I was able to *control* them.

Sunitra slumped against the wall, panting heavily. "You couldn't have done that before the fighting started?"

"I—" I wasn't even sure what I was doing. I just wanted to stop Oman from killing Bidal.

Bidal heaved. "Let's go before your magic wears off."

I led us past the group of demons, their hungry eyes glued to me like sap on a tree. In truth, I didn't think my magic would ever wear off. If I told these rakshasas to bow, they would. If I told them to tell me their deepest sins, they would. If I told them to slit their own throats, they would.

If I willed it, I could dominate their hearts and minds.

We were almost to the exit when I spotted a figure waiting by the entrance. The Asura of Pride leveled a look at me. "So, you *are* much more than a courtesan."

Dread poured into my chest. "I don't know what you mean."

"In my existence, I've only ever seen *that* kind of power once. But that can't be, because Rati destroyed it when she ascended this forsaken realm."

A bitterness filled my mouth as Abhi stared with keen interest. He was shorter than the other Asuras and his hair was combed over. His posture gave off an air of indifference.

I needed to tread carefully. Zehan had made it clear that he did not want Rati or the Asuras to know the full extent of my powers, but it was too late for that. "I was gifted this power when I was twelve by a stranger. I was young. I didn't understand what I was getting into."

"No, I imagine you didn't." Abhi tilted his head in assessment.

His deep hazel eyes drifted toward Zehan, who was still slung over Bidal's shoulder, and then back to me with quiet assessment. I hated the way the Asuras did that. Like they could see the inner workings of my soul.

"I'll keep your secret." His expression turned cold and menacing. "But when you find the person responsible for the missing souls, I want to punish them first."

He didn't say *if* I found the person responsible. This was another sneaky bargain. If I didn't find out who was behind the murders, he might reveal to everyone—and, more importantly, Rati—what power I held.

My fingers twitched in warning.

Mere moments ago, I would have used this opportunity to ask for a boon, but then remembered Hans's words. *None of the Asuras can give you a boon.* The implications of this new fact had yet to sink in.

Abhi clucked his tongue. "Are you truly pondering my question?" Sunitra nudged me with her large elbow. He lifted his hand. "One snap, Niya. It takes one snap of my fingers to open every single cell door in this hellhole and release the hungry demons."

I swallowed the bile that had risen in my throat.

This wasn't really a choice. If I didn't want him to sound the alarms or go straight to Rati, I had to agree.

"Done," I said. "But you let us leave here and never say a word about what you saw to anyone. And you'll make sure none of the guards come after us."

Word of this incident might get out anyways. Humans were not able to feel my magic on them, but the Asuras could. As for the demons, I suspected it was mixed. Those naturally stronger may be able to tell they were being manipulated.

Abhi barked a laugh as he stepped aside. "Shama and Lobha were right about you. I agree to your terms. But remember, Niya, I want to be the first to greet the culprit behind these disappearances."

I dipped my chin in confirmation. Why was Abhi so invested in this killer? Had one of his souls been taken?

Bidal walked slowly past Abhi, keeping one eye on the Asura. Sunitra clutched her sword tight. She stayed behind me as we made our way out. I felt Abhi's deep stare drill into the back of my head as we left the cavernous palace.

Damn Asuras and their games.

As soon as the heavy stone door closed with an echoing thud, I released the hold of my magic, imagining Oman punching the stone wall in frustration.

I plopped down on the last step where the stone met snow. A let out a few short exhales, each forming a visible puff of white vapor. For once, I was grateful for the cold.

"By the Asuras, I am never going in there again."

Sunitra dropped next to me. Her sword clattering to the stone. She looked at me as she rested her forearms on her knees. "That was..."

"Intense?" I finished for her.

"I was going to say *interesting,* but *intense* definitely describes it."

Bidal grunted and dropped Zehan onto a mound of snow like a dead carcass. He fell onto his knees next to him and laid back. "When he wakes up, I am going to kill him."

Sunitra and I stared at the rakshasa then back at each other. Laughter bubbled out of me. Perhaps it was the near-death experience or the fact that my plans to get a boon were now utter shit, but full belly laughs escaped my lips.

Overwhelming. Irrational. Carefree.

Bidal and Sunitra stared at me like I had gone mad.

Perhaps I had gone mad.

Zehan groaned and jolted up, making sense of his surroundings. He found me instantly and frowned when he saw the delirious smile on my face.

Bidal tossed some snow at Zehan. "Good of you to join us, Your Highness. We almost died while you were sleeping."

Zehan looked around, his wolves reappearing. "What do you mean you almost *died*?"

"Oman," Sunitra said as if that explained everything. She took a handful of snow and smacked it onto her face.

Zehan growled. "He has a death wish."

"Perhaps another day," Bidal nodded.

He fell back into the snow, his shoulders relaxed. "Trust me. I would have taken that fight over this pain any day," his voice strained. Sorrow dimmed the normal blaze that resided there. "I'm sorry, Niya."

The snowy air didn't feel refreshing anymore and the stench of Kalank returned.

A million unsaid words and questions hovered in the air between all of us. The snow flurries fell faster, yet time seemed to slow. A sick, sinking feeling hit me like a wave, and I felt the pain of a soul being ripped all over again.

Ruhi.

CHAPTER TWENTY-ONE

The sharp sounds of birds chirping served as my music this morning. I spun, and my payals let out a soft clink. It was the earliest hours of the morning, where most patrons of the palace were still asleep. The sun hadn't even reached the bottom curve of the moon, but I preferred the serenity and silence.

It normally allowed me to focus on my form and posture. However, that was not the case today.

"Ugh!" I groaned loudly. My frustrated echo cut threw the earthy air. My footwork was sloppy. One of the greatest dancers in Tyaga, unable to run a simple series of tight spins. I stumbled on the next sequence and let out another curse.

I pulled the ribbon holding up my hair and ran my fingers through it, relieving the tight pressure that had built at the base of my bun. I paced around the bright courtyard, attempting to calm my breath back down so I could start again. Guards stood mutely at their stations, watching me warily.

I had been here for hours, attempting to get the sequence perfect. Yet, it was anything but, and I knew the reason why.

Ruhi.

Anger fueled my steps. I hadn't been on Prithvi when she died, so I didn't feel grief at her death, and even when I did see her here in hell, it was oddly comforting to know she was happy and at peace and was about to embark onto her next life cycle.

But now, her soul was gone from the very threads of existence. I would *never* see her in any lifetime. I felt her loss so acutely through Zehan that I knew I wouldn't feel peace until I avenged her.

Which is why my new bargain with Abhi didn't feel like a chore. It felt like a calling. I *wanted* to find who was responsible for her death. I *wanted* the culprit to pay for this sin. Whoever they were, they deserved to be punished.

Ruhi was another soul that had been snatched from their next bright life. A soul who was my only friend. This heinous act didn't have a strong enough explanation.

It was just as well, given my plans to get a boon were now destroyed.

Being under Rati's rule for so long has slowly stripped us of our power. If the Asuras could not give me a boon of freedom, that left me with only one option. One that I had already fully come to terms with.

I let out another throaty growl as I fumbled the second count of eight. *Again,* I said to myself. The only way to burn through my heart-ache was to dance.

Bidal, Sunitra, and I explained to Zehan what Hans had revealed about the missing souls and what transpired with the demons on the carriage ride home. He hadn't uttered a word, but at the mention of my new bargain with Abhi, the tension in his shoulders and grip on the leather seats illuminated his wrath. As soon as we arrived back at the palace, he quickly went up the stairs, leaving me standing at the entrance.

He had avoided me since.

Glimpses of what my magic revealed when I used it on him cycled through my mind. The boy with almond-shaped eyes, a grief-stricken mother, Rati choosing her dark prince. My head pounded at the remnants of the fractured memory of Zehan writhing in pain as he felt Ruhi's soul being ripped from the realm.

It's why I had spent most of the night pacing my room wondering if he was okay, if *we* were okay. *There is no we,* I reminded myself. Zehan and I had struck a bargain. That's all. There was *nothing* else between us. I lifted my hands to start the routine again.

"Twirling won't resolve your problems, courtesan," Sunitra observed. I stopped mid-spin. The rakshasa hands rested on her utility belt.

"Spinning in circles is all I know," I reminded her. I never had the luxury to venture into anything else. Dancing was the only skill that repeatedly saved me from my own fate, and so I gave myself fully to it. As soon as I moved into my starting pose, nothing else mattered. I could be me.

"I don't think that's true," Sunitra said. "You are far more skilled than you give yourself credit for. And you have the resilience and stubbornness of a warrior."

"Dancers would make excellent warriors," I agreed. "It's a shame they don't enlist females into the armies on Prithvi."

"I agree," Sunitra chuckled. "Imagine female humans beating men with their own blade."

I smiled and jerked my chin at her sword. "Who taught you to fight?"

"My father. He was never for conventional approaches, believing everyone should know how to defend themselves. Though, I am challenged all the time for being a female in a male's profession." She pointed at my feet. "Who taught you to dance?"

I blinked at Sunitra. No one had ever bothered to ask me that question. "My mother. She taught the dance of the devas in our village."

"She must have been a hell of a dancer."

"She was." Despite the belief that the devas had abandoned us, my mother believed the opposite. She believed it was *humans* who abandoned them. She taught the girls and boys in my village how to tell stories with movement, an art form that was rare now.

Sunitra sat on the edge of the fountain and propped one leg up onto the ledge. "What happened to her?"

"King Murkha decided he wanted Khoya for himself." I stared hard at the fountain. "I had just turned twelve when his armies ransacked our village."

At the time, war raged between the various kingdoms like a wildfire. Everyone wanted more land, resources, and gold. King Murkha was vicious in his conquest and ordered his men to kill anyone who hesitated to give their loyalty. He didn't want to deal with an uprising down the road. It was easier to simply kill people off.

"Your father was a soldier?"

I shook my head. "He was a messenger for Queen Orna." My father spent most of his time traveling between kingdoms with special permissions. "I wish he had been a soldier, perhaps then he would still be here."

I had blocked out most of the details of that fateful day. My mom's piercing scream when that soldier drove his blade across my father's neck still haunted my dreams.

"If you could not fight, how did you survive?"

"One of your kind saved me." I didn't know who or why. While a large majority of rakshasas lived in Naraka, clans lived in remote areas on Prithvi. Some kingdoms had become allies with the demons, while others wanted nothing to do with them. Queen Orna had been the former.

The rakshasa that had saved me didn't stay long enough for me to thank him. Instead, he had walked off to kill more of King Murkha's men. I was young, and everything happened so quickly. I still remembered the final look the beefy demon gave me before turning away and disappearing into the sandy wind. His eyes had been the most disturbing shade of blue.

Even then, I had been helpless and dependent on someone else to save me. I spent most of my life in the same state. It was an emotion I had become too accustomed to feeling.

Sunitra watched me carefully. "I am truly sorry, Niya, about your friend."

My head felt heavy. "Me too," I said.

I looked up at the sky, feeling the weight of both white and orange orbs fall onto my shoulder. I looked back at the demon before me. "Could you teach me to fight?"

Sunitra's smiled. She unclasped a small dagger on her belt and tossed it to me. I caught it with my right hand. "It would be my honor."

I smiled as I studied the dagger. It was approximately the length of my forearm. The pommel was black with a small yellow ribbon tied at the end of it.

Sunitra pulled out another identical one from her utility belt. "First lesson," she said. "Blocking."

She sidestepped with small shuffles, jabbing her dagger at various angles.

I barely blocked her movements. "Wait!" I yelled between each sharp clang of our daggers. "You're. Moving. Too. Fast."

"Your enemies will not wait for you to catch your breath," Sunitra said. "Spin toward me with your dagger up."

I did as she commanded. At the end of my spin, I blocked her oncoming strike, pushing her back a few steps.

She shoved my dagger down with hers. "Fighting is just another dance sequence. You don't break your performance until you've delivered everything you've got."

I pulled my shoulders back, feeling the release of energy I had been seeking all morning. A new itch. "Again."

We went back and forth until the sun rose higher than the moon and the palace started to bustle with maids and guards. If we had been in Khoya, sweat would have soaked through my tunic by now, but Naraka's cold climate just made my chest tighten with trapped breaths. My hair plastered to the sides of my face.

"Do you not tire?" Sunitra asked between pants. She walked over to the fountain and stuck her head underneath one of the spouts and took a few loud gulps.

I smiled. Baanu's rigorous training schedule was proving useful in a new way. "I have the endurance of a horse."

Sunitra snorted. Bidal appeared under one of the many alcoves that surrounded the rectangular garden. "Niya," he said, offering me a head bow.

"Is he awake?" I asked quickly, then instantly regretted it when Sunitra's lip curled.

Bidal only nodded. "He requests your presence."

Bidal led me through the wide corridors that had symmetrical carvings on either side, his feet clacking on the stone floor. Each of his steps forced me to take two-and-a-half to keep pace.

"I've never been to this side of the palace," I muttered, looking at the large statues of devas that were carved into the wall after each door. Even though I had lived here for weeks, dozens of rooms remained to be explored.

"We are in Zehan's private wing," Bidal said. "Folks are rarely allowed to venture to this part of the castle. Only a handful of servants and select guards." He gave me a pointed look. Heat traveled to my cheeks. I cleared my throat. "Have you spoken to your brother?"

"He is not my brother," Bidal said sternly. "Not anymore."

"Can I ask what happened?"

Bidal sighed. "Oman was part of this guard. It is an honor for us to serve the prince, or any Asura, but Oman did not like how Zehan behaved as a ruler. He felt that it made us look weak, and that he did not fully embody the ruler of hell."

That didn't surprise me. Zehan was different from what humans have been led to believe. "Do you feel like that?"

Bidal glanced at me with curiosity. "I admit Zehan's approach is unconventional. Rakshasas are bred to be hunters and destroyers. It is in our nature to wreak havoc and fight amongst each other. Those qualities have only been further encouraged by humans and the devas. But then Zehan came along and made us see that we did not have to be what everyone expected us to be. That notion was not well perceived by everyone." We turned another corner that led to a curved staircase.

"What did Oman do to make Zehan send him to Kalank?"

"He was aiding traffickers into various territories through Zehan's check posts. One of Zehan's human confidants, Ameel, found him smuggling five young girls in chains." Bidal's features twisted like he had tasted something sour. "Zehan took him to Kalank himself. Unfortunately, Oman is rather good at talking his way into things. He managed to get a guard post there after about five years of rotting in a cell."

I stopped in my tracks. Bidal turned over his shoulder, his brows pinching at the center. "You all right, courtesan?"

"Zehan stops the traffickers?" All my life I had believed that Zehan and his demons were promoting traffickers through those check posts, but it was the exact opposite.

Bidal scratched his chin. "Ah, shit. I thought you knew." He half shrugged. "That is the purpose of Sahra. Zehan has created a network of check posts to watch for signs of trafficking but also to manage who goes in and out of all the major territories."

I frowned at the demon. "It's all a front? Zehan is *saving* those women and children. Why not just tell everyone that is what he is doing. Why let all of Prithvi believe that he is the bad guy in all of this?"

"You should understand more than others, Niya." Bidal knocked on the large wooden door and without waiting for a reply, he tugged it open motioning me to enter. "Sometimes the good guy has to be the villain."

CHAPTER
TWENTY-TWO

Aging maps and scrolls littered the brown floor. A wave of heat embraced me as I moved farther into the small room. The aesthetic was similar to my father's office where he kept important missives and documents as records for the Queen Orna.

Zehan sat at his desk, intently reading a document, feather quill in hand. He wore a plain white tunic and dark-blue pants. The lace strings at his neck were undone, revealing his sternum and cuts of his abdomen.

Relief, similar to when I yanked open tight drawstrings on my lehenga, washed over me.

His haunted eyes sparked when he saw me. The air between us thickened with something other than the smell of moldy parchment.

I finally broke the silence. "Still summoning me like one of your wolves I see."

His body tensed, but a smirk crept onto his face. "You are my courtesan, are you not?"

"I wasn't sure," I said carefully. "You've avoided me since Kalank."

His expression softened. "I am sorry for that." He lifted one of the two small ceramic teacups at the edge of his desk and held it out to me. "Chai."

I slowly took the cup, and my fingers brushed against his, sending a bolt of heat straight to my head. I took a sip. "Are you feeling better?"

"Immensely. Thanks to you." Zehan leaned back in his chair, studying me. "Care to share how you managed to put fifty demons under the trance with one shout?" He glanced at my fingers that were tapping against the armrest.

"It was adrenaline," I answered quickly. Though, that was only partially true. It was like my magic felt the need to respond. Even now, I felt my magic itching to come out, to *seek* him out. "Sometimes when I get lost in a performance, I let the trance fully capture the crowd. It happens," I said airily.

Zehan didn't look convinced. I placed the cup down; the spicy notes of the chai hit the back of my throat. "Did she suffer?"

Zehan tugged at the roots of his hair. "I owe you an apology, Niya. It's my fault Ruhi is gone."

My constantly frozen insides thawed at seeing him so disgruntled. "No."

"Yes, it is." Zehan stood up and paced. "Ruhi wasn't supposed to stay here. She did nothing wrong. She was murdered. She was to move into her next life cycle immediately."

"I don't understand." My forehead creased. "Then why did you sentence her to one full moon here?"

Zehan came and stood in front of me. "I knew how much she meant to you." I blinked up at him.

"I knew after that night in Khoya how much she meant to you, but when she appeared here, and I used my magic on her, I saw the memories of you in her last life. It's the only time I've ever seen you genuinely smile."

My mind raced. He kept Ruhi here because he knew she was my friend.

"I decided to keep her here for a month to give you both more time before she reincarnated into her next life. I let my guilt for hurting her in the first place get in the way. And now, she is another soul I've failed."

"Why do you care so much?" I whispered.

"It is my job to watch over the souls," Zehan said, his expression darkening. "Every soul is precious to the overall balance of the world. Even one soul unaccounted for is far too many."

Bile built in the back of my throat. How many times had Zehan had felt that same pain? After seeing him thrash like that, I had no doubts about his motives for this bargain. He genuinely wanted and *needed* to find who was doing this. Zehan was the villain to everyone outside of Naraka, but to the people within...

He was their relentless protector.

I pushed my lips together. "When you felt the soul being ripped from the realm, I used my magic on you. I saw a boy."

Zehan's eyebrows flitted up a millisecond, but the rest of his features remained unchanged.

"He chased a black carriage that carried a crying woman into Naraka. Rati appeared before him, and he crossed the veil into Naraka. That was you, wasn't it?"

"My mother..." Zehan whispered, his voice sorrowful. "My father was not a kind man. He was the king of a small town south of Khoya, and he was ruthless. All he cared about was obtaining more land and destroying more kingdoms so he could be the sole ruler. He practically achieved it. He never treated my mother with any sort of respect nor showed her any form of love. After they had me, he tossed her to the side for his many mistresses. My mother found love with another." Zehan exhaled. "Her only mistake was that she got caught."

The room suddenly felt cold.

"My father set out to destroy her and ensure that no one ever found out. The world was different back then. Devas and humans interacted regularly, and he meditated and called upon the Devi of Naraka to take his wife away."

I swallowed. "Rati granted him a boon."

Zehan nodded. "Devas grant boons if they are pleased with your devotion. They don't distinguish between right or wrong requests. By that point, Rati had already locked away the other devas in Svarga. No one could stop her from granting his wish."

Zehan pinched the bridge of his nose. "When I saw rakshasas shove my mother into the carriage, something in me snapped. I lost all sense and chased after her. My father didn't stop me. I suspected he thought I would get tired and eventually find my way back, but I didn't stop. I ran until my legs were numb. Rati must have seen the determination in me because eventually she showed herself to me and offered me an exchange. If I took my mother's place for eternity, she got a one-way ticket to Svarga. She wouldn't have to enter her next life cycle."

I instinctively clutched my chest. In the vision I received, he was so young. How long has he lived alone in this cold, isolating place? "Did you ever see your mom?"

Zehan shook his head with a small smile. "She was sent to Svarga as soon as I crossed through the Gate of Three."

"I'm sorry," I said quietly, realizing how wrong the humans were about Zehan. How wrong *I* had it. I believed that Zehan was here because he made a deal with the devil for his own gain, but that wasn't true. He made a deal for someone he loved, and since coming here, he had made this place better for everyone in it.

Zehan gave me a small smile. "Don't be. I take comfort knowing she reached Svarga and is living the rest of her life in eternal bliss, hopefully now with the man she truly loves." He reached out and tucked a small wavy strand of hair behind one of my ears. Even the brush of his fingers sent a streak of heat to my toes.

"It's unfortunate you do not extend your generosity to *every* soul," I said stiffly. Zehan claimed every soul was important, yet he continued to take Chosens against their will.

Zehan has created a network of checkposts to watch for signs of trafficking.
Sometimes the good guy has to be the villain.

"I don't understand you." On one hand, Zehan deeply cared about the departed souls here, and yet he didn't extend that same favor to all living souls on Privthi. Why?

Zehan walked around his desk. "I know what you're referring to, and it isn't what you think." Zehan leaned against the edge of the smooth wood and folded his arms.

"You've claimed before." He was both evil and good, and it confused the hell out of me.

My next words were barely a whisper. "So why take a Chosen each month? You said you release them after they fulfill whatever bargain you offer them. I believe you, even more so after Bidal told me the real reason for your check posts." His fingers froze at the ends of my hair. "But I've never seen any of the Chosen return to Khoya. So where are they? You understand what it's like to be ripped away from those you love, from a place you love. How can you consciously do the same thing to so many others?"

He folded his arms to mimic my stance. Conflict raged in his eyes, but he finally sighed.

"They are in Varnasi."

My back straightened. "What?"

"Being the Prince of Hell gives me the ability to be ruthless and merciless. It does not shock anyone that I take young females against their will, so I've used that to my advantage. I take a young girl who is stuck in a horrible fate, and I give her a new life. None of my Chosen have ever set foot in Naraka," Zehan said. "Aside from you."

Suspicion laced my tone. "And you simply do this out of the goodness of your heart?"

Zehan shrugged. "It isn't purely selfless. I get intel out of it. Courtesans are well versed in court matters and have inside information about a multitude of traders. For example, by taking a girl from Tavas, I was able to learn of a revolt against Queen Oeshi. That revolt would have caused a war that impacted the other kingdoms, so I put a stop to it before it truly even began. Being immortal makes me bored sometimes. I like having a silent hand in things."

That's how Zehan always knew everything about everyone. He didn't have spies. He paid attention to the most undervalued people in every king's court. The dancers.

Aside from you.

That's why the Asuras—and even Rati—were surprised to see me here. *You're the Chosen he decided to keep.* When I initially made the bargain with Zehan, I had thought I would need to seek out a boon with the Asuras because he wouldn't uphold his end of our deal.

What if trusting Zehan *was* the only way to get my ticket out of here?

If he had sent dozens of Chosen to Varnasi, he knew how to get inside the city. Before anyone was admitted, Varnasi's ruler personally greeted them to ensure they had no ill intention.

Zehan observed me processing. "I've told you before, courtesan. Help me find the missing souls, let's work together as equals, not as two strangers in a bargain, and I will ensure the gates to Varnasi open for you."

I hated when his reasoning was rational. But I had heard similar words before from so many others, but it had always led to broken promises. This was the same man who hurt Ruhi, forced me to leave Khoya, and threatened to reveal my power to the world so a target would be placed on my back. Yet, he was also the same man who gave Ruhi back to me for a day and has not forced a shackle on me since I've gotten here.

"In the spirit of resetting our partnership, there is something else you should know." I nervously fidgeted with the end of my braid. "I only agreed to our bargain because I knew that I would be able to speak with the Asuras. I wanted to try to obtain a boon from them."

"That is why you jumped at the idea to speak to Hans alone." A slow dawning spread across his face.

I launched into the details of my interactions with the various Asuars. "I'm not sorry. I did what I thought I had to. I didn't know if you would actually keep your bargain."

I expected Zehan to be angry, but instead he half shrugged. "I knew you were up to something, I just didn't know what. I don't blame you for trying to find another way out of here, Niya."

There was more meaning behind those words than he let on, but I didn't question it. For once we agreed on something.

"But it is curious," Zehan ruminated. "Why are the Asuras keeping your secret? Why not tell Rati about your magic?"

"I don't know." I said. And I wasn't sure I wanted to find out. "But if we can find out who is stealing souls, we can give them all something else to focus on."

Hans admitted he was seeking out the culprit. Abhi had struck that bargain with me. It was likely all the Asuras had vested interest in finding the person responsible. And if we delivered that person to them, they would owe us.

Zehan didn't look convinced. "I don't like it."

"You don't like many things, so add this to the never-ending list," I snapped.

"This is different. *You* are at risk."

I stilled. "Are you forgetting that *you* brought me here? That I'm always at risk because of your demons?" What a hypocrite.

A muscle in his jaw ticked. "That's different. I always place you in *controlled* risk. If anyone had laid a hand on you, I would have killed them."

"That's—" My stomach flipped at the resolution in his voice. *Where did that come from?"* I shook my head. "Then, I have nothing to worry about," I said lightly, breaking the tension simmering between us.

"Rati is different. I can't move against her."

"Then we need to stop wasting time." I placed my hands on his desk. "We need to go see the rishi," I said.

Sunitra had explained to me that the rishi was a seer of sorts, he could read the cosmos or the stars. She thought it was a bunch of gibberish, but many souls went there to obtain some sort of peace from their last life.

Zehan let his shoulders drop a smidge. "I agree."

I nodded, feeling our new truce solidify between us. Whether I liked it or not, working with Zehan was my path to Varnasi. Finding the culprit behind these disappearances was now a mutual interest. I wasn't above any sin. I'd partake in them if it meant getting my revenge for Ruhi.

Which made the Prince of Hell my closest ally.

CHAPTER TWENTY-THREE

Snow flurries descended upon us as we trudged the uneven grassy ground. It had been mid-day when we left the palace, but now the moon was higher in the sky and the clouds hid the sun. We had walked for miles, surrounded by the smell of dead leaves.

"Remind me why we have to t-travel to the rishi's cottage by f-foot?" I stammered.

"The rishi's cottage drifts within the forest," Zehan explained. "It is never in the same location twice and as you can see, it's off the local path."

Sunitra and Kal walked twenty paces behind us, bickering as they frequently did. Zehan hadn't bothered to bring additional guards with him.

I heated my hands with my breath in a meager attempt to bring feeling back into my fingers. I had wrapped my dupatta around my face to keep my ears warm, but as the temperature dropped, it helped little. "Why?"

Zehan weaved in and out between trees. "The rishi moves to where the cosmos speaks to him. Like the devas, he uses the energy from the universe to help him understand the crisscrossed paths of life, death, and fate. He can read lifecycles more intensely than I can."

I fell into step beside him. "Was he given that power?" There were hypnotics and prophetics on Prithvi but I'd never heard of any being so sophisticated in their practice.

"I've never asked," Zehan admitted. "But I presume it was a boon from a deva. Power like that doesn't just materialize. It is asked for. I can see a small thread of a person's life, while he has no limitation, he can see everything about all of your lives."

I looked sideways at him, my curiosity peaking. "What have you asked him?" What would the most powerful man in Naraka need to ask for?

"Me?" Zehan stopped walking and faced me. "I asked if my mom truly made it to Svarga."

I pulled my overcoat around myself, tight enough to squeeze my ribcage. "And?"

"She made it to Svarga, at least, that's what the old man told me." Zehan sighed. "It's possible he told me that to make me feel better. No one truly knows what state Svarga is in after Rati destroyed the Gate of Two. But I choose to believe that she is in a better place with her soulmate. I know it's foolish–"

"No it isn't." I understood that reasoning and the need to believe something better was out there. "If it helps you keep your sanity, it isn't." It was as simple as that. No good came out of dwelling on the unknown.

We continued walking in silence, only the bustling of our steps filling the void until a small cottage appeared in the distance. "Is that it?"

Zehan nodded. The small structure looked quaint and peaceful. Another gust of wind whipped around us. My dupatta flew off my head and snagged onto a tree with lower branches. "By the Asuras, the cold here is insufferable."

I went to the tree in question and tried to reach for the burnt orange fabric. I hopped once and then twice, until I grabbed the corner and tugged, the fabric started to tear. I cursed. Gauri was going to kill me for ruining her creation.

Zehan hand-covered mine, drawing it down. "Do you have that much pride that you cannot simply ask for help?"

"If I'm asking from you?" I laughed. "A-absolutely."

Zehan eyed me but pulled the dupatta off the branch and placed it on my head, looping it off on one side. I tracked his movements, feeling my cheeks go impossibly red when his knuckles brushed my neck. I shuddered.

Zehan sighed. He snapped his fingers, and warmth created a silhouette around my body as he walked away. "That is the last time I help you with that, courtesan. The next time you want warmth, you'll have to find another way."

I snorted. "Fine. I'll just wrap myself around you."

I froze, realizing what I had just said. *What in nine hells?*

Zehan's chuckle made my toes curl. He prowled closer to me until my back hit the bark. "Is that so?"

I lifted my chin. "You haven't bothered to teach me how to perform that bit of magic. How am I supposed to learn it."

"You're right," Zehan said, relaxing his posture. He folded his arms. "Do it now."

"I don't think you understand the method of teaching. I can't just snap my fingers like you and summon the Deva of Heat"

The corners of his eyes crinkled. "The Deva of Heat? I don't believe there is one, but I could be him."

I let out a groan of frustration. 'You know what I mean." I shoved past him.

Zehan grabbed my wrist and pulled me back into his chest, smiling. "I do–"

"Zehan!" Sunitra called.

I yanked my hand out of his hold. Sunitra and Kal caught up to us. A very large black bird with a massive wingspan and razor-sharp teeth was perched on Sunitra's shoulder. She handed an untied scroll to Zehan.

"It's from Ezhil. It's Oeshi. Her army is headed towards Khoya as we speak."

"Shit," Zehan read the scroll with pinched brows.

My eyes widened. This is what Ezhil, Zehan, and Ameel had been referring to when I overheard them. "Oeshi is seeking conquest?"

"Has been for years," Zehan tucked the note into his coat pocket. "Oeshi could give Murkha a run for his money in terms of greed."

"Ameel and Bidal will need to go support Ezhil to talk her out of it. We don't need a full out war between the territories. It will draw more travelers and monarchs' towards Naraka."

Of course. Zehan's interest in keeping peace stemmed from not wanting anyone to look closer into his realm, where there was an abundance of resources.

"But no one can get into Naraka right?" The gate only appeared when Zehan marked someone.

"Yes, but there are enough demons going in and out of the Gate of Three that it could become apparent where the entrance is. And as you are proof that humans can possess magic, there is always a risk of someone entering and

Naraka cannot be infiltrated. I must go brief Bidal." Conflict weighed down his shoulders. "We will come back another day."

I placed a hand on my hip. "Do you really want to risk another departed soul being taken?" I shook my head. "No, Kal, Sunitra, and I will go on." The cost of delaying even by a day was too steep. The Rishi's cottage could also move locations and we would have to start our search anew.

Zehan lifted his brows at my resolution, but did not argue. "Very well. I'll be back as soon as I can." He nodded to Sunitra and Kal before vanishing through a plume of white mist.

***

The rishi's cottage was nestled between a few lanky trees. Vines spidered across the rustic roof and walls. It couldn't be more than two rooms on the inside.

"Are you all right?" I asked Kal.

As soon as we spotted the cottage, the butler had gone oddly quiet, fidgeting with the lapels of his uniform. I had become accustomed to his cheery demeanor, but today his squirming was slightly unsettling.

"Fine, fine," his voice wavered. He scanned the forest with wariness. "I just don't like this part of Vajra."

"Didn't think you were spooked so easily, Kal." Sunitra laughed.

"I know what you mean," I reassured Kal. I felt like the landscape watched me, waiting for me to trip on its gravel or become lost on its twisty paths. The sky flooded with red and black streaks, like it too grieved at Ruhi's unjust passing.

"Why were the departed souls here in the first place?" Why would anyone want to come here?

"Normally, departed souls seek the rishi out to see the living. For some, it's hard to let go of their last life, especially when the death was unexpected and the departed soul still has family on Prithvi. Death does not destroy love," Kal said softly.

"Sunitra and I should wait outside," Kal said, throwing himself into the rickety chair on the small two-person porch. "The old man gives me the creeps. And he will likely be more responsive if Niya were to go in alone."

Sunitra glanced at the rishi's door and then me. "I think it would be better if I went in with you."

I snorted. "I'm more than capable of handling an old man. I stopped a whole gang of demons from shredding us apart."

Sunitra didn't look convinced, but she nodded. Even she seemed off.

I knocked once on the door. Then twice. Finally on the third, the door creaked open.

"Hello," I whispered into the room. No one was there. It was tiny on the inside, with only a small circular wooden table and four chairs. The air smelled like sage incense and burnt wood. Flames roared in the fireplace, easing my nerves.

A red curtain swung back to reveal a frail old man with a braided gray beard. He wore a flimsy dhoti that wrapped around his bare torso. His eyes were the oddest shade of amber—light with black streaks.

"You've finally come," his voice sounded like sandpaper being rubbed together. "The return of death could not be hidden for so long."

I kept my expression neutral. "Were you expecting me?"

"The stars told me you'd come with him." He jutted his chin at the door where Kal stood outside. The small man started moving around in the space, muttering to himself. "He works from the shadows, rolling the dice, waiting for the devi's own forged destruction to come to fruition." He opened various clay jars and pulled out matchsticks and herbs. "Death of desire will lead to life of death. Sacrifice of death will lead all into final breath."

I swallowed. Zehan and Kal had both said that he spoke in riddles that hardly ever made sense. I wasn't sure how to respond, so I didn't bother with any other pleasantries. "Did Ruhi come here? A girl with long black hair?"

"No. Though I wasn't expecting her. I expected you." He moved to the table and started lighting his divas with a long incense. The small oil-dipped lamps flickered to life one by one.

I frowned. So, Hans's intel was correct. Ruhi was the only soul to not visit the rishi before she died. I had been with her the day before we went to Kalank. Something had happened during the night.

"What about the other departed souls that have visited you recently? What did they want?"

"They all want the same thing," he muttered, motioning me to sit in front of a cluttered table. "To *see*."

My patience thinned. "To see what?"

He lifted his hands, a bundle of incense around a series of candles, or divas as they were called by the devas. His body shook with the cosmos vibrations. Smoke wafted in the air and down my throat. I coughed.

"To see what they need and what they want."

Beautiful white and terrible black shadows rose over us, mesmerizing yet horrifying. Then the smoke floated above me, patiently waiting. The rishi watched me with rapt attention. He was waiting for me to do something.

I shifted uncomfortably. "Do I just ask?"

The rishi nodded eagerly and gestured toward the smoke again, like I was a child that needed to be encouraged to eat.

"Show me who took Ruhi," I whispered. Something thudded outside, but I was captivated by the deep gray smoke circling in front of me.

"Bladed bone will take divine power in its wake. Return of the right will force the cosmos into a rueful shake," the rishi spoke with finality.

The smoke formed first into a crown and then a trident and then two hands joining. A body started to take shape, followed by a head, and then a strong face, two familiar horns with piercings along the side...

No. The walls of the cabin closed in. I knew that sharp-featured face.

Sunitra.

CHAPTER TWENTY-FOUR

"Your mistaken," I glanced at the door. "Sunitra couldn't...she wouldn't."

The rishi smile held gaps where his teeth had fallen out. "The smoke never lies, meri mara."

My lips parted, but before I could protest, the door splintered causing a mess of wood to crash into the small room. Rough winds ripped through the cabin, toppling over the table and chairs, spearing through Sunitra's face in the smoke.

One second, I was sitting on the wooden chair, staring wide-eyed at the circling gray fumes, the next, I was flung out of my seat. I screamed. My head hit the wall with a sharp whack, and my entire body vibrated with aftershocks.

I groaned as I stood back up, disoriented and aching. Something warm trickled down the right side of my face. My attention turned to the large monkey-like rakshasa that blocked the exit. He had tawny, waxy skin, and blackened eyes. He bared his teeth.

The rishi yelled louder, like he had to get the words out of his throat. "Surrender and love will open the deva's gates. Ensuring darkness and light entwine into bonded fates."

Right before the beast could claw me in half, a diya struck him on the side of the head. It clunked as it fell to the floor, drawing his attention toward the rishi.

The rakshasa was on the old man in a blink of an eye. He flung the rishi, and his body *cracked* when it hit the wall. The rakshasa prowled toward the man like he meant to eat.

"No!" I yelled.

I picked up a wooden plank and whacked the beast as hard as I could. It bounced off him like a marble striking another ball.

The rakshasa twisted and wrenched the wood out of my hand. He growled, backing me into a corner. The claws on his hand elongated further. Fury funneled through me. I had not come this far in this realm to be killed by a rabid demon. I lifted my hands and unleashed whatever magic I could muster.

Obsidian ink poured from my fingertips.

Lethal. Sleek. Inviting.

Shock filtered through me as my magic took on its own form and path. The shadows gripped the rakshasa's body and mind. I felt them slide down his throat and constrict his lungs. He grew less crazed as the trance flooded his senses.

"What the *fuck?*" Zehan's lethal voice boomed into the cabin. He looked around at the mess of wood and blood and darkness. And for once, I was grateful to see him. Relieved even.

"Kal?" My voice strained as my magic kept the beast in a deathly choke hold.

Zehan was in front of me in a second, his eyes roving over every inch of me and freezing on the blood that trickled from the side of my temple. "Knocked out, but alive."

The rakshasa sputtered. I pulled back some of the shadows. "Who sent you?" I whispered.

"*He* did," the rakshasa boasted with a thick voice.

"Who is *he*?" My magic fumed. I was done with the riddles and the unsaid truths that this realm offered. I could do it. I could kill the rakshasa right now.

But that would make me no better than my creator.

The rakshasa let out another half snarl. "I do not regret my actions, for I will be rewarded."

"Perhaps you would have been." I gritted my teeth, flicking my wrist. I acted on pure instinct with the shadows as my guide. "If you had not been caught." Black translucent ropes squeezed around the rakshasa's neck, causing his now orange eyes to bulge. I could taste the fear in his aura. I closed my fist, and the rakshasa's neck cracked, filling the cabin with a satisfying echo.

Maybe I wasn't better than my creator.

Maybe I was worse.

Zehan didn't even wince. He simply stared at the crumpled form on the floor and then at the charred tendrils that leaked from my frame and then at me. *All of me.*

My shadows rattled with rage.

"Niya." Zehan lifted his hands that held white wisps of light. He inched closer to me. "You need to relax. You're using magic too fast."

I looked down at my hands. Velvety magic poured out of me like a bottle of sura without a stopper. I moved my hand away from me, like it was a flame too blue to touch. But the shadows continued to stream out. I clenched and unclenched my fist, but it did not help. My magic had always been elusive, not tangible.

"I don't know how to stop." My voice broke. All of Zehan's jabs at me for not training, for not learning about what this magic truly was and could do. My lack of courage was all backfiring.

The shadows covered the entire floor of the cabin and leaked outside. Chills traveled down my spine. Kal and Sunitra were out there. What if they hurt them? I stared at the rakshasa lying motionless on the floor, a pool of black had formed around him.

"Y-you need to leave," I stammered.

He scoffed, taking a step closer. As if my state of panic and the disarray around us was simply another inconvenience. "We both know that won't happen."

The pitch of my voice increased. "They are capable of *anything,* and I can't—" *What if they hurt you?*

"Niya *Jaan,* look at me."

That word tugged at the taut strings of my heart.

"You are the sole master of this power. *Breathe.* Take control of them," he commanded.

I'm trying. I stared into those sharp, witty, beautiful eyes and tried to calm down, but my body shuddered with effort. The shadows relented. My pulse sped up.

Two fingers tilted my chin up, and Zehan dipped his face. I stood still as his lips tentatively brushed mine once, then twice.

He pulled back slightly, his eyes flickering around us, but my focus was entirely on him. I gripped the lapels of his embroidered sherwani and pulled him toward me so our bodies were flush, and our tongues and teeth clashed with vibrant force.

Restraint snapped. And my emotions of worry were replaced with vital need.

Zehan's hands wandered down the sides of my cropped blouse, his fingers brushing the underside of my breasts. The pads of his fingers dug into the bare skin at my waist. A low moan slipped from my lips.

Dying like this wouldn't be so bad.

"You are not going to die." Zehan cupped my cheeks, slowing down the kiss. I hadn't even realized I had said the words out loud.

He nipped my bottom lip one more time before pushing his forehead against mine. His breath was so intoxicating that if I thought hard enough on it, I would be done. He swiped my cheek with his thumb and stepped back. His gaze heated.

My dark tendrils vanished from sight, and it was only then I realized what he had done. *He had distracted me.* Coaxed my magic back into its harness.

Coldness set in, the fibers of my body felt drained. "I'm sorry," I struggled to say through the shooting pain that pounded at the back of my head. "I didn't know that I..." I trailed off. I've never wielded shadows. I didn't even know I possessed them.

"I know," he said softly. White tendrils of magic floated around me, menacingly slow, herding me closer to him.

Zehan waited, like he knew I wanted to say more. To explain. I couldn't hide what this power was or where it came from any longer.

Later. I would explain everything later, but right now, he needed to know.

"Sunitra," I whispered to him, my throat burned with disgust. "The person responsible for the missing souls. It's Sunitra." That's whose face I saw in the smoke.

Every fiber in me wanted to protest. Why would Sunitra do something so horrible? My head pounded harder with each question that arose. But if there was anything I had come to learn in this realm, it was that nothing was ever as it seemed, and no one could ever be trusted.

Zehan's pupils became jagged pieces of coal. His bright threads of power vibrated with a silent scream of betrayal. I opened my mouth, but words failed to form. Naraka's sky suddenly felt too heavy and the ground too light. I swayed forward, falling into his awaiting embrace.

CHAPTER TWENTY-FIVE

W arm, strong arms cradled my body, enveloping me in fierce protection. Heady magic thrummed in my veins. A heavy voice barked frantic commands. I tried to pry my eyes open, face whatever havoc I had imparted on the cabin and demon, but I had no energy left.

Tired. I was so incredibly exhausted, but the repeated hushed murmurs along the edge of my consciousness encouraged me to stay partially aware. Memories from years ago unlocked, featuring a quiet meadow full of magenta hyacinths. Even now, I could smell the potent spicy and sweet floral notes of the tiny buds before viscous shadows turned them into death-filled ash.

More soft whispers of strength, beauty, and sin traveled across my skin.

I know that voice.

I wanted to listen to him, to stay present with him, but the black tendrils of power called to me like a child lost from its mother. One I could not ignore. I felt the magic wrap around my mind, body, and soul, reminding me what I was and who I would become.

Light twisted around me, generous and giving, and for the first time in my very short life, the yearning for more left me.

I was at peace, finally succumbing to the beckoning darkness.

CHAPTER
TWENTY-SIX

Coal and mint tickled the tip of my nose. My lashes fluttered open. I was back in my ornate room, cocooned in silk sheets and a heavy velvet blanket. The curtains had been drawn. The only source of light coming from the soft, glowing flames in the fireplace.

I slowly sat up and rubbed the grogginess from my eyes along with the remnants of what had transpired. The rishi's crumbled cabin, the rakshasa's prideful expression, my tar-colored power that exploded from me like a murder of crows.

My hand went to the side of my head, expecting a wrapping, but the wound had been healed.

"You're still a bit pale," Zehan said gently.

I twisted toward his rumbling voice. He stood at the entrance of my room, standard teacup in hand. Hues of purple circled his eyes, and his hair was disheveled. The night-colored strands pointed in all directions, like he'd been tugging at the roots. And, he was still painstakingly handsome.

Even more so after that damn kiss.

He had kissed me like I was a dance that had just begun. One that still needed to be finished. *It was only to get my magic to calm down,* I reminded myself. It meant nothing at all. It couldn't mean anything beyond what it was.

A *distraction.*

"How long have I been asleep?" My voice was raspy. My hand traveled down to my throat, which ached. Had I been screaming?

"Two days." He said slowly. "And the answer to your unsaid question is yes, you were screaming." His grip on his cup was so tight I thought it would shatter. "I doubt anyone in this palace slept very much."

Two days. I shoved the covers off myself. "Where is Kal?" I looked down at my clothing. I was out of the lehenga. Someone had changed me into a cream salwar kameez with maroon embroidered cuffs. A blush crept onto my cheeks. "And who changed me?"

"He is fine, back to his chirpy self." Zehan smirked. "And I didn't change you. Gauri did. I didn't want demon blood getting all over my sheets."

I rolled my eyes. Did I even care if it *had* been him?

No. Yes. Maybe.

I hugged myself. "And Sunitra?"

The tops of Zehan cheeks reddened. His voice dangerously sharp, "Sunitra has admitted she was involved with the disappearances."

I stood up. "I want to see her." Even though the rishi had procured her face in the smoke, I was in disbelief. I needed to question her myself.

"You should rest. You took a rather hard hit to your head." A muscle ticked in his jaw. "Besides, it's too late. I sentenced her to Kalank without trial, after Abhi is done interrogating her per the agreements of your bargain."

I flinched. "Did she say why she did it?" I hadn't realized she would be imprisoned so quickly. There had to be another explanation.

He set his cup down on the small end table. "No. She only said she did not regret her actions," he said harshly. "Abhi is determined to break her. But I've warned him it won't be easy. Sunitra was my best guard."

My stomach lurched. "What will happen to her?"

"That will ultimately be up to Rati. I finally told her about the souls going missing."

A tingling sensation traveled along the nape of my neck. What motive would Sunitra have to take departed souls? The rakshasa seemed content with the way things were in this realm. She was happy, was she not?

"I just don't understand why she would do this." There had to be a reason.

"She admitted guilt, Niya," Zehan said quietly. "She is responsible for the deaths of ten souls. She is the reason Ruhi is gone. She deserves whatever comes to her."

Renewed vengeance sparked at the mention of that fact. Zehan was right. Whatever her motive was, she had to be held accountable for her crime.

"The rishi, he recited something. At first I thought they were just empty words, but the more I think about them..."I pressed my temples, trying to remember the exact words. "'Bladed bone will take divine power. Return of the right will force the cosmos into a shake. Surrender and love will open the gates. Ensuring darkness and light entwine into bonded fates.' I might be missing a few words," I said. "What do you think they could mean?"

Zehan stepped closer and heat wafted off him. "The rishi is known to speak in riddles. I would not pay any heed to his words. They likely mean nothing of importance. And besides, we have bigger things that happened at that cottage that we need to discuss, courtesan." Zehan moved closer to me.

He is referring to the kiss. I gulped. "Which would be?"

He lifted my chin. "When did the Deva of Naraka give you a boon with his magic?"

I pulled my face out of his grasp. "Where and how I got my magic is irrelevant to our bargain."

"By the Asuras, your stubbornness," Zehan snapped. *"Everything* about you is relevant to me."

My lungs felt like they were encased in iron. Magic flared in my veins, like something ancient had been awoken.

"No more feigned ignorance, courtesan. The power and shadows you wield originally belonged to Yama, the Deva of Naraka."

"I didn't know they belonged to him," I blurted. Shadows pooled into my palms as if they'd sensed a threat.

"After Hans revealed that he and the other Asuras can sense my magic, I suspected my power had come from this realm, but I had no idea it belonged to the actual Deva of Naraka himself."

Yama had been defeated when Rati took over this realm, which was over two centuries ago. How was it even possible that I possessed his magic?

Zehan filled his hand with beautiful white light and clasped my trembling fingers, sending calmness into my veins. "While humans can possess magic, it is rare. I knew you had magic when I saw you at Khoya, but I didn't know where it had come from. I thought perhaps you received your magic through a lesser demon, but when you were able to pass through the gates of Naraka so easily, I became skeptical."

"Wait. You've suspected since then? Why didn't you say anything?"

"I wanted to be sure." He ran a knuckle down my cheek, sending shivers of warmth to my bare toes. "That's why the Asuras can sense your magic, and they likely feel a sense of loyalty to you. I'm surprised Rati hasn't sensed it yet. How did you get it?"

I froze, squeezing my eyes shut.

He slowly tucked a couple pieces of hair behind my ear and then twirled his index finger around the end. "Tell me how you got your magic, Niya Jaan. I need you to trust me."

As he said the words, I realized I did. Completely. Probably more than I should. I pushed my lips together. Eventually, he would find out. This was Zehan. A part of him probably already knew.

I sighed. "After my parents died by King Murkha's men, I was on the streets, with nowhere to go, no way of surviving. So I prayed. I prayed to any gods who might be listening, even though I knew they were gone, because I couldn't accept their absence. I was young, desperate, and had nothing else to do or lose. I went to the ruins of my village, where there was a meadow of hyacinths." My voice dropped into a whisper. "I used to frolic in it as a child, while my parents watched. That day, I spent what felt like ages in the field, meditating and praying to the forgotten devas. I clung onto the hope that they would give me a way forward or take me to their abode. Right when I was about to give up, a young man dressed in a black sherwani materialized."

Zehan was so still I would have believed he was a statue if it wasn't for the subtle rise and fall of his chest.

"Pleased with my devotion, he offered me a boon. The power of trance and truth. I was so shocked that I hadn't even thought to ask who he was or what that magic entailed. He placed his hand on my head, started muttering a chant. Black shadows rushed out of him, flooding the meadow, killing everything in it, aside from me." I wrinkled my nose, remembering the smell of burning flowers. The way the spicy and floral scents had turned rancid. "I was so afraid of what had just occurred that I ran from the meadow, believing it all to be a dream...until the next day when I tried to steal a mango from a food cart, and a woman caught me. The magic pushed out on instinct a second later, and her eyes glazed over and she let me go." I swallowed. "I knew then that whatever had happened was a gift from that mysterious god.

"Baanu ran a small veshyaa in the city's darkest corner. She was well-known for making deals with helpless young girls. She took them in, shaped them into beautiful playthings, and locked them into lifelong contracts."

Zehan stayed thoughtfully silent, but he took a step closer, like he couldn't stand the inches of space between us.

"My mother was a well-respected dance teacher. I had started training from the day I could walk. I performed on the streets for whatever spare coin people tossed at me. My magic helped me, and Baanu noticed. Two of her men stole me away in the middle of the night and brought me to her establishment. I tried to use my magic on them to escape, but I was still new in wielding and became tired too quickly. Baanu realized what I could do, and she threatened to tell everyone and place a ransom on my head, if I didn't agree to work for her."

Zehan's eyes darkened. It was the same thing he had done to me the night he selected me as his Chosen. "Baanu's karma will pay her back. I will ensure it," he promised.

My cheeks warmed. "I was so tired of being hungry and alone and sad. I thought that at least this way, I could do something I loved. I could dance. And so I made a bargain with her." I twisted my fingers. "I served as her dancer and spy, and after seven years, she was to arrange for my passage to Varnasi. She invented the stage name Mohini, and my popularity grew over the years. It was how we ended up in King Murkha's court. I've always known how incredible this power is. But I also knew that if I went against Baanu and King Murhka, and they told the world about it, I would always have to hide."

All because of me. My power. My dangerous gift from the Deva of Naraka.

Zehan's brows shoved together then. "If you've known how powerful you are, why are you so afraid to embrace it? You could control your own fate."

"Because I've seen what my power can do!" I flung my arms into the air. "I had just asked for a boon that would let me survive my fate. I never expected him to give me all his power. I always felt the shadows willing me to do more with it, but I never did. I've held it back because I've witnessed how horrifying and wretched these powers are."

The meadow of hyacinths still haunted me. The destruction. The sheer force of darkness that had swallowed that field. "I didn't know I had that much power until I came here, until I used them on you in Kalank." Tears swelled until my vision became blurry. "Until I killed that rakshasa."

Zehan slid his hands to cup my face. "Your powers do not control you, Niya. It's the other way around."

The tears fell freely. "It isn't me wielding them that I'm afraid of."

"Ah, you're afraid of others forcing you to wield them."

I nodded. "If I don't accept the powers fully and refuse to use them, if I am not capable of wielding them, then how could anyone seek me out for their own gain?" I'd been used as a game piece since the age of twelve. I didn't even know what it was like to not be under someone else's command.

"That is why you wanted to go to Varnasi?" Zehan ran his hands through his hair.

I nodded. "I thought I could start a life. Maybe even open a dance school. Teach girls how to dance for themselves, not for others."

Thoughts rapidly fired off in Zehan's mind as he searched my face. "And you never heard from Yama again?"

I shook my head. "I tried to call him back sometimes, whenever I felt too guilty or wrong using his power. He never answered. I didn't even know who I was calling for."

Zehan brushed his hands down my shoulders and clasped my hands. He stared into the darkest part of my soul. "Having power does not make you bad, Niya. No power is inherently good or bad. It's how we, the wielders, choose to use it. And though the power was originally a boon, it is now *yours*. Not Rati's, and not even this realm's. You've been treating them as separate entities, but really, the power is you."

The power is you.

It all seemed to click into place. Why magic felt stronger here, why the Asuras were drawn to me in a weird way, why I felt so comfortable in hell. The darkness I held designed this entire realm. Yet, knowing this truth did not lessen the weight bearing on my shoulders.

"I was like you once," Zehan said, squeezing my hand again. "Afraid to use my power, afraid to see what it was capable of. I realized that if I didn't, it would hurt more people. I am responsible for so many souls. If I didn't use my ability, it would be a disservice to them. I'd fail them, and I'd fail my fate."

My throat constricted. The fact that Zehan even believed in fate and cared about souls... he was a living contradiction. He was an enigma that I wanted to completely uncover. I stepped closer to him. "What happened at the Rishi's cottage..."

Zehan dropped his hands, causing my skin to become cold. He took a small step back and dug his hands into his pockets. "I promised you that I would take you to Varnasi if you helped me find out who was behind the missing souls. As you have fulfilled your part of our bargain, it is time I uphold my end."

I opened my mouth and closed it. I don't know if what I felt was disappointment or surprise. "You're letting me go?"

Zehan nodded, his eyes flitting to me, then darting to the window as if expecting a creature to soar through it. "I am a man of my word, courtesan. I won't give you another reason to delay what you've been working toward. Nor will I make this harder on us."

Meaning nothing more would happen between us.

Because if it did, we both knew that it would make it harder, maybe even impossible, to not explore whatever this was between us. I was so close to getting my freedom. Why did I feel this pull to him that forced me to abandon my own vows to myself?

"All I ask is that you stay through the Grahan," he added.

The solstice festival was two weeks away. Kal had mentioned it the day we went to see the rishi. "Why?"

"There are some things that can't be described with words, and the Grahan is one of them. I want you to experience it before you go back to Prithvi and resume your human life. I don't want you to have to wait until you're dead to experience the one night in Naraka that makes everything I do worth it," Zehan said. "One more night. Give me one more night to show you what Naraka is at its core, and then you're free."

"You seem confident that I'll wind back up here when I die." I lifted an eyebrow. The dark prince who scared all of Tyaga and the man standing before me now were so at odds with each other.

He gently tapped one of my heavy earrings. My chest fluttered at his boyish grin. "Oh meri jaan, I'm praying for it."

CHAPTER TWENTY-SEVEN

I twirled on the balls of my feet and stepped into a lunge, jabbing my small dagger forward. Kal yelped, leaping back in surprise, causing sand to fly around us.

My face broke into a grin. "That's three."

Ezhil whistled from the side of the sparring circle. "Not bad, courtesan. In another life, you must have been a warrior."

Kal wiped his brow with the back of his arm, his silver blade flickering with the sun's reflection. "I let you have that one."

I snorted. "Keep telling yourself that."

Every morning I dragged Kal or Bidal to spar with me at the back of the fortress. I took a swig of water out of the satchel as Kal wiped his forehead with a damp cloth. At first, I dreaded it, but now, I've found that releasing the pent-up energy helped with managing my new power and the constant tension that radiated between Zehan and me. He came to my room every damn night to maintain appearances and then proceeded to ask me one or two questions about myself before using the Vayu to disappear.

What is your most hated color? What is your favorite fruit? When did you start dancing?

Questions that were personal and easy and thoughtful. Our new friendship unnerved me. Yet, we had silently agreed that nothing more could happen between us, and neither of us had taken any initiative to break that truce.

It didn't help that Zehan had taken it upon himself to train in my new form of magic. *We can't have you leaking darkness all over Varnasi,* he'd said with a sarcastic smirk during our first session.

This morning's lesson focused on forming shapes with shadows. After several attempts, I procured a shadow beast similar to his wolves, but Zehan claimed they looked like fluffy cats.

A quiet fire lit his gaze, his expression remained boyish. "Don't get cocky. Don't forget I'm the weakest link here, being a butler and all." Kal dipped his chin at Ezhil. "Perhaps the commander would be a better partner to spar with."

I opened my palm with the dagger and let the shadows lift so that it circled in the air. "By all means."

Ezhil lifted an eyebrow. "You sure about that, courtesan? The butler is right. I'll have you pinned in thirty seconds."

I smirked, as I retied my dupatta around my waist. "I'd like to see you try, Commander."

Ezhil watched me with a tilt in his gaze. He peered over his shoulder and then shrugged. "Fuck it. Challenge accepted. I'll even use no weapons to make it fair."

I planted my feet into the dirt. Ezhil stripped himself of his weapons and stepped into the circle. "Zehan is going to have my ass."

I laughed. "Not if I win."

"True," Ezhil agreed, "but you won't." He lifted his hand and motioned for me to come to him.

I ran toward the commander, but he blocked my first jab with his forearm and second and third.

He pushed me back and grinned. "That all you got?" He threw a punch.

I ducked. "Not even close," I bit out. I swiped my foot underneath him so quickly that he fell onto his back but quickly rolled to his hands and knees.

We cautiously circled each other as if we toed on thin ice, unsure which step would cause a crack. Ezhil's expression softened as he looked directly into my eyes. "I'm sorry about your friend."

"Thank you," I said. Uncomfortable heat itched beneath my skin. "Have you heard anything about Sunitra?" The question burned the back of my throat.

Ezhil's shoulders tensed. "She is still being held captive by Abhi. He has informed Zehan that she has yet to provide an explanation for her actions despite multiple attempts to break her."

To break her. My sweat turned cold. What had the Asura of Pride done to her? "Did Abhi say why he wanted to interrogate her first?"

"One of the departed souls that was ripped from the realm was from his court. Asuras may be tormenters and executioners, but like Zehan, they are loyal to their subjects. They do not take lightly to others encroaching on their domain."

"I just can't believe it was Sunitra." My gut twisted. I knew I should be relieved that we found who was responsible for Ruhi's death, but something felt off about all of it.

"I admit I was surprised as well. Sunitra is one of the toughest rakshasas I know," Ezhil said, "but she was always challenged by the other guards for being female. Bidal protected her by threatening the others to not mess with her, but that didn't always work. Both Zehan and Bidal knew that. It's why they placed her with you. They knew it would give her a bit of a reprieve from the constant bullying. It isn't common for female demons to learn how to fight, and serving as a royal guard was unheard of. She was made an outcast by many of her kind."

"Perhaps she thought she could gain more power by taking the souls," Kal offered.

Sunitra had admitted to me that she had faced her share of challenges by becoming a royal guard. Bullied or not, it didn't give her the right to hurt other souls for her own gain.

I rotated my wrist. "Something still doesn't add up. The rakshasa that attacked mentioned he had been sent by a male." Sunitra had been knocked out by the demon as well and originally, Zehan was to be with us. Why would anyone arrange for one demon to attack all of us?

"She could have had it organized through someone else," Kal said. "To hide her tracks."

I shook my head. "No, this demon was possessed or under some kind of curse." He had been feverish before my magic took hold of him. "What if one of the Asuras sent him?"

Ezhil frowned. "I agree with you that there could be others involved. But the Asuras…they wouldn't."

"Why are you so sure?"

"Because the Asuras and Zehan may not love each other, but, there is an unspoken agreement amongst them to not kill each other."

I scoffed. "There are no truces between demons. Who else knew that we were going to see the rishi?"

"Bidal and a handful of guards." Ezhil said, eyes widening. "I'll question them myself."

I nodded, flipping my dagger in my hand. "All right, Commander, break over."

I charged at him, and in one second, he twisted my arm behind my back. I flung my head backward, but he ducked out of the way with a grunt, pulling my arm tighter. I switched tactics, kicking backward in between his legs.

He cursed as he pushed me forward so I missed. "Shit, you play dirty, courtesan."

I grinned. We continued sparring until we were both sweaty messes. I knew Ezhil wasn't using his full might and skill, but he gave me the space to fight until my muscles couldn't take it anymore. After losing for the fifth time, I placed my hands on my hips, lifting my face to the sun, trying to catch my breath.

"Your endurance is insane," Ezhil said, bracing his hands on his knees. "Don't you ever give up?"

Don't you tire? Sunitra's words rushed to me. This was supposed to be her training me.

"No," was all I could manage to say before lifting my arms again for the next round.

***

I didn't think anything could outshine the dress from Antam, but the peacock-personified ensemble that I currently wore did a hundred times over.

Silk-printed gold vines and leaves crept up the teal skirt in a chaotic fashion. The matching blouse had a deep V for the neckline and cinched at the back, leaving a two-inch gap from my navel. A gold dupatta twisted across the front and looped into one side of my hip. Even my jewelry had been curated with the outfit in mind. Sapphires and emeralds plated in gold encircled my neck, paired with massive drop earrings that stretched my earlobes down.

"You've outdone yourself, Gauri," I said as she finished pinning up my hair.

She smiled, her kindness was infectious. "You've given me something to do these past few months. I'll be missing you when you eventually depart."

I watched her in the mirror. "If you don't mind me asking...why are you here?" She didn't fit the mold as far as sinners went.

Gauri's expression turned sad. "I had been a seamstress for Queen Oeshi. She is a fearless but ruthless leader. We were not allowed to ask questions, our jobs were to do what we were told. About a decade ago, she asked me to make her ten shawls with poisonous dye." She avoided my gaze. "It was a tedious task to create a fabric where one side keeps you warm and the other kills you. I did as asked and hand-crafted ten magenta wool shawls."

My saliva turned sour, but I stayed silent.

"I was the only one who knew how to put them on without getting the poison on my hands. At the time, a large rebel group threatened her reign, and she had caught ten females who had infiltrated her staff as spies. One by one, she made me put those shawls on each of them. Many of them were my friends." Tears streaked down her face.

I took Gauri's hands in my own. "What happened is not your fault."

"It is." Her wrinkled face sagged. "I made the decision to follow orders instead of choosing the harder path that was the *right* path. My sin was sloth, the decision to not do anything at all."

"How long is your sentence?"

"I died naturally. My body finally running its course. Initially, I was sentenced to Shama's court for a few years for what I did, but when I was told I could enter into my next life cycle, I chose not to. I'm not done repenting my mistake. Zehan, learning who I worked for, gave me a place here at the palace in exchange for intel on Queen Oeshi."

Of course Zehan saw an opportunity for intel and took it. However, It didn't leave a bad taste in mouth like it once would have; Zehan was doing what he needed to keep his realm and people safe.

"I know it may not mean much, but I believe you've repented for your mistakes over and over again." It was clear that the guilt was eating her alive. "You should give your next life a chance. There are others who don't get that."

Like Ruhi. Like the ten souls that Sunitra killed.

Gauri sniffed. "I will consider it. Thank you, Niya."

The old woman pulled me into a hug before I could say anything else. At first I stood awkwardly, not sure how to respond, but slowly I wrapped my arms around her small shoulders.

"Now, now. Enough sad talk." She released me and wiped her eyes with her plain dupatta. "You've got a solstice to attend."

CHAPTER TWENTY-EIGHT

"**Y**ou are not as snarky tonight," Kal said. "Is there a reason for your unnatural silence?"

We weaved through the crowded palace toward the hefty sound of barrel drums. Colorful and vibrant drapes decorated the palace. Excitement swirled in the air and the bounce in everyone's step was hard to miss. Grahan was a big deal here.

"Gauri told me how she ended up here," I stated, explaining my mood.

My mind felt heavy with all that Gauri had revealed, further complicating my emotions about Prithvi and Naraka. The simple truth was that I'd miss this realm. The enchanting landscape, the gray personalities of the departed souls, the gruffness of the rakshasas, and the dark ruler with a benevolent heart.

Kal's grin faded. "Yes, her fate was rather unfortunate. Though the decision to leave now rests with her, she has more than paid her repentance. Naraka doesn't just force a soul to rue their sin; it also encourages them to reflect on their karma."

I let that truth sink it. It was a shame, really. Humans were misguided in believing that Naraka was a place for the worst of humanity. But people have multiple sides to their personalities, characteristics that are good and in some cases, bad.

Another pound of the drum drew my attention. The crowd grew with every passing minute. "What happens at this festival?"

"Has no one told you?" Kal winked at another rakshasa. He had joked and spoken with souls and demons alike as they passed us. He knew everyone here.

I shook my head. Prithvi did not celebrate the Grahan, so I did not know what to expect. Zehan also told me that I am simply a guest at this event, no longer a courtesan, and I wasn't sure *how* to be one. I was always the entertainment; restricted in what I could eat, see, or do.

Two guards opened the throne room's doors, causing a gush of hot wind to brush my face. He placed a hand around my shoulder, beaming down at me as he pulled me into the vast room. "We dance."

The music hit me first. The strings of the sitar and steady pound of drums struck the chords of my soul. Thousands of tiny yellow lights strung across the ceiling, reflecting onto the pale blue-and-white flowers that covered every pillar and every wall.

But it wasn't the music nor the décor that made my lips fall open.

No, it was the concentric circles everyone danced in, the sweeping motions and twirling and organized clapping. I had seen this style of dance before, during the harvest festivals in my village, around a large community fire.

Recognition dawned on me. "This is..."

Women, men, children, and rakshasas danced together with smiles and jest. Some circles were moving clockwise while others counterclockwise, but they all uniformly wove together without obstacle.

"This dance is a tribute to the devas," I finished. My mother had described this event to us as an old tradition, one that was no longer practiced. But her dance teachings stemmed from this style.

"It was and still is." Kal's expression turned serious. "Zehan holds this festival every year to honor them. I think he hopes they still watch and see that not everyone has forgotten them. He remembers the time when humans and devas coexisted. He misses it." The butler suddenly looked decades older in his burnt orange sherwani, which fashioned a raised collar.

Zehan sat on his embellished throne, wearing a forest green sherwani with gold detailing. I drank in the sight of him, with his lopsided grin and gold vintage crown. He regarded his subjects with not just power but compassion.

He caught my gaze. Heat instantly pooled into my core. We never acknowledged our kiss or the way the air thickened every time we stood within a foot of each other. Given my departure tomorrow, I think we both decided not to address the unnamed feeling that raged between us.

We'd figured out who was behind the missing souls. Zehan, true to his word, was granting me my freedom. I'd be in Varnasi, free to do whatever I pleased. And with the help of his training sessions, I'd never have to use the dark power that flowed in my veins again.

Zehan rose from his seat with enough bravado to challenge the Asura of Pride. The orchestra dropped their timbre, like they've done this act with their prince before. Zehan swaggered down the steps, each one marking the earth-shattering pound of the bass drum.

The horde of subjects broke their circles, creating room for their ruler to grace the floor. With one more quick smirk at me, Zehan broke our gaze and spun. The orchestra picked their tempo back up with every instrument joining in to form an intoxicating harmony.

My jaw dropped.

Because the Prince of Naraka, the ruler of the underworld and caller of demons and sinners, began to *dance.*

Zehan glided across the slick floor with wide, powerful strides and perfect posture. His barrel spins had more air than I'd ever seen a man produce and his confidence was so contagious I felt like I could trance every rakshasa in this room with a simple snap. Zehan knew his power and owned it, making him a force I constantly wanted to entrench myself in.

He was *my* Mohini. *My enchanter.*

Baanu created that stage name for me because she said I could use my dance to bring any man to his knees, and now Zehan was doing that exact fucking thing to me.

My heart thrashed in my chest. A need. An urge. A soul-deep want that I could no longer shake. An essence of possessiveness washed over me. I couldn't peel my eyes away from Zehan as he lifted his arms in invitation to his subjects and to the devas above, as if in calling down the entire cosmos. Without hesitation, people joined in, recreating the circles with no care for tomorrow. Fully immersed in the daze of this dance.

Kal laughed. "The look on your face." He shook his head. "Aren't you glad you didn't miss this?"

I elbowed him sharply in the shoulder, and he just laughed again. I looked at the butler, who had become a friend during my short time here. "I'm glad I met you, Kal."

"Likewise, courtesan." Kal patted me on the back. "I'm sure His Highness would make an exception." He gave me a meaningful look. "If you wanted to stay longer."

I gave him a sad smile. The thought of living here was not as tantalizing as it once had been. "I will have my time here," I said, though my gaze reluctantly went back to Zehan. "But I need to live out there."

Varnasi had always been the end goal, and it would remain so.

The circle widened as more dancers joined in, moving closer to us. Zehan appeared mere steps from me and held out his hand with a dare in his expression.

I placed my hand in his, and in one fluid movement, he tugged me into the circle next to him. I stumbled the first round, but halfway through the second, I was comfortable. The style was rhythmic. Meditative. Powerful.

Zehan looked at me with every pivot back, the heat in his expression becoming more pronounced with every beat. His body perfectly followed and formed to the music, and a subtle sheen of sweat glistened on his forehead.

I felt lightheaded, and my breathing turned shallow. But it wasn't from the dancing, or the relentless pounding of the drums, or the stifling heat that was building in the room.

It was him.

My eyes dropped to his mouth and quickly swept back up to meet his gaze. I wanted him. Adrenaline surged in my veins like a tide rising during a full moon.

Zehan's gaze narrowed. Without a word, he clasped my wrist, leading me out of the ornate throne room. The crowd easily carved a path for us as we exited. The souls of Naraka watched us, but no one dared snark or even look sidelong at Zehan.

He led me into one of the many shadowy alcoves. My ears rang from the loud music. He twisted me around so my back was against the concrete wall. He leaned against the opposite wall with a foot propped back against it, creating distance between us. The bastard folded his arms, letting a dark smile grace his lips, and patiently waited. The unsaid challenge hung on a thread between us.

When you're ready to take the edge off, courtesan, just say the words. Any time. Any place.

My cheeks were impossibly hot. My chest bled with need, and my mind teetered on the threshold of right and wrong. Everything was muddled when it came to Zehan. I felt an unavoidable connection to him, and whenever I tried to ignore the link, my insides burned. I wouldn't see Zehan again until this life was over. What was the harm in indulging in whatever sin continued to spark between us? To satiate the building ache between my legs.

I flicked my wrist, causing shadows to yank Zehan toward me. He snapped his fingers, and the opening to the alcove filled with white shadows, blocking us from anyone wandering out of the throne room. My lips clashed with his. His tongue swept in, deepening the kiss further.

Minty. Smoky. Freeing.

I was pushing to go faster, but Zehan moved slowly. *Too slowly.* My hands roamed every inch of him. He pressed me against the wall, trailing heated kisses down the column of my throat.

"Zehan," I groaned as his hands moved down my sides. Slowly, he lifted my heavy skirt, bunching it at my waist, letting the cool air hit my legs. I tugged at the golden clasps of his sherwani with trembling hands. Too much painted silk fabric separated us, and I needed it *all* off.

Zehan chuckled against my mouth. "Patience, courtesan." He bit my lip and tugged slightly. His fingertips brushed my inner thigh. "Do not rush me, or I'll draw this out for hours before you get your release." He shoved the thin cotton to the side and slid his fingers between my legs. He pressed his thumb right at the apex where it ached the most.

A shiver racked my body, and my head fell backward, but Zehan caught it with his other hand. He brought his mouth into the crook of my neck, so his lips were right underneath my earlobe, pressing in my earrings. "And then I'll start over again."

By the Asuras.

He hadn't even really touched me, and I was already unraveling. I only made it to the third clasp of his top, which revealed inked lines, before he slid a long finger into me. Raw carnal hunger filled his expression, setting me ablaze.

I squirmed as he held me at an edge, not giving in fully. I tried to reach for him, but like his dance movements, his shadows smoothly grabbed both of my wrists and placed them above my head.

Oh. My. Devas.

He tugged the string that held my blouse, and the fabric fell forward, revealing my bare shoulders.

"Please," I pleaded with a breathy voice.

His eyes went wholly black as he pumped his finger once. Then twice. "What have I told you about begging?" He ran the tip of his nose along the long column of my neck.

"It's unbecoming." I gasped as he lifted me up so that my legs straddled him, and my back pressed harder into the wall. I gripped his shoulders tightly as he kissed me once again, silencing the moans that tried to escape my bruised lips.

"Precisely." He added another finger to the first, creating even more luxurious pressure. A release began to build in my core. I became drunk on him. His voice. His scent. His *presence.* All of it.

"Centuries," he said in a husky voice. "That's how long I've waited to do this to you."

One of his shadows slid down my arms and caressed my throat, squeezing slightly. I tightened my legs around him, finally managing to tear the fabric.

"Well, this is rather interesting," a voice tutted.

Zehan and I each twisted our head at the same time.

Rati stood there wearing a deep red and white lehenga that had black thread checkered at the borders. Her eyes had a wicked glint to them as she tilted her head at us. Her silver crown glimmered in the lowlight along with a a matching trident, that was almost the same height as her.

I quickly unwrapped my legs, letting my skirt fall back into place. A fresh flush bloomed the tops of my cheeks.

Zehan slowly dropped my legs and stepped slightly in front of me so I could fix myself. "Actually, I find it more interesting that you are here when you don't find the appeal of events like these." Zehan shrugged his hands into his pockets, seemingly unbothered by the fact that the Devi of Naraka just caught us engaging in unspeakable activities.

Rati smiled with her teeth. "Zehan Jaan, you know I'm a fan of the Grahan. Besides, I wanted to extend my personal thank you for capturing the demon responsible for the missing souls. It will give our subjects some much-needed peace."

My back straightened. Rati hadn't bothered to find out who was behind the missing souls. Zehan was the one actively trying to provide peace to the people who lived here.

Rati turned her attention to me. "Your Chosen here was how you figured it out, correct?"

"Niya played a role, yes." Zehan treaded carefully.

The corner of the devi's perfect lips ticked up. "You used her magic. There is much talk about her power amongst the Asuras. They are calling her *meri mara,* from what I hear. The bringer of death."

The Asuras told her. Just like Zehan had suspected. My fingers trembled as anxiety took hold.

"Many humans are born with magic in their veins." Zehan did not let his expression falter.

"Hmm, yes. Though it is quite the gift, is it not? A bit much for a normal human to possess without receiving a boon."

The heat that I had felt moments ago vanished as ice filled my veins. Dark shadows flickered in my palm, and Rati's lips pursed as she caught sight of them.

She knew. She knew that I was not born with this magic. She knew it was gifted to me by a deva. A very specific deva. But how had she figured it out? The only person that knew the truth of my magic was Zehan. I hadn't considered the ramifications of having Yama's power within Naraka. The alcove felt claustrophobic.

"I don't have any interest in this power," I stated. Once I was in Varnasi, I wouldn't need it any longer. I'd bury it deep and let the threads of black shadows be forgotten.

"It doesn't matter if you did or didn't." Rati's eyes bore into me. "Zehan did."

Zehan visibly stiffened next to me. Rati looked positively delighted.

I narrowed my gaze at the devi. "What do you mean?"

"Oh, did he not tell you? You weren't just here to help him with a petty mystery." Rati feigned surprise. "He brought you here to kill me."

CHAPTER TWENTY-NINE

I blinked, unsure if I should laugh at the absurdity. "That's ridiculous."

"Is it?" Rati asked. "Have you not wondered why *you*, out of all his Chosen, are still here? The other Chosen barely spent any time here. They were here one morning, martyred the next." She said this with such melancholy that my insides twisted. "Although I can't imagine why he would try so hard to overthrow me when his magic, his being, his very existence is because of me."

Martyred. Unease trickled through me, the sensation similar to cold water slowly dripping onto the top of my head. That couldn't be true. Zehan had said that he had offered a similar deal to his other Chosen. That they were now in Varnasi. Safe and living their new lives. "His other Chosen are—"

"Where they belong," Zehan interrupted. His eyes gave me a cold, harsh warning. I pushed my lips together. Rati didn't know they were in Varnasi. Or was it possible Zehan had lied about what really happened to them altogether?

Rati chuckled, not bothered by Zehan's interruption. "You're the key to his freedom. *You* are part of a prophecy he has been trying to fulfill for decades."

"Prophecy?" I twist my head sideways to look at Zehan. "What is she talking about?" Strands of his hair were wayward, a mark of my fingers tugging at the roots. He didn't meet my gaze, keeping his stony expression locked on Rati.

Rati answered. "Long ago, the rishi foretold a prophecy that a girl with unknown magic in her veins would be the one to break the curse I placed on Zehan, freeing him from this realm. But she would have to do so willingly." Rati lifted a long finger to trace a sharp nail down my cheek. Disgust rolled within me. "Who would have thought a lackluster courtesan from a mediocre kingdom would be the determinant of his fate."

"That can't be true." I shook my head. I would have known. Zehan would have told me.

"Who told you?" Zehan's voice held a dangerous edge.

My next exhale froze. *No.*

He couldn't be asking that question. If he was, that meant Rati spewed the truth. The whispered words the rishi spoke... Was that the same prophecy Rati referred to? Zehan had dismissed them as riddles, but what if that was because he was trying to hide the fact that he needed me to kill a devi?

The throne room thumped with bass. The laughter, chatter, and shouts of glee drowned into static noise that hurt my ears. Revelation made my head spin. I ran through our conversations over the past few months, had they all been a lie? Was he even going to let me go to Varnasi?

"I have my ways." Rati shrugged. "You should know better, Zehan Jaan, to be so *loose* with your conversations. You know that I have spies *everywhere.* I had always wondered why you created the concept of your Chosen. I thought it was a silly pastime, but then I came to learn you've been selecting them to see if they have a certain type of magic to supersede my throne."

I felt like I was falling.

Rati beamed. "Don't be too hard on yourself, Niya dear. You were not the only one who was fooled. Zehan is a master charmer."

The amount of breathable air in this alcove diminished. How had I not realized? I knew Zehan used his shields against me. But I hadn't really tried to use my magic on him again, especially after our truce.

I clamped down on the rising humiliation. "That is why everyone was so surprised that you kept me here," I stated. *The Chosen he decided to keep.* All of the Asuras had said that repeatedly. Zehan claimed they were in Varnasi, but what if that was all a ruse? What if they were martyred like Rati said because they didn't have the magic he was looking for?

Zehan reached for me, but I took a step back. His shoulders trembled. "I wasn't planning on following through with the prophecy."

"But there is a prophecy," I said. He originally brought me here to take Rati's place and chain me to this realm like he currently is. He'd repeatedly lied to me.

Rati scoffed. "Do you really expect us to believe that? You were testing and assessing her magic all these weeks by having her act as your courtesan. Her assistance in finding those behind the souls was a way to gauge her abilities."

Zehan's silence felt like a jeweled choker being fastened too tight. It was all part of a grander plan.

Everything now made sense.

The constant intrigue with my magic, the push to use it more, the series of tests with the Asuras. It was all helping him figure out if I had enough power to take down a devi.

Because my power belonged to the Deva of Naraka, I was the only one who could rightfully take his place. Bile gushed up my throat.

Rati thumped her trident on the floor. "I admit I felt an odd draw to you when I first met you, but I passed that off as you being human. But then, I learned you were able to use your magic on the Asuras, and you destroyed the rishi's cottage with remarkable *shadows*. I realized that you must be the one Zehan has been seeking all these decades."

Decades. Zehan had been working on this plan for *decades*. Before I had even reincarnated onto Prithvi. I shook my head, not wanting to believe it, but unable to find any way to dismiss it.

I turned to Zehan, his expression grim, yet his features still so beautiful. "Were you actually planning to ever let me go? Or was that all part of the ruse so I'd continue to do your bidding?"

He reached for me. "Niya, you have to understand—"

I took a step back, so his fingertips grabbed air. "Answer the question," I snapped. "When you first brought me here, when you first made the bargain, were those just empty words?"

Zehan swallowed. "Yes."

Was that why he had been flirting with me all these weeks? Had it all just been some sick way of keeping me here willingly?

I laughed bitterly. "It's my fault. I knew you only wanted me for my power but I convinced myself that you were a different kind of ruler."

The realization stung like a bee defending itself. Zehan was no different than Baanu, King Murkha, or Queen Oeshi. People in power always played for their self interests.

"These theatrics bore me." Rati waved a hand lazily at us, yet her eyes gleamed with satisfaction. "Come now, courtesan. I haven't got all night."

I froze. "What?" I would not be going anywhere with her.

Rati smiled with her teeth. "You don't actually think I came here to simply tell you that Zehan brought you here to kill me and then leave, right? Your current life is forfeit. As long as this magic swirls in your veins, you are a danger to those around you, a liability."

Numbness spread into my limbs. Rati saw me as a threat and only one thing would make her see otherwise. "Then take my powers from me," I said quickly. "All I ask is for my freedom."

"No." Zehan paled. "Niya, wait, use your power on me. See that I am telling you the truth."

I ignored him. "I don't want the shadows."

The power in my veins twitched with aggravation. To be rid of the beckoning shadows would be a saving grace. No one could ever use them against me again. And once I was in Varnasi, I wouldn't have a need for these powers anyways.

Rati paced in front of me. "If only it were that simple. A boon given by one deva cannot be outright stolen by another deva unless there is a vessel by which to transfer the power. I do not have a vessel, so my option is to take you as my prisoner or kill you outright." Red waves of light pooled at her feet.

Shadows fought to come out of my hand in protest. "No," I said, burying the magic. This was no time to test power that I knew could potentially harm every single soul dancing in the adjacent hall. "I am not your subject, nor am I even here by my own sin. I was Chosen by him." I didn't dare look at Zehan. That would only sting. "I belong on Prithvi."

Streaks of bloodred light circled around my feet. Fear and anger gripped the sane parts of my soul. The thought of never being able to leave here closed in. My vision blurred.

Zehan stepped in front of me, using one hand to shove me back. A flare of white left his frame in ripples. "Your fight is not with her. It's with me. I'm sure we can come to some sort of arrangement." I almost let out a hopeless laugh. We both knew he couldn't act against her.

How long would she keep me as her prisoner? Would she just wait until my soul truly departed from my current existence? No, I wouldn't settle for new ownership. "What if I swear to never use my magic again in exchange for a boon?" Rati was a devi. She could still hand out boons at will. "Then I would be bound to not use my magic against you."

Rati tilted her head, her red hues fading. "An interesting proposition. But boons are boring, and I have something better. You will go through the Asura Trials. Pass, and you'll be released from this realm and never allowed to return, even after death."

Of course Rati would dismiss the idea of a boon. It was too simple for her. Rati didn't care about power because she knew that no one could challenge her. She was the last standing devi in this realm after all.

"Don't do this," Zehan pleaded. His voice caressed my spine like the softest feather.

The idea of never seeing Zehan again stung more than it should. Passing the Asura Trials would not be an easy task, but at this point, a life that wasn't free was one I no longer wanted to live.

"I agree to your terms."

"Wait, I'll do anything you want." Zehan's shoulders vibrated with suppressed anger.

I whipped my head sideways to look at him.

The pained look on his face did something to the fury that had built a wall around my heart. A part of me wanted to scream in protest, and the other part wanted to shove him into the concrete wall that he had just pinned me up against.

I ignored the emotions raging through me, and let logic take over. Zehan needed me to stay alive because I was his ticket out of here. I needed to think about the best option for me.

And that was partaking in the Asura Trials.

"This *is* what I want, Zehan Jaan." Rati smiled again and lifted her three-pronged staff and pointed it at us.

Zehan didn't wait, he waved a hand and ghostly white light gathered in front of us like a shield. He couldn't use it against Rati, but he could use it to protect us. Rati's brows lifted in surprise. He slipped a hand around my waist. "Now would be a good time to use your magic, courtesan. Hold on to me."

"And what is your plan?" I hissed. I moved out of his hold. It wasn't like we could whisk away to somewhere Rati couldn't follow. His light covered us from her sight. "It's not like we could get very far." As long as I possessed this magic, Rati would find a way to control me. I would never escape her clutches.

I always thought I could change my fate and stop being played as a pawn. But perhaps, it was time to accept defeat and admit that a pawn was what I'd always be.

"I'm working on it," he said tightly. I could practically see his mind assessing each option and consequence.

"I'd listen to the girl, Zehan Jaan. You'll only make this harder than it needs to be," Rati said, watching us with equal parts amusement and annoyance. "There is nowhere for you to hide, and what can an untrained, common courtesan do? Your attempts to overthrow me have been futile since the beginning. This realm is and will remain *mine.*"

I grated my teeth. Every time she called him *Jaan,* I wanted to claw out my own ears.

Zehan yelled, crumpling to the floor.

"Zehan!" I knelt beside him. His shield of light dropped. "What are you doing to him? I already agreed to do your stupid trial."

Rati blinked with surprise, but then quickly masked it. "This is not me."

Zehan cried out again, the sound cutting through me like a newly sharpened dagger.

I lifted my hands again to suffuse the pain with shadows. "The missing souls," I whispered. The shadows glided over his form, coaxing the pain away.

Another soul was being ripped from the realm.

Which meant...Sunitra wasn't the killer. Or she hadn't been working alone. The departed souls here were still at risk. Someone was still targeting them.

"Interesting," Rati said lazily, appearing to be unbothered by the new development. "I thought we had closed that chapter, but apparently not." She looked down her perfectly long nose, pointing her staff at me. "It is no longer your problem." Warm tingling fell over me, and then my fingers started to fade, turning into shimmering translucent droplets.

Zehan yelled something, gripping my hand to hold me close, but it was no use. Rati was using the Vayu to whisk me away, and I had no idea how to stop it. I was translucent, like a shining ray of sun. There one moment, gone the next.

I blinked, and Zehan's crumpled form was replaced by blackened blood-smeared floors. His cries of pain were replaced by distant screams.

Rati stared coldly at me through iron black bars. "Welcome to the real hell, courtesan."

I was back in Kalank, only this time, I had no idea if I was ever getting out.

CHAPTER THIRTY

The cold that took residence in the dungeon had turned the tips of my fingers white. My head rested against one of the bars of my tiny square cell. On one side, there was a twin-size cot with a bundle of dust-filled blankets, and on the other, a brown chamber pot that I was pretty sure had never been cleaned. It reeked, placing me in a constant state of nausea.

Food and water came at odd intervals. The only light was a single fire torch at the entrance of the corridor. It would be easy to lose my sanity in this constant state of solitude, with only my sinful thoughts for comfort.

Rati had dropped me off here with no mention of when the Asura Trials would take place. An error on my part. I should have specified when I wanted to take part in the trials. For all I knew, the Devi of Desire could keep me here until my soul decided to become one of the departed.

A famed courtesan forgotten in the depths of hell.

I knew escape was not possible, yet I had repeatedly tried to break through the lock on the cell with my shadows. Repeatedly, I threw them at the iron bars, hoping they would sear through the metal while also knowing they wouldn't since the bars were warded against magic.

I shifted to rest my forehead on my knees. Silent tears slid down my face, and my sniffles bounced off the walls in soft echoes. My beautiful dress was now streaked with grime and whatever remnants lingered on this infested floor.

I felt like I was falling. I was a fool for letting Zehan worm his way into my heart. Something no one had ever done in the twelve years since my parents died.

I had closed myself off from forming any new relationships for a reason. Grief was hard. I knew that better than most. Whether in death or drift, losing someone you had formed any kind of bond with cut deep.

"I hadn't pegged you as someone who gave up," a raspy voice cut through the drowning silence.

I squinted at the cell diagonal from mine. The previously still lump shifted. It moved into the small shred of firelight that sliced through their cell. My gaze latched on their horns.

"Sunitra?" I crawled towards her, letting my skirt drag behind me. Bruises and cuts scarred her arms. One of her eyes was swollen shut. "What happened to you?"

Sunitra laughed morbidly. "This is courtesy of Abhi. I was brought here yesterday on Rati's request, shortly before you arrived."

Unease pricked me like a clasp snagging on skin. "Why haven't you said anything?"

Sunitra shrugged. "I woke up a little while ago. Didn't think you would want to chat to the person who stole your friend from you. But my existence will end soon. Might as well make what amends I can. I take it the devi found out about Zehan wanting to use you to fulfill the prophecy?"

My stomach hardened. "You knew?" Did everyone know about this damn prophecy? Kal? Ezhil? Bidal? Were they all just helping Zehan gain his freedom at the sacrifice of mine?

Sunitra nodded once. "Zehan told a select few of us his plans. I understood. An eternity here with no one like you can be lonely."

I blinked at the rakshasa. Zehan trusted her enough to tell her about the prophecy, about his desire to *leave* them. Now seeing her here behind bars for a heinous crime...it didn't sit right.

"Why did you do it?" I asked. I had thought Sunitra was different from other rakshasas. "You knew how much Ruhi meant to me."

The rakshasa winced. Barely. If I hadn't been looking right at her features, I would have missed it. "I didn't have much of a choice," Sunitra answered in a monotone.

"We always have a choice," I shot back.

"If that was the case, why are you here?" she asserted.

"That's different."

"Is it?"

"My choices have not led to souls *ceasing* to exist."

"I will not apologize for what I've done," she said stubbornly.

"I'm not looking for an apology, just an explanation," I said sharply. The Sunitra I had come to know would never willingly hurt others. She wouldn't have just stood by and watched a soul be destroyed.

"It was those souls or my family."

I frowned. "What are you talking about?"

She dug a fingernail into the ground. "My family lives on the outskirts of Naraka. My parents died when I was young, leaving me responsible for two sisters and a brother. Months ago, I received an anonymous missive instructing me to steal a bone dagger from the prince's art collection."

Curiosity trickled through me. I tilted my head. "You mean the Ashti?" That had been the blade I admired when Kal gave me a tour. He had pointed it out. *It is said to be carved out of a deva's bone and possess untold power.* But why would someone want to steal it, and how did that connect to the missing souls?

Sunitra nodded. "It stated if I didn't follow their instructions, they would hurt my siblings. At first, I thought it was one of the other guards pranking me, so I ignored it. Being one of the few females, I didn't want to make a fuss, so I kept my mouth shut and didn't tell Bidal or Zehan. Another two missives arrived the following week with the same handwriting and request, but I burned them. And then"—Sunitra took a deep rattly breath—"my youngest sister went missing. My brother searched everywhere for her." Her voice broke on the last word.

I clutched the loose fabric of my skirt, scrunching it tightly in my fist.

"Another missive arrived, except this time, the request was to bring a departed soul to the outskirts of the village *alive* in exchange for my sister. I didn't know what to do, I couldn't just take anyone. So, I sought out someone who didn't have very many friends. I saw a man leaving the rishi's cottage and knocked him out." Sunitra let her forehead rest against the bars. "My sister returned home the next morning, shaken up but not harmed."

"Did she see her captor?"

Sunitra shook her head. "That was the first question I asked her, but she had been blindfolded and bound the entire time. After that incident, the missives started to appear like clockwork with requests for more souls. Those souls didn't die by my hand, but I'll never forgive myself for the part I played in their deaths."

"I'm sorry." I couldn't use my magic on her to see if she was telling the truth, but her words did not feel like lies. "I believe you." It was an impossible choice. If I had someone I cared about enough, I would have made the same one. "Why didn't you tell Zehan?"

"I couldn't risk losing my siblings again. Whoever sent me the missives also prepared for my eventual capture. They said if it were to happen, I was to take the full blame. They said they would know if I didn't." Sunitra shrugged.

"It has to be someone inside the palace then." How else would they have so much information and intel on Zehan and his guard?

"Yes. I've been trying to find out who but never got close to deciphering who the missives were from. Though my time is running out."

"Maybe your silence isn't fully necessary anymore."

Sunitra snapped her head up, her nostrils flared. "What do you mean?"

My voice dropped. "Another soul was ripped from the realm."

"Shit," Sunitra clipped. "That means whoever is behind these attacks has already found another demon to do their dirty work."

Dread curled in my chest. "Or they've just decided to do it themselves. You should plead your case during your trial. I understand you're afraid of what will happen to your siblings, but Zehan will protect you." If I could trust anything about Zehan, it was his care for the people and creatures here.

"I could give the same advice to you," Sunitra said.

"No." Shadows flickered around me. I wasn't *his* subject. I wasn't his anything. "Zehan won't protect me. He only wanted to use me for his own gain"

Sunitra shook her head. "Do you really believe that?"

"Yes." I paused. *No.* I closed my eyes, hoping that when I opened them, I would be back in my beautiful room where I could see the sun and moon greet each other. I wanted all of this to just be a horrible nightmare. "I don't know what to believe anymore," I admitted. "I don't even fully understand what the prophecy means."

"It foretells Rati's ultimate destruction." Her voice sounded brittle and faint. "A few decades ago, Zehan learned of a prophecy claiming a mortal girl would possess the power to take Naraka's throne. As long as Rati is alive, Zehan must follow her orders. He knew it was unlikely he would find the one the prophecy spoke about, but he still tried, which is why he created the entire concept of his Chosen. He would use it as an excuse to assess them with his magic, and then he would send them to Varnasi. He had been trying to see you perform for years, but Baanu and King Murkha always pulled you out of the performance." Sunitra's expression turned solemn. "He was suspicious that Mohini, whoever she was, had magic, and I think he got the confirmation he needed as soon as you entered this realm, but after getting to know you these past weeks, I think he had a change of heart."

You're not the only one chained to a fate that you're trying to escape. His soft words came rushing back.

I had been rash when Rati revealed Zehan's lies. Perhaps too rash, but it was too late now. I couldn't take my actions back. "It doesn't matter now. The rishi's words can't be taken as complete truth." He had shown me Sunitra's face in the smoke as the person behind the missing souls, but that was only part of the story. The killer was still out there.

I still could hear Zehan's anguish in those final moments before Rati brought me here. Had he recovered? There were so many unsaid words between us, and now I may never get the chance to say anything to him ever again.

My spiraling thoughts shattered by the clanking sounds of heavy chains. Three guards approached my cell, one with thick shackles, another with a bundle of bloodred cloth, and the third with a tray of what was undoubtedly yesterday's leftovers.

They dropped all three things right outside my cell just within arm's reach.

"Eat, get clean, put the clothes and shackles on," one of them grunted. I recognized his grotesque features and foul mood. *Oman.* "It's time for you to finally face what you deserve, whore."

"Do you really think it's wise, Oman? To threaten one of Zehan's Chosen."

Oman pounded his large fist against the bars. "Keep talking, and we'll see how long you really last in this cage, Sunitra. I'll take being a bad brother over being a disgrace to your race any day."

Sunitra glared at the demon with enough hatred to disintegrate the demon where he stood. I eyed the rakshasa with my own loathing, not letting his monstrous features instill terror.

Oman spat on the ground. "Her Highness demands your audience. You have fifteen minutes, whore. And unless you'd rather me come in there and dress you myself"—he smelled the air and his pupils dilated—"I'd finish up in ten."

The other two rakshasas snickered.

I clicked my tongue. "I assume monsters have no sense in offering gentlemanly privacy." I reached for the clothing that was flimsier than any dress I had worn in Khoya. Two silver payals were also wrapped in white cloth.

"You assumed right." The rakshasa with the horn in the middle of his head flashed his teeth in a wide smile, causing disgust to lick down my spine like an uncomfortable bead of sweat.

My fingers trembled as I changed. The shadows wanted to savagely attack the rakshasas' faces, but I held them at bay. They whistled and laughed, but I didn't let their jeering humiliate me. They would meet their end.

Everyone had to face their fate at some point. And right now, it was my turn.

CHAPTER THIRTY-ONE

Oman tugged me towards my trial like an animal on a leash. The blood-rusted chains were connected to a steel choker around my neck, the weight causing my shoulders to hunch over. My bare feet shuffled along the gritty gray floors, my payals ringing out with every forceful yank.

I glowered at the demon's back. If my wrists weren't bound, I would have coerced him with magic to stab himself. "I'll never understand how you and Bidal are brothers."

Oman looked over his shoulder. "Believe it, whore. Bidal is loyal to a fault. He forgets whom this realm was built for. I do not."

We entered a vast circular room that was domed at the top and fully lit with roaring fire torches. Rati sat above us on a massive throne that was encrusted with gemstones the shades of the Naraka's sky. She wore a midnight-blue lehenga that was paired with a bright-silver dupatta.

She smiled sweetly at me, making my insides churn. "There, you see, Zehan Jaan? I told you I'd take good care of her."

My eyes immediately swept to him.

He wore a black sherwani with white-and-maroon accents. He gripped the armrest of his chair so hard that his knuckles turned white. He assessed every inch of my face and body.

I blinked away the tears. I wouldn't give Rati the satisfaction. I didn't want her or anyone to know that I had missed him, that being apart from him, even for just a few days, had impacted me.

The nine Asuras were seated in their own thrones. I met each of their gazes before locking in on Hans, who was no longer in his obscure wraithlike form, but a human one. The giveaway was his rust-colored eyes. *You all betrayed me,* I spoke into my mind, wondering if he could hear it. They were the ones that revealed my powers to Rati. Who else could it be? No one else knew about my abilities aside from Zehan's close confidants.

Do not be fooled, courtesan. We Asuras did not betray you. Rati has other ways of gathering information. It wasn't Hans who spoke, but a female voice I heard in my head.

An Asura with snakelike features and long plaited black hair stared down at me with such intensity it made the hair on my arms rise. *Nadi.* The Asura of Fear. She was the only Asura I hadn't yet seen in the flesh, and she held the same mind reading capability as Hans.

Nadi speaks the truth, meri mara. Hans gave me the barest of nods. *You've come far with your magic.*

The other Asuras held expressions of indifference. Could they all hear what he had said to me? I spoke back to him mind-to-mind. *You knew whose magic I had this entire time. Why keep it a secret?*

As soon as you crossed the veil, we felt you but could not intervene. Our power is limited. We had to let you tackle and come to terms with your fate on your own. You are more powerful than you believe, meri mara.

I wanted to yell at him and his riddles. Why couldn't they speak in plain terms? But now was not the time to process the hidden message behind his words. I lifted my chin, refusing to cower before hell's leaders.

Rati stood and placed both hands on the balcony to look down at me. Assess me, more like it. "Leave us," she said to the beasts beside me.

Oman bowed with a slick grin. "I hope they eat you alive, whore," he muttered in a low voice. He threw the chain a few feet away. The weight caused me to fall onto my hands and knees.

Zehan growled with sheer wrath.

White smoke wrapped around the demon's torso first and then spread to his limbs. Oman clawed at his throat. Zehan watched with no remorse as the rakshasa fell to his knees so that we were eye level.

"Apologize," Zehan whispered in quiet rage.

I swallowed. I had thought he couldn't use magic here. But Rati shifted in her chair to become more comfortable, simply observing. Not even a flicker of regret crossed her features.

Oman gurgled a response as black liquid dribbled from the corners of his mouth. It sounded like an apology, but Zehan didn't pull back his magic. Seconds passed, and no one made a move to stop Zehan as his magic forced Oman to choke on his own blood.

I should have stopped Zehan from blackening his soul for me, but I didn't. I relished the small glimpses when he completely lost all control over the good in him.

The rakshasa fell with a heavy thud to the ground.

"You two, take him," Zehan commanded, though they weren't his servants. "And make it known to the rest of your guard that anyone who touches or *looks* at her with ill intent faces a worse fate."

The rakshasas had the decency to look afraid as they nodded quickly. One took the dead demon's arms and the other, the legs, and they hobbled out of the room.

Zehan twisted his head. "Release her, Rati." His smooth voice rippled through the room with checked fury. "End whatever sick game this is. I will send her back to Prithvi and make it so she will never be able to step foot into this realm or use her magic against you. Hell, I'll even commit to being your whore. *Release. Her. Now.*"

No. My body trembled as the shadows communicated they also hated the thought. But they couldn't come out, not when the chains remained fastened on my wrists.

Rati tsked. "You've grown soft, Zehan Jaan. It's customary for every soul that passes through Naraka to face some sort of trial."

"*A* trial, not *the* trial," Zehan argued.

Rati smiled with her sharp teeth. "Welcome to the Asura Trials, Niya."

My blood turned cold. This was my stage, but it was their show. I lifted my chin. "And what does the trial entail," I said as evenly as possible. These trials were reserved for people who had passed on Prithvi but had committed sins that were far too great for Zehan to pass judgment on, but I wasn't a departed soul.

Rati's brilliant white teeth glinted in the lowlight. "One final dance, courtesan, or *Mohini* as they call you. That is the price of your freedom. I want to see your soul laid bare. You dance for us right here, right now until the last fire torch winks out."

The shadows rose within me to take a stand, but they hit the invisible wall created by the shackles. It seemed simple, but I knew it was a trap. The problem was that I wasn't seeing the door to get out.

"One dance," I repeated, "in exchange for my freedom. What happens if I fail?" Rati had told me when I agreed to partake in the trials what my prize would be, but she never clarified what would happen if I lost.

"If you stop before the last flame flickers, you forfeit the rest of your human life to me, serving as *my* courtesan."

The shackles became heavier.

"That is absurd—" Zehan started angrily.

"Ah," Rati cut him off. "Do not force me to make the deal sweeter, Zehan Jaan. Look at it this way, if she loses, I'll grant you visiting rights."

Zehan pursed his lips. White light escaped in frenzied wisps around him.

My anger had diminished after my conversation with Sunitra. He wanted to use me to gain *his* freedom. Zehan should have told me the truth, but I understood why he did what he did. We both essentially wanted the same thing.

"How can I be sure that you haven't magicked the fire torches to stay on indefinitely?" I couldn't dance forever, but I wouldn't put it past Rati to not make me try.

"Clever girl." Rati waved her hand, a small lamp made from red clay appeared in front of me on a dais. A cotton wick dipped in oil sat on the edge of the bowl. The end had a bright flickering flame. "Dance until the diya burns out then."

Rati likes to play games. Zehan's original warning rang through my mind. *She always saves a twist for the end.* Those wicks were not like a regular matchstick that would quickly fizzle out, they could go on for minutes, even a full hour depending on how long the cotton wick was.

"Are you open to adjusting the terms of our deal?" I asked.

Zehan tensed. The Asuras around the circular balcony shifted in their seats. It was a risk to bargain in my position, but Rati enjoyed the game, and negotiating was part of it.

Rati ran her long fingers through her hair. "I'm listening."

"These shackles must come off for me to dance."

"Obviously."

"I will need music."

"Zehan will play his oud."

I blinked but barreled on before I could linger too long on how that new fact made my heart melt. "Sunitra is to be released from your hold, as she is not the one who killed those souls. Someone has been blackmailing her." I looked meaningfully at Zehan.

The Asuras and Zehan all exchanged looks.

Rati paused but then said, "I'll consider it."

I knew it was a slim chance she would agree, but I wanted the others to know that departed souls were still at risk. I stared at Rati with all of my resolve. "And"—my voice dropped—"you release Zehan from his bind to Naraka and to *you*."

A muscle in Zehan's jaw twitched. I was angry at him for his lies, but I couldn't hate him enough to keep him in his horrid, cursed fate.

"We like to play, I see." Rati's brows lifted. "That's quite a steep bargain, courtesan."

I shrugged, holding back the shudder that wanted to rack my body. "I have nothing else to lose."

Being a courtesan had made me observant. Through my few interactions with Rati, it was obvious she got high off the stakes of the deals she made. She enjoyed watching people's hopes and dreams shatter into tiny shreds of glass by their feet. Her soul was charred and blackened by her own broken love. She wanted to make sure those around her were constantly grieving the loss of something or someone, just like her.

Which was why I was risking everything I had. I was betting that she wouldn't be able to refuse a gamble like this.

Silence filled the large hall. The Asuras watched Rati carefully, while Zehan willed me to finally look at him. Pain, anger, and something else that I refused to name glared back at me. I shoved it all away, waiting for the Devi of Naraka to make her decision.

"Very well. I agree to your terms." Rati raised her hands as if she were inviting the abandoned devas to come down and join us. The shackles vanished off me. "Begin."

I shook out my hands, readying myself while simultaneously realizing I hated that summoning word. Like I was a pet to be controlled.

Focus on the trial. I had done this a million times. What was one more dance? Even if it struck an arrow through my remaining dignity.

Rati nodded at Krod. The Asura of Anger bowed his head and stood. He winked at me with arrogance and lifted his hands in concentration.

I jolted as the edge of the circular floor roared to life with flames. The stone below my bare feet suddenly became too warm. I backed up, but the entire stage glowed like hot embers.

"Oh," Rati said with mock surprise. "Did I forget to mention that small detail of the trial? Your dance floor will shift with each Asura's sin."

Well, fuck.

The trap was laid out well indeed.

CHAPTER THIRTY-TWO

My head hammered wildly. What in nine hells kind of trial was this?

Krod lifted his hands like he was directing an orchestra and flames encircled me, producing suffocating heat. His sin manifested through fire so that is what the stage became.

My soles began to burn. *This was madness.* I attempted to bring the shadows forth into my palms, but they rebelled against me.

I was in over my head. Perhaps I should surrender now.

The taut sound of strings drew me from the rising panic in my bones.

Zehan's fingers oscillated over the strings of a small mahogany instrument. His fingers moved like his footwork, rapt with precision. He played as if he were in my head, knowing the song I wanted to dance to.

Zehan wasn't an amateur with the oud, he was a fucking master.

His night-personified eyes lifted to meet mine. *Deep breaths,* he seemed to say. *Dance like it's just you and me."* Eyes on me.

The room and sound and everything around us suddenly vanished. I inhaled and exhaled. *Show them why they call you Mohini.* He dipped his chin.

Another dance. That's all this was. Another deva-forsaken *dance.*

I bowed from the waist creating a large circle and launched into a set. After years of guiding the dance, I let it guide me. The floor became increasingly hot. Sweat beaded down my exposed back and belly. One breath after the next, I continued to gracefully skate on bare feet, using fast footwork so my feet didn't scald completely. It was the same tactic I used in Khoya when practices carried on into the middle of the day.

Rati lazily sat back on her throne. She had been driven into a darkness that she could not leave, no matter what light was placed on her. The situation I was in now was entirely my fault. I had agreed to the devi's terms knowing she would likely play dirty.

The stage pivoted, shifting from fire to shimmers. Gold liquid cascaded across the floor. I let my eyes travel up to the Asuras seated along the edges as I twirled. Lobha had a small smile on his face, and his expression gleamed at the dramatic color that adorned the floor. *Greed.*

The slimy sludge of gold was impossible to move in. It reminded me of the wet sand Baanu made us spin through when she wanted to challenge us. Perhaps all those brutal practices had been in preparation for this exact moment.

On and on it went. Each Asura's sin presented itself as a dancer's worst obstacle. Shoka's sin of despair caused freezing water to pelt down at a vicious pace. My fingers and toes became numb. Shama used his influence to horrifically slow down Zehan's pace, forcing intense strain on my muscles as each pose had to be held for a full count of eight. The Asura of Pride created winds that made the slick slips of fabric that had been plastered to my body from the gold liquid flap away from me, leaving little to the imagination.

My calves ached and my arms strained as the dance went on for what had started to feel like eternity. Issa, the Asura of Envy, tossed back the rest of her sura and then viciously threw the glass onto the stage. Shards of glass shattered onto the stage.

Until the wick burns out.

I glanced at the small diya. It was two-thirds gone. I bit my cheek to stop my scream as the sparkling glass dug into the bottoms of my feet. It was a hundred times more painful than Baanu's leather whip.

Zehan's anger radiated through the sporadic strings of his instrument as smears of crimson joined the leftover gold. His shadows turned into wolves at the front of the stage, next to the oil lamp that toyed with me. A sign of solidarity.

A reminder this dance was the embodiment of my repentance.

This is ultimately what Rati wanted. For me to be tortured through something I authentically loved. My steps became frantic; my movements turned desperate. Tears mixed with sweat ran down my cheeks. It was only Zehan's strings of melancholy that urged me to continue when Nadi shrouded the stage in dark shadows, making it impossible to see. Each sharp twang of Zehan's oud reminded me what was at stake.

My freedom. *And his.*

I couldn't fail.

Despite what you believe, you are not a prisoner here. I had thought that being physically stuck within the confines of Naraka was imprisonment, but now I realize Zehan had given me freedom all along.

And I had taken those small liberties for granted.

Rati eyed the diva that mocked me from its pedestal and I thought I caught a flicker of doubt. She jerked her chin at Hans, who slowly rose from his seat.

Spots formed in my vision as the strongest Asura lifted his hands, his features full of foreboding. My sweat turned cold. Hans had the gravest sin, which meant his would be the worst obstacle.

I'm sorry about this, meri mara.

Another turn, another twist. The blisters on my feet burned and pricked ruthlessly, but I didn't stop. I couldn't stop. Not when I was so close.

Hans stared directly at me. The edges of his mask dropped for a millisecond, in the form of a defeated breath. However, his features quickly became sharper than a newly made blade. He snapped his fingers, and Sunitra appeared in front of the diya chained to the floor.

The sudden change of scenery left her bewildered as she looked around, her eyes darting from the audience and then to me. "Niya?" Her expression turned frantic when she realized who she kneeled before.

"Sunitra," I panted. *No.* Including others in this twisted scene was not part of the bargain. I almost stopped dancing to demand that Hans release her, but Zehan's oud kept me focused.

If I stopped now, I'd lose the trial.

Sunitra's reluctance twisted into agony as she crumpled to the floor and started to scream.

No, no, no. Disgust and panic racked my brain. Rati was forcing Hans to do the unthinkable. But how could I even be sure this was real? What if it was all an illusion to get me to stop dancing? What if Sunitra was still in her cell?

Her piercing shrieks drowned out Zehan's oud. His wolves whined and growled.

Zehan's strings faltered slightly, but he continued to play his small instrument. "This is immoral," he boomed. "You are a devi, for Asuras's sake. Act like one."

"Including others in the Asura Trials is not our way, Rati," Nadi added with a buttery soft voice, though I sensed the deception underneath. Zehan had said she specialized in being able to reveal a person's underlying fear. She tilted her head at me, like she could pluck out every single fear I had held through my life. Her yellow eyes narrowed into slits. "This goes against our creation."

"I agree," Hans grimaced, maintaining his hold over Sunitra. "Punishments are only meant to be given where they are due. Stop this, Rati, before it goes too far."

"You forget, Asuras, that I determine our way," Rati said as Sunitra screamed again. "And need I remind you, Zehan Jaan, that you have your own subjects to worry about. Is one life worth thousands of others?"

A wave of nausea rolled over me as I entered my next spin. I was fatigued. My footwork was messy. My muscles were stretched like worn-out cloth. Sunitra's screaming would not relent, and the wick had far too much left to burn out.

"You can end her suffering, Niya dear. All you have to do is stop dancing." Rati's eyes flashed brightly, like gemstones caught in sunlight.

I heaved as my knees slammed into the floor. My head fell back so that the tips of my hair brushed the stage, and I could look up at the monsters above me. I slowly slid my hands behind me so I could prop myself up and roll my stomach in a seductive wave. Floor choreography provided a moment of reprieve.

Zehan looked mutinous. The Asuras stayed silent, but their wary expressions told me they were nervous. Sunitra's next scream took all of the oxygen from the room.

I wanted to help, but what could I even do? The pain Hans inflicted was internal. Like a long-lost answer, my power rose within me, heckled by the injustice of this wretched court. The shadows rattled and reached my fingertips, begging to explode.

I could use my magic.

For my entire life, I believed I had to earn everything I desired by someone who held power or sway. It's why I struck such horrid deals with Baanu, and it's why I originally agreed to be Zehan's courtesan. But the truth was, I could have reached for what I wanted all along if I had stopped letting my inner resistance win.

I was *tired* of everyone forcing me to perform on gilded floors. Tired of believing that freedom was a reality I did not deserve. And most of all, I was exhausted from waiting on my bargains to benefit me.

You are more powerful than you believe, meri mara.

Han's words finally held so much more significance. If Yama's power ran through my veins, I didn't need to depend on anyone to get what I wanted. Ever. Again.

Magic rushed through me like water bursting through a dam.

Sunitra's cry stopped my shadows in their tracks. I could win this trial and snatch everything I wanted right now, but doing so would come at a price.

One I wasn't willing to pay.

I stopped dancing. The shadows chaotically twisted within me. "You win," I said through hard pants. In this moment, I didn't need to be victorious. My magic could be used at any time, but right now, Sunitra's life hung on my next choice.

Zehan's eyes widened.

Hans frown deepened.

"Let her go. I'll serve as your courtesan," I said.

Sunitra's screaming finally stopped, and relief in the form of tears escaped me in earnest.

"Niya, no!" Zehan stood up, the fervent emotion in his voice zinging through me. I shot him a look, trying to convey to him that it was all right. *I know what I'm doing.*

The Devi of Naraka rose in her seat, looking slightly disappointed. "I admit I'm surprised. I was sure you wouldn't stop," Rati said with that same sweet voice. "Your compassion will be your downfall, Niya. I, too, was once like you. Determined. Always giving. Always waiting for good things to come my way. However, hope is fickle, and it is best you don't cling onto it." Rati lifted her staff and pointed the three prongs directly at Sunitra.

"Wait—" I lifted my hands, but Rati's power barreled through Sunitra, leaving a gaping hole in her chest.

CHAPTER THIRTY-THREE

The scream that left me was pure human rawness. I covered my mouth with both hands. My heart stopped beating. *This was only an illusion. It's not real.* Any second, Sunitra's still form would vanish and, in her place, the laughing, kind rakshasa would return.

But the form stayed still. Silent. Unmoving. Desolate.

"I did say I would end her suffering," Rati said casually.

I slowly approached Sunitra's motionless body, ignoring the deep ache that radiated on the soles of my feet. When I reached her, my knees buckled, and I dropped to the ground. Pain shot like a lightning bolt from my kneecaps into my upper thighs. Darkness released from my frame in dozens of tiny spirals.

Zehan yelped with pain. My head snapped up. He clutched his chest, like whatever tether connected him to this realm and people had given out for a second.

Sunitra's soul was gone.

I looked back down at Sunitra. Her expression was frozen in pain. Rati had given her no mercy, not a single ounce of empathy.

A form crouched next to me, the smoky sweet scent of mint cocooned me into an embrace. Her death was my fault. I killed her.

"You did not kill her," Zehan said softly, addressing my inner thoughts like he could hear them loud and clear. Zehan kissed the top of my forehead. He carefully brushed the pads of his thumbs across my cheeks, wiping away tears that streaked through the grime on my face.

I couldn't even look at Zehan, couldn't see the disappointment flicker back at me. "I failed her. I failed you." I had bargained on his freedom, too, but didn't deliver.

"You could never do such a thing," Zehan said, holding me like I was a glass doll. I said more words, but they were incoherent. His magic flooded over me, coaxing me into calmness, bringing me back from the darkness that beckoned in the deepest pits of my mind and soul. "I'm so sorry. For everything."

I felt the truth in his words. I didn't even need to use my magic to feel it in every bone. Another voice neared us, but I heard the vicious snarl and flash of white that left Zehan's unfiltered anger teetering on the edge of a full-blown lashing.

My sorrow shifted into anger. A tremor racked through me. I locked onto the devi. "You." *I was going to kill her.* Rati's reign would end with me. I let the shadows rise around me. But silver clamps appeared on my wrists, dampening the rising darkness. Shit. "What are these?"

Rati laughed as she thumped her trident on the floor and red pooled beneath around my feet. "You lost the trial."

Which meant I was her prisoner. She was going to place me back in my cell with no Sunitra for company. I tried to use my magic to get the wristlets off, but searing pain traveled up my arm when I tried. "I never agreed to shackles," I said angrily.

Zehan looked at Rati with sheer loathing. "You killed one of my subjects for no reason. Sunitra didn't kill the departed souls. She did not deserve death merely because you found it entertaining."

"Sunitra was unfortunate collateral. And she may have not killed those souls, but she played a role in their deaths." Rati's sly voice sounded like a knife sliding against stone. "Say your goodbyes, Zehan Jaan. Niya is now and forever the courtesan of Naraka."

"Wait," I said, clearing my throat, "the terms of our agreement state that I am your *courtesan*, not your *prisoner*." Rati's features twisted, but I continued to press on. I doubted she would take off the clamps that held my power at bay, but I wouldn't stay here a second longer. "It was you who failed to specify the terms of my commitment to your court. You never said I had to *live* in Kalank or even Naraka."

Rati opened her mouth with a snarl, but Hans intervened. "The girl is right, Your Highness. You did not specify where she had to live. She may be your courtesan, but no magic can keep her physically here. You can summon her when you require her services." The Asura turned to Zehan and gave him a meaningful nod. "Take her home."

Home. The word felt right. Somehow along the way, Zehan's palace had become my home.

Rati yelled a curse and pointed her staff at us as Zehan wrapped his hand around my upper arm and whisked us away into nothingness.

We landed in a luxurious bedroom with high ceilings and dark walls. The curtains were closed. A grand four-poster bed was at the center with smooth indigo sheets and white feather-filled pillows.

Yet, I couldn't even take the moment to admire it. Instead, I bowed forward, wrapped my hands around my torso, and let my grief finally emerge.

***

I wasn't sure how long silent tears slid down my cheeks. Zehan held me through it. He did not speak or say anything, he simply stayed with me until I was coaxed into a deep slumber by his silvery magic.

When I woke, I flinched at the unfamiliar surroundings, wondering if this was my new room in Kalank. But after seeing my feet wrapped in gauze and new comfortable clothes, my nerves calmed.

Every inch of me ached with exhaustion and anguish. The clamps Rati had placed on me were still on my wrists, though power thrummed underneath my skin. It was unusually warm in the room, or maybe it was my anger causing my blood to boil.

I winced as I stood, a sharp pain shooting through my leg. I placed one hand on the bed to steady myself.

"Careful there," Kal said. He placed a tray on the small table and quickly moved to help me.

"Kal!" I threw my arms around him, squeezing his neck and shoulders, ignoring the pang that shot through both of my arms.

Kal chuckled as he hugged me back. "I'm glad you're okay."

Tears would have formed if I hadn't run out of them. I released Kal, scanning the rest of the room. It was more magnificent than my own one, and at least twice the size. Paintings in palettes of blue and beige adorned the walls. Clay sculptures of Asuras and devas alike graced the surfaces. This could only be one place.

Zehan's bedroom.

Kal held his hands up. "Before you ask, you are here because Zehan lost any semblance of control and demanded that you be under his watch."

My knees weakened, but the wave of emotion was quickly replaced by a resounding truth. "Sunitra—" I closed my eyes, unable to even complete the sentence. The image of her fractured body was still too vivid.

"I know," Kal said quietly. His expression was sympathetic. "But you cannot blame yourself, Niya."

I shook my head. Rati may have dealt the strike that killed, but *I* was the reason Sunitra was even there in the first place. "Sunitra was innocent. She didn't have anything to do with the murders." If I hadn't bargained for her freedom, maybe she would still be here.

Kal's brows shot up. "What do you mean?"

I sat on the edge of the bed and quickly told him all that Sunitra had revealed to me in the cell. Her role in the disappearances and the fact that someone had asked her to steal the Ashti. Even when the rishi revealed Sunitra's face in the smoke, it felt wrong. My power had been trying to tell me that something was off this whole time, but I ignored my instinct. A mistake I would never do again.

"We had already suspected the killer was still out there," Kal said. He slouched forward, resting his hands on the tops of his legs like he, too, was battling exhaustion. "It was the only explanation for why Zehan felt another soul be ripped from the realm."

I nodded, hugging my knees. Hollowness settled in the pit of my stomach. Why would someone ask Sunitra to steal the Ashti? "And we have no more leads."

We. No, this was no longer a joint effort, because at any moment, Rati could summon me to perform. My gaze traveled back to Kal. "I failed the Asura Trials—"

I trailed off as I saw Zehan lean against the doorway with his hands in his pockets. His hair was damp, and a few stray strands stuck to this forehead. The sleeves of his midnight-blue tunic were rolled up to his elbows.

All the air in the room suddenly thickened.

"I am excusing myself," Kal said quickly before dashing out. The door softly thudded behind him, leaving us alone...in his room.

"I—" we both started at the same time.

I swallowed.

"I've found a way to end Rati's reign once and for all," Zehan said, his voice barely a whisper. I swore the fire torches in the room flickered around us.

My throat dried. "Zehan, what did you do?"

"Not nearly enough." He pushed off the doorframe. "I know an apology will never make up for—"

"Don't." I lifted my hand. "I hate that you lied to me, Zehan, but I understand why. You were trying to get out of your cage. I know what that's like." I didn't blame him for not telling me. If I were in his place, I would have done the same. "Why would you trust a human with a secret so detrimental to not only your fate but this realm's?"

Zehan stepped closer. "At first, I was going to convince you to help me take Rati off her throne. But after..." He sighed. "It truly was my intention to send you to Varnasi. I had accepted my fate."

"I know," I said softly. "Tell me all of it," I pushed. I wanted his side of the story, not just the one I'd heard from Rati and Sunitra.

Zehan understood my unspoken question. "After two centuries of doing this job, I wanted out, but Rati would have never granted it, and I had also become attached to the souls here. I couldn't just abandon them. I needed to find someone who would see them for all they are, the good and the bad. It was then I learned about the prophecy from the rishi. After that, I made it my sole purpose to see it fulfilled. Taking a Chosen was the easiest way for me to assess females, to see if they were 'the one' destined to change my fate. For the next several decades, I entered their politics and created routine visits at the various courts to keep a foothold in Prithvi. I knew the chances of finding you were slim, but then I heard of the famed *Mohini* in Khoya."

My pulse raced as he twisted the end of my braid.

"The way people described you made me wonder if you had magic, perhaps an ability that you didn't even know you possessed. I found out everything about you. I knew you were orphaned, knew you had been in Baanu's employment from a young age. I knew I had to see you, but Baanu and King Murkha were hard to convince. Despite my long-standing relationship with King Murkha, they refused to entertain any negotiations." He said the words with disgust. "It took years before they finally agreed, and even then, they tried to squeeze as much as they could from me."

Stillness settled over me. He had been trying to take me from Khoya for *years?*

"So Baanu and King Murkha had already agreed to send me off with you before they asked me to dance that night?" I had assumed as much, but getting the confirmation made me realize how much of a fool I'd been. They manipulated me into believing I was making a bargain for my freedom, but it was all a sick trick.

Zehan shifted on his feet. "By that point, I had also learned how they were using you. Khoya grew too quickly in its territories for it all to have been merely a successful strategy. If I didn't have to maintain my diplomacy, I would have killed them for what they forced you into. I would have done it slowly, leaving a scar for each one they created on your feet."

His words settled into me like a promise. "When you appeared on that stage, you were like an answer to an unsaid question. Fierce, determined, and everything in between. I immediately felt drawn to you." He brushed his knuckles against my cheek. "My plan was to assess your power and then convince you somehow to take a stand against Rati.

"But then, you danced in my court, swayed the Asuras with ease, and challenged me in ways that I thought weren't possible. I fell for you completely." His voice was hoarse. "And in many ways, it broke me. Because chasing my freedom meant pulling you away from yours."

I licked my dry lips, and Zehan tracked the movement. "I didn't know Rati knew about the prophecy. I was sure if she did, she would have confronted me about it or prevented me from leaving the realm. But now, I believe she was waiting for me to find you."

"She wanted to remove me as a threat to her throne," I said.

He nodded. "When she saw you in my home casually eating breakfast with me, she became suspicious. It's why she pulled me into a baseless meeting. She was trying to understand why I kept you out of all my other Chosen."

"Because you sent all your other Chosen to Varnasi? But how did you manage to do that?" Varnasi was supposedly safeguarded to extreme levels. No one could get in or out without approval. I doubted the king there would simply allow Zehan to pop in whenever he wanted.

"Varnasi is my territory."

I rapidly blinked. Positive that I had misheard him. "What?"

"After I found out about the prophecy, I knew the chances of me finding the destined girl was slim, and I still needed to maintain my stature as Prince of Hell. So I took courtesans and let everyone believe that they were brought to Naraka. But really, I sent them to Varnasi. All the prisoners I've taken in war, refugees who make the dangerous trek through Chayya Forest, all of the trafficking raids my demons have intercepted at my check posts, the women and children who the perpetrators were smuggling...they all now live there. I wanted to create a haven for people who had nowhere else to go."

"You are the ruler of Varnasi?" I was dumbfounded. I had dreamed about the kingdom for so long, devoutly believing it would give me the independence I craved. Yet, I had refused to see that Zehan had given me that in his own home repeatedly. And now, my stubbornness had potentially trapped us both. "I'm sorry I failed us."

"You *never* need to apologize to me, meri jaan. I don't believe in failures, only pivots. What is fated to happen will happen, just perhaps not in the way we expect it." Zehan cupped my face, willing me to look up at him.

"I'm going to help you fulfill the prophecy." I had made the decision during the Asura Trials. I lost on purpose. I wanted Rati to believe she had the upper hand, and I needed her to stop torturing Sunitra. But my plan had backfired in more ways than one. I looked down at the silver clamps around my wrist. "As soon as I figure out how to get these damn things off."

Zehan laughed. "I have accepted my fate, meri jaan. I no longer want you to save me." His eyes glistened like obsidian stones. "If you are free, I am free."

Since arriving in this realm, Zehan had pushed me to accept who I was deep down. To let this power manifest. To find freedom where I was because no one could control how I felt. I stepped closer to him so our mouths were inches away from each other.

"That answer is not good enough, Zehan *Jaan*." I rose on my tippy-toes and let our lips meet with finality.

CHAPTER
THIRTY-FOUR

This kiss, like our previous ones, was equally unhinged. As if we fought against time, before some unknown force tore us apart and whisked us away into the mist.

Zehan's hands skimmed up the sides of my waist and slowly lifted to cup my face. I clung onto his tunic, afraid to let him go, surrendering to the unspoken current we'd been resisting all these weeks.

He tugged on my bottom lip with his teeth. "You should know that if we do this, there is no turning back. Your soul is mine in every one of your lives."

My toes curled into the wool rug. "Deal," I whispered against his lips.

He kissed me again, tilting my head back to deepen it. The truth was my soul had already belonged to him for a while. I just had to find him. He was the song I never wanted to stop dancing to.

I heard the door lock click. Zehan reached behind me and pulled one of the strings of my blouse. "Where should I start, meri jaan?" The timbre in his voice turned my core molten.

Tendrils of his magic had already gotten to work, curling around my fingers that were gripping his tunic, tightening around my ankles, and snaking up my calves.

I don't need my fingers to make you beg.

I was beginning to believe that statement would turn into reality. An airy sigh escaped my lips at the sheer feel of his magic possessing me, overtaking my senses. Shadows wanted to escape my fingers. Adrenaline pounded in my veins, my core throbbed with need, and every part of me hyper-conscious on the man standing before me.

I lifted his tunic off over his head. Multiple tattoos—words in a forbidden language, symbols that I didn't understand—ran up one side of his chest and wrapped onto his back and down his right arm. I wanted to trace each one with my tongue while he thoroughly explained what they meant.

Zehan herded me backward until the back of my knees hit the large bed. "Sit," he ordered.

I didn't protest as I plopped down ungracefully, letting my hands roam his coppery skin and slowly make their way to his upper thighs. Zehan pulled out the ribbon that held my braid. He ran his fingers through waves of brown-black hair that cascaded down my exposed back. Goose bumps erupted all over me, but Zehan did nothing to warm the air. He wanted me to remain sensitive for whatever he was about to do. He let his fingers leave a searing trail of heat down the column of my neck, in between my breasts, and over the center of my navel.

He stopped right before the string of my lehenga. "Lie back," he commanded.

I raised an eyebrow. "Still ordering, are we? You know I'm horrible at following them, Prince."

"We'll see about that, courtesan."

A shiver crept up my spine at whatever promise his words held. Normally, I would not yield, I would argue, but at that moment, I craved for him to satisfy the need that was becoming unbearable, to quell the fire that blazed all over my body. I shuddered. From the cold or lust, I had no fucking idea. I clucked my tongue in frustration as black power rippled within me.

I wanted him *now*.

His light magic snaked along my limbs, caressing every nook and groove. It would itself around my neck like a thick dupatta. The more the tendrils closed in on me, the more pronounced the throb between my legs became.

I eyed him darkly. "Stop teasing." I sat up again and ran the heel of my hand along the bulge in his pants which earned me a deep groan. It brought a pinch of satisfaction, but it was not nearly enough.

He chuckled as he fell to his knees and bunched up the flowy chiffon lehenga that started white at the bottom but slowly faded into blue at the top. He yanked my thighs forward and tossed my legs over his broad shoulders.

The first cold lick made me whimper.

The second made me convulse.

My back arched as he used his tongue to bring me to the edge of combusting. My hips bucked off the bed, but Zehan's hand pinned them down. Getting air into my lungs became harder as he lazily swirled his tongue at the apex.

Then he added his damn finger.

I cried out as he settled in, like he had nowhere else to be. My hand fell into this thick hair, and on the next graze of his teeth, I tugged the strands close to the roots, encouraging him to slide his tongue between my wet folds with a faster pace. He switched back and forth between languidly licking and sucking until my eyes rolled back into my head.

I held on to the smallest amount of sense I had left, *clung* onto it with everything I had. But he abruptly pulled away.

"No," I whimpered.

Zehan, the bastard, grinned as he looked up at me from his kneeling position. "Now, meri jaan…" He added a second finger, filling me up to the brim. "Beg."

By the Asuras. I didn't have to be told twice. "P-please." I felt him smile and cursed as he sucked the small bundle of nerves. I pulled his hair harder, unsure if I was telling him to stop or continue.

"Surrender to it." His words were a summons.

On the next tortuous stroke of his tongue, I shattered. Pleasure rippled through me like a dark reckoning. A storm that had finally unleashed its fury. Power vibrated fiercely down my spine but met a wall when it tried to come out.

"You are stunning," he whispered, slowly rising and staring at me in awe. "And every part of you, your very existence, *belongs to me.*"

The conviction in his words made any remaining control I possessed snap like a twig. I pulled him over me and kissed him, tasting a familiar smoky sweetness. He wasn't the only one capable of dominating.

I boldly ran my hands down the stack of his exposed muscles and pulled the string of his pants so the knot loosened. I refused to wait any longer.

A heavy knock hit the door, sobering me from the intoxicating desire.

"Ignore it," Zehan muttered as he gently squeezed one of my breasts through the blouse hanging over my shoulders by one loosely tied string.

My head fell back, but the knocking quickened.

Ezhil's voice traveled through the door. "You can't ignore it."

Zehan cursed. "This better be fucking important, Ezhil." His voice was hard.

"Do you really think I enjoy interrupting you right now?" Ezhil said through the door.

"You do. It's why you ran here all gleeful," another voice said dryly. It was familiar, but I couldn't pinpoint where I had heard it. Another knock hit the door. "Zehan, the Asuras are here."

My pulse quickened. The Asuras would only be here for something serious. Had Rati already summoned me?

"All right, I'm coming." Zehan pressed his forehead to mine in apology. "I thought we would have more time." He dropped his voice. "Stay here."

I nudged his nose with mine, slowly unwrapping my legs that had wound themselves tightly around his waist. I smirked. "You know I'm coming with you." If they were here for me, I'd have to go with them anyways.

"They want to speak to Niya, too," Bidal added.

"How in nine hells did he hear that? And just how many of you are out there?" Zehan snapped, but his expression was that of bemusement. "Remind me to soundproof this room. I'm not sure I want the entire palace hearing you scream my name."

"Gah. Please fucking do," Ezhil added.

I blushed and shoved his shoulder, but he simply took my hand and placed it over his chest. He kissed me one more time. Deeply.

I quickly readjusted my blouse. Zehan tugged his kurta over his head. "Before we go, there is something else I need to tell you." He turned me around to tie the strings at the back.

I peered at him over my shoulder. "More secrets? Don't you think we've had enough between us for this lifetime?" Skepticism laced my tone.

Zehan grinned. "It's not really a secret, more of a surprise."

I raised my eyebrow as I finished pinning my dupatta that had small pearl diamonds embedded across my shoulder. I didn't comment on the fact that my outfit matched his.

Zehan didn't strike me as someone who would be good at surprises. Yet when he drew the curtain back and bright sunlight streamed in, my mouth fell open.

If I had been dancing, I would have forgotten the next step. I rushed to the edge of the balcony, letting the warm breeze brush my cheeks.

A luscious sea of azure abodes stretched across a wide span of arid land. The room we were in led out onto a white concrete terrace where hot winds whipped my hair back. The sun beamed down on me, welcoming me like an old friend. Horse carriages and people and rakshasas crowded the streets, engaging in bustling bazaars.

"Welcome to Varnasi, meri jaan."

I turned around to Zehan as he waited at the entrance of the terrace, watching me with bright eyes.

"What...when?" I turned back to face the striking city before me. The warm breeze caused my lehenga to lift a few inches off the ground. "How?"

"I used the Vayu to transport us here instead of the palace," Zehan said as he walked over and entwined our hands.

I couldn't find words. I took in the various shades of indigo across the buildings. I instantly wished Ruhi were here to see this.

Zehan lifted my hand to his mouth to brush his lips against my knuckles. "I will not keep you in hell any longer."

Even if it meant he had to stay in it for eternity.

"But how are the Asuras here?" I thought they couldn't leave Naraka.

"I've given them permission to be here. They know better than to abuse my generosity." He clasped my hand. "Shama found out about my connection to this place years ago and of course, my attempts to make him keep this a secret from the other Asuras failed miserably."

The Asuras knew that Zehan ruled this territory. "And they haven't told Rati?" I asked as we walked through the palace. I couldn't stop admiring the warm and open aesthetic of the structure, which featured beige walls with red-and-brown accents.

All nine Asuras were seated around a very long and narrow wooden table. Their hard expressions and dark clothing were wildly out of place in the balmy and bright room. Bidal, Ezhil, and Ameel were also seated on the table. *That was the voice I had heard.* The soldier nodded his chin at me. Zehan held on to my hand as we entered, everyone fell silent as we took seats at the center.

"Well, whoever was betting they wouldn't get together owes me five souls," Lobha said, leaning back in his chair. The others sniggered.

Rahas's dark turquoise dress shimmered in the golden light pouring through the open-aired ceiling. "I never thought I'd see the day Zehan took a consort."

Consort. We hadn't even discussed what we were yet. My cheeks felt warm. I dropped Zehan's hand, but he quickly pulled my fingers back into his, resting our joined hands on the table. He clicked his tongue. "I assume all nine of you are here to discuss my missive, not my relationship."

I looked at Zehan with confusion. What missive?

The Asuras shared a look between each other. "It can be done," Nadi said, her snakish gaze landing on me. "But there is a risk."

"What can be done?" I asked.

"Zehan wants to open the gate to the devas," Shama said. "Essentially free them from their imprisonment."

I exhaled. "The Gate of Two."

Zehan's eyes slid to me. "Kal found an old scripture that said the power of all nine Asuras and their creator could close and open the gates. At one time, it would have been impossible, but now we know whose power you have..."

I could help the Asuras open the gate. Because I held Yama's power.

"What's the risk?" I asked.

"We don't know what state the devas will be in. Rati allegedly took their power from them before she left, but we are not sure," Rahas said. "Not to mention there are also lesser demons in their realms, magical creatures that could wreak havoc if they are not controlled."

"The devas may not want to help us. Devas are not beyond revenge. They may be bitter and angry," Shama argued. "They could take it out on us."

"Their anger will be directed at Rati," Zehan swiped his thumb on the inside of my wrist. "If we open the gates, I'm positive they will leap at the chance to rid the cosmos of Rati."

I straightened. I wouldn't have to remain her courtesan and Zehan could also be free. But I no longer had access to my magic. I lifted my wrist, displaying the silver clamps. "There is still one problem."

"I think I can help with that," Nadi said. She reached across the table and lifted my wrist. She waved her hand over the silver bracelets and they clicked open, clattering to the table. Nadi smiled at my surprise. "I created these as a way to torture departed souls with magic. Rati likely didn't bother to learn who created them."

Right. Of course. I was in the company of the most feared creatures in the entire cosmos. Shadows instantly filled the room like dark fog. I sighed with relief. This magic had become a part of me, losing the ability to use it was like losing the ability to dance.

Placing his heavily ringed hands on the table, Abhi chimed in. "Now that that is settled, even if we agree this is the path forward, Rati is still a problem. She could summon Niya at any second, and she is angry enough to completely lose it if she finds out what we are up to. And if we are forced to face off with her, none of us can use our power against her, except Niya."

"I will handle Rati," Zehan said. He turned to me. "Once you open the gates, come back here." Not *if,* when. Zehan held zero doubts that I could do this.

Hans's words created a kernel of doubt. "And if we aren't successful...?" I stared at Zehan. "I can't just stay here." Rati was the Goddess of Death for Asura's sake. If she wanted, she could make our lives even worse.

Zehan squeezed my hand. "You might if I offer to take on your debt—""No." The aching memory of Sunitra screaming in chains pivoted in my mind's eye so it was Zehan in her place. My stomach clenched with nausea. "Zehan, she will *torture* you until you bring me back."

"You dance for no one but me, meri jaan. No deva will ever earn that right." White shadows pulsed off of Zehan's frame. "Besides, there is no *if* in this scenario. You will be successful."

I glared at Zehan, knowing he wouldn't be swayed. But I didn't like it. We were basing this on a hypothesis that the gates could be opened and that the devas would be able and willing to help us. This wasn't a foolproof plan, but it was also our best shot at taking Rati down once and for all.

I turned to the Asuras. "Where is the gate?"

It was Issa that spoke with a slight lisp. "In Chayya Forest."

CHAPTER THIRTY-FIVE

S unny skies lit the streets of Varnasi the next morning and I could taste the salt in the air. Beyond the front gates of the palace, I could make out clusters of homes and colorful shops that I hadn't had the chance to visit. After years and years of yearning to come to the kingdom of paradise, the circumstances under which I had ended up here had turned it into something bitter, like an unripe berry.

Sleep had been difficult to come by, knowing what today held. I had stared at the ceiling for hours, restless, watching my shadows glide around the room until Zehan slipped under the covers late in the night and pulled me close. He had been planning with Ezhil, Ameel, and Bidal. He didn't say it, but I knew they had been preparing for what would happen to Naraka and Varnasi if we failed.

Zehan watched me approach with a rueful smile. He opened the door to one of his sleek black carriages and drank in my face and clothes. Instead of my usual lehenga-dupatta fashion, I wore wide-legged dark-brown pants and a shorter kurta that cinched at the back. It was comfortable, easy to move in. I didn't hate it.

He wrapped an arm around my waist, tugging me close as the pads of his fingers dug into my back. "I think I prefer this attire on you." He kissed my temple.

"Your preference is noted, Prince," I murmured.

He rubbed my arms and tucked a stray strand of hair behind my ear. The severity of his features had smoothed, as if Varnasi brought out the real version of him and the person he was before he became the ferryman of souls.

Zehan did not belong in the shadows, he was destined for the light.

He kept his eyes on me as his other hand went to his pocket and he pulled out a small sheathed dagger with a familiar black pommel.

"The Ashti," I said.

"I don't know why Sunitra was after this, but whoever asked her to steal it likely had a reason." He handed it to me. "Take it. You need to carry a weapon anyways."

The blade was cream white and sharp at the very tip but dull farther down towards the curved edge. Now, upon a closer look, I could make out faded words and symbols on the pommel. They matched the inscriptions on the front walls of the palace and Kalank.

Bladed bone will take divine power in its wake.

This had to be the same bladed bone that the rishi had referenced, it was too coincidental for it not to be. My hand hovered over it.

Kal stepped up next to me with a large scroll tucked under one arm. "The Ashti." He fumbled with his fingers, eyeing the blade warily with that same fear that flashed across his face the day he gave me a tour of Zehan's collection. "What do you plan to do with it?"

I deliberately picked up the dagger, feeling the weight fill my palm. Magic shook through me with fervent force. "Maybe it will tell me when the time comes," I said.

"Kal will accompany you. He is the one who studied the locations of the gates," Zehan said. He pulled me into an embrace and kissed the top of my head. "This is not goodbye forever, meri jaan."

My limbs felt heavy. Zehan was going back to Naraka to appease Rati while the Asuras and I went to Chayya Forest to reinstate the gates to Svarga. It was only a matter of time before she learned that all nine of her Asuras were on Prithvi.

"It better not be," I whispered, nudging my nose against his playfully. "I'm not done dancing with the devil."

"I'll hold you to that promise, courtesan. Keep falling into that wondrous power of yours." He took a step back and stuffed his hands into his pockets, like it took significant restraint to maintain the distance.

I got into the carriage. Hans, Shoka, and Kal were already waiting inside. The other Asuras were in the carriage behind us. We were keeping the entourage small to not attract too much attention to ourselves. The Asuras looked human, but their features were too sharp

Don't look back. Don't look back.

With a jolt, we lurched forward, and the hooves of Zehan's black stallions clattered against hot street stones. Chayya Forest would take a few hours of travel through the Drifts. I stared out of the window, keeping my eyes locked on the dark grey overcast in the distance.

This is not goodbye forever, meri jaan.

Then why in nine hells did it feel that way?

***

The further we ventured into Chayya Forest, the harder rain pelted down. Thunder boomed. Ominous gray clouds grew large above us, though I relished each raindrop, even going as far as sticking my fingers outside to feel them splatter on my hand. It had only ever sprinkled a handful of times in Khoya.

Rain, in many ways, was a luxury.

Kal had been unusually quiet, frequently glancing between the scroll in his hand and outside to verify our location. Dusk would soon turn to night if we did not hurry.

A vicious gust of wind blasted through our small caravan. Anticipation warred within me. I didn't know what to expect. I fidgeted as I studied my companions. Hans also stared out the window while Shoka had his head resting on the leather, like he was deep in meditation.

"What happened to Yama?" I asked. Shoka's eyes remained closed, but his fingers twitched, indicating he had heard me. If anyone would know what happened to the deva I assumed it would be his Asuras. I held his power, which meant he had never actually been killed by Rati. "He appeared to me years ago and gave me this power, but Zehan had thought he was killed by Rati."

"We also believed he was dead," Hans said.

That got Shoka's attention. "After Rati took over Naraka, Yama was her prisoner for a long time. He lived in Kalank but was too weak to rise against her. He has not been seen for over a decade. One day, we all felt his power vanish, it was as if someone had snapped and the power that connected us to him, broke. We all thought Rati had finally finished him off. But then, you came along. And we knew that was not the complete story. Your power...it calls to us," he explained.

Hans crossed his legs. "We saw that you were reluctant to accept the shadows, for fear of what they might do to your nature. But you surpassed our expectations in the trial. We are sorry for our part. While we can move against Rati through loopholes, we must obey a direct command."

It was humbling to realize that even Asuras, who were believed to be the worst kind of being, had emotions and depth. "I understand," I said. "I will prove that I am worthy of this power."

"We don't doubt it, meri mara," Hans replied.

"Why do you call me that?" Rati had told me that it means bringer of death. It wasn't a nickname I particularly was keen to have, although it sounded better than courtesan.

"We're here," Kal interrupted. He thumped on the roof of the carriage, signaling the guards to stop.

We found ourselves in a large clearing that smelled of moss and damp leaves. Trees towered over us, prohibiting our view of the sky. The only sounds were the faint rustling of leaves and water splashing against bark. Disquiet settled over me as we formed a small circle. Kal stood to the side, watching us curiously.

"How does this work? If the gate is completely destroyed, how do we know what to fix?"

"Rati used the combined power of the devas to destroy the gates all because she wanted to exact her own revenge," Kal said. "The gate is a living thing that ties the cosmos together. He placed a small rock in the grass."

"Something destroyed does not mean it cannot be recreated," Nadi said.

The Asuras held their palms out and forced their vibrant power to seep into the damp ground right over the rock Kal had placed. They began to chant. It was a prayer I had never heard but was easy enough to recite. I lifted my hands and let my magic pour out, night infested spirals wrapped around the powers gathered at a central point in the grass.

Slowly, like a widening hole, space opened within it, large enough for someone to fall right through. Our chants became stronger and deeper, the vibrations of them making the trees around us tremble. A symmetrical curved archway, similar to the one I had passed through to enter Naraka, rose through the floor.

Kal's eyes widened with awe. He smiled so that every single one of his teeth shined. "Keep going, it's working!"

The gate rose further. My voice strained from the chant. Gold accents began to mark the edges of the arch followed by a shimmering veil of red and orange formed between the two white pillars.

The Gate of Two.

We did it.

Suddenly, tendrils of red smoke crashed into the arch. The ground trembled as the forest floor was engulfed in a sea of red. I looked around for the source but then Issa's piercing shriek sliced through our chant.

A silver trident slid clean through her stomach.

Issa's form vaporized. Rahas scream caused the forest birds to flee.

Rati stood in Issa's place, her skin deathly pale. Her hair flew back in wild waves. "Stand down," she commanded. "I will deal with all of you later."

The Asuras didn't move or speak, but their fractured expressions said it all. Hans clutched his chest like his heart had stopped beating. The others held similar shock in their features. They had felt Issa's death, likely the same way Zehan felt his souls leave him.

Shadows burst from me. I was done with her games.

She tsked and waved her hand. "Careful now. We wouldn't want Zehan Jaan to pay the price for your recklessness."

Zehan appeared through a red Vayu, kneeling on the dirt floor, bare chested and shackled at the wrists and throat. An immortal warrior bound by his burdens. His mouth parted when he saw my shadows dancing around me. Dozens of rakshasas stood around him with black-tipped blades.

"Zehan," I whispered.

Rati's smile made my skin cold. "Did you all really think you'd be able to enlist the help of devas to kill me? Trust me, the devas are no better than me."

I threw my shadows at his chain. He yelled in pain, like another soul was being ripped from Naraka. His yells grew the more I tried to unlock the chains with magic.

I reeled in my power. Zehan was imprisoned. The Asuras couldn't use their powers. It was me against a devi. *I can't win this fight.*

I glanced at Hans, whose tight-lipped expression gave nothing away, but his voice filtered through my mind. *The trident and its power can release Zehan,* he mind-spoke.

Relief washed through me. I may not have the might of the Asuras, but I had their support.

Tell Kal to be ready, I said back to him.

I kept my expression neutral as I refocused on Rati. "I don't understand," I said, relaxing my muscles slightly. I needed to distract her until an opportune moment. The Ashti's presence at my waist increased. It burned as if it were awoken by being in close proximity to the devi and the immense power she unrightfully held. "What do you gain by doing all of this?"

The Asuras believed everything she did was out of boredom, out of desire to be in total control, but I wasn't convinced.

"You know my story," her voice was vicious. Even the trees stilled to listen to her. She walked closer to me, leaving her trident a few feet behind her. "You know what was done to me, what was *stolen* from me. Kama. My *soulmate.* Devas feel emotions tenfold compared to humans. When we hate, we bring earthquakes. When we cry, we bring storms. When we love, we forge new worlds. Knowing that I was hopelessly in love with Kama, they still killed him for simply falling into his nature. He was the Deva of Love, he needed to receive love from everyone. That is why he used his arrow on the Devi of Wisdom."

I shifted uncomfortably. Even though Kama was wrong in his actions, Rati had still lost what she believed to be the other half of her soul. I glimpsed back at Zehan and felt our truth slam between us.

If I lost Zehan, I'd break every cosmos law to get him back.

"You asked what I wanted," Rati said with quiet calm. She was mere feet from me now, her floral scent filled the cold, stale air. "I want this." She pointed at Zehan. "His *grief.* No one in this cosmos should be able to have love when I cannot. I see his yearning when he looks at you, and that won't do. *No one* should be free to feel love when all I feel is hollowness."

My shadows tittered at that. Rati hated universal laws, so she set out to make her own, but she failed to see that there was a reason for them. They played a critical role in the crisscrossed paths of life, death, and fate. The blade tucked safely at my side became searing hot, to the point that I was sure my skin burned. Like an answer I had been seeking, an idea clicked in my mind.

"You are an abomination to the *devas*," I said quietly. "It is your job to watch over the souls and help them become more resilient, not torture them because you feel like the cosmos has wronged you." Kal inched towards Rati's trident. "But I'll do you a favor, I'll free you from this grief." In one swift movement, my shadows swiped the dagger from my waist, so it hovered in midair next to me.

"Kal, now!" I yelled.

Kal reached for the trident, but as soon as his fingers brushed the long handle he yelped, jumping backwards as if he'd been branded by the metal.

Rati whipped around, her hair flying in all directions. "You!" She yelled. The distraction was all I needed to send the Ashti flying until it plunged into Rati's chest.

CHAPTER
THIRTY-SIX

The Ashti barely missed Rati's heart, but I was sure that her cry could be heard throughout the forest. The ground trembled as if the forest would cave in on itself at any second. She hovered a trembling hand over the small dagger protruding from her. It glowed bright red.

Her eyes widened when she recognized the blade. "No."

Bladed bone will take divine power in its wake.

Kal had once told me that devas could not be killed while they had their power. The power was what made them immortal. It must be stripped first.

There are laws, even amongst gods. Zehan couldn't use the Ashti against Rati because of the boon she bore him, but I, having no connection to her, could. This blade was the vessel that could hold her power, I just had to get it in her first.

The Ashti glowed white-yellow as it siphoned the devi's power. Rati was a goddess being undone. Her features twisted into something from a nightmare.

The Asuras stood on the sidelines as spectators, watching the events unfold with rapt attention, unable to intervene. *We serve the true power of Naraka.*

Zehan yelled my name, trying to tear his arms out of his shackles. The rakshasas, wary of Zehan's power, held their swords at the ready. Sparks flew from his wrists, his magic repeatedly snuffed out by the bruising chains. Sweat glistened across his face, he looked terrified. I started toward him, but movement caught my eye.

I watched it all happen in slow motion. Rati's lips pulled back from her teeth as she reached for the dagger lodged in her flesh. *No.* She was going to yank it out. While the dagger had stolen some of her power, she held the power of *all devas.* Even a drop of power left within her was enough for her to maintain her throne.

I ran toward her, but her hand gripped the hilt and yanked it out. She tossed the blade onto the floor, where its glow faded like a dying pulse.

"You think you can *best* me?" Rati's voiced deepened in an unnatural way. Her beautiful features engorged into something beastly. "I am the supreme devi of all devas. The *only* devi left in the cosmos. It'll take more than a thin knife to destroy me." But her breathing was labored.

I took a few steps back as she moved toward me in her shredded, gaudy red dress, a creature returning from the brink of death. Her silver jewelry clunked with each step like a chime signaling an approaching end.

Rati lifted her hands, curling her fingers, causing lightning to strike above us. Her black hair lengthened at a rapid pace. I watched with disgust as the thick strands became alive, turning and twisting on the ground.

My eyes flickered to the dagger glimmering in the darkness. *Another stab.* I had to get to it. I ran toward it, but her hair wrapped around my ankle and tugged. I face-planted.

I spat out moldy dirt, twisting around. "I do not have to *best* you," I said. Shades of black and stormy gray released from my fingertips. I smiled as the magic came to me effortlessly and hid me in a dark cloud. "I just have to make sure you don't win." I kept the shadows around me and darted toward the small dagger. The piece of bone that could end this once and for all.

I only traveled a few feet before Rati used the Vayu to appear inches away from me. She shoved me back with invisible force, causing me to slam up against a tree like I weighed no more than a bundle of blankets. Pain shot through my side, and my breath *whooshed* out of me.

Rati lifted her arm out, and her staff appeared in her hands. I rose onto my hands and knees, trying to rid the vibration I felt throughout my body from the impact. I threw out my fingers, urging the shadows to bring the dagger to me, but Rati destroyed their path with her own magic.

She slowly pointed her staff at my face. "This is your end, courtesan."

I sat back on my heels, making the twenty or so paces the dagger sat from me. *Travel by Vayu.*

I had never learned how, but I could try. She was going to kill me if I didn't. I rolled on the cold earth, barely missing the cataclysmic strike of her power. I briefly shut my eyes, focusing on vanishing with the air to the dagger.

Nothing happened.

Rati looked like she could spit fire. "I had hoped we would find equal footing, Niya, but it appears you have chosen a path that will not end well for—"

She gasped. The Ashti had been stabbed through her heart this time. The tip of the blade boar-berry red. Silence rushed over all of Tyaga as dropped to her knees, bringing us to the same height.

The devi lifted her pale hand as if she meant to tuck back one of my strands of hair. Her mouth parted, and she fell to her side with a thump. She craned her neck to look up at the one responsible for her fate.

Kal.

I felt paralyzed, like I had also been struck by the blade. Kal stood above us, staring down at the devi with not just apathy, but quivering wrath.

"What—" The question froze on the tip of my tongue; I didn't dare move for the trident or the Ashti that was still buried in Rati's chest. The more she stared at Kal, the rounder her eyes became.

The Asuras were silent and rooted to their spots. The rakshasas guarding Zehan slackened their stances. They all stared at Kal with a mixture of awe and fear.

Power twitched between my fingers. The signal from it clear, *Be on guard.* But this was Kal. My butler. My friend.

Kal squatted so he could bring himself closer to Rati. A large sword magically appeared in his hands.

He had magic.

But how was that possible? He was a departed soul.

Rati snarled. "No! Y-you w-will face their w-wrath for this." Blood dribbled from the corners of her mouth.

"Oh my dear, I doubt that. Not when you've turned the heavens into a prison." His voice was richer, smoother, almost velvety. Without hesitating, he flipped the sword and pierced Rati straight through the stomach, silencing her once and for all.

I winced as Rati's blood mixed with wet mud. Her immortal gaze now dull and lifeless.

Kal's attention was fixated on me. Unease trickled over me. I couldn't reconcile the person standing before me now as the same quirky butler who'd been clumsy and fretful.

"Who are you?" The new depth and familiarity in his features set my senses on alert. Power in an unmagical form seemed to radiate off him now. It was similar to the way Zehan and Rati tampered down their godly characteristics.

I blinked rapidly as his form started to shift between smoke and veils. His features sharpened, his hair lengthened until the tips brushed the tops of his shoulders, his skin darkened to the color of mulch. His clothing also shifted into a deep black sherwani with glimmering rhinestones on the cuffs and collar.

I stumbled a few steps back as his form enhanced with more clarity and the smell of hyacinths and ash wafted off him.

"Hello, little flower." The black in Yama's eyes grew starker as bright purple ringed his irises. "I've come to take my throne back."

Kal was the Deva of Naraka.

CHAPTER THIRTY-SEVEN

"Y ou?" My eyebrows reached my hairline. "But you're—"

"Supposed to be dead?" He grinned wickedly. "Devas are hard to kill." He opened his palms and black smoky flowers bloomed from them.

The hair on the back of my neck rose. The swaying forest stilled. The sounds of the night drowned out. My magic—*his magic,* thrummed in my veins. This darkness. The shadows. The ability to destroy and coerce.

All of that power belonged to him.

I slowly rose. His appearance was identical from all those years ago in the meadow of hyacinths—long face, pointed nose, high cheekbones. I swallowed hard. Ripples of alluring energy leaked from the deva's handsome form.

Kal, who was no longer *my* Kal, flashed his brilliantly white teeth. "How beautiful and famous you've grown, *Mohini.*"

It was triggering. My palms became clammy. That damn name. It represented years of swooning men and constantly being a pawn in a larger game. Living to only be shredded of my dignity.

Behind him, the Asuras stood in varying levels of shock. Shama's expression had wilted. Hans grimaced. Even Krod was wary. *They had not known Kal was Yama.* Somehow, Kal had hidden his identity and lived amongst them for decades without them being any wiser.

"I don't understand," I said slowly, trying to determine where to start. What question to ask because as the seconds ticked by, more and more rose within me. "How are you..." I trailed off. Was he considered alive or dead? "Existing?"

"Patience, little flower," Yama chuckled. "Decades of *tortuous* patience. For a while there, I was worried you wouldn't succeed in beating Rati." He tilted his head. "I'm glad I was horribly wrong."

Zehan attempted to free his arms from his shackles again, blood streamed down the metal with every shake. I thought that killing Rati would have released his shackles, but it hadn't. The magic on them must be too strong.

Panic shimmied its way down my spine. "Why did you give me your power? Why have you been hiding while Rati rules on your throne?"

"Rati was a truly vengeful bitch." Yama twisted his features, which made him almost resemble Hans's inhuman form. "When she came for my throne, she didn't just want to kill me. She wanted to make me suffer for my hand in her consort's death. Kama was pathetic and constantly felt the need to be loved by others. When Svaya found out he used his arrows on his wife, Vani, he enlisted me to help him punish him. I obliged and kept Svaya here for centuries, but then Svaya killed him instead of letting him go free, sending Rati on her eternal rampage.

"Instead of taking my power from me outright, she kept me a prisoner for decades, letting my power dwindle to a mere fraction of what it was. I knew the only way to beat her was to bide my time, earn her confidence, and convince her to let me serve her in other ways, outside of those wretched prison bars she kept me in. After a century, she released me with the expectation that I would act as her spy in the realm." The deva paced in front of me. Faded power sparked off him. "With my newfound freedom, I sought a way to rise against her. She held the power of multiple devas, but the rishi revealed another way."

He works from the black shadows, rolling the dice, waiting for the devi's own forged destruction to come to fruition. The rishi's words came ringing back. He had been referring to Kal. He knew that the Deva of Naraka was alive and attempting to take back his throne.

Adrenaline pounded through my veins as realization dawned on me. "You had the rishi killed. You sent that demon into his cottage." Kal refused to accompany me inside that day, excusing it to the rishi's strangeness, but it was because he worried the rishi might reveal his identity. *Kal* tranced that rakshasa to attack us.

Yama had the audacity to frown. "A rather unfortunate death. I don't like killing those who have been useful to me. The rishi revealed to me that a living human with the power of a deva would be the one to restore me back to my seat. I couldn't understand how that was possible. The devas were all trapped in Svarga. I thought the old man was mistaken. I had lost any hope of revival, until Rati brought you into the fold." His turned to Zehan.

Zehan stiffened. "And why is that?" His voice was hoarse.

Yama smiled again. "Rati brought you into Naraka because she was bored of harboring and punishing the departed." The deva shook his head like it was preposterous someone could tire of torture. "By bestowing both a curse and boon on you, she unknowingly created a path to her own destruction. She gave you the power of a deva."

"That's why you wanted to be my butler," Zehan said. "You thought I was your way to destroy Rati."

"I told Rati I would act as her spy, but my real goal was to gain your trust. I wanted to be there when you eventually tired of Naraka and wanted out. But Rati was smart. She hadn't given you power that was destructive in nature, it was soft." Yama huffed. "Not to mention the changes you started making in Naraka. Demanding obedience and properness and *understanding*. It was all very frustrating." He made a face. "I started to lose hope, again, but then..." The deva ran a smooth knuckle against my cheek making my gut twist.

Zehan yanked against his chains, growling.

"I heard a young girl's prayers." His long fingers hovered around my cheekbone. "It had been so long since I had been prayed to, and you were so innocent and fierce, I let the cosmos take me to you in the middle of that meadow." Yama was close enough to allow me to catch his scent –burning coals and patchouli. "You were so small and fragile, but I knew at that moment that you were the mortal the rishi referred to. So, I gave all the power I had and vanished. It was perfect as my power continued to grow in you.

Of course. A deva's power grew because of the devotion they received. Over the past decade, I drew in praise from thousands during my performances and my trance magic intensified my allure.

"I came back to Naraka and launched things into motion." Yama looked at Zehan. "I fed you a version of the prophecy and helped you come up with the Chosen idea so that you started hunting human girls. I started working to retrieve the Ashti, knowing that you would need it eventually, which is how it ended up in your collection."

The ground's coldness seeped into my skin. He blackmailed Sunitra. He killed Ruhi.

Anger pounded against my temples. "And the souls? Why take them? Why enlist Sunitra to get the Ashti when it was already in Zehan's possession?"

"I had no power left, and with no one praying to the Deva of Naraka, my power continued to dwindle. I needed the energy from the departed souls to maintain my form and existence. I could have done it myself, but if I was caught, it would place me back in Kalank." Yama shrugged. "Sunitra was close enough to Zehan to be able to move in and out of the palace without being questioned, and she was strong enough to bring the departed souls to the edge of the forest, where I was able to take power from them."

Zehan dropped his head. His guilt was so potent I could feel it leaking from him.

My head spun. Yama had mobilized every piece on the chessboard so that we had no choice but to fall into checkmate.

"So, now what? You have what you want." I stared at the deva. His height was similar to Zehan's, but he was broader around the shoulders. "Rati is dead. You can have your throne."

Everything. My entire life felt like it had been designed for this moment. For him.

"Oh but, little flower, my power still flows in your veins," Yama said with a quietness that sent a trickle of cold down my spine. Black shadows formed around him into carnal beasts with horns. "And I would like it back."

I instinctively took a step back. "I thought a boon could not be taken back." How does a deva take back a boon? Zehan struggled against his shackles.

Yama snarled. "My deva kin were obnoxious with their righteous laws, but they are gone, along with their morals." Yama's black shadows moved in closer to me, herding me like a lost calf. He kneeled and pulled the Ashti out of Rati.

Fresh blood dripped off the ivory surface. "I have plans for the cosmos, and I cannot succeed without all of my power."

My knees locked. He meant to use the Ashti on *me.* "There has to be another way," I protested.

"I'm grateful for you and your dance, because I will be more powerful than ever before."

Yama snapped his fingers and black smoky vines wrapped around Zehan's legs, arms, torso, then throat. "But it's your life or his, little flower. The decision is yours."

Zehan yelled something, but it was quickly muffled by another vine that wrapped around his neck and mouth. I ran toward him, but Yama grabbed my wrist, holding me back.

I whirled on him. "Let me go."

Yama kept his expression blank. "Running will get you nowhere."

Rati was gone, was she not? But now, Yama was here. They had to obey whoever was in power.

Remember who you are, meri mara. Hans's voice spoke in my mind. *Yama is holding us with his power.*

They were unable to do anything because their old master had returned. Next to them, the gate to Svarga shimmered, still very much present.

I sought out Zehan, who stood in a large puddle of his own blood, trying desperately to break out of the heavy chains. Exhaustion smoothed the sharpness in his eyes, even through whatever pain he felt, he mouthed three simple words.

Hot, panicked tears burned paths down my cheeks. Those words were ones I never thought I could have. Especially not in the darkest corner of the cosmos.

"Goodbye, little flower." Yama lifted his arm with the Ashti. "Take comfort in knowing you're finally getting freedom from your fate," Yama said quietly, so only I could hear the words. His shadows swirled by my feet and in the air around us.

But he wasn't freeing me from my fate, he was simply entrapping me in a new one. A fountain of power rose within me—rage and defiance and hope. This wasn't just about me.

With the other devas gone, if Yama took back his throne, there would still be no checks and balances. No one could stop him from taking all the power in the Ashti and continuing the corruption inside and outside of this realm.

"No," I breathed. I refused to stand aside. I had been so afraid to accept the light and darkness that lived inside me. But not any longer.

Yama's shadows banked. He arched a brow, and I lifted my own arms, letting black tendrils of my power rise like a tide in the night. I wouldn't let Yama become the next version of Rati. The black rippled through the air, heavier and fiercer than ever before.

Yama barked a laugh. "You cannot win against me, little flower. Like Zehan could not wield his magic against Rati, you cannot wield against me."

"Perhaps not." I flicked my wrist and Zehan's shackles clinked open and fell to the dirt. The rakshasas around him were forced to their knees by my power. Incandescent branches of white light formed around Zehan, streaming into the forest floor like roots. A smile crept onto my face. "But he can."

Zehan, now released from his chains, walked purposefully, like a deva in his own right. His magic burst around him like piercing stars.

I moved my arms so the shadows enclosed Yama, briefly obscuring his vision, giving Zehan a chance to get closer. "This is for Ruhi."

Yama snarled at both of us. Black vines streamed toward Zehan with rapid speed, but Zehan crashed through them with a flick of his wrist, his power illuminating the forest. Zehan slammed his fist into Yama's face, causing the Ashti to slip from his fingers.

When I picked up the Ashti, it felt heavier, like it carried the weight of the world in its hilt. "You said it yourself. Your power flows in my veins. Naraka is *mine* to rule now. The souls, rakshasas, and Asuras within it will all bow to *me*." I was tired of people tossing me aside as an afterthought. Perhaps at one point, this magic had belonged to Yama. But not anymore, he had given me a small bud of power, and I'd groomed it and grown it into a flower with life and depth. "I am a devi. And I'm claiming what is rightfully mine." I turned to the Asuras and whatever hold Yama had on them and crashed through it with half a thought.

Zehan again punched Yama on the side of the head, then in the gut, then on the temple. He continued until the deva dropped to his knees. When he wanted to be, Zehan was a force to be reckoned with. The darker parts of him, the ones he hid from others and himself, I *loved* them.

The truth was, I craved the moments where his mirth outweighed his mercy.

Zehan kicked Yama again, moving them closer to the Gate of Two. Yama laughed hysterically. He spit out a mouthful of blood. "What are you going to do, boy? Kill me? You can't. I am the damn deva of this realm. This place would be nothing without me. I created suffering and torment. You can't break me."

Zehan gripped Yama by the roots of his hair and tugged his head back. His shadows shook with revenge. "You're right, which is why instead of torture and punishment, I plan to give you nothing but peace and solitude with death." Sweat had caused the loose strands at his forehead to curl up. Blood coated his hands like a loosely fitted glove.

Yet, I saw no monster.

Just the devil in all his glory.

Zehan glanced at me, raw and unruly. I threw the Ashti. He caught it by the hilt without any effort and stabbed it firmly through Yama's gut.

CHAPTER
THIRTY-EIGHT

T he whites of Yama's eyes became black as my shadows. His roar of betrayal and vengeance shook the forest floor. Wind and shadows gusted around us, causing the trees to bend wayward.

Yama turned to the Asuras, the veins in his forehead bulging. "Kill her. I am your creator. You answer to *me*." The Ashti's pommel glowed gray as it extracted his power.

Hans placed his hands behind his back, his expression full of indifference. "Your *power* is our creator, and we will only answer to it. There is no loyalty amongst demons, Yama. You were a fool to forget."

Yama growled as he attempted to lunge toward the Asuras, but Zehan held him firm. The deva was so small now. Yama's attention focused on me. He half laughed, flashing his scarlet teeth. "You think you've won? No, you've just started a new game. One that you won't know how to play. Heed my words, little flower. You will come to regret this."

The warning and threat in Yama's voice should have created fear, but it didn't. "I highly doubt that." I had no interest in games. I never did. And I never will.

My voice was hard as I stared at the deva lying at my feet, attempting to breathe without sputtering blood. "The cosmos is better off without you." That much, I was sure of.

The brewing atmosphere calmed as whatever existence lived within Yama slowly diminished, leaving only a man no greater than a departed soul. My shadows faded to mist. Zehan lifted his hands, filling them with white light, meaning to strike.

"Wait," I said, "he needs to live."

Sacrifice of death will lead all into final breath. I wasn't precisely sure what the rishi's words meant. But I suspected that Yama was the reference to death. *Death of desire will lead to life of death.* He killed Rati who was the Devi of Desire before she took over Naraka and resumed his true form. If my suspicions were right, I didn't want to take a chance at the second part of that line coming to pass. The rishi may have been a mumbling old man, but his words held truths. I wasn't going to take his riddles for granted. Until I could figure out what they meant, Yama needed to stay alive.

Zehan tilted his head, waiting for me to explain, but with so many listeners around us, I just added, "For now."

Zehan nodded curtly in understanding. He released his grip on Yama, letting the man fall to his knees. The Ashti had stopped glowing. I slowly pulled the blade out of his body as his breath trembled, eyes glazed as his existence slowly began to fade. He needed a healer soon.

A single crease formed on Zehan's forehead as he studied the blade that now comfortably rested in my hand. No doubt he had the same thoughts I did. This small piece of bone now held the power to destroy realms.

"This needs to be kept away from those seeking to gain power," I stated. If it fell into the wrong hands, there could be detrimental consequences.

Zehan nodded. "I agree, but I do not trust it in the palace." He was right. Zehan's palace was an open door to anyone.

"Leave it under our protection," Hans suggested. "People fear Kalank far too much to attempt to steal from it, and we Asuras cannot wield it. Yama was a smart creator, he ensured we could not steal power from devas unless we received a boon to do so."

I contemplated. Kalank was likely the safest place for it, and now that I had my own power, I could also place protections over it. "Very well," I said. "It stays with you, along with him. Find him a place with little comfort." I jutted my chin at Yama whose jaw was set tight.

Zehan stared at the Gate of Two that still glimmered. "We should keep it open."

I hesitated. I wasn't so sure that was a good idea. I worried the gods would be bitter at being locked away for so long. "Do you think they are truly on the other side of it?"

"I do," Zehan said with resolution. "They have to be."

"Very well. We keep it open, but we should place guards around it so humans do not venture in or in case someone appears."

Hans mind-spoke to us. *What has transpired here today will have ripple effects.*

Too many ears around, listening. Who knew who was in this forest? Everything that had been done and said would no doubt spread across all of Tyaga.

"We will figure it out," I said confidently. Zehan and I could do anything together, I felt that in my bones.

We are never far away should you need help, Hans said. *After all, you are now Naraka's true ruler.*

"I—" My fingers went numb. *Naraka's true ruler.* The reality of my fate hit me with full force like a smack on the back. I didn't know the first thing about leading. Where would I even begin? How would I earn the loyalty of a bunch of demons?

Zehan, sensing my hesitation, moved to stand next to me. He was coated in dirt and blood. He placed a hand on the small of my back and looked down at me with so much understanding and gentleness. His warm fingers drew a small line at the center of my lower back causing my pulse to tick faster.

You were made for this.

His presence next to me grounded me in reassurance. I should have felt suffocated by Hans's words, trapped by the prison of my own making. But I didn't, because this was a choice. I could leave now and go to Varnasi and let Naraka figure itself out. But deep down, I knew that wasn't the right choice. I belonged in Naraka, where the sun and moon constantly fought to be in the same sky.

I was fated to be here and become this. Somewhere along the way, hell had become my home, and I felt free within its walls. My magic hummed in agreement. I looked up at the too dark sky. The stars glimmered back at us through the cracks of the forest ceiling, but it wasn't the same without both the sun and moon fighting to be in the same space.

"Naraka is my Varnasi." I slipped my hand into Zehan's. "But you are free," I said softly. I couldn't ask him to stay with me. His purpose here was to help souls face their sins, but now that job fell to me.

With Rati gone, there was no curse holding him here. He was free to go to Varnasi. To rule over that land like he had always desired. He could finally have the life he wanted, and I wouldn't be the reason he gave up that dream.

Zehan tucked a strand behind my ear. "You are my—"

He was cut off by a vicious snarl. Yama charged toward us. The fallen deva snatched the Ashti out of my palm, shoved a gust of wind toward me and sank the blade deep into Zehan's side.

I screamed as I was slammed into a tree. Yama pulled the Ashti out and began to slice his own hand with a chant. He was trying to take the power from the blade.

A knot formed in my gut as the blade flared with color. If Yama was successful, he would obtain the power of *all devas*. I tried to stand and felt a sharp shooting pain running from my right hip down to my leg.

Zehan's coal-colored eyes found mine. Full of glimmering strength, power, and that foreign emotion we both had yet to say out loud. "I'll find you in the next life, courtesan."

My heart thudded. What was he doing?

Zehan ran and crashed into Yama but instead of falling to the ground, he pulled the deva with him through the veiled gate.

"Zehan!" I yelled. But I was too far, and it was too late.

As soon as they tumbled through the ethereal light, the gate vanished and only twilight remained.

"No," I whispered, my voice drowned out by the peppering rain and rushing winds.

Zehan was gone.

"We have to open the gate again," I demanded.

"We cannot," Rahas said. "It takes nine Asuras and the power of Naraka to open it."

Ice filled my veins. Rati had killed Issa.

Yama had injured Zehan with the Ashti. A wound like that could not mend itself without magical intervention and a healer. Did the gate even lead to Svarga? What if we didn't open it correctly? What if they were stuck somewhere in limbo between the realms?

"Niya," Shama said. I startled, facing the Asuras who appeared to be waiting for something. "You must act now."

"I—"

Hans handed me Rati's trident. *Steal your rightful place. Time is of the essence, meri mara. The cosmos is imbalanced and Prithvi has monarchs that will fight to enter into this realm. You are not only the bringer of death, but the rightful Queen of Shadows. Accept your fate like you have accepted us.*

With a slight tremble in my hand, I took it and felt the rightness crash into me like waves pounding into rock. My power rose within me with confidence, no longer meeting resistance.

The Asura of Sloth turned to the dozens of rakshasas who stood with shock frozen on their faces. "Kneel," he demanded in a low, calculated voice, "to your new queen."

For a moment, nothing happened. I was sure that the rakshasas would revolt, but then, one by one, the Asuras knelt on either side of me. Hans was the first to take a knee, followed by Nadi, and then the rest. The rakshasas followed suit.

"The Asuras accept your rule and all that comes with it, meri mara," Hans said as he dipped his head forward. *As will all who step foot in Naraka if they wish to live here without suffering,* he hiss-spoke directly to me. The threat to my future rivals was clear, even if they didn't hear it themselves.

I smiled at the Asuras, my inner circle that I had yet to figure out. Somehow, I was not afraid. I felt utterly unbound by the prospects of shaping this realm. *My* realm. But there was still one missing person here that I would go to any length to get back.

Zehan.

My fingers trembled as power funneled into them. No matter where he was, I would find him. His soul was mine in every lifetime.

Even an immortal one.

Turbulent magic streamed through my veins. I waved my hands, and the wind and rain morphed into a tune that matched my gait as I walked towards the small crowd, holding my head high despite the grief I felt by Zehan's absence. A quiet hum that caused my chest to vibrate.

I briefly closed my eyes, drowning in the triumphant call to both the dark and light parts of my soul. Dark shadows streamed out onto the forest floor creating a sea of black. The trance had never felt stronger. One snap. That's all it would take for every creature here to fall into its thralls.

I was unleashed. Made anew with power that couldn't be trusted. I smiled at my new subjects, letting the essence of darkness settle over me.

A new dance in hell was beginning, except this time, I controlled who went on the stage.

ZEHAN

Heaven smelled like ripened fruit.

Whispers raced across my skin in a warm embrace like they were welcoming me home. The ground trembled and a distance roar reached my ears. I grunted as pain laced up my side. I turned to lie flat on a cream-tiled floor. Yama hadn't stabbed me deep enough to be debilitating, but I felt the sharp ache nonetheless.

The fallen deva was a few feet away. He had been operating on final reserves of energy, tumbling through the gate must have knocked him out. The Ashti laid idly between us. I quickly grabbed it, tucking it into my ripped sherwani.

I stood up and took in my surroundings. I was on the terrace of an intricately carved white palace, one that overlooked a wide landscape of lush greenery and waterfalls in the distance. All sitting under the brightest blue skies I'd ever seen.

Svarga. My eyes traveled along the walls and up to the ceiling where more chiseled stone formed a perfect symmetrical pattern. My magic thrummed in my veins like it was responding to whatever power threaded the air.

Yet, I felt no awe, because I had to leave my other half behind.

Surrender and love will open the deva's gates. Ensuring darkness and light entwine into bonded fates. The rishi's words clicked into place the moment Yama had started to chant with the Ashti in hand.

I surrendered for love by taking Yama through the gates, not knowing where it would truly lead me. I hadn't been thinking about my destination. I just knew I had to get Yama far away from Niya so he could not take what now belonged to her.

Naraka.

Diving through that gate had been the only way to keep Niya, Prithvi, and Naraka safe. If Yama took the full power from the Ashti, the two realms would fall into chaos. The souls there would all be under Yama's rule. I had heard stories of Yama during my time in Naraka, and if I was confident about anything, it was that Yama was no better than Rati. The devas were always out to only solve their needs.

More than once, I had wondered if the universe was truly better off without any of them.

But I also remembered the time when the devas were very much present on Prithvi. Mortal souls held more unity with each other when they had someone higher to look up to. There was less war, less corruption, and more distribution of power.

When Rati offered me that bargain over a century ago in the middle of the Drifts, I had no idea what I was signing up for. Fatigue, thirst, and grief had all taken their toll on me. The sun had been beating down on my head, causing sweat to soak through my fine sherwani. I couldn't fathom my mother being trapped in a horrible fate because of my father's pathetic ego. When Rati offered a way out for her, I grasped onto it for dear life. I was foolish. I never imagined the loneliness and burden of responsibility I would feel by accepting that bargain.

Until I saw Niya dance. She was the only bright light that could match my magic.

Every time I saw her, it was like I was doused in water and fire. She was breathtaking. A completely perfect soul and mine from the moment she first took that golden stage in Khoya. I loved her. I hadn't said it out loud yet, but the next time I saw her I would. *I vow it.*

"Zehan."

I turned around to face a beautiful woman. She wore a mustard and gold gown that pooled to the floor and a woven crown of gold petals sat on her head. She did not compare to Niya's sharp beauty, yet she was alluring, and I couldn't seem to peel my eyes away from her. I was going to ask how she knew my name, but the answer popped into my mind before I could voice the question. *She is a devi. She knows everyone's name.*

"Which devi are you?"

"The Devi of Pyre." She smiled, the gold thread on her outfit sparkled. "And you need no introduction. We've been waiting a long while for you. I believe you've brought something with you?" She glanced at the dagger that peeked out from my hip.

The Devi of Pyre. It sounded familiar, but I couldn't pinpoint if I had ever heard about this devi. There were many devas that I hadn't heard of, as they were an entire community of their own. I pulled out the Ashti. The woman's eyes burned into the blade like she needed to get her hands on it.

The hair on my arms rose as the silence of Svarga became overly apparent. It was too quiet here. Too...empty.

My fingertips, where my white shadows stood ready, tingled. "Where are the rest of the devas?"

Her teeth flashed. "Away for now, but they will be back."

Something about this female wasn't sitting right. Magic curled in my palms. She noticed. "I would like to speak to the Deva of Creation," I said. He was the ultimate leader, the one who instilled order and rule amongst the immortal.

"Of course." She studied me as I paced around the room. Half of it was cut off by a massive floor-to-ceiling curtain. I heard a muffled sound. I walked closer to inspect it.

"You fulfilled your end of the prophecy," the female stated, drawing my attention back to her.

It didn't surprise me that she knew about the rishi's prophecy. I knew they could somehow see what occurred on Prithvi and Naraka. "I did."

She tilted her head, perplexed. "Why?"

"Naraka needs someone rational in the seat of power, and it cannot be him"—I jutted my chin toward Yama. Her composure slipped, and a bit of softness passed over her features—"and it cannot be me."

I knew little about the way devas' magic worked, but I was convinced that if Niya were to leave now, after accepting her power, Naraka would begin to fade.

The realm didn't just belong to her, it *was* her.

"You entrusted the realm of demons to your soulmate, knowing that doing so would force you apart." She ran a finger down one of the long columns.

"I—" Words stopped forming. My ears began to ring. *You entrusted the realm of demons to your soulmate.*

Who was this female? How did she know the truth I'd kept hidden from everyone, including myself? My back straigthened. "How do you know that?"

"It's true then, Niya is your soulmate."

I didn't answer. The simple answer to her question was yes. Niya was my soulmate. It wasn't some possessive comment when I said her soul belonged to me. It was sheer fact. Soulmates were rare. Finding the one who is equal to the very threads of one's being was nearly impossible, yet she was mine. The longer answer was something I hadn't come to terms with yet.

But this devi knew all of that. There was something off about her, but I couldn't place what.

"Who are you?" I asked again, my tone darkening as I let magic gather at my fingertips. I looked down at my hand. My power felt different here. The shadows were richer, more velvety. *Assess later.* My shadow wolves took their place beside me, pawing at the smooth floor.

The devi smiled with all of her pearly teeth. She flicked her wrist, and the curtain behind me swept aside, unveiling an enormous gold cage that glimmered. Confusion and panic rippled through me as I recognized the girl inside.

Her almond-shaped eyes widened. "Zehan?"

"Ruhi?" But how was it possible? I felt her soul shred when it was ripped from the realm. She couldn't exist. The ground trembled again, and I widened my stance to keep from falling. *What in nine hells is going on?*

Ruhi's frantic eyes met mine. "Zehan, it's a trap! They only want you because—"

A yellow shadowy clamp appeared over her lips. Alright, I was done being calm. I twisted around to face the Devi of Pyre. "Who the fuck are you?"

Yama let out a low groan as he stirred awake. His sights immediately landed on the devi. My senses heightened when recognition ignited between them.

"You're back," the devi said with an airy voice, like she feared if she said it too loud he would vanish.

Yama suddenly appeared centuries younger as he approached the female with slow steps. Adrenaline pounded through me like I was getting ready to enter another fight. Yama looked at this female the same way I looked at Niya.

A grin tugged at the corners of his eyes. "Hello, wife."

THANK YOU

Dear Reader,

Thank you for reading this Bollywood-esque romantasy. I hope you enjoyed reading this as much as I enjoyed writing it. I'd greatly appreciate if you would leave a review on Goodreads and / or Amazon.

Again, thank you for taking a leap of faith on this story and supporting me as I chase this dream. Niya and Zehan's adventures with the Asuras and Devas will continue in 2027 – follow me on instagram @npatelbaxi to stay updated on book news, releases, and much more!

ACKNOWLEDGEMENTS

I've always been a daydreamer. Since I was young, I found it so incredibly easy to detach from my current environment and let my imagination take over. I would use music (Bollywood, of course) to explore stories and ideas, which is why it is so fitting that Dance of the Asuras is my debut fantasy. It has *everything* I craved in books – a brown girl heroine and hero, dancing, music, South Asian clothing and aesthetics, and even chai! This story is the product of so many early mornings, late nights, spirals, edits, and brainstorms; but it would have not been possible without my incredible and very large support system.

To my husband, Raj, thank you for believing in me and giving me the space to write my words. Your warmth, your humor, and your love is always *exactly* what I need. You read me better than I read books, and *that* is an incredible feat. Thank you for being the best partner to me for fifteen years!

To my son, Yuvaan, you were the catalyst that finally pushed me to embrace my own potential. This past year with you has been one of the greatest joys of my life. You are, without a doubt, a bright light, and my hope for you is that one day, you will embrace your courage to pursue your own unique dreams.

Mom, Dad, Samit, Alyssa - I'm so grateful for your unwavering support. You all celebrate my successes like they are your own and also wallow in my losses the same, and having that kind of love makes me feel like I can take anything on. I know that any problem is never too big for our small group to solution on. If you could, I know you would move mountains to help me and that means the world to me.

To my incredible in-laws and brother in-law thank you for your full acceptance of *me* and my particular-ness. I told you I was going to write a book and you all immediately showed enthusiasm. I consider myself so lucky to have your understanding and compassion.

Ciara, I honestly have no idea where to begin, and a simple 'thank you' will never be enough. This book would have never gotten past the first draft if it wasn't for your feedback and faith in this story. Your friendship and advisory has been critical to getting to this point. I'm so grateful that you reached out via Instagram all those years ago; it is because of you and your belief (like Evelyn

Carson) that I am now a published author. I know you know this, but you're stuck with me now.

To my Hendo Gals—Shannon, Gopali, Khadija, Arham—thank you for being my silent cheerleaders. You all have known about this secret quest of mine for over a decade, and you've always believed in me more than I believed in myself. Thank you for pulling me out of every spiral with pep talks, providing unsolicited advice knowing that I won't like it, understanding me when no one else does, and being truly the best friends a girl could ask for.

To Emily, thank you for helping me become a writer and pushing me to always trust my instincts. Your guidance and coaching were critical unlocks in my author journey. To Brit, thank you for reading the early draft of this and always reminding me that it will all work out and sometimes to move forward, you just have to let things go.

To my Beta Readers – Rachel, Binal, Saajana, Sonali – thank you for being early readers of this story. Your feedback on the plot and characters were crucial and helped me make some necessary adjustments that have enhanced not only Niya and Zehan, but the corrupted and complex world of Tyaga.

To my Editors – Emily, Mallori, Taylor, and Krista – thank you for your constructive feedback through multiple drafts of Dance of the Asuras. Publishing a book is no joke, it takes time, effort, and a lot of collaboration with many different people. You all helped ease my anxiety about having a story that was steeped in South Asian culture and instead of shying away from it, you all encouraged me to embrace it fully.

When I announced I was going to publish a book, the love and support I received was overwhelming and gave me the necessary push to follow through on this scary but rewarding journey. So to every single person that sent me words of encouragement, checked in with me through the process, interacted with me on social media, believed in me when I didn't—thank you.

ABOUT THE AUTHOR

N. Patel Baxi (also known as Neerali) has always been a 'What If' girl, forever thinking about the future and asking impossible questions. Her stories come from a lifelong love for the magical and unreal. When she isn't busy imagining new worlds, she spends her time sipping on chai, watching Bollywood, and traveling across the world. She currently lives in Atlanta, Georgia with her husband and son.